STONE
At Your Service

Carolina Bad Boys, #1

RIE WARREN

Stone, At Your Service
Copyright © 2014 by Rie Warren
Excerpt from Love, In the Fast Lane copyright © 2014 by Rie Warren

https://www.riewarren.com

Cover Design
By Jada D'Lee Designs
https://www.facebook.com/JadaDLeeDesigns

Editing
By Gilly Wright
http://www.gillywright.com

Printed in the United States of America
Stone, At Your Service / Rie Warren – 1st ed
1.Contemporary Romance—Fiction. 2. Alpha Male—Fiction. 3. Romantic Comedy—Fiction. 4. Erotica—Fiction. I. Title

First Edition
ISBN: 978-1500744786

Chapter One
Full Service Friend

MY PHONE JITTERED ON the nightstand, dragging me from a fitful sleep. "What?" I croaked into the receiver.

I was used to getting woken up at all hours of the night by JJ's soft little snuggles or—more often—his screaming wide-awake nightmares that seemed to get worse with every year his mom was gone. One look at the name flashing across my phone screen and I knew this call had nothing to do with the kid though, and everything to do with a dumbass obligation I'd made to my best friend, Nicky.

I'd barely yanked a bundle of sheets from under my ass when Nicky spoke with suppressed laughter, "This is your call service, sir. I'm to remind you you're settin' off to Atlanta, Tuesday morning, nine sharp."

"Yeah, whatever. I'll be ready. Don't get your panties in a wad, Nicky."

Speaking of wad, I hopped from the sheets bunched between my ball-sack and armpits. The cotton entanglement mimicked the death-by-python thighs of the chick I'd fucked earlier in a fit of *I am the man* mentality.

It happened every Friday night.

I liked to screw; ladies liked my looks. Love 'em and leave 'em was my style, and Friday was my only night off without the kid. With him safely getting spoiled by my ma until his little milk teeth probably ached from a sugar overdose, TGIF was the one time I got to indulge in a little indiscretion. And I took full advantage.

Being ball-and-chained for thirty-one motherfucking months to Crazy Claire had taught me two things: expect the unexpected and keep your heart to yourself. She'd done a runner on me, our son, and our marriage. No way in hell was I ever letting anyone in enough to walk out on me or break the kid's heart again. No way was I going to risk the small slice of a comfortable life I'd carved for us through sheer hard work and long, long hours. But that didn't mean I didn't take care of business.

"I bet you look like shit, Josh. Hope you clean up some over the weekend." Nicky's voice carried over the phone, and I considered whirlpooling it with a fast flush in the toilet once I'd tripped into the bathroom.

"Let's put it this way. If your gaggle of girlfriends is expectin' pink oxford shirts, pressed chinos, and goddamn penny loafers, they're outta luck," I joked.

"You fucked her, didn't you?" Accusation dripped from Nicky's tone. He referred to the woman I'd made eyes with at Richard's Bar and then made love to for several hours afterward.

And following approximately fifteen minutes during which I'd caught my breath, blinking back a few conscience-driven recriminations, I'd slipped from the woman's clingy embrace. I'd swept my arm toward the bathroom door, thinking that was at least one gentlemanly thing to do, giving her some privacy to clean up after our fuck-fest. Before I gave her the signal to clear out.

"Nah, I baked her cupcakes, painted her nails then made her a strawberry daiquiri." *'Course I fucked her. Tits out to there. Legs up to here. Ass tight enough to withstand my smacks and writhing back for more . . .*

2

"Name?"

I jiggled the loose toilet handle. "Heh?"

"What was her name?" Nicky pressed.

"Julie, Janey, it's all the samey. Who cares?"

"I care, since you're gonna be my boyfriend for the week."

Filling the sink with hot water, I wiped the last red lipstick stains from my chest, my abs, from my cock. "Damn, you get bitchy when you're not gettin' serviced regularly."

With my disposable razor in the crapper after one day's use, I tore open a new package with my teeth and jetted foam into my palm.

Nicky heard the aerosol can go off. "Shaving?"

I slathered my upper cheeks and lower throat just enough to maintain the five o'clock shadow I never shaved off. "Nope. Puttin' frosting on those cupcakes I told you about."

"Do your nads, too."

"No fucking way." A razor was getting nowhere near my balls.

"If you're gonna be my boyfriend, I need the tail feathers and drop-nest gone. The twinks like it that way."

My morning boner deflated like a balloon with a pin stuck through it. "I gotta do this?"

"Yup. Save my ass so I can sodomize yours." Nicky—Nick—Love, my best bud and best-selling paranormal romance writer, chuckled at my expense.

"We're really gonna play gay at your writing convention?" I tucked the phone against my shoulder, smearing shaving foam all over it.

"It's for my career."

I groaned and resumed shaving, my face only.

Viper growled in the background from Nicky's end. Talk about a man-hungry bitch. Viper the Rottweiler ate shoes, carburetors, car fenders for supper. So sweet as a puppy, such a pain in the ass as an adult—typical female.

3

"Nine a.m. Tuesday, Josh. Get your *Glee* on." He hung up on me with a final laugh.

I dipped toward the mirror, scowling at my slightly furred chest, stomach, and balls. If Nicky got me started manscaping the undercarriage, the bastard wouldn't stop there.

"I am not shaving my gonads," I muttered, tossing the barely used razor into the trash can.

* * * *

On Tuesday morning, the thought of leaving town without a final look at the kid almost made me cancel the whole trip. Instead, I took a detour to my ma's on the way to work. She'd kept him since my Friday night with "Julie, Janey, samey" so he could get settled in, because Ma and I were both a little wary. This would be my first time away from him since Claire pulled up stakes a year and a half ago.

Letting myself into the house, I bypassed the creaky floorboards I'd memorized from years of sneaking in and out as a teenager. In the room decorated especially for JJ, I scowled at Viper—also a houseguest for the week—and gingerly stepped around her bulk at the side of the bed.

Mostly hidden beneath the quilt, only JJ's sweet little face was visible, along with the index finger he always sucked to sleep. I slipped onto the bed and gently folded myself around him. He scooted into me like I was his own personal teddy bear, which I suppose I was. At three years old, he still felt so tiny to me. I feathered my fingers across his brow and his nose wrinkled. Combing the dark blond hair aside—the color he got from me—I nuzzled my face against him, breathing in the baby and boy scent. I cuddled with him a while longer, careful not to disturb his sleep, thankful it was peaceful for once.

Even with my side trip to Ma's, I was at work almost at the crack-of. The garage was quiet, nobody else due for another hour. I walked through the first three bays whistling through my teeth as I inspected the cleanup from the previous night. My dad would've been proud. All the tools were tidy in their cubbies, the cars left inside the night before swathed in cotton-flannel covers, a touch that never failed to impress the customers. I walked past the office into the reception area, flicking on the computers, faxes, and two flatscreen TVs on the way through. I replaced the out-of-date magazines with a new batch Ma had delivered yesterday. *Motor Sport, Garden & Gun, Charleston Magazine, Cosmo* . . .

Stepping out the opposite side of reception, I surveyed the last two bays of Stone's Auto Service. We specialized in tires, but we could hook up just about anything. Stone's had stood in this exact spot on 17 North in Mt. Pleasant, South Carolina, since my dad's father—Billy Stone—had opened the doors in 1960.

I'd spruced the place up a bit, added perks for the clients while never losing the down-home family appeal from my granddaddy's day. We were kid friendly for the moms waiting for their cars with children in tow. The female customers also didn't mind hanging around with a nice glassed-in view of the bays as they watched the guys at work. I'd modernized as new technology became available, but we still worked to the same standards. It was all about doing your best, keeping your crew and customers happy, and having some serious fucking pride in your work.

Yeah, Dad would be happy.

I looked down at the white badge with *Stone* embroidered in red on the chest of my coveralls. It was the same nametag my dad had worn. I'd painstakingly snipped it from his uniform three weeks after his death and stitched it onto my own with shaking hands and falling tears that made me take half an hour on a five-minute job. Because I was taking up the helm of Stone's Auto Service a good twenty years before I expected to, and it wasn't because

5

Dad had retired early.

We still gave out a single red rose to every female customer, a tradition my granddaddy had started. Grandmothers, cougars, snooty princesses, gawky teenagers, and even little girls . . . it didn't matter. The smiles on their faces—after coming in pissed off and impatient—were worth it. Of course, it didn't hurt none that our smooth move collected a few phone numbers in the process.

The phone stationed on the wall in front of me rang. I answered, "Stone's, at your service."

Chicks eat this shit up.

I listened to the customer, moving to the computer when the door jingled open. Squinting at the monitor, I raised a hand in greeting as the guys streamed in. Red-haired Mick, young gun Javier, big, black Gerald, who was built like a plow horse and could probably bench press a Jetta—maybe even my '94 Ford Bronco—and Ray, as handy as a mechanic as he was with the mathematics. The squat blond man was my second-in-command. Another ten strolled in, hitting the Mr. Coffee and the Krispy Kremes before heading out to the bays.

It wasn't long before the hiss of air compressors, the fresh smell of solvents, and the sight of the parking lot filling up filtered in to tease my senses.

"This is gonna be your first week off since I started." Ray took over my station at the counter, bringing up the day's work tally on the computer.

"Yup." I narrowed my eyes around the reception, straightened a few chairs, and strode to the door. "We ready?"

His bushy eyebrows jerked in my direction. "You betcha."

I flipped the lock, turned the *Open for Business* sign over, and stood back as people tramped inside. My chest puffed up with pride as the room filled, Ray handling the workload he'd grunt off to the mechanics, flat tires already rolling out the back of the bays.

Patting Ray on the shoulder, I headed for the office. I peered into the garage for a minute more, the floor humming with activity and energy, telling myself the guys would do okay in my absence.

The navy blue carpet in my office matched the navy blue of my coveralls. Both were oil-stained, an occupational hazard I loved. I'd already scrubbed my fucking nails raw and my fingers red trying to get rid of the ingrained grit and grease, but I sure as shit hadn't shaved one single pube, Nicky be damned.

I eyed the clean clothes piled on my desk. Pulling the zipper down, I shucked my coveralls, the ones I often wore draped down to my waist when the summer heat got too heavy. Under the badge that had belonged to my dad, beneath the dark blue uniform and the white tank I dragged off, I looked at my tat. The red heart almost pulsed on my chest, running from my left shoulder and over the hard slope of my pec. Wrapped in chrome pipes, the heart bore the words *Joshua James December 13, 2009*, symbolizing my three-year-old kid and cars, the two loves of my life.

Right down to the tattoo on my chest, which I'd gotten one week after JJ's birth, I was a man's man. Just not *that kind* of man's man. Except for the purposes of helping Nicky out this week. I pulled on a new red T-shirt, a pair of old jeans, and brushed my short hair back. After pocketing my phone and wallet, attaching the chain to a belt loop, I anxiously waited for nine o'clock to arrive and willed the days to leapfrog forward at the same time.

In about fifteen minutes I'd be on a road trip with Nicky. One unlike we'd ever taken before. Not camping, fishing, horsing around. Nothing like that.

The only campy thing about it would be us.

Nicky Love was my best friend, and he had been since high school when we'd joined up over pranks that usually caused fire alarms, full-scale school-wide evacuations, and a lot of detentions. It was probably a miracle either one of us graduated.

I didn't have enough fingers and toes to count the number of times Nicky had saved my *cojones*. For starters, there was my marriage bust-up. Thirty-one motherfucking months in and Claire just up and left, no note, not even a postcard *ever* to let me know she was okay. Nothing of JJ's taken with her—not a single memento of our life—to say she'd be thinking about our son but just couldn't stick it out. I'd been seven years into the job by then, up to my eyeballs in money and management crises, not to mention diapers and nightmares and Nickelodeon when Claire disappeared.

Nicky—unmarried, unattached, guy's guy Nicky—pretty much moved in the first six months. *My manny.* Best man and best break-up buddy ever. Hell, he even did short-time at the garage like he used to fourteen years ago, when we'd wise off at Wando High School during the day and come work for my dad as soon as last bell rang.

I owed the man, big time. He never told me who or how, but his Yankee legal eagles located Claire, served the papers, notarized her signatures, requested a hearing, and Charleston County cut me loose faster than it took to tie the knot. So if he needed me, no matter what, I was there. I just hoped I didn't crash and burn and bring him down with me. I was determined to be successful . . . as a gay dude.

Stepping out of the office, a blush burned my face. The guys all knew where I was going and they'd spent the past week taking cracks at me. Add in my clean gear—as if I'd never done neat and tidy before—and they were yapping up a shit storm, me at its center.

"*¡Ea diablo!* Knock me on my ass den fuck it hard." Javier's gaze passed over me then he got on the intercom. "*Mira*, come get a load of Stone!"

I was gonna give the squirt a load. I put my hand on my crotch and pumped it as the boys crowded into the small space behind the counter.

"Fuck you all very much."

"That's what we hear you're supposed to be doing to Nicky." Gerald winked.

Right on cue, Nicky arrived, not in the nick of time, because—*holy fucking shit*—he cruised into the lot in a g-damn shiny white Volvo station wagon rental that screamed queer-mobile, and all the guys guffawed again.

"Dude, I'm tweeting this," Mick remarked.

Nicky, Nick, Nicholas . . . I loved the guy. And gave him as much shit as he shoveled out. But right now? I hated him so goddamn hard. In fact, I hated them all. I glared from one of the idjits to the next as I slid my duffle over my shoulder and a garment bag over my arm. Stepping out beneath the bright red awning, I faced the garage, giving it one last once-over. Nicky climbed out of the car with a wave and popped the back of the Volvo.

Catcalls and earsplitting whistles resounded out the bay doors when I strutted across the lot in the simmering May heat.

Ray shouted, "Shake that ass, Stone!"

I flipped a stiff middle finger over my shoulder, growling, "This place better be standin' when I get back, dickheads."

"Oh, yes sir!"

Nicky chuckled when I reached him. "You know they could probably sue you for harassment the way you talk to them."

"Yeah, they probably could. But they get too much tits and ass from my business to give it a legit shot."

"You practically run an escort service from Stone's, *at your service*." His hazy purplish eyes twinkled.

"It's not my fault half the women who come in here are horny." I wasn't above partaking myself.

"Well, if you need a sideline . . ." He waggled his hips around, causing another round of whistles from the garage.

"GET BACK TO WORK!" I yelled. Then I muttered

to Nicky, "They're gonna destroy the place."

"Nah, man. They love it as much as you do. You got a tight crew here." If anyone knew how much I busted my ass for this place, or how the guys met me with just as much blood, sweat, and tears, it was Nicky.

"Yeah." I smiled, slinging my gear and a case of brews into the back of the car.

Nicky rolled his eyes and started to the driver's side as I slammed the hatch. I could feel his huff coming from a mile away. I slipped in beside him, sniffing the *ooh new car* smell of the clean upholstery, completely unlike the red-blistered-to-pink Jeep Cherokee he drove all over the lowcountry, Viper the bitch-hound his sidekick.

"We're so queer."

"About that." His lips compressed into a thin line. "Beer?"

"Yeah."

"Beer does not say queer."

"Now that's just plain discriminatory."

"I'm not trying to be a jackass but look at you, Josh. We're gonna have to work extra hard to tone down your—"

"Manly studliness?"

His eyebrows rose in response. "More like obvious heterosexuality, especially when there are women around."

"I think this car and your duds shout we're bro-mos loud enough." I checked out his pink oxford—the exact same shirt I'd sworn I wouldn't be caught dead in—tight jeans, and the long medallion hanging from around his neck. "Well, aren't you all dolled up, darlin'?"

His eyebrows remained hairline high.

"I am not cashin' in my beer, man. Besides, it's Heiney, that should work, right?" Met by more silence, I slouched further in my seat. "Fine. I'll hide it."

I got a fist bump in agreement. That was good enough for me.

"Let's get this ass and pony show on the road!" I

rolled down the window and rapped on the roof, sending a wave to my grease monkeys who were still goddamn gawking at us.

Nicky hit the horn several times as he cut into the morning traffic, pointing us westward.

* * * *

We were on hour three, had just stopped for a refill at Wendy's, and I'd taken over the driving. I eased back onto the highway, glancing at Nicky. "So lemme get this straight."

"Har har." He rested a foot on the dashboard.

"No pun intended." I winked. "You've got this awesome job guaranteed to snag you some pussy. You're basically surrounded by hot, smart, and horny honeys all the time, but instead of diving head first into the buffet of broads at these writing conferences, you told them you're homosexual."

Pulling the leather band off his low ponytail, he dragged both hands through his hair. "It's not all glamour."

"Oh, believe me, I know that." I looked pointedly at the mess he'd just made of his hair.

He shut me up with a punch to my arm. "*Anyway*, you know I thought it'd be hard as hell to break into the romance writing biz as a man. Women wanna read what a *woman* wants, not what a guy *thinks* a woman wants."

"Yeah, but you're a best seller, man."

He snorted through his nose. "I am now, six years later, because of the loyal readers and being able to get my stuff out there, bam-bam-bam. But being a guy who writes sex and romance—even you didn't think that'd fly. You know that's why I went with my pen name." His mouth slid into a half smile. "'Course, what the fuck do I know, huh? My sales didn't really take off until it came out that I *am* a guy who writes steamy romance, fangs and all."

"Fans and all, you mean." I waggled my eyebrows.

"Don't remind me." He groaned. "How many times did I get hit on by chicks asking me to act out sex scenes from my books with them?"

"Quit your bitchin'. You gotta admit the revolving bed of fangirls had some perks for a couple years."

"Yeah, well that bed rotation got old fast. I'm not the fantasy they want, and they sure as hell weren't mine. Remember the one who showed up on my doorstep in the dead of night? She swore she was Alaina deChristiane from my—"

"*Vampires Do It in the Dark* books?" I swiped a hand down my face. "How could I forget your very own bunny boiler? She promised to be your immortal mate. Oh! And she tried to kiss your face off while wearing fake vampire teeth, right?"

He shuddered. "Maybe Nicky Love wasn't such a good idea after all."

Nicky Love. The name sounded totally feminine, which didn't match the man sitting beside me at all. Nicky could be a bruiser. Just over six-feet tall with a wiry, muscular build, he'd been my wingman in more than one bar fight during our early days after we'd gotten fake IDs. We certainly got a name on the bar circuit before my dad had found us out at the Kickin' Horse Saloon and busted our chops. Then he put us both in front of Ma for her own brand of ass whuppin'.

The funny thing was, Nicky Love was almost his real name. He'd practically fallen into his calling, much like me. Nicholas Loveland. I'd called him Nicky from the get-go and when he started writing he took it up and shortened his last name. Presto-fucking-bingo, for all intents and purposes in the anonymous age of the Internet, he could be a woman writing chick-shit.

He'd carried on, flying under the radar and writing his love stories until he started going to these damn writers conferences. It wasn't like the word got out after he *came out* as a guy to his fellow writers, but there was speculation among his growing readership. The mystery surrounding *Nicky Love* heated up his career.

"A couple years ago I started hating going to the conventions. Being one of the token males?" He shivered and it had nothing to do with the A/C blasting over us. "It gets a little uncomfortable. They don't mean any harm. But who doesn't like a little attention from the opposite sex, right?"

Who me? I mouthed, wide-eyed and innocent.

"I was gettin' drunk-groped like I was one of the Coverdales—"

I spit a mouthful of Coke all over the steering wheel. "Cover what now?"

"Coverdales. That's what we call the male cover models who usually make appearances, meet and greet, and get groped . . . the ladies love it."

Groped, huh. Maybe this gig isn't so bad after all.

Nicky must've recognized the predatory gleam in my eyes because he wagged a finger at me—obviously getting into role—and continued. "Aside from the off-their-meds stalker types, I was in too much danger from the women in my writing circle trying to set me up with their daughters, nieces, younger sisters . . ."

"*Ah*. The rarified breed, a male romance writer."

"Fuck you, Stone." He elbowed me in the ribs. "My crew is as awesome as yours at the garage, but they excel at henpecking. You'll see."

"Not sure I want to." My hands started sweating on the steering wheel as I reconsidered the five-day LitLuv romance convention I'd signed up for.

"Being gay was a good solution. Bonus? Saying I was in a permanent relationship kept the hens off my back, until they kept hounding me about my partner." He looked over, sizing me up. "Now you're my bear."

I gave him a jaunty nod. "Stone, at your service."

Scrubbing both hands over his face, he mumbled,

"What the fuck was I thinking? Macho mechanic who can't keep his cock holstered, with sex on the brain and grease stains on his knuckles?"

"Hey, asshole, that hurt. I'm sitting right here, and I goddamn scrubbed my knuckles until they were chapped, I'll have you fuckin' know."

He peeked out at me between his fingers. "Holy shit, Josh. That was really gay of you."

"Really?"

"Yeah."

I jerked my chin down, weirdly pleased. "Right on. See? I can do this, *lover.*"

Nicky snorted until I burst into laughter too.

After another driver switch, I pulled one of his bags onto my lap, intent on doing a dive for the romance-y shit he always packed for these getaways. I already had all his books—signed, naturally. I'd even opened an account on Amazon to post reviews for him. He was a talented dude, even if I had to pretend it wasn't him writing stuff that made me a little turned on because that would just make my nuts dry up. Nicky could joke about Stone's Escort Service all he liked, but I was his biggest pimp, handing out his postcards and business cards at the garage. Because the ladies liked romance and red roses with their lube jobs.

I pulled out a wad of white cards. "What's this? Notes for your next story?"

"Uh . . . actually, they're note cards, for you."

"Me?" Didn't I feel overwhelmed by happy. I flicked through them. Then I didn't feel happy-frigging-happy at all. "Notes about how I'm supposed to dress, act . . . who I'm supposed to be?"

The asshole kept mum.

"Art dealer? You're shitting me, right?" I tore that card in two and stomped it beneath my feet. "I know jackshit about art. How's that gonna fly if someone with a clue starts talkin' to me? What's wrong with a fella owning a garage?"

14

Nicky frowned so hard I thought all the words he kept inside his head were going to spew all over the dashboard. Then he grinned slowly. "Foreign car dealer."

Smug motherfucker. I bumped his fist. "Yeah." I settled back in my seat. "I still don't understand why this is necessary. Can't you just do the holy water, wear a cross, garlic thing to keep the crazies away?"

"Try being a single male surrounded by thousands of female romance writers and fans . . . in an enclosed space."

Hell yeah, game on.

"Sounds like my kind of heaven. PS. you ain't that hot."

He cracked a smile and managed to deliver two birds my way while keeping his eyes on the road.

Talented mo-fo, like I said.

"I hate taking you away from home, man. Do you think JJ will be okay?" he asked.

I rubbed a hand over my chest, the place that ached whenever anyone mentioned the kid and I wasn't close enough to see him. "I haven't been away from him for more than a night at a time since he was born."

"I know."

I sucked it up. "It'll do him good to be away from his pops. Ma's plans to spoil him will take months to undo."

"She's the best."

My throat tightened when I thought about her, alone in that big house, without my dad. The way she welcomed everyone from her grandson to my best friend to my crew and all their hangers-on made it a home even with one vital part missing. *The Stone family is everyone's family.* "Pretty much."

"So's JJ."

"Yeah," came my raspy reply.

"Let me talk to him when you check in later?"

"Okay, Uncle Wicky . . . just don't rile him up before bedtime."

"Rile him up? C'mon. When've I been known to do

15

that?" He gunned through the midtown Atlanta traffic, as much as he could in a not-so speedster Volvo.

"Let's see. Usually every Saturday night, eight o'clock, on the dot." I dug through his bag again, determined to leave off the heavy. I had a few days off to hang with my best friend, see him in his element, and I was gonna make the best of it. "You brought new swag?"

"Yeah, check the main pocket." Nicky leaned over to slap my thigh. "Like a kid in a candy shop."

* * * *

Ramada's valet parking sucked balls and cost a mint. The hotel was lit up like a fairytale palace—or a whorehouse, depending on how you looked at it—with convention attendees coming and going. It was busier than Stone's before a holiday weekend, when everyone in Charleston's tri-county area seemed destined to get a flat tire. Bellhops wearing pained grins pushed overflowing wheeled-carts through the carousel doors.

I wielded our cart into the lobby, following Nicky as he strolled up to the check-in desk. His demeanor changed the instant we walked through the doors. Gone was the scrappy South Cackalackee bad boy. He rolled up the sleeves on his oxford twice, neatened his hair back into a sleek ponytail, and greeted people with effortless charm.

While we stood in line, a commotion at the back of the queue drew my attention. A woman wrangled with her cart and then watched—eyes wide and mouth open—as four boxes crashed to the floor. Books, dresses, shoes, wigs . . . *lingerie* swam onto the polished marble floor.

I noticed her cock-up with the cart first.

Her legs second.

Her tits third.

Her face last.

Holy fuck.

"Who the hell is that?" I whispered, pointing at the

babe surrounded by ten tons of shit spilling all over the floor.

Nicky glanced over his shoulder. "No idea. New kid on the block, I guess."

"I'm gonna go help her." I shouldered through the crowd and squatted down next to her. "Need a hand?" Because one thing Ma had taught me was always help out a lady in distress.

She blew a tendril of the lightest red hair from her brow. "I'd sure appreciate it."

I helped pack her things back up and tidily stacked it on the cart. I willed myself not to look at her as I stepped back. *Definitely not remembering the lace, the frills, the full-on feminine lingerie I'd handled.*

"My knight in shinin' armor?"

Shaking my head, I backed away. I saw Nicky at the elevators, waiting for me. "Not really, miss."

New kid on the block. There was nothing kid-like about her. She was voluptuous, a handful from hips to hourglass waist to perfect breasts. The southern drawling miss in a knee-length skirt and clinging top didn't seem to realize she'd made my cock railroad-spike hard. I walked away, mesmerized by her feminine-fuck-me appearance up to her goddamn adorable face. A killer combination. Full throttle attraction the likes of which I'd never felt made my head spin, my heart speed.

And there was no way I could act on it because I'd just signed up for five and a half days of Gaydom at the Rom Con.

Chapter Two

Tuesday: Gamecocks and Henpeckers

LITERARY LOVE CONVENTION 2013 had kicked off with a bang all right, just not the kind I suddenly needed care of the lusciously curved lady who'd caused a heavy ache to settle low in my groin.

As I approached Nicky at the elevators, he asked, "Do what you needed to do?"

I shrugged. "Sure." *Not really, since my dick's still in my pants.*

To offset the fact I could barely keep from looking back at little miss sex-on-legs, I grabbed Nicky's hand and rubbed my thumb over his knuckles. His forearm tensed as he fought against pulling away from the unexpected caress.

"Goin' up, babe?"

I thought he was gonna snort, which would really kill the mood I was going for. Holding himself in check, he twined his fingers through mine and gave me a peck on the cheek. "Sure, love."

Motherfucker better not try to one-up me in the gay-

stakes. 'Cause I'm gonna bring it.

We pushed into an empty elevator and broke apart as soon as the doors closed. Nicky knocked his shoulder against mine, laughing when I alternated between rubbing the heel of my palm against my just-kissed cheek then my hand against my thigh. To wipe off boy cooties presumably. Christ.

"You're gay!" He nearly cackled.

I hit him with a broad smile. "Only for you, babe."

He was still chuckling when we made it to our room. He waved the key-card in my face, and I snatched it from him as we went inside. A Fabio wannabe with some half-dressed pirate's booty babe decorated the card—someone's book cover. *Oh, good for a buy one, get one free appetizer at the mezzanine level Grille on Tuesday.* I had to hand it to the writers, customers loved BOGO. I might learn a thing or two.

I unloaded shit. Nicky checked out the bathroom and the freebies before chucking everything off the desk to set up his laptop. I cracked a beer then growled, taking in the one and only bed in the room. *Keepin' up appearances.*

He shucked his jeans, pulling on the same pair of University of South Carolina sweats he'd been wearing for over ten years.

I tanked the beer and went for another, checking my iPhone. There was an urgent message from the garage. Imagining fires, destruction, utter fucking mayhem, I opened the attached file . . . then wished I'd never been given the gift of sight. The knuckle-draggers obviously thought they were funny as fuck. They'd stepped out behind Stone's to drop trow and shine their moons for the camera. I pushed the phone as far away from me as possible with a loud groan.

Nicky looked over. "What?"

I pointed at the cell with a firm shake of my head.

Undeterred, he reached for the phone and reeled back when he saw the photo. In the next second, he fell all fricking over himself, laughing it up. "Ray looks like his ass could use a weed whackin', dude, yeah?"

I grabbed the phone back, quickly texting, "*All y'all are FIRED.*"

"*See ya Monday, sport!*" Ray replied.

"Meatheads," I muttered.

Nicky continued to rock with laughter. Meanwhile, I was scarred for life. I ignored the rest of the buffoons' incoming bullshittery and settled back onto the bed, pressing the most used contact on the phone.

"Stone's! At your service, y'all." The sweet voice humming over the wire warmed my heart, her greeting not so much.

"Ma, you're not supposed to answer your home phone that way. Gives people the wrong idea."

"Joshy! We were wonderin' when you'd call. You get to 'Lanta all right? You know those people out there drive like it's the Indy 500. Like to take your life into your own hands. You stopped to eat, now, didn't you?"

I waited for her to take a breath. "Yes and yes, ma'am."

It didn't take her long to gather more speed. "You tryin' to sweet talk me? Five days away is a long time to get into trouble. Now I know Nicky's a good boy, but I don't approve of you spendin' all that time around all those ladies. Y'all best make sure to mind your manners and your morals."

Unlike everyone else on God's green earth, Ma didn't know I was playing *Queer Eye for the Straight Guy*.

Nicky had heard her rant from half a room away. He shouted, "Hey, Gigi! Don't worry, I'm keepin' Joshy here under lock and key."

That calmed her down some. Nicky always had that affect, while I riled her up by breathing the same air, simply because I was, and always would be, her baby boy. Not that she was much for babying, unless it came to JJ.

"The kid there, Ma?" I asked.

"Oh, he's sittin' right here. Had him some pulled pork for dinner, your memaw's old recipe, and a tiny piece of cobbler. And then we went to the Piggly Wiggly to get some Popsicles. I think he's about tuckered out."

Tuckered out? JJ was gonna be bouncing from his sugar spike for the next three hours. I listened to the patter of little feet while my heart flip-flopped in my chest.

"Daddy?"

It never goddamn failed. I shifted to the side of the bed and stared at the wall, quickly blinking. "Yep, I'm here."

"Miss you, Daddy." His squeaky voice cut a path straight through my heart.

I cleared the gruffness from my throat. "Me too, kid. But you're havin' fun with Jamma, right?"

That was the right tactic because he launched into a tale of all the crap Ma had already done—including a trip to Target capped off with a "gween shushy"—which I'd have to unlearn him from when I got home.

"And then Jamma lemme swim in the deep end of the pool wiffout fwoaties!" He finished on what he thought was a high note, but what gave me the forerunner of a heart attack.

I imagined his mussed up hair, his hazel eyes he got from me. The fearlessness of the Stone family that had me worried like only a dad could be from those first wobbly steps and every day since.

"Can I talk ta Uncle Wicky?"

I beckoned Nicky over.

"Hey, dude-man." Nicky's deep voice rumbled out as he greeted my son.

The rest of what I heard was a series of high-pitched nonsense and Nicky rambling on, a huge smile on his face. "Nah, I ain't famous."

There was a pause, then Nicky's loud chuckle. "No, I don't know Mickey Mouse."

A couple minutes later, he handed the phone back. "He's winding down."

21

"Sugar crash," I mouthed.

"Daddy?"

"Yeah, baby boy." I listened to him yawn, that soft pop of his innocent mouth.

"Do Baloo for me."

I fell back on the bed. "'Bare Necessities'?"

"*Mm hmm.*"

I shut my eyes and curled against the phone like I folded around his little body when I sang him to sleep. I'd employed every trick I could think of when he suffered from colic the first nine months and Claire was battling postpartum depression. Disney characters were the old standby. Putting on my best Baloo-bear voice, I sang him the song as he sleepily harmonized as Mowgli.

The song ended and all I heard were soft breaths, deep and heavy. Ma came on the line, whispering, "I don't know how you do it, Joshy. He's already asleep. You're a good daddy."

I crooked my arm over my face, swallowing a few times. "Thanks, Ma. Thanks for takin' care of him."

"Oh hush now, you do all the work. I just do the spoilin'."

"You know he's gonna be up pissing all night because of the sodas and ice pops, right?" A grin slid across my mouth.

"*Hmm.* I hate to break it to you, but you were the same way. And I done been through the wars with you."

"Love ya, Ma."

Her voice softened. "I love you too. Behave, or I will break out the willow switch when you get home. On you and Nicky both."

Ending the call, I kept my eyes closed. JJ still asked about Claire, wondering why his momma left him, why he could only remember me singing him to sleep at night. I didn't believe in sugarcoating the truth, but I did believe in protecting him. Most times I told him she wasn't ready to be a mom. "*But she sure missed one helluva a kid.*"

Then I'd sit in the rocking chair beside his bed all night, making sure his dreams didn't turn into nightmares. That's why I'd never left him before.

"Still hurts?" Nicky read my mind.

"Yeah. But not because Claire left me. Because she left JJ high and dry." I propped up onto an elbow. "Man, what if I'm not good enough to be everything to him?"

"That's bullshit and you know it. Anyone who sees the two of you together knows it, too. Besides, you're not doing it alone. You've got me and the guys, you've got Gigi."

"You think?"

"Yeah. But, if you stopped sowing your wild oats around the lowcountry and settled down, maybe he could have another mom." He knocked into my shoulder.

"Well that isn't gonna happen now that I'm your lover, right?" With a grin, I pushed him right back.

Sure, marriage had never been a cakewalk. That had been blatantly obvious as soon as Claire smashed a piece of our pretty wedding cake into my face after the shotgun-she's-pregnant ceremony. But I'd been determined to give it my best shot, which meant putting up with all of Claire's worst ones. I'd stuck it out for the kid because family was important. Now I didn't give any woman the chance to shake me up, shake me down. There was too much at stake.

It wasn't as if I didn't have offers. Half the female population in Mt. Pleasant—including a good quarter of the married ones—acted like I was a high commodity. They saw the surface only: tough guy, big muscles, successful business owner. They didn't delve into the single dad working all hours, whose personal time was spent with his son, his family, his friends. The Friday night freebie-fucks were what I needed to de-stress from a week full of worries, bills, and bitching.

And I sure as hell was not looking for anything else.

At least here I'd be somewhat anonymous. Nicky's

love muffin, not Mt. Pleasant's most-wanted bachelor.

I sat up when Nicky popped the cork on a bottle of wine, wedging a few more inside the mini-fridge. He took a sip of the pink-colored fizz in his glass. "Done moping?"

"I wasn't moping, I was thinking," I replied.

"I knew I didn't recognize that look on you."

I chucked the hotel menu at him, which he swiftly deflected. "Blow me."

"Might have to before the week's out." He gave me his best attempt at a leer.

"Speakin' of, the cost of registration . . . that's a write-off, right?" I'd have to sort through all these receipts when I got home or, better yet, hand them off to Ray.

"Yeah. If you're a writer." Nicky tossed a red-ribboned lanyard at me. "You can get a thirty percent deduction as my assistant though."

"And this is?" I looked at the thing he'd thrown into my lap.

"That's your name badge."

"I gotta wear it?"

"Yep, at all times." Then he threw something else over and I grabbed it midair. "Don't forget to pin your pretty silk flower onto it. It's the same as mine."

What the hell? A corsage too?

I dutifully pinned the peach-colored flower to my name badge and did a double take. "Stone?"

"Straight up Stone." He swigged down the rest of his wine.

"No pun intended, huh?"

Ambling closer, a seductive swagger to his steps, Nicky bit his bottom lip.

I hustled back on the bed, laughing nervously. "Uh, Nicky? You're kind of giving me the heebie-jeebies here."

He ran his fingers through the shoulder-length hair freed from his ponytail, peering at me with eyes that suddenly smoldered. *Jesus, this is scary. Is this what he does to the ladies?* He stopped right in front of me, breathing into my ear until my shoulders shot up. "Stone. Hard Stone. It adds to your aura, lover."

I gulped. "I can work with that."

Canning the Casanova crap, he started crowing loudly, enjoying every second of my discomfort. "Dude, you actually thought I was hitting on you? I already told you you're too hairy for me."

I punched him in the stomach. "Douchebag."

He continued to laugh as he began his total transformation from plucky Nick Loveland, to natty dresser Nicky Love, *New York Times* best-selling paranormal author. Changing into a flowing poet shirt, tight-ass charcoal gray slacks, he finished it all off with a slash of guy-liner and the long silver medallion that sat in the open collar of his shirt.

I strolled up behind him in the bathroom and pinched his ass. "Lookin' good, babe."

"Maybe you should take a lesson." He scraped a blunt fingernail down my dark stubble.

"I am not going clean-shaved. It hides my weak chin," I grumbled quietly.

"You do not have a weak chin!"

"How do you know? You've never seen it. I was growing this when I was fifteen." *Jesus, I already sound like I'm flaming.*

He looked at me in the mirror from all possible angles. Then he nodded. "Designer stubble."

I could work with that.

"Yeah, butch gay instead of pretty underwear model gay, you can pull it off."

I nodded. "Right on."

With that huge problem solved, i.e., my hairy face, he left me to my cleanup. I changed again, feeling like a frigging clotheshorse as I pulled on another pair of jeans, my shitkickers, and a navy button down shirt. I brushed my teeth, slapped on some aftershave for the shave I hadn't had, and left the bathroom.

Another beer from the mini-fridge in hand, I quickly found ESPN on the TV. Nicky settled at the desk doing his conference shtick. He used one hand on the laptop, the other on his cell, both flying with speed as he pounded out . . . something. His tongue stuck out of the corner of his mouth, and a frown dug deep lines into his forehead.

"Dude, you look like you're about to drop a double deuce over there."

He looked up with glazed eyes. "Huh?"

"Straining, like you're about to drop a load."

"Facebook and email." He waved at the computer. "Twitter, tumblr, and texts." He shook his phone.

I didn't know twatter from tumbleweed from fuck-all, and I definitely didn't have a Facebook account. "You look a little stressed, my friend."

He chugged a glass of wine. "Well, how many accounts do you have?"

I held up my thumb and fingers in a big fat zero.

Pressing a hand to his heart, he gasped. "That's— that's—social media suicide!"

"Hey, I've got a website for Stone's and it's on Facebook, as you well know, but Javier handles that crap. I don't have time to diddle around on the Internet."

"It's not diddlin'. Where do you think my readers come from? How do you think I get the word out there?"

"Whoa, hoss, no need to get your nuts in a knot. I just don't want you to stroke out because of social media before I get a chance to get in your pants."

He pressed a key on his computer and hovered over something on his cell simultaneously, grinning at me.

I shrugged and muttered, "I even hate my iPhone, man."

"You are such a throwback."

"Yep, that's me." I retrieved the fedora from my bag and set it on my head at a rakish angle. The hat combined with my smirk was a guaranteed pussy-magnet. Hell, maybe it worked on dudes too.

"So you're okay with PDAs?" Nicky turned his attention away from the Internet to me.

"Portable electronic devices?"

He walked up and rapped his knuckles against my forehead beneath the hat brim. "Public displays of affection. Asshole. With me."

"Yeah. Already done it, didn't I? But just so you know, rimming is off the table."

"Gotcha," Nicky said with a wince. Then, not to be outdone, he widened his eyes. "What about tea-baggin'?"

My nuts shriveled up. My voice raised one notch higher. "No balls goin' anywhere near each other's mouths. Jesus."

He flopped onto the blessedly massive bed after snagging one of my brews. "Is there baseball on?"

"Dude." I settled next to him, watching him closely in case crazy was catching. "Gamecocks versus Clemson, you forgot?"

He suddenly perked up with a clink of his bottle against mine. "Go Cocks!"

We watched the game in soothing male camaraderie, chugging beers and booing and hissing along with the televised crowd.

The umpire made a bad call and I sat up to shout, "That was not a foul ball!"

"That was clearly a foul ball." Nicky got in my face.

So I decided to take him down. We traded mock punches, pulled a few wrestling moves, the game forgotten for good ol' scrapping. Then it got serious. Clambering on top of me, the wiry bastard practically shoved his crotch in my face.

My head tipped back as I snarled, "What'd I just say about balls in my mouth, you dirty whore?"

Nicky scrambled to his knees and grabbed his johnson. "Foul balls! Foul balls!"

I'd just beaten him down to the mattress with his arm jimmied behind his back when heavy pounding on the

27

door cut into my three-count victory moment. "Who the hell is that?"

His head shot up. "Oh shit."

"Oh shit?"

Bucking me off him, he quickly tied back his fucked-up hair. "My crew."

More hard knocking ensued.

His crew? Sounds like Gerald's out there with a battering ram tryin' to break the damn thing down. Not a bunch of female romance writers.

I watched in amusement as Nicky shoved our beer bottles behind the nightstand, whipped out a fresh bottle of pink fizz and two plastic wineglasses. He chewed his lip, skimming TV channels until he got to a cooking program. *From bros to boyfriends in twenty-five seconds flat.* For my part, I thought about straightening up but then figured what the fuck? We looked like we'd just been catching an early evening canoodle, right?

Nicky arranged himself on the bed with wineglass in hand, pinky finger quirked. Waving like the sultan of some Middle Eastern country, he gestured for me to let the henpeckers in. I kicked his foot—hard—when I walked past the bed.

Pulling open the door, I was almost stampeded into the carpet. A flurry of ruffles and hair and perfume swept past me. Counting the ladies off in my head and matching the numbers to the women I knew were part of Nicky's gang, I started to shut the door.

"Wait!" The last lady's hand shot out. She grabbed someone beyond the portal, pulling her hastily inside.

I flattened myself to the wall and shut the door, listening to the hustle and bustle just beyond the short entryway, gathering my courage . . . and my balls.

Stepping around the corner, I faced the firing squad headed by an elegantly dressed, mid-fifties-something woman. Giant diamonds glittered from her fingers and long strands of pearls hung off her neck.

"Missy Peachtree, BDSM. We simply couldn't *wait* to meet Nicky's partner. Now, we didn't interrupt anything, did we?" she asked with way too much interest.

I straightened my collar, scanned the room for my fedora—the one Nicky was twirling on one finger with a cool smirk on his face—and offered my hand to Miss Missy Peachtree/BDSM. "Pleased to meet you, ma'am."

"Oh my. He's just delicious, isn't he, ladies?" Her hand, released from mine, fluttered to her throat . . . and pearls.

Titters abounded and I curbed the impulse to strut around.

A short round woman in peasant gear with bangles running up and down her arms knocked Missy out of the way. She looked me over from behind green-tinted Lennon glasses. "Divine, I'd say. Where'd you find this tall drink of water, Nicky?" Before he had a chance to answer, she pulled me into a long hug. "Janice Ranger, Steampunk."

Steamwhat? That was a head-scratcher.

No sooner had she released me than a dark-skinned lady glided up to me. "Utterly fuckable."

My eyebrows ratcheted sky-high.

"Don't mind Jackée, she has no filter." Janice butted in.

Lifting her hand with a snap of fingers, Jackée said, "Bitch, don't be callin' me Jackée, this ain't no *227* up in here." She gave a mighty exhale through her nose before her brown gaze walked all over my body. "Jacqueline, Gay Male Romance. I might need to get with you to work out some ideas."

Oh God, meat market. And I'm the grade-A beef apparently.

I stood stunned until another one was pushed forward. I started at the shoes— heels to be absolutely fucking correct—because they were red, with ribbons wrapping around nicely toned calves. A scarlet dress halted just above her knees, cinched in at the waist, cupping her

29

breasts as if offering them for dessert. Sexy round shoulders and the palest buttercream skin brought me to instant hard-on. Then there was her bow-shaped pout and sexy-secretary glasses over guileless green eyes, all set off by clouds of strawberry hair.

It was the woman from the lobby whose shit had dumped out all over the floor.

The babe. The beauty. Right here in our room. In red. *How the hell does she wear a dress like that and manage to look . . . innocent?* My eyes weren't the only thing bulging.

"Leelee Songchild, New Adult." She lifted her hand.

Boing. And I almost swallowed my tongue. Sliding my palm against hers, I curled my fingers and brought her hand to my lips. "Stone. At your service." This time it wasn't a line.

Heat rippled between us as Leelee—*Leelee*—flushed from the top of her breasts to her cheeks. Her lashes fluttered, the pulse in her throat skipped. My cock throbbed in time to it. I only broke away from her when Nicky coughed-swore in the background, probably to remind me my place was supposed to be at his side.

I cleared my throat, glancing around the group. "Stone, foreign car dealer."

"Swoon." Steampunk Janice fanned herself.

"More like sex on legs." Jacqueline picked up her purse.

Missy adjusted her pearls for the umpteenth time. "I'd love to suspend him in a hogtie and try out my new Evil Stick on those thighs."

I choked through a forced laugh and looked to Nicky for help. In return, he grinned and sent my fedora sailing toward me. I caught it behind my back, rolled it up the length of my arm and flipped it off my shoulder to sit at just the right angle on my head.

"Ice, girls, I need ice!" Jacqueline wailed.

I looked to Leelee, my gaze drawn to the red-dressed

minx. She dipped her head and gave a slow clap. No rings on her fingers, she was fair game, except I already had a boyfriend.

"Dinner!" Missy was clearly den mother as well as Domme—another, even more alarming, prospect.

We filed into the hallway, Nicky and I in the center of the chickens who carried on clucking around us. Guiding him along with a hand pressed to his lower back, I earned a half smile and batting eyelashes from him—*Jesus, even I'm convinced*—and giggles from the gals.

"I could get used to this," he whispered.

I growled in what I hoped was a suggestive manner and tightened my fingers just hard enough to cause a twinge of pain with any luck. "Used to what?"

"Being out and proud with my boyfriend."

Yeah, I'm gonna have them all eatin' out of my hand, including Nicky, by the time this shindig's over.

"Which one's the groper?" I whispered.

"Jacqueline. Janice after a successful book signing. Missy after one too many martinis. I don't know much about Leelee yet."

Fuck, I hope Leelee's a groper.

We lagged back and I said, "She's the woman from check-in."

"Oh yeah." He smiled absentmindedly.

Oh yeah? As if Leelee was anything less than spectacular. "You said you didn't know her."

"She just joined our Facebook group a couple months ago, doesn't have a selfie up. I didn't recognize her." He shrugged, again with the nonchalance.

I watched her ass move ahead of me, the loose skirt settling against those round cheeks with every step. I adjusted myself as discreetly as possible.

Leelee came part and parcel with the Henpeckers. This didn't bode well at all.

* * * *

A couple hours later, I was squished into a booth with Nicky on my right side and Leelee on the left of me against the wall. Against a wall was right where I really wanted to fuck her as soon as possible. I let loose a low groan, trying to figure out how to hide my ever-ready erection.

We'd spent an hour and a half in the bar of the barbecue joint waiting for our table. The bartender had flirted shamelessly with Leelee, and I'd wanted to pound his head with my fist until he got a case of cauliflower ear. I'd flirted shamelessly with Nicky, hoping to cement our relationship. I'd totally failed at keeping my eyes off Leelee. But I hadn't put my hands on her yet.

I decided that was a victory.

In the booth, Nicky scooted closer, if that was possible, and laid his hand on my thigh. "Okay, lover?"

Giggles rose from the gaggle of geese on the other side of the table.

I dropped my chin and lifted an eyebrow. "*Peachy*, babe." I glared at Missy Peachtree.

"Ready to order?" Our waitress tapped a pen against her order pad.

I hadn't even looked at the menu because Leelee sat stacked and ready beside me. Her shorter stature made it real damn easy to take a gander at all the creamy skin that was strictly off-limits.

"The fish is supposed to be good." Her soft voice scattered across my skin in slivers of heat that spread to my groin.

Jesus. "Can't. Allergic to shellfish." And then I decided to break out my Will Smith impersonation from *Hitch*, contorting my face and saying, "It is *not* that serious!"

My face suddenly scorching, I hid behind a long drink of goddamn fruity something or other while Leelee Songchild giggled beside me. "That's one of my favorite romcoms. I can't believe you can pull off Will Smith. My ex hated watchin' stuff like that with me."

I dove after that nugget of info, desperate to have her relationship status confirmed. "Your ex?"

She laid a hand on my wrist. "Long story, not a happy ending."

I got my *Glee* on for that, until Nicky narrowed his eyes at me.

Orders were placed, food was eaten, and I kept my damn mouth shut after that. *Doing impressions for the kid was one thing, but Christ.*

Nosy Missy leaned forward over dessert. "So, Stone, the hat . . . is that your signature?"

I twirled it off my head to the tips of my fingers and back again. "Just one of my things, ma'am." Damn, she probably liked it when I called her that. I'd have to knock that shit off. "Y'all should see my cowboy hat," I drawled. "'Cept I only wear it when I ride Nicky hard and put him up wet."

Jacqueline slammed a palm to the table. "Booyah! I knew it! You're the top." She waggled her fingers. "Pay up, bitches."

"So butch." Janice practically eye-fucked me across the tabletop after she handed her cash over.

I fought a grin. Butch sort of worked as a compliment in the macho column. I'd take it, especially when Leelee suddenly jerked away from the heat of my thigh pressed against hers. Her skin turned rosy, and she wouldn't meet my eyes even when I placed an elbow on the table, bracketing her in.

"Okay?" I asked.

"*Mm hmm.* Just parched, I don't think the A/C's high enough in here." She drank from her glass of ice water.

If she was overheating, I was on fire. My body tingled from my fingertips to my toes, and I wanted to get closer to her sun. Nicky bumping against me broke the spell of attraction enough to make me slide an arm across his shoulders.

We spent another hour at the restaurant, filling up on coffee and convention gossip I listened to with half an ear. I was too distracted by Leelee next to me as she sent zingers in reply to Jacqueline's fast-fire questions. Basically working myself up to a long cold shower or a quick, quiet jerk-off session later.

Catching the shuttle back to the hotel, I felt a little lazy, a little drunk. I hauled Nicky closer for an *affectionate* skull rub. He gave me a *loving* elbow jab to the ribs. It was a war between feeling warm-hearted and welcomed by his crew, pretending I couldn't wait to grab Nicky and fuck his brains out against a wall, and pretending I *didn't* want to grab Leelee . . . and fuck her brains out against a wall.

The possibility of wall-fucking came a lot sooner than expected when we returned to the hotel and the hens prodded me to escort the *little miss* to her room.

"Leelee's new to all this." Missy the Mistress explained with a twist of her pearls.

"Uh, so am I." I really didn't need an excuse to be alone with Leelee, in a hotel. *Alone.* Where there were beds behind every door.

Janice's bangles jangled in my face. "Yes, but you're a man."

"Double standard much?" I groused. "What happened to feminism?"

Nicky covered his mouth with his hand, no doubt smothering the ha-ha chuckles.

Jacqueline's head swung back and forth like a snake charmer's. "Please, second-wave feminism is so passé. A woman likes to be walked to her door. Besides, Stone, you look rough—"

"And ready," Janice chimed in.

"Like a bouncer. Have you ever thought about wearing leather?" Missy colluded.

"She's just a babe in the woods, only twenty-seven and getting her first taste of fame. Leelee has people after her, and we wouldn't want anything to happen to her, would we?" Jacqueline crossed her arms.

"People? After her?" I turned to Leelee—innocent, sexual, extremely fuckable Leelee—in disbelief.

"She's being courted—" Missy whispered.

"By agents and editors." Janice shivered and her jewelry shimmied too.

I glanced at Leelee. She stood with one leg braced against the wall, drawing my gaze to the long slit up the thigh of her dress I'd missed earlier.

Holy shit, that's hot.

Jacqueline stamped her foot to drag my attention back. "She just happens to be the latest self-pub whiz kid, her first book went viral. Now everyone wants a piece of her pie."

Leelee's pie? Count me in.

"Fine." I jabbed the elevator button. "I'll take her."

I prayed the elevator would be bursting with people.

It was empty. Of course it was.

I thought about attempting small talk, but it took all my damn concentration to keep from staring at Leelee in the mirrored surrounds. I held my hands loosely cupped in front of my crotch and tried not to fidget. My cock ached, my jeans were too tight, and the only thing working to my advantage was my hat, which hid my lust-hungry eyes from sight.

On Leelee's floor, I followed a staggered step behind, because I wasn't dumb enough to pass up the chance to eyeball her ass one more time.

When we reached her door, she took out her key and smiled. "So . . ."

"Yeah."

Her green eyes flickered up. "My knight in shinin' armor again?"

Scam artist, maybe. All my natural tendencies urged me to kiss the hell out of her. I really wished I could follow her into the room. I'd give my left nut to find out

35

what kind of whimpers she made when my head was buried between her thighs, my hands pulling down the straps of her dress to get to her tits. The fact my hands—and tongue—were tied made me ornery as hell.

"I'm nobody's knight, lady, least of all yours." My voice came out flat and hard.

A veil dropped over her eyes, making them brittle as green glass. "My mistake. And here I thought chivalry wasn't dead," she said with all the haughtiness of a true southern woman before slipping into her room.

The door slammed in my face.

Pissing Leelee off might not have been the best idea because that spark of hot temper was even more attractive than her angel-vixen looks.

Babe in the woods? Bullshit. This woman was hell in high heels, and I had designs to fuck her against the hood of my '69 Camaro.

Chapter Three

Wednesday: Y Chromosome and Testosterone Overload

I SKIPPED THE COLD shower, the quiet jag-off session, kicking myself in the ass instead for putting that *you're a dick* look in Leelee's eyes. After stripping down, I shoved Nicky aside in the bed and started worrying. About the garage, the kid, the sudden wanna-fuck-Leelee-outta-my-system fantasies. Nicky tossed a handful of pillows at my head, and we ended up fighting over blankets until we finally passed out.

I woke up in the night, sweating my balls off from all the blankets I'd stolen from him. His breath tickled my ear, his arm slung across my torso. *Fucking cuddler.* I pushed him to the knife's edge of the bed, only slightly tempted to nudge him that extra inch until he fell off. He snorted-snored and smacked my hands away. I sprawled on my back, enjoying all the room, and fell back asleep.

A mash-up of nightmares chased my dreams. Boobs, broads, faceless chicks, and nameless conquests caught up

37

with me.

At one point I groaned awake with Nicky hanging over me, his jaw clenching. "Stop fuckin' snoring, dude, before I duct tape your mouth shut."

Washy lines of sun slanted into the room from behind the blackout curtains when I came to from a restless sleep. Nicky dressed in the weak light of what had to be barely half-past the crack-of, a time I was all too familiar with from the kid's early morning wake-up routine. It usually included JJ pouncing on my head, pulling on my toes and—the joy—pretending to be a big, slobbering dog called Viper. I rolled over, burying my head under a pillow. I was gonna milk this gay-cation for all it was worth.

"I've got a roundtable to chair at . . ."

Bla bla bla.

The bed dipped when Nicky sat beside me. "Then a panel at nine, a meeting with my editor at ten-thirty." I heard him flicking through his notes about what he had to do, who he had to meet, and where he had to be every fucking second of the next four point five days. "A meeting with Warlocks and Witches at eleven-thirty, another panel at noon, and then a pitch session to work after that. So, you're on your own this morning."

Jesus, and I think my days are busy? "Yeah, yeah." I dove farther under the blankets until I was in a tight cocoon and his voice sounded muffled by cotton.

"Lunch . . . 1:30 . . . text . . ."

"Fuck off already," I grumbled.

"Love you too, darlin'."

I reached out a hand and swatted his ass. "Get lost, shithead."

When I finally heard the door close, I yanked the covers off and thought about jerking off too. But would that count as cheating on Nicky? I tugged at my hair, glaring at the morning wood pushing up the waistband of my briefs. I decided to snag a couple more hours of shuteye. I could be faithful to *my man* for at least one day, right?

Roused by my alarm at eight o'clock, I stood and stretched then dropped for five reps of good old-fashioned sit-ups followed by four sets of one-armed push-ups. After I finished, I kicked off my briefs and considered leaving them under Nicky's pillow just for shits and giggles. Strolling into the bathroom, I scowled at my rejuvenated erection. Cold shower? *Screw that.* If I had to fuck my fist to make the bastard go down, I'd do it.

One palm on the wall, my head bent under the hot spray, I wrapped a hand around my cock. I was so hard and sensitive the first few strokes hurt like a bitch, but the water and a few squirts of shower gel took care of the shock of touch. Pumping in and out of my fist, I braced my legs wide and groaned. It sure as hell wasn't *Nicky* that came out of my mouth.

I ran the flat of my palm over the swollen head, closing my eyes as I imagined Leelee's mouth sucking slowly over my cock until she couldn't swallow any more. Muscles from my chest to my thighs to my ass shook. My forehead fell against the shower wall. I dragged my fingertips up, coasting them across the crown, lightly fingering just beneath until my thighs quivered. I'd never wanted a woman more than I did Leelee at that moment. Naked, wet, glistening. Nice tits, big hips, soft ass. Hungry and begging for my cock.

I knocked my fist against the tiles. Throwing my head back, I chased after the come filling up my balls until they felt like they'd burst and blow the top off my dick too.

I heard another knock, and that time it wasn't me.

Then another as I stroked faster, swearing, so close . . . *Jesus fuckin'* . . . "Aahhhlmost!"

Then full-on banging. At the door.

I pulled my hands off myself and flipped my head up with a loud, "Fuck. I'm comin'!" Or I would've been. I nearly was.

"Maid service better not expect a tip at the end of the week." I cut off the water. I tied a towel around my hips. I swore some more. "Knock knock knock, my cock was about to go off." I flung open the door and almost dropped the towel.

"Hi, Stone. Nicky was worried about leavin' you to your own devices. He thought you might be lonely." Leelee's pretty eyes wavered for a second, lowering to my chest where drops of water clung.

Nicky was a dipshit *and* a dipstick for sending her to check on me. As for lonely? I was horny. I was the very last thing from lonely especially with the walking, talking, blushing visual of Leelee right in front of me and my cock ready to explode. She was soft to look at, but I reckoned there was hot fire just beneath the surface. Once unlocked, she'd be a wildcat the likes I'd never tangled with. She could easily win my heart, cut it out, crush it beneath her unreal high heels, and be on her merry way.

She stood in my doorway. With a bed behind us and my gay-mance cockblocking cover story between us. I tried not to crowd against her when all I wanted to do was take her in my arms and kiss her for all she was worth.

That was when I noticed her outfit.

Leelee. Holy. Jesus. Christ.

"What the hell are you wearin'?" I asked before my mouth caught up with my brain.

"Oh! I don't usually dress like this. It's for the convention." She smoothed one hand along her hip and angled an ankle behind her.

She continued talking, but I was done listening because every ounce of my attention was aimed at the disarming display—*disarming display? I need to stop readin' Nicky's shit*—of hotness in front of me. This dress was going into the Handjob Hall of Fame. V-neck, off the shoulder, rose-colored. Leelee's hair was twisty and perfect for grabbing while I rode her hard from behind. And the shoes on her feet should be outlawed in all fifty states for being unlawful very-fucking-hot violations. They were spiky and showed sexy toe cleavage.

I brushed up on this Queer Eye shit, fat lotta good it did me.

"Besides, what are *you* wearin'?" I watched her cherry-red lips move, thinking I better act like I had half a brain in my head rather than a full quart of come ready to rocket from my other head.

"A towel?" A hard-on and a smirk. No hat. Stone. Rock hard stone.

Leelee took in the ink on my chest. "This is gorgeous, the rendering's exquisite." Her fingertips brushed against my tat and the heart—my heart—pounded double-time. It felt like she'd taken jumper cables to my nervous system.

I was supposed to be unavailable, and I most definitely shouldn't be alone with Leelee. So of course I did the stupid thing. Stepping back, I invited her inside.

"I brought you coffee, black." She thrust a cup in my hand. "You don't seem like the type of man who takes sweetener."

If only she knew how much I liked sweet things like her. "Thank you, Leelee."

"Um, I'll just wait and you can finish what you were . . ." She trailed off, her gaze skimming down my body. My towel was quickly becoming the *most unseemly mode of dress* as it reached the danger zone of my pelvic V cut. She swallowed and looked away. " . . . doing in the shower?"

Yeah, I didn't think I was gonna whack-it with her present. What I'd been doing in the shower was her. And if I kept at it, I was gonna be real goddamn loud, especially with the living masturbation-material sitting in the next room.

Returning to the bathroom, I gulped down the coffee and slammed the cup into the trashcan. I gritted my teeth and grabbed the base of my cock, squeezing hard. My eyes teared up, but I managed to go from full to semi, at least until I got dressed and walked out of the bathroom and

41

decided a hard cup jockstrap might be in order whenever I was near Leelee.

* * * *

We made it to the lobby to hang with Jacqueline without any further suggestive comments. I averted my eyes from Leelee's legs, her breasts, her dress, and most definitely her stilettos. Jacqueline waved at us from a clutch of couches at the far end of the room. I almost ran to her. I needed a goddamn safety net or back-up plan, anything but a wingman, if I was going to make it out of this conference without dragging Leelee to a bed—any bed would do, hell, the elevator was beginning to look mighty tempting—and keeping my ruse intact.

The overlarge room held a party atmosphere like Mardi Gras—or Savannah on St. Patty's day. People greeted each other with air-kisses and almost-hugs, wearing the lanyards that listed them as writer/aspiring/agent/editor/gawker. And then there were the Coverdales Nicky had mentioned. They were unmistakable as they strutted around looking big and beefy and romance-cover worthy. Now I got it. These dudes were a cross between Chippendales, cover models, and, holy shit, Clydesdales, because some of them were as big as horses.

The lobby definitely wasn't Stone's staff room.

But there were pastries.

I loaded a plate. Leelee served herself beside me, and I saw her to a seat before I pulled up a chair next to her and across from Jacqueline.

Jackée's fingernails were long, sharp and sparkly. Peering closer, I saw they were decorated with tiny book covers. Inventive marketing—writers had it going on. She tapped them like knifepoints on the table, a wicked glint in her shrewd brown eyes. "Damn. How is it you look hotter this morning than you did last night, Stone?"

I ripped into a gooey pastry, chewing instead of answering.

Her nails struck the table in a faster rhythm. "Was it something Nicky did to you last night? Did he pounce on you as soon as you walked through the door? I always figured him for a freak in the bed."

I swear, my nuts got smaller and smaller, shrinking from her unveiled interest. It didn't help any that Leelee barely managed to muffle a laugh behind an éclair.

Finally Jacqueline sat back and crossed her arms. "What good are you? I'm just looking for a little sinspiration for my love scenes."

Right, the gay male writer.

"'Fraid to say, I don't kiss and tell."

"I wasn't talking about kissing," she replied glumly. "All right, keep your secrets for now. But don't think I'm letting you off the hook, Stone. I will get it out of you if I have to get Missy to beat it out of your beefcake ass."

Fuck, I hope not.

With renewed spirit, she turned to Leelee. "So, what's your story, girl? You ain't never said so much as boo in our Facebook group."

"Who says I have a story?"

"You're a writer, you've got a story . . ."

Touché.

"There's no one. Just my folks, my friends, and my writing." Tight face, tight-lipped, Leelee obviously didn't want to spill.

Jacqueline kept at it like Viper, the princess Rottweiler with a rawhide chew toy—or my boots. "C'mon now, give me *something*. I swear, if it wasn't for the fact Stone likes the man-love, the pair of you would be two mute peas in a pod, and all this girl wants is a little story. Took us two years to get Nicky to even breathe a word about this one over here." She pointed those claws at me. "Are you really gonna make me wait that long?"

Leelee slapped the half-eaten éclair onto her plate and

muttered a quiet *dammit*. "Fine. I'll tell y'all."

I felt bad about her being in the line of fire because I hadn't made up some lusty tale about Nicky and me. "Leelee, I don't think you need to—"

She held a hand up in front of my face. "You don't need to stand up for me. Remember, you're no one's knight in shinin' armor."

I opened my mouth to apologize for being a complete asshole, but Jacqueline beat me to the punch, hooting, "Told!"

"And you can shove it too, Jacqueline. I'll tell it 'cause I need to get it off my chest, but don't think I can't see right through you. You want the lowdown on the new girl, to see if I stand up to inspection with all y'all veterans. I swear. Goddamn writers, sometimes it's like a hazing ritual."

Listening to Leelee put the beat-down on Jacqueline was some seriously hot shit.

An approving smile curved Jacqueline's glossy painted lips. "I'm happy to see you show some balls, Leelee."

"Oh, I got balls, balls of goddamn steel."

So do I after that display of utter fucking brass.

"That's what I thought, girl."

Leelee sat back and glanced at me. "It ain't gonna be pretty."

"*Mm hmm*, the real stories never are. And that's why we keep at the romance writing." Jacqueline gave a little gospel.

I wasn't all that fond of chick-talk. The most I came close to it was when I caught the boys snorting in the staff room over that *Real Housewives* train wreck or when they showed up at Ma's with their women for the monthly Stone's potluck. But I was all for learning more about Leelee, so I put my listening ears on. Just like Ma always told me to do when she used to give me the what-for.

"I was real serious about this guy, Patrick Waddell."

I instantly hated the schmuck because she said *this guy* and *serious* in the same sentence.

"I thought he was just the most wonderful man there ever was. Successful, smart, sweet as could be. Sweet on me, at least I thought he was." She twirled one long curl around her finger then snapped up in her seat, pressing her hands together in her lap. "Good lookin', a real sharp dresser. A total scammer, it turned out."

"Oh Lord," Jacqueline breathed out.

"You see where this is going?" Leelee's head dipped toward the other woman, who nodded in response.

Color me goddamn stupid because I have no clue at all.

"We were engaged, the wedding date was set. One Saturday we were picking out china at one of those precious little boutiques. And Patrick just started layin' into me, right there in the middle of the store. He didn't like the colors, didn't approve of the patterns I'd pre-chosen, wanted to get right back into the car and go home. It was just china! It turned out it wasn't the patterns he was worried about at all. The man helping us out, he stepped off a bit while Patrick blew up in my face. But I saw him watchin' us, his lips pursed like he was suckin' on a sour lemon."

Jacqueline reached across the table to lay her hand on Leelee's shoulder. "Oh, girl, he wasn't, was he?"

"Yeah, yeah, he was." Leelee's head bent low as she sighed.

I was crawling out of my skin. *He wasn't, he was what?* The Y chromosome plus a boatload of testosterone meant I missed out on a whole lot of feminine intuition, apparently.

Guarded eyes flew to mine and away. "Patrick said 'I can't do china, I can't do a wedding with you, I can't do you anymore!' He shouted at me, but he looked at the other man, the very gorgeous man who'd messed up our order and dropped a few plates and muttered some cutting

45

comments all the while he'd attended to us. And I was just naïve enough to ask Patrick what he was talkin' about."

"The kiss of death," Jacqueline said.

Leelee mumbled, "The kiss of death."

The kiss of huh?

"My fiancé left me for the clerk while we shopped wedding china in his store. He came out by accident, practically on the eve of our wedding, because he'd been two-timing me with that man!"

Wait, what?

"Now that right there is a second chance love story." Jacqueline tapped those fucking outrageous fingernails again.

"Oh, trust me, there's no second chance for Patrick or any man. The wedding invitations were followed by regrets and a cancellation notice." She flicked her fingers at the éclair in front of her. "My life is worse than a romance novel."

"That definitely counts for a black moment, baby-doll." Jacqueline clucked her tongue. She stared at me over Leelee's bowed head as if I had the feel-better answers to something I'd barely understood.

I held my hands up in an I-got-nothin' move.

"'Course, as the fates would have it, this all went down last fall when every other huge thing was happening for me. My writing took off and my world fell apart at the same time."

Jacqueline silently urged me to do something again, her hands spinning furiously in the air.

"I turned him gay," came Leelee's suddenly tiny voice. That cut me harder than any knife to the heart . . . or the other woman's nails.

"Bullshit, Leelee. You can't turn a straight guy gay, right, Stone?" Jacqueline glared at me for the third time.

Not unless it's for the purposes of pulling the wool over y'all's eyes. "'Course not, that's fucking ridiculous." I hooked my foot around the leg of Leelee's chair and pulled her closer. Cupping her face, I did something immensely unadvisable and placed a light kiss on her cheek. Then the other one. Where I lingered much longer than I had any right to do.

From beneath long eyelashes, dewy eyes sought mine. Leelee's lips quivered. *Please don't cry.* I decided right then if I ever got the chance to meet Patrick the dick Waddell I was gonna beat his face all to bloody motherfucking hell.

Leelee pulled herself together and pulled away. I didn't know whether to be thankful or regretful. Most of all I wanted her back in my arms.

"You must really hate people like me and Nicky," I blurted.

Jacqueline snickered, "Oh, snap."

"No!" Leelee patted my thigh, way up high. *Danger zone, danger zone.* My legs twitched, my cock throbbed, and I fought down the animal inside. "I feel safe with you, Stone."

Bad move, babe. The side of me that wanted to protect her from pain warred with the part that wanted to prowl all over her body. Safe was the very last thing she should feel around me.

Jacqueline's chair screeching back hauled me away from the edge of proving just how dirty and dangerous I could be for Leelee.

Jacqueline stood to shout through megaphone hands, "It's that famous writer, Nicky Love!"

Several heads from the surrounding tables swiveled to watch his approach. Next to him, Janice wasn't to be outdone. She pointed and waved. "I don't believe it! The most prestigious male-male author, Jacqueline!"

"What're they doing?" I mumbled to Leelee.

"No idea."

Having caused a stir, Jacqueline returned to her seat with a pleased hum. "Oh, we just like to get a little attention."

"Or annoy people?" I asked.

"That too." She grinned.

I stood as Janice, Missy Beat-me, and Nicky approached. Leaning in to nuzzle his neck, I wrinkled my nose where no one could see. "Interesting way to make an entrance."

"You like that?"

"I had no idea you were such a showman, might have to get you around the gara—I mean around the dealership more often, babe." I slid my fingers through his hair, working the enamored lover angle to the max.

He spoke just loud enough for those around us to hear. "I'm pretty sure you know exactly how much of a showman I am from bein' in my bed every night, lover." Dressed in pinstriped tuxedo pants, a ragged maroon T-shirt and black suspenders, he lowered his voice. "From skirt-chasin' rogue to queer and en vogue overnight, Josh? I'm impressed."

"Just makin' sure we look good and spending some time with the ladies."

"It's that last part I'm worried about," he hissed.

Me too. I was enjoying the ladies' company—one in particular—a little too much.

Janice shoved Nicky out of the way. I did a double-take. Gone was the hippy peasant look. She was dressed in some kind of kinky Old West saloon-madam get-up complete with a tight corset she almost busted out of. I guessed Nicky wasn't the only one who dressed the part. She reached up to grab my face for a smack on the lips.

"What was that for?"

"I'm a hugger." She shrugged.

"That was more than hugging."

"You can take it." Janice winked from behind a pair of old-fashioned goggles instead of last night's John Lennon glasses. A large pendant of what looked like clock gears rested on her bosom.

"So, is this the Steampunk thing?" I asked.

"You got it, hot stuff." She reached around for a quick squeeze of my ass.

"Hands off the merchandise, wench, he's mine." Nicky towed me toward to the table.

They all crowded around, mouths gunning a mile a minute about the big book fair on Saturday, the morning's *epic* triumphs and *fail* moments. Then there were things called *flail* moments. I was lost again, especially when Missy did a lot of flapping of her arms at me. Maybe she was trying to be a human flogger?

"How about you, hon?" Janice waved her hand in front of Leelee's face, a burnished antique timepiece replacing her bracelets.

"Oh, I'm just takin' in the scenery." And I swore her gaze slid to me before skipping away.

I decided to take in the scenery too, going so far as to angle my chair more toward Nicky and less in Leelee's direction. I worked my arm around his shoulders, ignoring the chorus of sighs from around the table. While they blazed on about the afternoon's agenda, I lingered on a woman across the room who danced aimlessly, with no music and no partners.

"What's her deal?"

Nicky turned to check her out. "Dances to the beat of a different drum?"

I watched the girl awhile longer—her tiny body and face almost completely hidden by acres of flowy shit and incredibly long blond hair. If the kid were here he'd probably ask for her autograph, mistaking her for one of Disney's cardboard cutout creations. "She reminds me of that chick."

"Which chick." He squinted at the nearly fairy princess.

I made sure no one else could hear me. "Angel or Erin or . . . fuck, I can't remember. The one who used to show up at Stone's to give me lunchtime blowjobs."

Snapping his fingers, Nicky said, "Angelica."

"Yeah, Angelica." Angelica with the long, long legs and the long blond hair. She was just about addicted to my dick. That'd been a good week.

"She was crazy."

"A nympho, maybe. Gave some crazy good head though."

His voice dropped even lower. "You really are a slut."

"Guys can't be sluts, can they? I think that makes me a stud." I pulled him right up to me and bit his earlobe. A love bite, not a sharp punishing pinch of my teeth at all.

"Double standards." He accused.

"Double penetration."

"Hopeless case."

"Yeah." I raised my voice. "Hopeless for you, babe."

More sighs from the chickens and a glare-grin combo from Nicky.

"You should join FetLife." Missy dragged Nicky back into the conversation.

"What the hell is FetLife?" I settled my forearms onto the table.

Nicky pointed to a lady dressed all in leather as black as the hair arranged in a wild formation on her head. "A social board for The Lifestyle."

He said "the lifestyle" like it was in all-important caps . . . and I stared at leather-lady. "Elvira has a lifestyle?"

Cuffing me with a *discreet* smack to the back of the head, he explained, "BDSM, remember?"

"Maybe that should've been in the note cards, never mind all the other shit," I grumbled quietly. Then I narrowed my eyes at him. "But you don't write BDSM."

With a sharp twist to her pearls and an even sharper smile, Missy said, "No, but I do, dear."

"You practice what you preach?"

One eyebrow arched in my direction. "If you walk the walk."

Her comment caused alarm bells to go off inside of me. Leaning in, I whispered for Nicky's benefit alone,

"Please tell me she's not already onto us."

"Better hope not." Clasping my hand, he spoke in a loud drawl, "Besides, you know how much you love bein' called sir, darlin'."

Hoots and hollers rose from our companions.

Missy and Nicky had both just one-upped me, assholes.

Half an hour later, some guy muscled in from out of nowhere. I didn't like him on sight, especially when he perched on the arm of Leelee's chair. His dark hair was slicked back from his face, his grin oily, his palms were probably greased too. Whatever he was trying to sell her screamed used car salesman, and I knew all about that. My territorial instincts went ballistic.

He kept leering down the top of Leelee's dress while she inched as far away as she could. He droned on and on about his pet bunnies, which I took to mean underage girlfriends. The longer he sat and chatted, the more Leelee looked shaken. A blast of protectiveness came out of left field and rocked me to the core.

Finally I glared at him long enough to scare him off. "Who was that dirtbag?"

"Andrew LaForge, big-time agent." Janice flipped her hand up as if that explained everything.

"He's one of those folks out to get you?" I asked Leelee.

"Get to her, sign her, same diff." Jacqueline leaned in close. "Last LitLuv, he walked away with so much ingénue talent, he could've worn a suit made of hundred dollar bills. No one knows how he does it. There's never been a report made against him, but I guaran-damn-tee there's some skeletons hiding in his swanky walk-in wardrobe."

I liked less and less the idea of Leelee the small town hit-it-big girl versus the New York City slicker.

Missy met my eyes. "Mark my words, he's a shark who can smell fresh blood from a mile away."

"Well. I feel the need for a long, hot shower after that." Giving a shaky laugh, Leelee got to her feet.

"Stone'll take you." Every single one of them rushed to volunteer me while I bit back a groan.

Yeah, I wanted to take her, in more ways than one. I also did not want to be alone with the woman for one damn second longer than I had to be. But she turned to me with such a weary smile there was no way in hell I could resist.

"It'd be my pleasure." I placed my hand on the small of her back, guiding her along.

We had to make several pit stops for fans who wanted pictures, so I played paparazzo while Leelee smiled and signed books. With each of her readers, she was gracious and genuine, a true southern lady, showing none of the earlier stress.

As soon as the elevator doors shut us in, she slumped. "I don't do well with crowds or attention."

"You could've fooled me."

She blinked and blushed. Silence—the tense kind that was usually the forerunner of clothes being torn off before some outrageous fucking—thickened between us.

I cleared my throat. "So. This is getting cozy."

"You, me, and the elevator . . ." Her voice lilted along my skin, tightening the muscles in my lower belly with wicked arousal.

I walked her to her room, unlocked it for her, and this time gallantly accepted her thanks. She rose to her tiptoes and slid her lips across my cheek. My groin thumped with heat, but I played it cool, stepping back and dipping an imaginary hat.

"Wait! I've got somethin' for you." She darted inside. Rushing back, Leelee thrust a book at me then, with a sultry drawl, a saucy wink and a "Happy readin', Stone," she closed the door.

I flipped the book over then slammed my eyes

shut.

The title? *Ride*.

The chick on the cover was riding, all right. Naked and back to, she straddled hard-muscled thighs. Her head was thrown back, the curve of one tit showed, and a pair of masculine hands gripped her hips.

The author? *Leelee Songchild.*

Holy fuck.

I am a dead man.

Chapter Four
Wednesday: Ride It Out

IN THE HOTEL ROOM, I flopped onto the bed and snagged a couple pillows behind my head. *Ride, huh? Let's see what Leelee's got.*

Avery heard him through the cracked bedroom door.

"Yeah, Ave. Like that, suck my balls."

Ave? She inhaled a shaky breath before pressing the door open. She and Jase had been roommates for approximately two months, and he'd never so much as given her a second glance. Or maybe she just hadn't noticed, her nose was usually buried in a textbook. Apparently he'd been saving up any careful consideration of her for something that sounded hypnotically raunchy, entailing things she certainly didn't do.

Gorgeous Jase cultivated a bad boy image, but he always got up early to cook her breakfast, usually in a low-slung towel fresh from a shower.

Peeking inside, Avery's face turned hot. His head tilted back, the cords of his neck rigid, Jase sat completely naked in the leather armchair across from her. One fist slowly pumped his cock as the fingers of his other hand slid below to cup his balls.

The door creaked, his muscles flexed, his head flew up. He caught her breathless and staring. Through the shaggy hair falling across his face, she made out his brown eyes, hooded by heavy eyelids.

"Avery, darlin'. Was just thinking about you."

Happy reading? Was Leelee fucking kidding me? More like horny reading and instant hard-on aided by the fact sometimes shy, sometimes spitfire Leelee had written some seriously kinky shit. At this rate my cock was gonna have an embolism.

"Really? Which head were you using?" She asked in a barely steady voice, her gaze straying low before boring a hole into the wall above his . . . head. The one on top of his shoulders, not the one glistening as it jutted against his belly.

"Now, don't bust my balls, gorgeous." He hooked a finger at her. "Why don't you come over here and suck 'em instead?"

She shook her head, intending to back away, determined not to become another of Jase Everly's needy little tarts. His flavor of the day. The boy was like Baskin Robbins . . . 31 flavors, one for every day of the month. "I don't think so."

I started laughing. Even worse, Leelee tickled my funny bone, as well as my boner.

"*Too prissy to suck cock?*"

"*Too discerning to blow yours, Jase,*" *she hissed.*

In a stern voice, he said, "I'm not gonna ask again. Come inside and close the damn door, Ave."

"*Go fuck yourself,*" *she shot back, turning to leave.*

He was there before she could escape, slamming the door shut and spinning her against it. She smelled him—spicy, a little sweaty—and it made her dizzier than she let on, glaring up at him.

Leaning to the side, he swept one hand up and down the skirt and blouse she wore. "I'm all for a little cat and mouse, but you're not as mousy as you make yourself out to be. And what you're hiding underneath all this? Really turns me on, Ave." He skimmed his nose along her jaw then nipped the sensitive skin beneath her ear. Jase whispered in a velvety voice, "Maybe you just need a little spankin' to loosen you up."

"*Maybe you want me to hogtie your hand to your cock!*"

His warm, rough fingers sliding across her belly to her hip, he jerked her against him so she felt his hot length pressing against her thigh. "I don't think you wanna do that. Nnh nnnh." When he retreated, Avery's body jolted with anger . . . with hunger.

"*No, you like this, don't you?*" *He gripped himself again and made a slow show of thrusting his cock in and out of his fist, already so erect he*

was dark red, shiny, and swollen at the tip.
She shook her head.

I laid the book down and dragged my arm across my forehead. Bashful, beautiful, blazing Leelee, who blushed at the drop of a hat, wrote hardcore smut to rival my old collection of *Penthouse Forum*. This wasn't good. I didn't need another reason to think about her and sex in the same sentence.

The steamy cover of *Ride* facing me made matters worse. My hand automatically reached to unbutton my jeans. Working one-handed, I plucked the buttons free, desperate for release before the built-up pressure in my cock caused irreversible injury. Freeing myself from the denim confines, I flipped the book over.

> *Jase gave her a wicked grin and tilted his head. A throaty growl escaped him. "I'm gonna come soon. If you don't want it in your mouth or on your body, you better go."*
>
> *Willing her eyes away and her legs to move, she scrambled for the doorknob, listening as Jase strained to say, "See you at breakfast, Ave."*

I'd just pushed my pants down my thighs when my damned iPhone blared the "Bohemian Rhapsody" ringtone.

"Sonuvabitch!" If it wasn't the maid service disguised as Leelee interrupting my session, it was Ma, instant mood killer.

After shuffling my clothes back in order and slowing my heart rate, I answered. "Ma."

"Oh good gravy, what have ya done now? You're all outta breath."

"Nothin'." Yet. Unfortunately. Her telling-off tone of

voice reminded me of every single time she'd caught me, and usually Nicky, up to some bound-for-reform-school hijinks. I'd hated her saying back then: *I got eyes in the back of my head, sonny, so don't you even think about it*, but I planned on being the same way with the kid.

"*Mm hmm.* Just make sure you keep it that way." She quickly shifted subjects. "JJ just had his lunch. We went to the Bojangles and then I made him some of my strawberry shortcake with the fresh biscuits I like, not that store-bought sponge cake crap that's no good for nothin'. He ate it right up."

"'Course he did, Ma. You just loaded him to the gills with fast food and sugar." I rolled my eyes.

"Well, that's what ol' Jamma's for." I could nearly see her preening her sharply cut, silvery-white bobbed hair. "He's just about to go down for a nap, and he wanted you to sing to him. Then later we're gettin' in the pool—"

I interrupted her. "Yeah, about the pool and letting him swim in the deep end—"

"Shush it. You think I'd ever let anything happen to him? I gotta remind you I've got an extra set of eyes—"

"In the back of your head, yeah, I know." Just what I'd been thinking. "Is he there now?"

"He's wrestlin' with Viper, that big old softie. Aren't they a pair?" Ma made soft cooing noises. Anyone would think she was talking about JJ playing with a cute little kitten instead of an eighty-pound Rottie.

It didn't matter that the kid had Viper wrapped around his little finger, that shit flipped me right the fuck out. "Please go get him, Ma," I gritted between clenched teeth.

"JJ baby, Daddy's on the phone. Don't let Viper kiss you on the face, hon, she ain't brushed her teeth today . . ."

Not to mention that they were big killer teeth. Fuckin' A. I was gonna have a heart attack during this trip, one way or the other.

I let loose a big sigh of relief when I heard the kid's breathless squeaky voice. "Hi, Daddy!"

My heart walloped in my chest. I smiled through the need to wrap him in my arms, keeping him safe from everything and everyone . . . including Viper *the big softie*. "Winding down for a nap?"

"Jamma says I gotta."

"Jamma says I *have to*." I reminded him.

"'S'what I said," he complained with that teetering-on-the-edge whine.

"That *is not what* you said." I gentled my tone.

"Daddy, why you talkin' funny at me?"

Oh well, we'd have to tackle grammar, sugar withdrawals, and dog avoidance behavior when I got home . . . after I hugged the almighty hell out of him. "I'll just sing to you instead, huh?"

"I like that best. And when you hug on me. And ice cream . . ." The sleepy ramble heralded an extra-long nap.

"Me too, kid. Which song will it be this time?"

"Not the scary lady with the horns," he muttered, taking his decision very seriously. He'd be frowning and pulling at the cowlick on the crown of his head.

"Got it. No scary Maleficent." I didn't do the chick parts very well anyway.

JJ hummed for about half a minute before shouting, "The Flynn one!"

I grumbled. That Flynn Rider dude was nothing but an itinerant playboy. I preferred the horse or the chameleon. "You're doing Rapunzel."

"*Mm hmm.*"

This one was pure schmaltzy romance, and I tried not to laugh as the kid mumbled through half his turn of "I See The Light". I'd sat through the movies on repeat so many times they almost played in the background of my head, which could become really disturbing.

We finished on a warbled, half-out-of tune harmonization that definitely wasn't our best work. I'd have to toss the *Tangled* DVD when the kid wasn't looking.

While I still had him half-awake, I rattled off the same list of dos and don'ts I had when Ma had picked him up Friday night. "Don't forget to say please and thanks and ma'am."

"Uh huh."

I heard him fading so I rushed, "And be careful in the pool and around Viper."

"Aw, Daddy. Viper wuvs me. Not as much as you and Uncle Wicky and Jamma, but she do."

"She *does*." I corrected him.

"I know, 's'what I said."

My life had become all about semantics.

Ma came back on after the kid and I exchanged I love yous, which I managed to get through without my voice breaking. She yelled across the room, "Don't let her lick your fingers, either!"

"Dog cooties," I murmured.

"Whatsa-coochies?" She'd finished getting the kid's fingers out of the mutt's maw, presumably.

My eyes lit on the Book of Torment beside me. "Hey, Ma, you read romance stuff, right?"

"Sure, and any lady who tells you she doesn't is a damn liar." She had a little book club that was known to get rowdy at times, what with the mimosas on tap and the bawdy books they read.

"You ever read anything by a Leelee Songchild?"

"Why? Is she good? Should I?"

"No!" I jumped off the bed and started pacing.

"I'm writin' it down, how do you spell her name, Joshy? Is that with four e's and two l's? Did you meet her at that convention? You know how I like my autographs, Nicky's done spoiled us." She clucked her tongue, and I heard her fumble for the pen she kept looped on a chain around her neck.

I rubbed my forehead in defeat. "I'll try to get something signed for you."

Her voice softened. "Now, reading these romances

sometimes gets me to thinkin' about your dad."

Suddenly it felt like I'd taken a crowbar to the stomach. "I know, Ma."

"I miss him. I sure do wish he was around to watch your baby boy grow up."

The dryness in my throat made it almost impossible to speak. "I think about that every day. He would've been a great grandpa."

We were both silent for a while, swimming in our own wishes for what should've been.

"You okay, Ma?" I rubbed my eyes, my fingers coming away damp.

"Yep. So long as I got you and JJ and those boys at Stone's, all those families, I'll be all right. Y'all don't need to worry about me, son."

"I love you, you know?"

"Oh sugar, save that for the ladies."

After we hung up, I fell back on the bed, staring at the ceiling. It would be nine years this November since James Stone had died. The pain had dimmed from the initial shock and disbelief to months of bewilderment. Even now it sometimes felt like my dad should still be in charge and large at the garage on those solitary mornings when I drove to Stone's. Sometimes I'd sit in my Bronco, cradling my coffee cup, remembering his long lope across the parking lot. The keys had always jingled from his belt loops. I held the mirage of him inside my mind those days when I couldn't shake the loss.

The biggest regret, the hardest sadness to swallow was he'd never met JJ.

So they'd always be close in one way or another, I kept a picture of Dad and me on my dresser alongside the first photograph I'd taken of JJ when he'd come out squalling his lungs off. With a wrinkly red face and unfocused eyes, he'd been a little shrimp I was too scared to handle in the beginning. But when he'd latched tiny fingers around my thumb and immediately stopped crying

61

like he knew I was his daddy, I figured out pretty damn fast being a father was going to change my entire life. He was and always would be the most beautiful thing I'd ever seen.

The photo of Dad and me was taken outside of Stone's when I'd joined the team straight from high school. I was a healthy six-foot-three and broad-shouldered, but Dad— who used to call himself the old goat—never failed to rag on me about the extra two inches he had over me. Handsome, rugged, and an old crooner of Chet Baker songs when he got his sauce on, he'd been Ma's silver fox.

She used to work the desk at Stone's back in the day, swishing around the place like it was Buckingham Palace and she the queen. Hell, she still did on Tuesday and Thursday mornings when the kid was at preschool. And she'd always had the smackdown ready for any dame making eyes at Dad—not that he had a tune for anyone but her.

I rolled over and shut my eyes. Behind them, I saw the dresser with his picture, him and me standing side-by-side, arms slung around each other. That photo was right next to where I dropped my wallet, keys, and grease rag so I'd make sure I said goodnight to him each and every night, no matter how much it hurt.

There were other framed photographs around the house, too. Mom and Dad's wedding picture, every milestone moment and then some of the kid, shit and shenanigans at Stone's . . . It was a good house, a good home I'd made for JJ. I'd bought it ten years ago as a bachelor during the bust, thinking of it as an investment. Later it became a place for my own family as it grew quickly with Claire and the kid. The two-story Victorian wasn't a spread by any means, but it was a prime piece of real estate in the middle of the Old Village, which I'd bought for a penny compared to what it would cost now.

I'd restored it that first year with Dad. Aside from the loose toilet handle in my bathroom, it was perfect. Neat as a tick just like the garage, the house was pretty as a picture from the white picket fence outside to the glossy finished floorboards inside. And it was nowhere any chick would expect to find Josh *bad boy* Stone. I intended to keep it that way.

But that jiggly toilet flush—we went way back, all the way to November 2, 2004, the day Dad and I were finally going to fix it together. The day he died. He went hunting that morning before our noon fixer-upper date. I'd been waiting for him to show when I got the call. It had been a hunting accident. That was the day the project stopped, that time stopped, and a piece of my heart broke away.

I could fix that damned toilet handle if I wanted to. Could've done it years ago. But I didn't because doing so would mean truly letting Dad go, and I wasn't ready.

That was why we'd named JJ *Joshua James*. And that's why I usually called him the kid, because most days I couldn't stomach the thought of Dad's early death.

I wiped my eyes then blinked them open at the same sterile hotel room ceiling. Yeah, it was time to get out of my head.

* * * *

In the hotel gym half an hour later, I was in full work-it-out mode the old-fashioned way. I grunted, groaned, and cursed my way through a circuit on the weight machines complemented with CrossFit training designed to make me keel over. At least then I could stop thinking.

Having to pretend I was into Nicky while ignoring the fact I was one hundred-percent attracted to Leelee was gonna make me mentally unstable. Not to mention her last relationship broke off because Patrick was bi and lied to her about it. I didn't stand a chance with Leelee even if I was on the up and up with her, not with her history and my Rom-Con con. Shit, her bad break-up story more than rivaled my own.

So my plan of the moment was sweating it—*her*—out of my system PD-fuckin'-Q. If that failed, I was going to masturbate over every single sex scene in her book until my dick was raw, even if I had to bust my nut in the shower with Nicky in the next room. Maybe then my bastard cock would learn to stand down in her presence.

Right then, as luck would have it in some form of twisted fate or some other writerly term—like foreboding or foreshadowing or whatever—the door swung open . . . and Leelee swished inside. Wearing exercise gear: hip-huggin', boob cuppin', ass-lovin' Lycra.

Her life might be worse than a bad romance novel, but mine was beginning to resemble a *har har fucking har* romantic comedy, minus the romance part.

Trying to ignore her so I could get my workout done and get the hell out of Dodge, I continued to torture my body. Sweat dripped like bullets down my bare chest and into the low waistband of my nylon shorts. My muscles huge and heaving, I rolled up to a squat from another set of sit-ups and came face-to-tit with Leelee.

When I rose to my full height, topping her by a good nine inches now that she wore sneakers instead of fuck-me heels, my gaze fell to her face. Her pouty bottom lip was tucked half between her teeth, and I wanted to use my mouth to tease it out. Her eyes were brighter than ever, her hair pulled into a high braid, all the better to wrap around my fist and draw her up for a long, deep kiss.

And the room just got a whole lot hotter.

I rolled my neck, bouncing on my feet while I reached for my discarded tank top to mop up my face. Pushing the neck of my tank top into the waistband of my shorts, I was well aware the extra weight dragged my shorts even lower over the cut muscles of my pelvis, almost to the point where my pubes peeked out.

I grinned when Leelee peeked too. "So, what brings you here?"

She took a seat on one of the blue mats, averting her

eyes. "The gym's a great place to hide. I only started workin' out when I began coming to these things. You know, me and crowds."

"Yeah, I'm hiding from those vicious writers too."

She laughed, and then her gaze flickered over me, not with a quick glance but with the attention of a woman who liked what she saw. I held still, held my breath and felt like she electrocuted every one of my nerve endings until my muscles jerked in excitement rather than exertion.

And that was all before she even stretched her legs to either side of her in a near split and began limbering up.

What had I thought this morning about wearing a hard cup jockstrap? Yeah, that. I needed one now. My cock rose and the thin material of my shorts was not gonna hide a single goddamn inch of thick erection for very long.

I covertly slipped the tank top over so it fell on top of my crotch. Resuming my workout on the pull-up bar, I watched Leelee as she watched me. I pumped up and down at a strong, measured pace. She performed some yoga-type moves that immediately put me in mind of inventive sexual positions. I hopped down and moved on to weighted squats, and she bent over from the waist, walking forward on her fingertips, round ass in the air.

The tank top wasn't gonna last very long concealing my raging erection at this rate either. And it was pretty damn hard to do squats with my dick as iron-hard as the barbell in my hands. I was so revved up, my only hope was to outlast her. My very, very best dreams come true . . . and my worst nightmare of the moment right in front of me:

Soft, voluptuous Leelee
Who writes fuck-hot, steamy sex
And works out
In tight ass Lycra and boob-hugging spandex
Long wavy red hair
Beautiful southern drawl
Hard as nails and sharp as a tack underneath it all

The kind of girl I could take home to Ma . . . and the kid. *Fuck fuck fuck.*

"Spot me?"

I almost fell on my ass when I heard her request. I brought the barbell slowly to my shoulders and then lowered it to the floor. "What?"

"Could you spot me?" Her face was flushed from all the yoga *cum* Kama Sutra contortions.

I groaned and pretended to massage a hamstring to cover the quick jerk in my shorts. *Jesus.* I'd spot her all right, all the way down to the mats. "Sure."

She lay back on the bench after calibrating the weights. I stood behind her, thighs opened on either side of her head. This was a very bad position for me to be in. If things went south, my cock was gonna end up in her mouth.

Through deep and determined inhales and exhales while she pumped iron, she asked, "Did you get a chance to check out *Ride*?"

I tried real hard not to think about where I'd left off reading: Jase and Avery desperate to fuck, yet deliriously as cockblocked as me. Every hot word written by Leelee. I definitely couldn't admit I'd been about to tug my tackle over it either.

"Yeah, a little. Not bad."

Leelee nodded her chin, signaling me to put the weight back on the rack. As soon as she was clear, she swiveled up and around. "Not bad?" She playfully punched me in the ribs.

I couldn't tell her what I really thought, so I shrugged. "The guy-girl thing doesn't cut it for me, ya know?"

"*Hmm.*" Leelee reserved her opinion on my opinion.

After that, we went around the machines together. Sexual tension hovered on the sidelines, but it was broken down with talking, teasing . . . and sweating goddamn buckets.

An hour later, we sat against the wall, arms hanging

over our knees.

"You remind me of my '69 Camaro." I had an oilgasm every time I thought about the muscle car I kept babied in the garage beside my house. Sleek, bright red, and just gritty enough, the car was an American classic, like Leelee. Not like the fancy foreign made motors I was making a fake career over.

I braced myself for the backlash. The last time I'd said something similar was to Claire about her resemblance to my full-sized Bronco. I meant she could handle anything, not her post-baby weight. Shit got ugly after that.

"That was supposed to be a compliment," I added when Leelee made no comment.

Her smile was slow in coming but it lit me up like the rays of the sun when it hit me. "I know. My daddy's a gear-head. He always wanted to get his hands on one of those. I grew up with my head under the hood."

Lovely Leelee, a tomboy in grease-stained coveralls? *Va va vroom and va va voom.* Damn if she wasn't the woman of my dreams.

"You're not the tough guy I first took you for, Stone." She patted my leg.

Begging to differ, I scowled in response.

She poked a finger at my biceps that didn't dent a centimeter. "Frown all you want, I'm still not convinced."

"It wasn't a frown, babe, it was a glower." I jumped to my feet and hauled her up with me, catching her when she stumbled.

Leelee's lips brushed my shoulder, her breasts skimming against my midsection. Her thighs hit mine as I clasped her waist. "Steady now."

Heat flared between us but I couldn't act on it. I couldn't swing her thigh up to my hip, grip her neck, grind against her. I couldn't do any of the wild and nasty things I wanted to.

I released her. Slinging a towel around my neck, I held onto its edges, shaking my head at the floor. I looked up

67

just in time to see her pitch a fresh bottle of water at me. As soon as I caught it, I twisted off the cap and spilled it over my head. I shook my wet hair all over her, just like Viper gnashing my favorite, scuffed-up work boots. Maybe that pup liked me after all. Not to be outdone, Leelee tossed the contents of her bottle down my neck too, laughing as I rained more water on her.

When I stopped, she looked at her top, which was almost as drenched as my hair. "You will pay for this, Stone."

"Lookin' forward to it, Leelee."

Walking out of the gym, we both grinned from ear-to-ear. Smelly, sweaty, and wet, we waited for the elevator to arrive once again. Other convention-goers gave of us wide birth, packing into the first elevator like sardines.

When the next one arrived, I bowed formally, bare-chested, wet body and all. "Going up, Miss Songchild?"

She started into the car, beaming at me. Two steps inside, she pulled up short, her face blanching. Against the back corner of the elevator, the creeper agent slouched, a slimy smile on his mouth.

Chapter Five
Wednesday: It Takes Two to Tango

THE AGENT DIDN'T LOOK so smug when I followed Leelee into the elevator. My bulky mass and heavy scowl put the fear of a beat-down in his deeply hooded eyes.

The doors closed and he straightened his tie, brushed off his cuffs. He held out his hand to Leelee. "We meet again, Miss Songchild."

"So it would seem." She gave him the barest amount of her fingertips to shake, and I tried not to chuckle. I didn't bother to hold back my laugh when she used my tank top to wipe off her hand after he released it.

From within his jacket pocket, he pulled out a business card, flipping it from finger to finger like a poker chip. "You know, you really should consider signing on. We have the power to get you where you need to go."

"Which is where, exactly?"

"The Big Six, of course. One book out in the *Ride* series and success on Amazon merely makes you a one-hit wonder. Without big backing, you'll likely be fly-by-night, forgotten-by-dawn just like millions of other writers."

Although LaForge appeared calm, there was something of a coiled snake in the way he sent his jabs, bearing his fangs before the strike. I was beginning to get an idea of how he worked, first using his glossed-over metro-man looks to hook his victims, and if that didn't work, he sank his teeth into the first weakness he could find. I maintained my stance just slightly behind Leelee, making sure he didn't forget I was there but letting her handle the scum herself . . . before I beat his head against the wall.

"But self-publishing has made me an instant hit and puts bucks in my bank instead of your pocket." Her braid swished back and forth across her shoulders in agitation.

"And how is that second manuscript coming along? Almost done, my dear? The fans are waiting. Isn't the point of doing it yourself to get your work out faster?" His lips curled in a sneer.

"The point of self-publishing is to retain control."

"Control, *hmm*? Is the lack of control around a lot of people why you're not much at handling crowds?" He continued to needle her. "An agent could help you navigate conventions, press, promotions."

Leelee paled as he hit her weak spot, and my pulse hammered.

The business card flew faster and faster between his fingers. "I can take you to the big leagues, Leelee."

"So you can take fifteen percent and the publishers can have seventy-five and I'll get less than one dollar a book." She threw her head back to glare at the numero uno asshole.

Asshole kept pushing it, leaning forward, invading her space. "You should really bite now. Offers like this won't last long, not with the non-stop crop of new writers popping up everywhere."

I broke from my self-enforced cage and rolled up in front of him. Menacingly huge, I was in his fucking face.

"Guard dog?" He stepped back.

Leelee opened her mouth, but I shoved the agent's shoulder before she could get a word out.

"Yeah, that's right. I'm the protection detail, so you might wanna rethink it before you open that mouth again." I grabbed Leelee's hand and gave it a squeeze of reassurance.

A frown formed between LaFuck's brows while he watched her hand gripped in mine. Then his face brightened. "You're Nicky Love's partner, aren't you?"

"Yeah. What's it to you?" Sliding my fingers from Leelee's, I crossed my arms over my chest.

The gleam in his eyes turned positively predatory. "So you, and Miss Songchild . . ."

"Are friends." I prodded him back into the corner, not liking the two-and-two connection he was making. It wouldn't be good for Nicky, Leelee, or me if he figured out the lie. I picked up the business card that had dropped from his hand. *Andrew LaForge. LaForge and Associates Agency. Helping you LaForge ahead with your writing career.*

"Clever." I slipped the card into my waistband and muscled up to him. "But don't you forget, I will LaFuck you up if I catch you skulking around Miss Songchild again."

The elevator pinged. Whether it was his floor or not, the dude slithered out. But he stood outside the doors, watching us until they closed.

Shaking him off, I looked over at Leelee. She stared at me, mouth agape.

A smirk playing on my lips, I leaned against the wall opposite her. "Still not buying the tough-guy image, babe?"

* * * *

After dropping Leelee upstairs, I banged through the door of our room. Nicky was in the bathroom, steam pouring from the shower. I reached in and shook the shower curtain. "I'm home, lover."

He yanked it back far enough to stick out his head. "You smell like a gym rat."

Perfect. Just the scent I was aiming for around Leelee.

I flipped him off and stalked to the bedroom area where my phone danced on the nightstand, lighting up with missed messages. Janey, Jamie, all the samey . . . plus the chick I'd fucked Friday night. Samantha, that was her name. *Delete, delete, delete.*

My finger hovered over the screen when I got to an attachment from the goons at the garage. Did I really want to know? I groaned into my hands before squinting at the image that popped up on my iPhone.

Someone—and my best bet was on Ray or Javier— had detailed their picture like they better be detailing the cars. Whoever the ha-ha-so-hilarious fucker was, he'd gotten his Photoshop on. Red flowers ringed every one of the guys' hairy assholes with the words *Stone's Roses* curlicued across the bottom of their butts.

Definitely delete, forever. I was never gonna recover from that picture. I put in a call to the office, trying to perform a mental brain scrub while the phone rang.

"Stone's, at your service," Ray answered.

"Next time y'all send me a photo of your fuckin' puckers, I'll pluck every single pube out and—"

Ray must've had me on the speakerphone because Javier yelled out, "*¡Ea diantre!* Tweeting that, Stone!"

"Wow, the thought of you tweezing our asses is really disturbing." My second in charge whispered in a horrified voice.

It truly was. I banged my forehead against the wall and said in clipped voice, "Just get back to work."

"It's closing time," Javier chirped.

"Then close up already 'cause I'm not paying overtime for shits and shenanigans."

"Sure thing, boss." Ray replied before I cut him off.

Imbeciles.

Nicky's head appeared around the bathroom door. "Grease monkeys?"

"They're fuckin' evil, man." Walking over, I lounged against the door. "How'd the rest of your day go?"

"Not bad. I spoke with my editor about the new series—the one with the witches—and shot the shit for a couple hours with some readers." Dark circles ringed his eyes from our late night and his early morning. "We have to hustle though, the hens are expecting us in the lobby in an hour."

"Okay, stud." Moving into the bathroom, I shoved off my loose-tongued sneakers and watched his face. "Never seen you like this, Nicky."

"Like what?" Foaming his face with one hand, he ran his razor under the tap.

"In your element." I air-quoted that shit. "It's kind of cool seein' you in action."

"You ain't seen me in action yet."

I snagged a towel off the rail and snapped it between my hands. "God, I hope not."

Whipping the terrycloth against his ass to get him to move over, I braced for the tussle to come. He didn't disappoint, going for a headlock skull-rub combo before he pushed me away.

"You still stink like a locker room."

I stripped down and staggered into the shower. The hot water eased my muscles, just not the one in dire need of relaxation. By the time I got out—no tugging, fantasy fucking, or raging hard-on release had—Nicky had shaved, dressed, and dabbed himself in fancy cologne.

"And you smell like a hooker."

"Get off my back." He *spritzed* one more time.

"I thought you wanted me to get on it." I slapped him, hard, between his shoulder blades.

"I lied, not into hairy bears."

I toed up to the fogged-over mirror beside him and

73

rubbed the tat on my chest. "I'll take that as a compliment."

"You shouldn't," Nicky sniggered.

Unzipping the garment bag on the back of the door, I began dressing. "I'm supposed to wear this getup tonight, right?"

"Yeah." He fingered the silk tie while I pulled out a pressed white shirt and put it on. "Nice suit, man. Tom Ford?"

"Yeah, yeah, I figured I'd splurge for a change, ya know? Not that I know jackshit about Tom Ford, but hey, it's a Ford one way or another." The new suit tailored for my big frame was the first I'd bought since my wedding, which had been the first I'd had to get since my dad's funeral.

Pulling on the slacks, I rasped a few fingers over my shadowed jaw. "By the way, dude, we're not doing this when we get back to Chucktown."

"What? Sharing the john?" Nicky stood at the toilet, shaking off and tucking in.

"No." I glanced at him. "Talking about clothes and crap."

He fistbumped me in reply to that, thank fuck.

Buttoning my shirt and tucking it in, I leaned a hip against the counter. "Ma said to tell you Viper's doing fine."

"Did you tell her I love her?"

"Yeah, I kissy-faced your pooch over the phone, asswipe." I started working on the tie.

Nicky brushed my hands aside and I tilted my chin up to let him do the honors. "I meant your mom, you dog hater."

I wasn't a dog hater, I was a Cujo hater.

He tightened the knot at my throat and ran a finger underneath to straighten the tie. "There you go, handsome, all set." He passed me my jacket.

And the fact that we'd just gotten ready in the

bathroom together with him fixing my tie didn't feel weird at all, because we were as close as brothers even if we weren't wholly embracing the true lovers role. I wandered into the other room to hunt down my shoes.

Nicky called out, "Did you get Leelee to her room all right after lunch?"

"Uh, yeah." At least one more time than everyone else knew about, too.

"Uh, yeah?" Appearing in the doorway, Nicky's voice rose and his face dropped. "Aw, shit. I know that sound. That's the *Josh Stone gonna-get-laid* sound."

"I haven't touched her, haven't kissed her." And I'd only eye-fucked her as little as humanly possible. "I'm not gonna mess this up for you, man."

Walking over to my side of the bed, he poked the lascivious book that lay face up and spine split on my pillow. "Wanna tell me about this, then?"

Frustrated—in more than one sense—confused, and completely out of my mind over Leelee, I swiped up the offending book. "She's not even my type, Nicky."

"Since when have you had a type? Your type is pussy."

"Hot pussy," I muttered.

He had a point, one I didn't like to admit at all when I thought about Leelee. The women I went for were easy on the eye, highly sexed, and ready and willing. A sense of humor helped, especially when I showed them out the door thirty minutes after our final fuck on a Friday night.

I slapped *Ride* against my thigh. "She's demure and sweet and really funny. Bonus? Her dad's into cars. She spent most of her childhood hanging out in the garage with him."

Ass planting heavily onto the bed, Nicky sighed. "Sounds like she's just your type."

I shook my head, hard enough to loosen a few brain cells, because I wasn't ever looking for more than a quick hook-up when the kid was snug as a bug at Ma's. I didn't need his heart getting torn apart again. "Nah. It'd take too much work to get into her panties."

"Especially since you're gay." His eyebrow lifted and with it, the corner of his mouth.

"Right." I sat in the chair opposite him, smoothing my hands over the cover of *Ride*. "Right. But why does she have to be so damn cute? And how the hell does she write this stuff?"

"You know what they say, practice makes perfect."

I pinched my eyebrows hard enough to blot out unwelcome images of her with other men. "Fuck. I hope not."

"Did you even start reading at the beginning?" Suspicion lurked in his tone as he squinted between me and the Book of Ball Busting Delights.

Surprise, he'd caught me.

"Skimmed for the sex."

He started laughing but I added, "Listen to this, man:

> *Breakfast. With Jase wearing his regulation low-slung towel and nothing else as he sat in front of Avery, watching her every move as she scooped up the delicious omelet he'd made. Nervous from his unwavering attention, she licked her lips. Jase's mouth dropped open, his dark brown eyes trained on the tip of her tongue. She repeated the same lick on her bottom lip, more slowly.*
>
> *Aroused awareness buzzed through Avery. She rolled her neck and arched her back. Then she blushed, as timid as a schoolgirl, which was exactly what she was. A shy college co-ed with a cruel, cruel secret she couldn't confess to anyone, because she'd already tried that, only to be told she was a pathetic little liar.*
>
> *Pushing away the past she couldn't change, Avery focused on Jase, a man she shouldn't*

want. She had no interest in her free lay roommate. None. She was sure of it. Baskin Robbins 31 flavors? More like Frito Lay. She giggled as she sipped from her cup of coffee, rich and dark from the beans he ground every morning first thing.

Setting his fork down, Jase elbowed his empty plate aside to put his joined hands on the table. That simple smooth move brought him several inches closer to her face.

"Is something funny, Ave?"

She gulped a little too quickly on the hot java. "No," she choked out, eyes falling to the fluffy remains of her breakfast and the last bite of toast on her plate.

"I don't think so either. You know . . ." He crossed his arms behind his head, leaning back in his chair. His biceps bulged, his pecs tensed, and he pulled his lower lip between his teeth before letting it pop back out. "I came all over my chest and belly last night after you left." One hand drifted down to rub the swath of tan skin and brown hair on his bare chest . . . all the way to the loose knot of the towel where the hair thickened.

Heat prickled Avery's skin and her mouth opened for a shaky breath. It pushed her breasts against the thin cloth of her top, and Jase hummed, "Nice tits."

Her nipples pearled to attention. "Jase—"

His voice smoldered from across the table. "So I was thinking. I help you out every morning." He waved a hand around the kitchen then stood with fingers slowly loosening the towel around his waist. "Maybe you could help me out, every night."

She shook her head but remained seated and

still, waiting to see what he'd do next.

His fingers unclenched, the towel barely held in place. Walking toward her, he hunkered down. The towel parted between his strong thighs, revealing a muscular landscape she wanted to explore.

"A little arrangement, Ave, that's all I'm talkin' about. Is that sweet pussy wet for me?"

"No." Urgency and arousal dripped into her voice no matter how desperate she was to deny it.

"I bet it is." A dimple dove into his cheek with his gorgeous smile. "I bet it is," he repeated, sliding away. Turning his back, he started running the water in the sink. "But that's okay, the lease is for another six months and I like a challenge."

"Great, hoss, that's just great. We're fucked, aren't we?" Nicky pushed up from the bed, plucked the book from my fingers, and tossed it beside the TV. "I'll take you to a strip joint, let you get your rocks off there."

"I don't want a strip joint."

"Yeah, I got that. You want Leelee friggin' Songchild." Flipping my fedora to me, Nicky held open the door to our room, hurrying me out.

I swatted his ass as I strode past. "Nah. I just want you, babe."

* * * *

The whorehouse-princess castle vibe was in full swing when we hit the lobby, only this time it was more dimmed lights, fake smoke, and speakeasy.

A squawking call went up from amid the overflowing chairs and sofas care of Jacqueline, who stood on top of a couch. "It's Nicky Love and Stone!"

I dipped my hat in her direction, murmuring to my beau, "What's with the glad rags?"

"They're videoing the flash-mob tonight." He one-finger waved at a behemoth male cover model dressed in a zoot suit being mobbed by a bunch of groupies.

"Flash-what?"

"It's a scene videoed with the Con attendees. It goes on the LitLuv website and YouTube, showcasing this year's theme."

I took in the feathers, beads, headbands, and sharp suits all around. "Roaring Twenties?"

"RAWRing Twenties," Nicky said before being enclosed in one of Janice's hugs that usually turned into full-on manhandling.

Jacqueline and Missy pulled me between them, but Leelee was missing. I scanned the party crowd looking for her, locking onto LaForge instead. He salivated over a group of readers, distinct with their red lanyards. Ignoring the ridiculous ache in my chest over Leelee's absence, I scarfed down several slices of pizza Missy plated up from the box in the middle of the table. I chased it with a red Solo cup of wine that made my taste buds burn. But who was I to complain, it was alcohol, and it was free.

The congested room quickly heated to inferno level. I stood to lose my jacket and threw it over a sofa. Preparing for a long, hot night, I pulled loose the tie Nicky had so meticulously knotted, rolled my sleeves up my forearms, and dipped the fedora farther over my right eye.

"Oh holy *hell*," Jackée breathed.

"Oh holy Stone!" Janice elbowed between her friends. "Back off, bitches." She scanned me from hat to toe, fumbling in a hemp bag that crossed over her chest. Tonight she was back to her John Lennon shades, this time tinted purple.

She pulled out her cell phone and caught me staring at the glasses. "Purple, as a reminder against purple prose."

"Huh?"

She buttoned my lips between two fingers, and I *flailed* for a second. "*Shh.* You don't need to worry about it, big bad beautiful man. It's a writer thing." Releasing my lips, Janice twirled a finger in the air. "Now, turn around for me."

I pivoted before I thought better of it then rolled my eyes when I heard giggles from the girls behind me and the click of cameras.

"Soooo hot."

"Le sigh."

"I'd die for a bite of that butt."

I recognized the last as Peachtree, and my now fully admired rump clamped tight as I spun around. Janice frantically tap-tap-tapped into her phone.

"Y'all are tweeting my ass?"

"Technically, I don't tweet." Missy hovered behind Janice who had dropped into a chair. Dressed in a silvery gray flapper dress with long strands of pearls, of course, she slapped a riding crop—or whipping crop, depending on how you looked at it, fucking semantics again—against her hip, probably just to watch me shudder. "I get other people to do it for me."

I pressed my palms onto the table, unwittingly giving a great view of my backside to a bunch of brazen women behind me. More smart phones started clicking on my posterior. *Posterior?* Fucking hell.

"His gorgeous glutes are going viral!" Janice showed her phone around.

"Meat market," Nicky murmured. Grabbing my hand, he whirled me around and into a dip, his hazy, evening sky eyes dancing above me. "Aren't you glad you're off the menu, darlin'?"

There were more claps, more camera flashes. I fought with my dominant side, willing myself to remain docile in Nicky's arms.

"As long as you don't drop me, partner," I drawled.

A young woman marched over as I straightened up.

She wore a white feather boa, a scarlet smile, and held a light meter in her hand. "Bravo! Bravo! Fantastic chemistry! Can you do that when we film the scene? A *leetle* more UST, yes?" She made a square out of her fingers with us inside the box. Backing off, she talked into the mic headgeared beside her mouth.

"What the fuck was that?" I asked.

"Jules Gem. She scripts this shit all year long. Don't mess with her. She'll cut your gonads off and send them home to Gigi in a gingham-wrapped package."

And here I thought that was Missy Peachtree's job.

He tugged me back to the circle of sofas where I squeezed between Jacqueline and Janice. All dolled up in beaded ivory, Jacqueline's mocha-colored skin contrasted with her dress. She turned slightly away to chat with a newcomer. Janice, on the other side, took the opportunity to run her fingers up my thigh.

I dipped the hat even lower over my eyes while I gently dislodged her hand from my leg with a tender *there-there nowhere near my groin* pat. As the huge lobby grew even more packed, I scoped the area from time to time, hoping to catch a glimpse of Leelee. The talk around me ranged from tweets and texts to something called Pinterest as we watched Jules Gem finalize her staging. When the conversation turned to shop talk—not the greasy, dirty garage shop talk I was used to—but New Adult, Romantica, Regency, and something called *mm mmm*, I gave up being subtle to stare unblinkingly at the elevators across the lobby.

When I turned back to the group to answer a question from Nicky that sounded like *wah wah wah* in my ears, I caught sight of a woman crossing the room. A pair of long shapely legs in fishnet stockings ending in spiky black heels filled my vision. I followed the clinging jet-black dress to curvy hips, full breasts, a pouty red mouth . . . and a razor-sharp, midnight black bob. The girl was stacked. Now not only did I feel like I was being unfaithful to

81

Nicky, I was cheating on Leelee, too.

Diving into the brightest green eyes as the woman slinked in front of me, I finally recognized Leelee. She wore one of the many wigs that had spilled from her luggage at check-in. I did a double take and came back for a third round. She looked vampish, not in an Elvira way but in a fuck-hot film noir Hollywood way. All the blood in my body took a southern route to my cock.

I immediately stood up and took off my hat. Ma had instilled southern manners in me from the get-go, and even though I was beginning to see myself as the manwhore my reputation made me out to be, this woman deserved to be treated like a lady. It all came back to me in an instant.

"Leelee, you look exquisite."

She blushed, the sweet pink color painting her cheeks. She kissed me to the side of my mouth, words heating against my skin. "My, Stone, don't you look rakish."

And the gawker-geese sighed altogether, "Swoon."

"Tweeted *and* Facebooked," Janice chirped.

Janice and Co. were cut short when Jules Gem started shouting. She could've stood on a table to be seen like everyone else did, but instead she'd been lifted onto the shoulders of two Coverdales.

Her boa flapped and her gums flapped too from behind a true-blue bullhorn. "Okay, kids! You have your instructions, yes? Make our viewers and friends who can't be here *feel* the vibe. This is our rendition of the RAWRing Twenties. The first dance is the Charleston, so step lively. Then we'll switch partners for the tango and canoodling. This is going out live, so I'll signal the change like this." She twirled a finger in the air just like Janice had to get a better view of my ass. "You can't *look* at me, because that would kill the scene, but you must pay attention to me at all times. *Capiche?*"

Thankfully, she shut the hell up and started a countdown with her fingers. *3, 2, 1* then she whispered . . . through the megaphone, "And action."

Big band music blasted out of the speakers, and Nicky spun me into the middle of the floor.

I stifled a laugh. "You're leading?"

"For a change, Butch."

We shuffled next to one another, grinning when the oboe cued in. The Charleston for two men from Charleston was a cakewalk. We had it in the bag, not that it was a contest but my be-the-best competitive streak wasn't something I could turn off, unless it was be-the-best boyfriend material.

Keeping up with the fast moves, we had little time to exchange barbs especially with Jules targeting us with the camera. The quicker we danced, the harder we smiled. Whistles and claps joined the music.

The song ending, Nicky performed his back dip move on me again. I clung to him in hopes he didn't marble-floor my ass. It probably looked like I loved this shit. The ladies certainly ate it up.

"OMG! I want to be in the middle of that Manwich!" Someone squealed from the background.

Nicky took me out of the back dive, his shoulders jerking with laughter.

Janice was right next to us, hair and glasses askew, mouthing and pointing at her cell, "Trending now!"

Jesus Christ, Javier had met his match. I was gonna make sure the two of them were never in the same fricking room together.

"Nice moves, Nicky." I ran my hand around his waist, just happy we hadn't been made to kiss for the camera.

"I learned from the best." He knocked against my shoulder.

Like me, Nicky had gotten a crash course in manners, mechanics, and cutting a rug from my parents. When his well-to-do, devil-may-care parents had decided they'd had enough of childrearing as soon as he hit sixteen, they Euro-toured it. They left him on his mimi's lowcountry doorstep and he'd become an instant Stone adoptee.

Jules Gem swirled her finger in the air, and it was time for the switch up. I located Leelee, struggling in LaForge's clutches. I did not want her tangling with him during the tango, especially since megaphone-mouth had added canoodling to the mix.

I waved off Janice, Missy, Jacqueline. I pushed through the crowd, intent on Leelee alone. The music started: hot, fast, and sensual. LaForge had his hands all over her, and I was two Latin dance steps away from wrapping my fingers around his windpipe. Coming up behind him, I trapped his foot with my leg. I twisted his jacket down his arms—with flair—and pushed him onto his knees. Splatting him face first to the floor with my hand to the back of his skull, I stepped over him.

It was all part of the dance, right? "Oops, my bad."

My hips moving in time to the music, I approached Leelee. Her horror from the moment before faded into a hesitant smile.

"May I have this dance?" I offered her my hand.

Her fingers laced between mine. "I'd be delighted."

We danced through the seductive arrangement, liquid as water, hot as fire. With Leelee's back to my front, my lips lingered too close to her bare shoulder. Her hips guided me against her bottom. Swiveling around, she flicked her dangerous heels between and behind my feet, matching every single one of my moves with a sinful come-hither combination of her own. Her eyes sparkled. A teasing smile canted her mouth.

I whipped her around on my hip, the slit of her dress parting up her thigh. My hand skimmed her sleek leg until I met soft bare flesh above the thigh-high fishnets. When her neck dropped back, my mouth was there. A solid shock went through me, an electric current racing to my cock. Slanted against me, Leelee slid down my thigh all the way to the floor.

I'd watched my folks dance so many nights, the kitchen table shoved out of the way, my dad singing in low tones as they swept around the room. I'd seen their connection but had never felt the same myself. Not with Claire, not with my Friday night babes. Leelee sang to every single part of me until my body felt singed with fire and all my thoughts revolved around her.

When she ran her palms up my arms and over my shoulders, I held her closer. "Maybe you should think about filing a complaint against LaForge."

She shook her head. She kept her face hidden against my throat until I tipped her chin up, spanning my fingers over her cheek as the song stampeded around us. The fear in her eyes unnerved me.

"Why not?"

"He has too many connections. As a pro he could ruin me overnight, and I'm just getting up to speed with my career."

"I don't like the idea of him sleazing all over you," I gritted out.

"I'm a big girl, Stone. And you said it yourself, you're nobody's knight in—"

Anger and shame boiled over inside me. "I know what I said, and I was a dick."

"No one's been there for me before, Patrick never was." Her fingertips skimmed my neck, spurring reckless need.

"He's a dick too." I spun her a few times, getting a contact high off her giggle.

The provocative song continued. Tight steps, smoldering looks. I bowed her back, pivoted her to me. She knew the rhythm as well as I did.

Fingers filtering through the short strands of her hair, I tugged Leelee to me. "You almost had me fooled with this."

"Did I?" she flirted.

"Yeah, but I prefer you red." I looked from her enchanting eyes all the way down her body to the killer heels.

"Why, Stone, I didn't think you were into the guy-girl thing." Her light laugh tensed all the muscles in my groin until they were taut enough to snap.

Leelee's gyrating hips were about three inches away from finding out just how much I was into the guy-girl thing. How much I was into her. My grip became tighter on her hand and waist.

She rode up from a low roll all along my leg, snapping her heel, tilting her head . . . and I was dead. Everyone else in the room disappeared. I deepened my stance before running my lips alongside her mouth. Our breath met. Our lips opened. The temptation too great, I twirled her away.

Some drunk fuck blundered into us, shoving us together. The near-miss kiss became a hot mesh of mouths. *Canoodle?* Hot arousal pounded through me when I tasted Leelee's lips on mine. I grabbed her ass and dove into her mouth, practically mounting her on a table.

"*Aaaaand* cut!" Jules called out just when my erection was about to detonate.

Leelee broke our kiss with a stunned look. "What was that, Stone? You're gay!" She pushed me away from her. "It's just for promotions, right?"

"Yeah, promotions," I muttered.

"You're a natural, Stone! You absolutely *have* to be in the cover model contest," Jules squealed beside us.

I batted Jules and her bullhorn away from my face. Lifting Leelee's hand, I brought it just below my lips in formal thanks—and dropped it.

"Stone?" Her confused voice cut me up.

I stiffened my shoulders and headed toward Nicky. "I can't walk you to your door tonight, lady."

Joining Nicky at the usual table, I spackled on a smile for my buddy as I listened to Leelee's heels snicking away. The gut-deep arousal I couldn't act on ate a hole through my stomach, but it wasn't half as bad as the horrible tightness in my chest. I would never have Leelee. I wasn't good enough for a woman like her. Hell, my own wife had walked out on me.

Chapter Six
Thursday: Mm Mmm (Not) Good

THANKFULLY, AFTER I GAVE Leelee the old heave-ho—a *so long, unlucky lady* move I'd perfected down to the don't-care-stare—the night wound down quickly. No one was the wiser, but who knew how long that would last since Jules's RAWR creation had gone up all over the Internet. And being the masochistic prick I was, I really wanted to see our kiss myself. A hundred times over. Then I wanted to run head first into one of the fancy marble columns in Con central command, because I'd fucked up with Leelee and potentially with Nicky too.

She wasn't just a piece of tail I could screw and move on from. All the signs so far pointed to romance with a capital *R*, and I'd never let myself get into this position before. The fact it was happening now, when I couldn't make a move if I wanted to, put a big neon billboard over the signs, reading: Josh Stone is Screwing the Pooch but Good. Add in the fact Nicky was my best bud and I was here to be his fake lover, and it all spelled Gargantuan Disaster.

In our room, I shucked my shoes and, shedding my

clothes down to briefs, flopped onto the bed.

"What was that *mm mmm* stuff y'all were talkin' about earlier?" I asked Nicky.

"*Hmm?*" He halted midway through hanging his shirt in the closet.

"Ha ha, dickface."

Nicky rummaged around his messenger bag—or murse, as I liked to call it—before tossing a book at me. "Male-male romance. Remember? That's what Jacqueline writes. She asked me to give this to you."

I glanced at the cover that showed two half-naked guys on the brink of a kiss. *Solar Flares.* Flipping it open, I shouted, "Sweet! She signed it."

He moved into the bathroom as I read the inscription aloud:

> *Stone,*
> *A fuckhawt read for a fuckhawt guy.*
> **le sigh**
> *xoxo, Jacqueline~*

Didn't I just feel warm and fuzzy—and a little like an all you could eat male buffet. I thumbed a few pages in, hitting a dog-eared page. "And she marked passages?"

"I told her what you're like." Nicky gargled through a mouthful of toothpaste.

Great, so now I'm the stud-muffin smut-reader of the group, with the Twitter-viral ass.

"So I should probably be readin' this, since it's written for dudes like us?"

The toilet flushed, the water ran, and he ambled back into the room. "Typically, male-male romance is written for the ladies."

I popped up in bed. "Women get off on two guys going at it?"

"Hell yeah."

That was a massive head scratcher, the likes that

would have Viper digging in her ears for days. "Huh. So how is this any different from me reading your stuff? That's for women too."

"I s'pose it's not, really. Have at it." He bundled into bed beside me.

"Well, Jackée did go to the trouble of giving me a signed edition. The least I can do is read."

"Yup." Laughter hovered around the edges of his agreement.

I glared at him. "Have you read it?"

"Yup."

"All righty then." True to my nature, I chose the third marked passage, in the middle of the book. There was nudity, cocksucking, kisses. It was pretty steamy. A tingle even started in my balls. Then it all went way the hell south, literally. Cranking my eyelids closed, I froze in a clenched-ass posture.

"Oh hell no. There's bunghole tonguing!"

The other side of the bed shook with Nicky's laughter. He managed to huff out, "You never tried it?"

"Dude, when has my mouth been near a man's butthole, ever?"

"What about women?"

"Totally different story. And maybe." Jesus, if this kept up we'd be trading fucking cupcake recipes next, while we lounged in bed together, talking about chick-or-dick sex, at a romance convention. Still, I was curious. "You?"

"Maybe." He smirked. The Don Juan probably thought he had more moves than me. He definitely didn't lack for bed warmers. He was simply more choosy, less promiscuous, more discreet than me. *Fucker.*

"Sweet dreamin', Josh."

"I hate you, Nicky." Which of course in our world meant love—in some sort of twisted, always have your back, gonna beat your ass kind of way.

* * * *

Dawn burned bright when I snuffled awake. Nicky snored beside me, half his head and all his hair hidden under a pillow. I checked the clock, thought about the kid probably jumping on Ma's bed at this precise moment, and went back to sleep.

Two hours had passed when I woke from nightmares of Leelee kneeing me in the nut-sack, Nicky smothering me with a pillow, and JJ running wild with the evil, grinning leprechaun from Lucky Charms.

I stretched my arms and legs, and groaned long and loud.

"Coming to breakfast?" Nicky stood from packing his daily dos into his man-bag. He'd left his brown hair loose and he hadn't shaved. He looked a little more rough and tumble—like he did at home—in shredded jeans and an old linen shirt.

Owning up to being a dick part II vs. laying low? I opted for the middle ground.

"Lookin' good, cubbie." I jumped up, scrounging for my gym shorts and sneakers. "But I think I'll hit the weights. Will you be in the lobby in a couple hours?" I hung the lanyard, carnation and all, over my *hairy bear* chest.

"I might be, but if I'm not, someone will be around."

Yeah, it was a specific someone I was worried about.

"Hey, how'd your dance with Leelee go off? I didn't get a chance to look at it online last night."

Think fast, shit-for-brains. "Uh, probably not worth a look. I don't even think Jules had the camera on us."

"Really? You mean you didn't put any famous Stone moves on her?"

Oh, I put the moves on her all right, with my hands and my mouth. And Nicky would shit a brick if he found out. "Savin' all those for you, babe."

Before he left the room, I reached over to pat his

91

cheek, which was the closest to a true lover's touch as we were ever gonna get.

I left not long after him. The gym was empty presumably because all romance writers already looked awesome, or they didn't know a barbell from a hand weight. Leelee sure had, but she wasn't there either. It was probably a blessing, yet I couldn't shake thoughts of her as I went through a workout regime that was more grueling than usual. By the time I finished, I could've sworn my brains, my guts, and my muscles were splattered all over the blue-matted floor.

After a hasty cleanup in the hotel room, I headed to the lobby: the epicenter or the aftermath, depending on how you looked at it. And it looked like a little unpleasant aftermath was coming my way since Leelee sat at a lonely table in the far corner.

I commenced my walk of shame. As soon as she saw me, she closed her laptop, unplugged the cord from coffee table outlet, and smashed everything into her bag as fast as she could. I swerved in front of her when she shot to her feet.

"Leelee." I placed a hand on her arm.

The instant she looked up at me, I wished I'd left my heart on the gym floor too because what I saw tore me up. Confusion warped into hurt, and then her eyes glittered, green and frosty.

"What were you sayin' about harassment yesterday?" She glared at my hand until I thought it would shrivel up and fall off. Something I needed my dick to do, because lo and behold, Miss Leelee Songchild was even sexier when she was pissed right the hell off at me.

I dropped her arm because it sure sounded like she'd call security on me even if she wouldn't do it on LaForge. "I'm not harassing—"

"No. You just kissed me," she hissed, tightening the shoulder strap on her bag as if it was armor.

"I'm supposed to say it was a mistake, Leelee."

"It didn't feel like one."

I swallowed roughly, gauging how much to admit. "To me either . . ." Fuck it. I never was a smart boy, so why start now?

The rapid pulse at the base of her neck, the nervous lick of her perfect pouty lips entranced me.

"I'm sorry." I got closer to her, slowly, one step at a time. Placing a hand over hers, I stopped her from fidgeting with the shoulder strap.

"Are you?" Her fingertips hovered over her mouth as if she still tasted my lips like I did hers.

How could I get through this week without lying to her through my teeth? And better yet, why wasn't the lobby bar open yet? It was my turn to fidget nervously, shoving a hand into the pocket of my trousers, jingling loose change. "I don't regret the kiss, but—"

"Nicky," she whispered.

"Yeah."

Her eyelashes fluttered to her flushed cheeks. "So maybe you can stop it with the mixed signals. Friends?" Leelee held out her hand.

"Okay, friend." I placed my palm in hers all the while knowing if I got the chance to plant one on her again, I was going to take it. Pulling my hand free, I ran it across my chin. "So, friend, I have a favor to ask."

She playfully rolled her eyes. "Well now, that didn't take long."

"I told my ma about your book."

"Stone!" She punched my arm.

"What'd I do now?"

"Your mom? *Ride* is full of sex." Leelee jutted out one curvaceous hip and wagged a finger in my face—I fucking liked it. "I can't believe you told your mother about it. You said you didn't even like the book."

"I never said that." I'd tried to beat off to it several hundred interrupted times already.

"The guy-girl thing?"

I shrugged. "Read some more. Changed my mind. It's hot as hell. Anyway, my ma reads that stuff, and she has a book club of horny old women. She asked if I could get you to autograph a copy for her. I'll pay for it, 'course."

Hell, I'd buy a dozen of her books if she'd keep talking to me. I threw in the puppy dog look—not like Viper the rabid bitch. And man, I'd never worked this hard for a woman, especially one who almost certainly *wasn't* gonna wind up on her back in a bed with me on top of her.

She huffed, fluffed her gorgeous strawberry blond hair out, and turned away on—*Oh, I'd missed those earlier*—peep-toed, toe-cleavage stilettos. "Fine. I'll do it."

Click clack went the heels, swish sway went her hips. I salivated behind her all the way to the elevators.

Friends, yeah, this is gonna be good.

There was a coy curve to her lips when she faced me. "Fancy meetin' you here."

An empty car arrived, and I bowed low. "After you, Madame."

Leelee entered, pressing the button to my floor and hers. "I'll just run to my room and sign up there. Doing that stuff in front of others makes me clam up. What's your mom's name?"

I was too busy staring at the new, life-sized decorations in the elevator to respond.

"Stone?"

"What the hell is this?" I gestured to the floor-to-ceiling posters of various book covers plastered all around the car. We were surrounded by half-clothed men and women in various stages of hot and heavy action.

Leelee sucked in her lip and let it pop loose. *Not helping.* "They only put them up once the Con gets rolling. Second-wave marketing."

Clever.

"Are any of these guys your type?" she asked.

"Heeeelll, no." She frowned and I hurried on. "Ya know, none of them are Nicky, so . . ."

"*Mm hmm.* I'll let you off the hook. Tell me your mom's name so I can get it right."

After I rattled off the details, Leelee smiled. "You, me, and the elevator again, Stone?"

I zeroed in on a hairy-chested, ruffle-shirted pirate who had a big-breasted bombshell fainting over his arm, presumably from his virile manliness. "And Captain Jack Sparrow does high seas porn?"

Her light laughter spun through me until I thought I'd swoon too, from lack of blood to my brain as it sped up the root of my cock. In an enclosed space with flirtatious Leelee, my friend, was not a good place to be right now.

So I asked the first thing that came to mind, of course. "You get into swashbucklin' sex?"

Her voice lowered to that luscious honey tone, and her gaze raked up my body. "If the sword fits."

Holy fuck. Heart attack, death by cock contusion, an aneurism from arousal . . . some motherfucking thing—named Leelee Songchild—was gonna do me in this trip.

I already knew she could write sex on the page. I was well aware she could move like a sex goddess and kiss as if her lips had been designed for sin. Add in her sweet personality, sharp wit, quick temper? She was one hot ticket.

I rasped, "A tight sheath is all that's needed, darlin'."

Her gasp was overridden by the ding of the elevator announcing my floor. Okay. Yep. And I was done. I put my hand in my pocket as I turned and strode out, this time to cover the large bulge in my pants. Rounding the corner, I hit the hall at a run, skidding to a stop at my door. *Let me in, let me in.* The goddamn light hit red, red—*motherfucker!*—green. *Yes!*

I tripped over my feet, glared at my shoes. Fuck it. They could stay on, it wasn't a first. Hitting the chair, I practically chewed through my belt, unzipped lickety-split and ripped those bastards open. Shirt buttons torn aside, I glanced at the desk. *Tissues, golden.* Two hard tugs at my nipples and my hand brushed down my belly, onto the thick cock rearing straight up in the air.

Leelee was due back soonish, but I was so keyed up, I couldn't wait. And it sure as hell wouldn't take long since I'd been holding back a massive blowout for forty-eight plus hours. The moment my hand curled around my cock, my back arched and a loud groan rumbled from my chest.

Then it was all about the pump action. I worked my shaft like a piston, all chambers firing. A twist at the plum-colored head on every upswing and I growled. Come boiled in my nuts, prominent veins teased my fingers. Air barely scraped into my lungs as my brain backfired.

"Fuck, yes."

Then it wasn't my hand jacking me off, it was Leelee's. I could see her, on her knees, free from her dress. Ample tits swinging, hips undulating back and forth, wanting my cock to fill her pussy.

"Oh, God, yessss."

I spat into my palm, added it to the precome slickness, and everything went smooth as silk, hard as stone. Gripping my shaft, I planted my feet and raised my hips in and out of the loose hold of my fist. *Oh yeah, so much better.*

One hand on the back of the chair, I drew in a deep breath that punched out of my nose. I lifted my eyes and barked out, "Leelee!"

Oh Jesus. Oh yeah.

She was there, just inside the room. A book in her hands and a rapt look in her eyes.

Oh fuck. Numbnuts here—literally—must have left the door propped open against the bar guard. Now things had gotten way out of hand. Or in hand.

Masturbating felt a million times better with her eyes glued to me. I spread my legs wider, lifted my balls out and fingered them good. Moisture rolled out of the broad head of my cock, and I used it to slick up and slide down the surface of my shaft. And just because Leelee didn't scream, shout, or run away, I slowed it all down. Rolling my hips, stroking my stomach, I leaned my head back with my eyes on her.

Her stare met mine. "You look so beautiful."

That did it. Tight fast strokes scraping over the flared tip, I went almost airborne as come triggered from my cock. Long, hot ropes of it hit my chest, my abs. "Leelee, *ah fuck*." It covered my hand, the chair, my pants. My dick pulsed as more come spooled out.

Recovery seemed impossible. My hips jerked, my breath rasped, my heavy hooded eyes sought her.

Leelee looked tense as fuck and fucking ready for a ride at the same time. Her words came out low and tight. "Life imitating art, Stone? Or smut . . . I guess."

It definitely wasn't Avery I thought about when I swirled two fingers through the come on my chest. "I read that chapter."

"Everyone does." A heated rash flashed up her neck to her face as she slipped the book onto the bed. She walked to the door to let herself out.

"Leelee," I groaned a second time. I started to rise, but my thighs were quaking with massive orgasm aftershocks.

There wasn't a slam of wood against metal. There wasn't even an audible snick as the door closed behind her. Come cooled on my crotch and just about everywhere else within spraying distance, and I still couldn't get Leelee off my mind—or in my pants.

Chapter Seven
Thursday: Hung Up and Strung Up

CAUGHT RED-HANDED, WET-HANDED, WHAT did
I do? I cleaned up, changed clothes, and glanced at
Jacqueline's *mm mmm* novel. *I am not ready for more
tongue-to-pucker probing.* Of course, Leelee's was right
beside it. I had all of lunchtime to lurk in my room,
pretending I hadn't just jerked my jock out loud over her,
in front of her. I sprawled on the bed to catch up on *Ride*,
because I was a schmuck looking for more punishment
anywhere I could find it. As long as Missy Peachtree
wasn't involved.

> *Jase thought his head was going to explode.
> The one hugged by a cranium and the one on the
> top of his cock. Every day with Ave it was the
> same: same sensible shoes, same baggy clothes.
> Same frumpy, old maid, bought from the
> Goodwill bargain bins shit covering up the hot-
> as-hell, sexy bombshell he just knew was hiding
> under that serviceable crap-colored sweater-*

blouse combo she wore.

From her bright blue eyes to the long chestnut colored hair untouched by highlights or hairspray, she was unexplored territory. Fresh, good, clean, wholesome, and hot. She just needed to be uncovered . . . unclothed. And on his cock.

He got a bad rap all around. Rich boy prince who lived off his daddy's AmEx, drove a motorcycle, had a tat or two, and liked to run around. It wasn't totally like that. Cut off from the trust fund tray at the age of eighteen because Daddy Everly was nothing if not a hard ass, Jase had put his other head to good use. Everly was raising an heir to the Texan oil field fortune, not a spoon-fed pussy with no business sense. Luckily Jase had the brains to match his brawn, as well as a few side projects that kept him flush enough to more than scrounge his way through college at A&M.

Bad boy this, bad boy that, gossip about his 'hit the tail and run' rep followed him like the exhaust fumes from his motorcycle. He didn't really give a bunny's cunt, unless it came to Ave. Until it had come to Ave . . . Avery.

Jase had a sweet side to him, too. At least he'd been told his come tasted sweet by a chick or three. Whatever. *He smirked into the mirror on his closet door, drawing on jeans that had been rumpled on his floor the night before when he kicked them off. Adding a T-shirt, his leather, a Marlboro Red dangling from his mouth, he made a clean sweep of the apartment on his way out.*

In the bathroom, Ave's towel flopped over his. He shook them both out and hung them over the towel bar. Inhaling her scent, he closed his eyes. Her natural fragrance was jasmine or honeysuckle or some summer-sweet perfume. The same flowers his mama let free-range in the back forty, the smell swilled to his nose and percolated his prick.

He wasn't making a full-on chef fucking breakfast every morning for Ave because he was a nice guy. Hell no. He expected some payback in return.

And he'd definitely expected a nice hard slap from across the breakfast table when he'd laid out his little dare. It would've been excellent to goad her out of her unaffected, smooth as ice shell, to see a spark of hot temper flare in her eyes. Instead, what he'd gotten was so much better he'd almost busted a nut in the breakfast nook. The lowering of her lashes, the tight hard peaks of her nipples—through another tent-like blouse, for crissakes.

Ave could deny it all she wanted but she was game. And it was on.

Striding outside, he smiled when he saw her standing beside his ride. She didn't have a car or a bike, and barely held down her job at Starfucks because she was so intent on getting the grades. She rarely made rent and he always let it slide.

The chinstrap of her helmet was so tight it cut into her neck. He loosened it, desperate to drag it off, push his fingers through her hair, make out with her right then and there.

"Loosen up, babe." He climbed on and patted the seat behind him.

The aged leather groaned, and Jase did too as her thighs wrapped around his. Timid arms trapped his stomach.

"I ain't gonna bite ya." He snapped his teeth in her direction, laughing when she swore *beneath the helmet in garbled words. "Hang on tight."*

Ave did. Her inner thighs gripping his legs through every corner made him hornier and hornier.

Maybe he was a fuckup. Maybe he had millions at his fingertips. Maybe he'd let that all slip through his hands, but as he put the bike into full throttle and held Ave's fingers at his waist, he knew he wasn't gonna let her slip away.

I recognized myself in Jase right down to the bad boy, fuck-that, take-this attitude. Not to mention the kid was as frustrated as me with his woman of choice. *Life imitatin' art?* Leelee couldn't have nailed me harder.

Placing *Ride* aside, I unearthed the Con planner-brochure-whatever from beneath a pyramid of pick-me-up junk food. I checked the afternoon's workshops and whatnots, circling one with my finger. *Writers' Widows: 2pm, Ballroom B*. Maybe that was for me, with Nicky working the circus all the time. At the very least, I could use a change of scenery and more hiding out from Leelee after my latest debacle.

* * * *

Ballroom B. Second floor. I navigated my way there, following the road map in the Con folder. A piece of paper taped to a door with *Writers' Widows* in blocky black ink let me know I'd reached my destination. Pushing through the double doors, I was faced with a mixed bag of bros and babes mingling around a Mr. Coffee burping out java-scented steam. Incomprehensible words streamed out of their mouths while they slurped coffee and munched from party trays.

"I flounced that one." A middle-aged woman with a frosted-blond blowout announced.

"I know. Total DNF." Her friend of similar age agreed, with whatever they were talking about. This one sported short black hair, impeccable legs, and horn-rimmed glasses.

A tall, athletic-looking African-American man nodded. "I remember that book. Porn without plot *plus* no HEA?"

"Fuck my life. What you need to read is *Ride*," horn-rimmed glasses said.

"Floved the UST in that book!"

I grinned because they were talking about Leelee's novel, even if I had no idea what they were saying.

"So fawesome."

Huh? What the hell with the codespeak? It wasn't enough I had to listen to Nicky banging on about hashtags and Facebook scandals? My retreat with a pack of people supposedly in the same boat as me, and I didn't even understand the lingo.

"You look a little lost. Are you new?"

Ah, normal words. Thank Christ. A big guy with the corduroy pants, an elbow-patched blazer, and a whole lotta clashing plaid strolled up to me, followed by the rest.

"First timer, yeah."

Corduroy slapped my shoulder in welcome. "I'm Fred, or as everyone else calls me, 'The Hubs'. That's Fawn, Felicity, and this here's Devon." He pointed at frosted hair, horn-rimmed glasses, and athletic dude in turn.

The rest of them, about a dozen or so more, introduced themselves. We all made our way to a ring of chairs.

Fred gave a jolly laugh, "So, does your partner refer to you as Mr. Pen Name online too?"

I rubbed the back of my neck. "God, I hope not. That'd make me Mr. Love."

That got a laugh out of everyone, and I eased back in my seat.

Fawn flicked her immoveable hair. "Tell us a little about yourself."

I had this part down pat. "Stone. Foreign auto imports." I looked around expectantly and they all looked back unblinkingly—like Stepford Wives for writers or something.

Big Devon smiled at me. "Not what you do but who you *are*."

"Uh, is this a therapy session?" Wiping my palms on my jeans, I eyed the fastest escape route to the door.

A deep chuckled rumbled from Devon. "Nah, man, not at all. We just like to know who we're getting in bed with."

From Writers' Widows to Stepford Wives to Swingers?

Felicity lifted her glasses to the top of her head. "Figuratively only, Stone." She reached over to slap at Devon. "Why do you always have to frighten the newbies?"

"Because it's fun to scare 'em."

I decided I liked the Widows-Swingers group. "A little bit about me, huh? Well, my partner and I have a three-year-old son. The sun sets on his shoulders, we love that kid." Everyone smiled encouragingly. "And a dog"—*bitch*—"but Viper is Nicky's technically. I'm not too fond of the mutt." Silence. "But we make it work!"

Claps and nodding ensued.

Phew.

"What about your SO?" Fawn asked.

My what?

It was my turn to blank stare until Fred saved me. "Your significant other."

"Right, 'course. Nicky Love. We've been together since high school, and he started writing about six years ago. We really connect when we restore cars together though, it's something we can do as a couple that doesn't have anything to do with his work, ya know?" I decided I wasn't half bad at this semi-made-up bullshit because everyone was eating it out of my hand.

"O-em-gee, I know how that is. John and I spend

every Saturday antiquing up and down the Maine coast, a new stretch each time. It helps him get ideas for settings for his cozy mysteries, but really, it gives us a chance to just *be* together that doesn't involve him being on his laptop at all hours of the night." Felicity slipped her glasses back onto her slim nose.

Murmurs of agreement and more mentions of what these writers' wives, husbands, lovers did to make their relationships work on and off the page followed. There was hugging, high-fiving, and a lot of bitching.

Fawn had just finished a story about her girlfriend's recent all-week, all-nighter final deadline bender. She capped it off by saying that during the course of writing her latest western novel, her lover had filled their spare room with chaps, cowboy hats, spurs, and lassoes.

"I'm not kidding, those spurs work almost as well as a Wartenberg wheel. And I won't even tell you how much those ropes came in handy, if you know what I mean." She winked.

Devon got up and proceeded to spank his ass while he went bull-rider with a lasso like he was John Travolta in *Urban Cowboy*.

Felicity snorted. "You dirty bitch, Fawn."

"You know it."

I couldn't stop chuckling, even when I said, "I got one, y'all. Last October, we'd just started potty training JJ, and he was hoppin' around on one foot like he was about to piss his pants. Now, Nicky writes paranormal, right? So sometimes he tries on goth makeup, fangs, the whole Bela Lugosi shit. Imagine that at Halloween time. So I've got the kid in the john, standing on his stool, and I'm waitin', and waitin', and he says, 'The peepees won't come out, Daddy.'"

"Isn't that adorbs?" Felicity piped up.

"I'm watching paint dry by this time, but the kid needs to piss in the pot. Bribery with Skittles, M&Ms, the whole nine yards, and still nothin'. All of a sudden, Nicky the

Vampire jumps through the bathroom door with red contacts and whiteface and bloody fangs. JJ screams, whirls around, and pees all over my boots. 'Course Nicky falls all over laughing, JJ gives him a pout that earns him a soup bowl fulla ice cream, and I get clean up duty, again."

True story. And that's how we potty trained the kid.

More sharing, laughing, complaining filled the next hour until I felt like just one of their group. We were from all walks of life with one thing in common: being tied to a romance writer, which brought an entirely new level of weird and wonderful into our lives.

Finally, Fred decided it was time for wine instead of whining, and we headed to the mezzanine level bar. I was in the middle of a conversation with Fawn about self-publishing trends and what it meant for writers—all ears because I wanted to glean any amount of leverage I could to support Leelee against LaFucking Forge—when Jules Gem legged it up to me like a really a tiny steamroller. And she still wore her mic and carried the bullhorn.

What the hell is she, some kind of roaming reporter?

She cut through Fawn and grabbed my arm. "Can I borrow him for a mo?"

"He's with us." Fawn went feral in front of me.

Patting Fawn's shoulder just in case she'd brought one of her girlfriend's six-shooters to the convention, I said, "It's okay, I'll meet y'all in the bar."

As soon as they cleared the area, Jules looked me over. "Enough small talk. I just wanted to remind you about the contest. I need you, your bod, your smirk and designer stubble on stage tonight." Her face dawned with evil delight. "These women want real men who walk the walk and talk the talk, trufax."

She shoved a sheaf of papers at me and marched off.

"Ma'am!"

Her back snapped straight but she didn't turn around.

"Sorry, miss. Miss Gem, could you wait a second?"

She pivoted around and returned. "That's better. Never

call me ma'am again. I assume you've heard of my rep? It's not all convention gossip. What do you need?"

"Isn't this a cover model competition?"

"That doesn't matter, you're purrrrfect. We're keeping with the RAWRing Twenties theme. Instead of Guys 'n' Dolls, we're doing Guys with Balls. And you, Stone" — she flicked my lanyard—"have 'em."

She wheeled away while I glanced at the papers in my hand. *Guys with Balls: Questionnaire. Favorite place to kiss a woman?* Lemme think about that. The cheek. Yeah, that would work with my gay persona. But to be honest, it was Leelee's soft round ass cheeks I was thinking about as I scanned the rest of the questions.

The papers crammed in my fist, I made my way to the bar and almost mowed Fred over as I entered. They'd gotten as far as the back of house and no farther. Felicity captured my hand and pointed at the bar. She jumped up and down on the balls of her feet like the kid did when he needed to take a piss but couldn't be bothered to go all the way to the bathroom.

"Fangirl squee!" Her *squee* pierced my eardrum and she gripped my hand so hard she almost broke bones.

The guys *and* dolls erupted into squeals, giggles, manly mumbo jumbo that went in one ear and out the other as I peered through the packed bodies to the bar. Whaddya know? They were flipping out over Leelee.

Fawn sidled over. "Do you know who that is, Stone?"

You bet your sweet ass I do. Leelee sat at the bar, a half-glugged glass of white wine in front of her . . . and unshed tears sparkling on her eyelashes. *Aw, shit.* Her mopey face was about a million times worse than the kid's.

"Give me a minute. I'll see if I can introduce you all to Leelee." I wasn't about to bring the wound-up Widows to her if she wasn't prepared to play the game.

Shouldering to the bar, I came up beside her. I gently ran a finger along her neck. "Leelee?"

One tear dropped onto the napkin she'd been folding and unfolding in front of her. "Stone."

"If this is a bad time, I can go away, but there's a bunch of people over there—" I hooked a finger over my shoulder. The gang saw it and waved in response.

Her wet green eyes slid past me to the doors. "Fans of Stone?"

"Actually, they're your fans. They just about burst my eardrums when they saw you." Pride filled my chest as soon as a slow smile washed away the sadness on her face.

"For me?"

"They're dying to say hi."

"Okay. Just give me a sec."

After she'd prettied up a face that was already drop-dead gorgeous, I wrangled the Widows over to her. The brilliant smile she gave each of them in turn as she shook their hands and signed whatever the hell they shoved at her really made me want to take her in my arms and kiss her.

We hung out with her through a round of drinks. The room filled with laughter while Leelee's eyes lit with happiness. She charmed every one of them just as she did me. Leelee didn't need to worry about not being able to cut her own path or do her own thing. She just needed to be herself.

And fucking hell, my heart squeezed tight.

One by one, the Widows filtered away. I waved them off with a, "Yeah, I'll catch you guys tomorrow."

Silence descended as soon as they left and I realized I hadn't seen Leelee since my masturbation muck-up earlier in the day. *Ah, so this is a WTF moment.* I ordered a second beer, another wine for Leelee, thinking about all the ways this could be imminently awkward, but hey, at least my vocab had skyrocketed being around all these writers.

"Hey," I said. *Or maybe not so much with the brainiac vocabulary.*

"Thank you."

"For what?" *For busting my cock out in front of you? Don't mention it.*

"For putting me at ease with your friends. Other people make me so frazzled. You have a way of relaxin' me."

Well, good. Too bad she does the opposite to me. Standing beside her, being near her, ideas of everything we could get up to jolted through my body.

"They were nice," she added.

"I think they're nuts. Besides, how good you were with them didn't have a damn thing to do with me."

Leelee's hair cascaded in loose waves down her back, and I wanted to tangle my fingers in it, follow the curled ends to her skin beneath. Instead I slapped my hand on top of the bar, crumpling the papers Jules had given me.

"What's that?"

Groaning, I dropped my head to the bar. "Guys with Balls entry form and shit."

"But you're not a cover model."

I peered up from my arms. "That's what I said. So you'd better be there later."

She spun toward me with a breathtaking smile. "You got it, hot stuff."

Framing her face in one hand, I ran a thumb over her lowered eyelashes that had glinted earlier. "The tears before, they weren't because of me, were they?"

She shook her head.

"Because I'm sorry you saw me, heard me . . ." I jerked my hand away and flipped the beermat up until it twirled on its corner. "That wasn't very gentlemanly."

"Probably not, Stone." She drained her glass. "But it was so damn hot."

Oh Christ.

DOWN BOY, JESUS!

Four deep breaths and one telling off to my cock later, I tried to make my voice work. "That bastard agent hasn't been at you again, has he?"

She nodded, setting off fierce instincts that had never been at work for a woman before.

"Tell me what he's done now," I gnashed out.

"He came at me during the self-publishing panel I was on—Surfing the Perfect Wave. His questions put me on the spot. I couldn't answer because I was so flustered, and what I did manage to get out just made me sound stupid. It was like bein' under interrogation." Her skin paled. "He knows how hard it is for me to be up behind the table, fielding questions."

An unreleased sob rolled through her body, and I just wanted to be there for her. Not Stone. Not fake-gay. But as a man for his woman.

" . . . and I have writer's block and he's right! I'm already twenty-seven and destined to be a failure. I can't do this on my own, and . . ."

I gathered her in my arms. "You're not doing it on your own, babe. You've got Janice and Jacqueline and Missy. You've got Nicky. You've got thousands of fans and friends." I brushed her tears away. "You've got me."

"No, I don't." She sniffed

I jumped onto that shit like a lifeline, albeit one that could tangle around me and drag me under. "Do you want to? Have me?"

"Stone . . ."

It seemed like she did. But she couldn't. Just like I couldn't tell her all I wanted to do was be with her, show her I was just a southern boy, a single dad, a car mechanic trying to provide a good home for his baby boy.

"It's Josh. My first name. Josh Stone, but we're trying to keep it under wraps."

One sodden napkin later, Leelee sent me flirty eyes. "Josh Stone, at your service?"

"Somethin' like that."

"In that case, Leelee Childes, from Shreveport." Holding her hand out, she smiled at me.

My fingers slid from her palm to her wrist as I bought her hand to my mouth for a soft brush of my lips. "Pleased to meet you, Leelee Childes from Shreveport." I released her fingers with another slow slide.

I took a swig from my beer bottle. I might not be able to tell her the whole truth, yet, but I could tell her some of it. I started unbuttoning the top of my shirt.

Her gaze flicked to my fingers. "You're not gonna practice for Guys with Balls now, are you?"

I chuckled. "No, babe. I have something I want to show you. It's about my tattoo."

Sitting back, she tugged in her bottom lip and let it out. "Then by all means, don't keep that under wraps."

I glanced up from under my lashes, taking in her swollen lip, so ripe for a kiss. Holding the shirt collar open over my shoulder, pec, and tat, I was really glad the Hens weren't around to molest me. Or tweet me.

Leelee's fingers hovered above my skin before pressing softly onto the heart surrounded by twisted chrome pipes. "It really is gorgeous." Her husky voice flooded me with a now-familiar ache.

Chills raced over my chest from one simple touch. Just when I wanted to press her fingers harder to the heart, my heart that had only held the kid for so long, Leelee withdrew her hand and dropped it to her lap.

"Who's Joshua James?"

"My kid. Joshua James. Josh for me and James for my dad." My throat was raw from emotion. "My dad died nine years ago."

"I'm so sorry about your father. I don't know what I'd do without mine." She let her fingers glance across the tattoo once more before drifting away. "Your son, huh? So how did that work?"

"There was a woman. We were married for a couple years." *Thirty-one motherfuckin' months to be precise.*

Leelee drew back, eyeing her wine, the bar, the door. "So, you're like Patrick."

It wasn't a question, it was an accusation, no doubt aided and abetted by hearing me grunt her name when I came all over my hand, chest, belly . . .

"No, it's not like that. I'm not like that. I'd never do that to you, Leelee." I wasn't bisexual, I wasn't bro-sexual. I was a one hundred percent pure hetero male who wanted to nail her on top of the bar right now. I groaned. "It's not like that."

"What was it like then, Josh? Because I don't get it." At least she stayed seated on the bar stool instead of bolting for the door.

"Claire, my ex, got pregnant just about four years ago, and we got married. I'd do anything to make sure the kid had a good, solid home. She never really took to the *until death do us part* bit. She had some problems after JJ was born, couldn't handle being a wife or a mother, and she left us. I never heard from her again. The divorce became final last year. She deserted JJ, signed it all away as soon as the papers were served."

A heavy stone sat in my chest as I confessed as much as I could. Maybe I should've tried harder with Claire, done more.

"That's horrible." Leelee swung back toward me.

"It's not. It really isn't. Claire wasn't a bad woman. She just wasn't my woman." I shrugged. "I'm a much better dad now that I don't have to worry about her and . . ." I stopped, really thinking about it. "It's been horrible for JJ, though. He still has nightmares, worries about me taking off and never coming home."

"But he has Nicky too, right?" She skimmed one hand up and down my arm.

My smile was forced because I didn't know what I'd say if she started asking about our relationship. He was a huge part of the kid's life, but as Uncle Wicky, not Daddy Number Two. "Yeah. Nicky stepped up."

"So, that explains it." She propped her cheek against one hand as she peered at me.

"Yeah. Wait, explains what?"

"Is that . . .?" She hesitated. "After Claire left, you and Nicky, is that why you're with him? Trust issues with women?"

Ah, shit. Maybe this is the therapy sesh I thought I was having earlier with the Widows. "Yeah, no. I mean, yes . . . trust issues and women." *But I'm not gay!* "Except for my ma."

"She accepts you two, that's sweet." She petted my hand.

She's goddamn petting my hand. This could not get any worse. Now I wasn't even turning over her engine, I was the pathetic lemon car, the last one left on the lot . . . a pitiful picture of a man to her. I had to turn this around.

"About earlier, Leelee." Once I had her attention— those big green eyes swerving to mine—I started buttoning my shirt. Slowly, very fucking slowly. "I'm sorry you saw me like that, but I don't regret it."

The same words I'd said about our kiss. Now she knew she was on my mind while I'd come, and I was glad she'd watched me.

"You looked amazing, stroking your cock like that." The more dirty words that slipped from her pert little mouth, the harder I got. She took a sip of wine and gave a laugh. "I might have to add that to my WIP."

I leaned closer, bound to her by the rippling tension between us. "Whip?" So long as it didn't belong to Missy the Mistress, I was on board.

"WIP—work in progress." Leelee looked me up and down, a gaze so intense it was as tangible as if her mouth, tongue, fingers slid all over my body.

"I don't give a shit about any WIP." It hit me then. I wasn't interested in taking what I could get from Leelee. And maybe being with her was a no-go for right now, but I could lay the groundwork for something longer lasting later.

"I'm sorry, that came out wrong. What I mean is, I care about *you*." Taking Leelee's hand in mine, I skimmed my fingertips up to her elbow. "I haven't made love to anyone for a long time." For years, maybe never.

Her back arched as if every part of her body was connected to the almost innocent stroking of my fingers on her arm. "What about Nicky?" she gasped.

I cradled her face in my hand, my thumb brushing her lower lip. "You can't tell anyone." *Josh, shut up, you big dumbass.* "It's over after the convention. I'm not in love with him, and he isn't with me." Not a lie.

"You seem so close . . ." Leelee leaned in, shivering from the heat of my touch.

I murmured, "We'll always be best friends."

Her eyelids grew deliciously heavy. Lips wet and parted. My thumb disappeared from her mouth, making way for my kiss. A small brush of our lips from side to side with her warm breath and hot wetness plucking at me. A kiss with all the promise of more.

My fingers trailed down her neck, which tipped to the side for my touch. I wanted to kiss her again, but I'd bide my time with a soft, slow seduction. I kept her hand in mine as I searched through my wallet for enough cash to pay the bill.

"We should get going. Headed to your room?"

She patted her bag, her lips, her hair. She stood on another pair of dangerous-to-my-dick heels.

"I'll take you, babe." With my hand resting on her lower back, I guided Leelee out.

My footsteps became heavier the closer we got to her room, and my heart decided to match that shit, dropping low in my chest.

Delivering her to her door, I asked, "You'll be at Guys with Balls tonight?"

"I wouldn't miss it for the world." She darted up for a peck on the cheek, no lingering. New lines drawn.

Lines I was determined to destroy.

113

Chapter Eight
Thursday: Balls to the Wall

I TREKKED BACK TO the room of my *inglorious* release, relieved to find Nicky absent. I stacked Leelee's and Jacqueline's books plus all the other freebies onto the overflowing nightstand and hit the bed. It was time to put my iPhone plan—not my palm—to good use. Or bad use. I almost kissed the damn thing when no messages piled up. Not another shove-a-pen in my eyes, pucker-up photo from the garage. Connecting to the Internet, I got busy on Google. The search engine spewed out so much Leelee Songchild info, I had to scroll down and down and down some more just to get my bearings.

Pinterest. That was the thing they'd mentioned last night. Quickly learning Pinterest should be called Pimpterest, I clicked, blinked, and backed away. *Twitter.* A bluebird, that didn't look like it would blind me with images of man-cock, right? I was immediately a fan of the little blue birdie because I didn't have to sign in or log on to follow Leelee, and she was online.

#LitLuv13 #WriteWidows Y'all r amazing! Thx for

drinks & luv

Huh, the Widows had their own hashtag thingamajig. That was cool. Maybe I'd sign up after all.

Another tweet popped up from LeeleesSong: *Lulz @Felicity Stone is yummy but he's off the market*

Oh Christ, she's tweeting about me? As soon as I blinked, before I had time to ferret out Felicity's leading tweet, @LeeleesSong flashed up again.

@Dev Nope just friends with Stone ;)

Hmm, I was working hard to change the just-friends status faster than I could change a flat tire.

Ohai @Jaque_line mm hmm defs Alpha Male material

Alpha male, was I? I Googled that . . . pronto, and was pleased with what I read, yeah, I could work that angle.

I leaned back against the headboard. Leelee had me tied in fucking knots and, as usual, rock solid. I went to the door, cracked it, and looked out into the empty corridor. Satisfied Nicky wouldn't burst in on me, I hurried back to my phone and searched for the LitLuv flash-mob. I hit the link and whaddya know? A video bloomed across my miniature screen. Forwarding to the tango, I waited until the camera zoomed in on Leelee and me. *Holy fuck.* Seeing it as a bystander was almost as hot as when she'd been pressed against my body.

Cursing the stingy display on my phone, I viewed the goddamn thing three more times, wishing for Surround Sound and a big ass, flat-screen HDTV. Nicky's laptop was on the desk, buried beneath a tower of papers and potato chip wrappers. Jumping from the bed, I double-checked the door this time. I wasn't a total schmuck.

I cracked the computer open, gave myself a free pass for breaking and entering, and attempted his password. *Nickyloveromance.* Master hacker? Hell yes, I was. I made sure not to touch any of his open documents. There were thirteen in all including his WIP, outline, upcoming Q/As, pic files, promo spots, and follow-ups. I hovered over his two open web browsers long enough to note what I expected: Amazon, Goodreads, Twitter, Facebook x two, Pimpterest, Instagram . . . and then a whole lotta what I could only call *research*. Porn in the name of his books. *The bastard's been holdin' out on me.*

Thinking about Ray and cookies and caches, I opened Google Chrome and left Nicky's Mozilla and IE tabs alone. I'd close Chrome out and he'd never be the wiser. Navigating to the convention homepage, I bingo'd the tango once again.

Then boing. Instant boner.

Big screen was even better.

Leelee in that svelte black dress and short black hair shook her hips to entice me. She blew me a kiss with cherry red lips over her bare shoulder to excite me. My hands moved up her back to her neck, meshing her against me so we met from thigh to hips to chest to breath. And then we kissed. Violent, frenzied. Tongues appearing, hands grabbing, mouths taking.

I wanted to see that kiss, to feel her lips blazing me up like a blowtorch, one more time.

Several loops later, I'd pulled the chair to the desk, the laptop to me. I was practically on top of it, my gaze glued to the image of Leelee and me kissing for all we were worth.

The only warning I had of Nicky sneaking in was a smack to the back of my head. I tried to shut down Chrome, but his fingers clamped down on my wrist.

He stared at the flash-mob video then spun my chair around. "Who's the stalker now, Stone?"

"Who's the creeper, dillweed?"

With an almighty slap he closed the laptop. His hair and collar were loose, his lips swollen. I narrowed my eyes when he accused, "You fucking kissed her!"

"And who have you been mackin' on, bro?" I stood up and pushed him back. "I recognize that *I'm-gonna-get-some* look." I sniffed his throat. "Lipgloss, watermelon flavor, right there, asshole."

"Guilty, but it wasn't with one of the insiders, and it certainly isn't gonna end up on YouTube."

"You smell like perfume."

He jabbed my chest. "You smell like spunk."

"You're a few hours late for that."

Sliding down the floral-papered wall, Nicky hauled his knees to his chest. "Shit, man. Just keep it in your pants for three more days."

I hunkered beside him. "You're the one who wanted me to settle down. Now I find a woman and I can't make a move?"

"I didn't think you'd find the girl of your dreams here, Josh."

"I didn't think I'd find her ever." Punching to my feet, I paced between our bed and the desk. "What am I supposed to do now?"

"Not here, Josh. Not now." Frustration crept into his voice.

I pounded the wall. "Goddammit!"

"We'll figure something out after."

"Yeah, and how's that gonna work? Leelee already thinks I'm gay, at best bi-curious. Her ex-fiancé is a two-timing, backdoor douchebag. She isn't gonna be impressed if I come out straight after the Con, and you still have your rep to think about."

He opened his mouth and then shut it tight.

"Exactly. I'm fucked."

Nicky glared at me with cool eyes. "So, you know the score. Why are you being such a bitch about this?"

The bitch comment wiped the scowl right off my face. "Holy shit. Who died and made you princess?"

"Fuck you. I'm the queen and don't you forget it." He lunged for my midsection and we crashed to the floor.

"Straight up," I wheezed with his forearm across my windpipe.

Grabbing a chunk of my hair, he thunked my head to the carpet. "Ha ha."

Incapacitating the slick motherfucker with my arms and legs, I used my superior body mass to flip him onto his back. "Who's the man now?"

"Me!" He gasped when I sucker-punched him in the ribs.

We rolled around, wrestling, laughing and half off our heads from sheer exhaustion. Finally he held up his hands in mercy, stumbling onto the bed.

I back-planted beside him and dragged his noggin in for a last noogie.

"You're still an asshole." Nicky rubbed his sore skull.

"But I still don't lick asshole."

Fist bump. All good.

Until Nicky turned on his pillow. "Remember the time that chick thought you were gonna propose to her—"

Her name I would never forget—but not for lack of trying. "Shayna." Single mom, wore desperation like the cloying perfume clinging to Nicky, and laughed like a hyena.

"—because she'd heard about your rep and you saw her three Friday nights in a row? What'd she do when you changed your cell number after she texted you every hour on the hour for five days straight?'

"She made a scene at Stone's. I think Javier videoed it on his phone. First she threw a chair at the reception window, and then she started bawlin' in front of the customers. When I tried to get her to take it to my office, she accused me of leading her on—which I never did. All the ladies know the deal with me. She finally left. Not before she slashed all the tires on my Bronco." *Great times with Shayna.*

"Good thing she never got her paws on the Camaro, since that's your one true love."

I flicked him on the end of his nose. "I think I might've tipped her over the edge when I offered to give her an *adios* fuck."

"Not your most chivalrous moment, my man." Nicky

closed his eyes, sleep about to pull him under. "'Sides, you attract crazy."

"That explains you, then, don't it?"

"Funny guy," he tiredly slurred.

"Tough guy." I gave him my butch voice and bunched up my muscles.

But I wasn't made of tough guy material at all, not when I thought about Leelee and everything I wanted with her. I didn't want her to become a girlfriend revenge story, and she wasn't even my girlfriend yet.

By the time I checked the clock, it was time to haul out. I set the alarm on Nicky's phone so he'd have a few minutes to wake up, freshen up, and make it to my debut as a strutting stud in Jules's contest.

When I opened our door on the way to Guys with Balls, the Hens about fell inside. They looked a little hectic from all the eavesdropping they must've been doing.

"Y'all got an appointment, ladies?" I tried to look stern, in the white terrycloth robe Jules had sent to my room, fedora in my hands.

Janice was back to the hippy look today, complemented by lemon-yellow lenses in her sunglasses. "Because of unnecessary lemons," she mentioned in answer to my pointed glance.

"Only lemons I know are bad cars," I said.

"Fanfic reference, hot stuff, never you mind."

Just when I was about to ask what the hell fanfic was, Jacqueline slipped between us. "Is everything all right in there?"

"Peachy keen." I smirked at Missy Peachtree.

Missy pushed a foot inside the door to keep it open and pierced me with an all-too-knowing stare. "Just rolling like a stone, right?"

Janice sidled up to me. "That sounded like a really big bust up in there."

"Trouble on the rough seas?" Jacqueline scanned my

119

legs and the loose robe as I turned down the hall.

"Or maybe just really rough sex," I called back over my shoulder. "Y'all will be at the contest?"

Swoons, sighs, tweeting!

Yeah, I'm all over this shit now.

* * * *

Feeling like a dude headed for a slaughter but dressed up for a spa day, I ignored all the camera flashes, all the giggles, all the titters sent in my direction as I motivated to the appointed room. Someone else had seen the tango-de-stupido and it wasn't just me. More like a thousand-plus someone elses.

As soon as I shouldered between the heavy black curtains to backstage, Jules pounced on me. "Stone! You're late." She pinched my ear and squeezed my ass. She ripped off my robe and hollered through the megaphone, "Clothes! Hair! Oil! STAT!" She slapped my chest. "Just remember, act natch but don't act. Make it sexay but not obvie, mm'kay?"

"Right," I replied as I stood bare ass naked in the middle of a bunch of similarly undressed beefcakes.

A pair of dark brown leathers was handed to me, and a pair of women barely waited until I pulled them over my legs before pushing me into a chair in front of a mirror.

"Spike it?" Female number one with fuchsia stripes in her hair asked her companion.

A glimmering tongue-ring appeared from the other woman's mouth as she tapped it against her teeth. "Fauxhawk?"

"Not long enough." Long-nailed fingers scraped along my scalp.

"Keep Stone *au naturel*. He's already fit, fine, and fu-hot," Jules barked through the megaphone, stalking past us.

Assured I was *au naturel* enough to pass muster, I was

released to the fitting area. Male models streamed past me as rock music blasted from speakers overhead.

"Gah! Exact fit." My seamstress slid her fingers around the waist of my pants, along the inseam and down to my feet. "Shoes?"

"Work boots." All-seeing Jules commanded the backstage chaos with one eye on everyone.

It was giving me the fucking heebie-jeebies.

A pair of scuffed up Timberlands were offered. I was prodded to a mirror. Wearing low-riding dark brown leathers and nothing else, the snug fit was downright indecent. They cupped my junk, my ass, and left little to the imagination.

"He's perfect!" Fuchsia-streaks shrieked.

Jules stopped beside me long enough to yank the leathers an inch lower so my Jesus crease showed. "Now he's purrrrfect."

"Ah-mazing." A lady with a mouthful of pins piped up. She accepted a bottle of oil and handed it to me. "Slick up, Stone."

I held the offending article up to my face. "Huh?"

Fuchsia hair called over, "To show off the cuts of your muscles."

"To make you a *cut above*," Jules confirmed. When I continued to hesitate, she took up a drill sergeant stance, bellowing through the bullhorn, "Do I need to make you drop for twenty?"

"No, ma'am," I replied sullenly.

I uncapped the bottle to pour oil into my palm. I rubbed it all over my chest, my abs, my shoulders. The atmosphere in the small backstage area was electric, filled with big men puffing up even bigger, herded from station to station. Our egos probably sucked all the oxygen from the room. Sweat dripped down the middle of my back as I tried to reach between my shoulder blades.

"You need help there, braw?" a buff blond dude asked.

"Nah, I got it." I stretched a little farther, twisted a

little harder.

He snatched the slick from me. "No need to be proud. I'll just do your traps and obliques."

I forced myself to remain still as he massaged my back, hitting all those places I couldn't get to on account of not being a contortionist. Thank fuck, Jules hadn't made this a backstage show; the crowd, Hens, Widows, women would've loved a view of this.

"Pull those pants lower." Big Blond's fingertips slipped just above my ass-crack before he smacked my left cheek. "Chicks like to see some of that. Nice bod, by the way. Are you auditioning for cover model?"

I thanked him for basically grooming and groping me and turned around. "Not really. Miss Gem roped me into this."

The guy before me had the whole package. Pretty boy face and dimples. Long blond hair. Shoulders ripped with muscles. If I didn't possess a healthy ego myself, I'd have gone off and cried in a corner.

"She's a right bitch, but she makes the magic happen." He patted my ribs. "Good luck, man."

"Places, people!" Jules single-filed us. I wasn't the show starter or the showstopper. I was the middle man, story of my life. "Don't make me regret adding you to the line-up, Stone. Now get that squee-worthy ass ready."

My nuts journeyed up into my body with her threat. No worries about sporting a woody now.

Several minutes later, from somewhere on the other side of the curtains came Jules's introduction: "Welcome to the 7th Annual Literary Love cover model competition—hosted in conjunction with Fever Romance Publishing—Guys with Balls!"

Screeches filled the air. It sounded like they came from a bunch of otherworldly banshees. But no, it was just the ladies revved up for the show. The blond Viking boy was up first. He took the house down. Shouts raised the roof, money probably fell into his jeans, and his jeans

122

probably disintegrated down to a vinyl g-string.

"Good crowd!" My masseur swaggered back through the curtains.

There were a couple more men before me, and I zeroed in on the hairy-chested, ruffled-shirted rendition up next. It was the guy from the book cover in the elevator. Pirate of the Happy Peen, aka Rafael. He must've already had a million fans, and they erupted with bloodthirsty screams while he swashbuckled his way up and down the stage.

I peeked out when the dude before me took his turn. He was built like an army tank. I almost felt inadequate until I watched him shake his ass and kiss his *guns*. That just made me roll my eyes.

Jules dj'd, "Say hi to Marko, ladies! The louder you yell the more votes he gets. Marko's fave place to make love is . . ."

The ladies beyond the stage went freakin' nutso.

"In his bed!"

Boos followed his *sooo* boring answer.

One of Jules's minions raced up to me. "This is fail. You have to bring 'em back online."

The shouts became rabid. "Eye candy! Bring on the eye candy!"

Catcalls and wolf whistles shot through the crowd. "Stone! We want Stone!"

I parted the curtains.

"Hard as a Rock" by AC/DC blared through the speakers.

Strobes blinded me, guitars deafened me, nerves chewed through me. Christ, even my palms were sweaty, not that anyone could tell. They were all greased up like the rest of me. But I sure as hell wasn't gonna pull some candy-ass move like licking my biceps.

"Introducing our Hard as Rock, smoking hot amateur. I give you STONE!!! Mr. Stone likes to take it all down low, down-home. Can I get a hell yes, ladies?"

123

The women positively salivated, and I hadn't so much as moved a step. Lifting my arms behind my head to tip my fedora forward, I scanned the feisty crowd. The Widows and Hens were front and center, seemingly competing for who could be the crudest, loudest, and rowdiest. Nicky winked at me. Leelee stood at the forefront, one palm pressed to her chest, her gaze penetrating me. With my arms raised, my muscles bunched and twisted, the leathers slipped even lower down my pelvis, and that was all it took to bring the noise level to an ear-bruising roar.

The song wailed even louder, the badass beat pumping through my body. One thumb hooked into the pocket of my snug pants, I strutted down the runway.

It was an all-male meatfest. So this was the magic happening. *Magic Mike* maybe. I just needed to rub my crotch on a broomstick handle and Show Over.

The guttural AC/DC lyrics punched through me. It was all about sex. Fucking. Leelee. I saw her below me, thought about her beneath me. When I reached the end of the mile-long runway, I rubbed a hand down my chest to my waist, tapping on a single silver button while I stared at her.

"DO IT, STONE!" Jacqueline crammed four fingers into her mouth and blew out a screeching whistle.

Felicity jumped up and down, her glasses knocking around on her nose. "Don't be a pussy tease!"

Pulling the button open, I slipped one hand inside the skintight leathers and touched the base of my cock. The shit was so tight I could hardly form an erection, but blood pounded to my groin nevertheless. Leelee unblinkingly watched every motion as I thrust my pelvis against my hand in time to the music. Dragging my palm up, I made sure the zipper pulled open, a thatch of pubic hair visible.

Swaying on her feet, Leelee skimmed her hands down her sides, swiveling her hips.

I'm gonna have that.

I doffed my fedora to the foaming-at-the-mouth melee, bowing deeply in Leelee's direction.

Hot spots shined on her cheeks.

Pretty damn pleased with myself, I made my retreat, catching a glimpse of Jules up and off to the left, urging the crowd on with her hands raised in the air.

I received a mess of back slaps backstage. Handed a bottle of water and a towel, I stood aside to watch the rest of the men do their thing. I had to hand it to them, it took some kind of balls to get their kit off on book covers for everyone in the world to see, mingle with the man-hungry mobs, and still stand around to cheer one another on. I clinked—or rather, smushed—my bottle of water to the blond's.

Things didn't go so happy for the next guy. He pushed through the curtains to a round of boos.

Army-tank gave him a burly hug. "You and me both."

"Bitches be fickle. One year it's blonds, the next it's brunets. No one can predict the trends, but you did great out there." My Viking mate soothed the man's busted ego.

He was almost in tears.

"Tough crowd, man." I patted his back.

"Got that right." He attempted a smile and glugged his water.

Four models later, the competition was over. I couldn't wait to get to Leelee so I rubbed as much sweat and oil off my body as I could and hurried to the front. The Hens and Widows had teamed up and taken over a couple tables where two pitchers of beer sat. As I approached, they all jumped up for a standing ovation and more whistles that made my footsteps stutter. My face got hot and I remembered I was wearing the bare essentials, *and* I'd forgotten to button back up. I hastily remedied my almost-flasher moment. Leelee followed the motion of my hands, making me even hotter as testosterone fueled every single cell in my body.

The bad news was there was nowhere to hide a boner

in these pants, and the length, curve, and head of my cock were clearly visible. *Shit.* Nicky splashed some beer into a cup and cruised up to me. His eyes bright, his smile loose, he was halfway to drunk already.

I accepted the drink with an arched eyebrow. "Forgive me for earlier, lover?"

He slid his cheek against mine. "Maybe if you stop making hot sex eyes at Leelee, *babe.*"

I needed to get him trashed to get him off my back.

My song came on again causing the entire throng of models, oglers, and me to dance. I pushed against Leelee's back, slipped my hand over her waist to the curve of her hip, my breath spilling against her ear. All my good intentions went right out the window.

She pressed her ass into me with a gasped, "Stone."

Jules's shrill voice jolted us apart. "And the winner of the Guys with Balls Contest and a twelve-month contract with Fever Romance is . . . RAFAEL!"

The porny pirate—that figured. I bet my sword was bigger than his. I cheered him on while he accepted hugs, kisses, and prize shit on stage from Jules and the Editor-in-Chief of Fever.

My friends weren't into cheering though, they started jeering:

"It was rigged."

"We demand a recount!"

Like I gave a fuck, honestly. The real win of the night was the unmistakable fact Leelee definitely saw me as a man, and the sexual interest sparking between us burned brighter than ever before.

Fawn opened her mouth to complain, but I clamped my hand over it before the Widows and Hens combined created a full-scale riot. "Don't worry about it, y'all. I mean, I appreciate your loyalty, but Captain Cock deserved to win. Besides, I'm too busy with the . . . car dealership anyway. I just did it as a favor to Jules."

Jacqueline's skin gleamed and her teeth glistened in a

grin. "Always stay on her good side, 'cause she will *cut* you."

Leelee's coy smile slid over me to land on Nicky. "*Mm hmm.* And besides, you seemed to think Captain Cock was kind of hot on the poster in the elevator, didn't you, Stone?"

Not. Nicky's eyes danced, mine flattened to a glare.

"I thought nothin' of the sort." I sniffed.

Before I could *defend my honor* any more, we were swarmed by groupies all looking to get my autograph. *Mine? This is some wild stuff.* I happily obliged as I'd seen Nicky and Leelee do, even when one buxom broad all but bared her tits for me to John Hancock.

As soon as the lusty ladies departed, Fawn sidled up to one side of me, Missy on the other. I didn't like the two of them in cahoots together.

Fawn slapped my ass hard enough to earn a feral grin of approval from Missy. "Next time, lose the leathers and just wear chaps."

The crew busted out laughing, and I backed into a corner so no one else could tap my shit. We continued to guzzle beer, the Hens kept peck-peck-pecking, and the Widows held their own in wit and one-liners.

The back of my neck prickled as I stood at the high top table mashed between Nicky and Leelee. Glancing aside, I saw two babes staring at me. They each crooked a come-hither finger at me.

"Uh, I think I have to go talk to some people," I whispered to Nicky.

He gave the girls a quick inspection. "Those two are the book reviewers and webmistresses at LolliPOP Grrrls. Go say hi."

At his prodding, I slipped away from the table, ambling up to the young ladies. They were opposites of each other. One dressed in a hoodie and all-black clothes, sporting an array of facial piercings from her ears to her eyebrows to her nose and lips. Her consort was a bottle

127

blonde femme in tight all-white neoprene. They both had bods any man with a working cock in his pants would appreciate. Miss Blondie sucked a lollipop with audible slurps and the dark angel smacked a piece of gum like she was chewing a cow cud.

They made me feel like a dirty old man, and I wasn't even the one leering; they were. At me. It was then I remembered once again I was bare-chested, almost naked . . . and not at all interested in them in any way.

The grins they gave me as I sauntered over were as saccharine as their treats. "Quite a show, Stone."

I pulled my fedora lower, wishing I had a shirt on, too. "Thanks, ladies."

Even though they looked like eye candy, Suck and Blow started in all business. "We run a review blog and we want you on it. *You write 'em, we suck 'em down,*" they said in unison.

Fuck, fuck, fuck. I was drowning in innuendo-ville.

"But I don't write." I shoved my hands into my pockets. That brought the leather low-riders another dangerous inch down my lubed-up body.

Their eyes riveted to the extra amount of skin on show, I withdrew my hands and crossed my arms over my chest. Half naked, oiled down like the kid's Slip and Slide when we squirted Dawn dish soap on it, I couldn't have made more of an *immodest spectacle* of myself.

The gum smacker said, "Oh, we don't care about that. We just think you're smoking—"

"Capital H hawt." Lollipop twirled a ringlet of white-blond hair around her finger.

Her kinky cohort snapped her gum. "Centerfolds? Nude?"

"Cover guy." They both sighed.

Yap, yap, yap, they went. I turned half around to the table so I could drink in Leelee's fresh-faced gorgeousness to find her . . . glaring at me. Glaring? *What'd I do now?* Oh. She was glaring at me *and* the two girls. Was she

128

jealous?

Hell yeah to that.

I took their card and promised to contact them. They sucked, smacked, and finally backed away, finding new prey to hunt down. I'd almost made it back to the table when I saw LaForge headed our way. Determination in his steady march, he glommed onto Leelee.

Hell no to that.

Whether the skuzzball was looking to get into her panties or her purse, both were a no-go. And I was gonna make sure of that. He got in Leelee's line of sight and she visibly flinched. I beelined for her before he made contact.

Her green eyes full of anxiety skipped to mine. "Can you get me outta here?"

Knight in shining armor, here I come. Grasping Leelee's hand, I sent an apologetic look to Nicky. Her fingers tucked around mine while I skirted the edges of the room.

We played a game of duck and dodge while our friends covered our retreat. The cover models had first string. Rafael, Viking, and Army Tank stood shoulder to shoulder, forming a solid wall of muscle between LaForge and our exit. Not to be outdone, LaFucker skirmished aside, intent on getting to Leelee.

The Hens held second defense, Nicky with them, his jaw visibly grinding. Mess with Leelee, mess with them. That devotion became apparent when from out of nowhere, Missy brandished a crop to beat him over the head. *Better him than me.* Jacqueline's nails were out, Nicky took up a boxing stance, Janice threw off her bangles. They converged on him, giving him a taste of his own predatory tactics.

By the time we reached the door, LaForge had hurtled past the Hens only to be foiled by the Widows. Fred, Devon, Fawn, and Felicity made a last stand as we broke through the exit. Nicky glared at me one final time. Noted. Ignored. I'd deal with the consequences later.

Reaching the lobby, we dived between masses of people. One of Leelee's heels broke off against an uneven tile. I lifted her into my arms.

"Stone! Put me down."

Not likely, not now that I had her with me. Once we reached our escape route, I slipped her slowly to the floor, cushioning her landing with my hands on the backs of her thighs.

"That was close, Sir Knight." Her eyes glittered. Amused Leelee was so much better than scared Leelee.

"Where to, Milady?" I bent low to kiss her wrist where the pulse raced.

Breathy from more than our mad dash, her voice slid over me like a caress. "My room, kind sir. I need to get out of this get-up." She lifted her foot and flicked the broken heel with a sigh. "These were my favorites."

Her room? *Danger.* Leelee getting undressed with me present? *Fucking perilous.*

I helped her hop aboard the elevator, pressed her floor number, thought about pulling the High Seas Hotty poster off the wall. Anything to take my mind off Leelee and the way she'd watched me during the contest.

The door of her room came too quickly. I wasn't prepared when she angled an inviting smile at me. "Comin' in?"

Pushing my thigh between hers until we met on the threshold, I moved her with me into the room. The door shut behind us.

No going back.

Chapter Nine
All Fuckin' Mine

I PULLED UP SHORT when I entered Leelee's room. *Holy shit*. The place looked like a tornado had touched down inside and, after that, maybe a hurricane. Suitcases exploded with clothing. Every available surface was crammed with books, paper, pamphlets, paraphernalia. It was worse than the sort of destruction the kid could easily cook up in less than ten minutes.

Leelee was a slob. Either that or she had some kind of personality disorder where she needed to see all of her belongings at once. I thought about Stone's, which was orderly and shipshape even if my employees were a bunch of boneheads.

I hesitated on the edge of the bomb site. "Uh, you need a minute to tidy up?"

From inside the depths of Hell, Leelee glanced around the room and shrugged her shoulders. Grabbing an armload from one bed, she tossed it onto the mountain of clothes and shoes on the spare one. Something slipped from her fingers, and I sauntered over to pick it up off the

131

floor.

It was lacey. It was silky. It was some kind of shimmery green that matched the color of her eyes. *Oh Christ.* Panties. Holding the scrap between both hands, I inspected them while her back was turned. Tiny, with bows at the sides, and—*fuckin' A*—there were two little heart cutouts that would probably sit over each hipbone.

"All set." Leelee whirled around.

I was not a creeper-stalker-lurker-perv so I pushed the panties into her hands and rubbed the back of my neck. "Um, those were on the floor."

"Thanks." When I looked up, her cheeks wore the most *fetching* shade of pink. But she met my stare with a wink, placing the miniature piece of Heaven on the bed. "I've got several more just like those in different colors."

I couldn't think of a thing to say because all my brain cells had simultaneously skyrocketed through the roof of my head, and I wondered if my cock had ripped through my pants yet.

Leelee probably wouldn't have noticed anyway, not with all the other shit she had going on in here. And her *all set* clean up had consisted of moving one pile to another pile, clearing off the quilt and pillows of the bed she apparently slept in. The fact that the mess didn't bother her at all might be a deal breaker.

As if.

I'd sleep in a freakin' pig sty if I had to, as long as I was with her.

Plucking a few items from the overspill of clothing, she glanced at me. "I'm just gonna go change. Sit tight, I won't be a second."

She headed for the bathroom, and I watched her ass all the way. I grabbed at my hair and took a minute to reconsider what I was doing. The moment fled as soon as I smelled a tantalizing whiff of her perfume. Leelee stripping down in the next room got me hot enough, but when I paced to the far end of the bed, the full-sized mirror on the closet door reflected a sliver of the bathroom. A sliver of her hourglass waist to the swell of her hips and a generous slice of backside.

Lush Leelee. She had the kind of pin-up body men salivated over. Curves big enough to fill my hands from her tits to her ass to her hips. All topped by that sweetheart face, the red rosebud lips, the dewy eyes. Not to mention the strawberry blond hair I'd never seen all the way down. Yet. That was gonna get remedied tonight.

I turned my back unless I got carried away and simply barged into the bathroom, bent her over the counter, and fucked her there and then. Facing the clutter and chaos of her room, I was tempted to tidy up a bit more, but I didn't want to get caught pawing through her underthings like I'd been caught pawing at my cock. Heaps of silky, frilly panties and bras and—was that a goddamn corset?—teased me. I stuffed my hands into my pockets. Or I tried to. Damned leathers were too tight.

When the door squeaked open, I turned, and Leelee appeared.

She brushed a hand down her front. "I hope you don't mind. It's been a long day."

Then she blushed, and that was so adorable I was one step away from jumping her bones. I couldn't have replied even if all my motor skills hadn't just taken a back seat to primal male urges. Leelee in the feminine dresses hinting at her sexy body, the heels that made me want to start at her ankles and head north, all of that did it for me. But this? My fingers itched to touch her, my breath turned ragged. All because of a pair of loose white sweats she'd cut off mid-calf, her fresh clean face, and the fact she was swinging free underneath an off-the shoulder LSU Tigers sweatshirt.

"Leelee." My voice rasped, deep and husky. "Christ, stop blushing. You're making it hard for me to think."

Sexual tension arced through the air, drawing her gaze to mine.

Her fingers slipped against her lips, and Jesus goddamn Christ, her tongue slid out to wet them. "Josh, that kiss earlier? Did you mean what you said about you and Nicky?"

Hypnotized by her shiny lips, I chewed briefly on my own. "Yeah. It's over. This is our last hurrah. It's not what you think anyway. There's so much I wanna tell you, but I can't—"

Before I could finish, she was in front of me, fingertips pressed to my mouth. "Just kiss me. Kiss me again." Her arms wound around my neck. Her fingers lacing into my hair, she pulled me down.

This time I wouldn't be stopped by phone calls or fake maids or my false conscience. Barely half an inch remained between my mouth and her upturned lips, but I held it. The feel of her breath racing with mine, the sight of her eyelashes lowered, I didn't want to forget this moment.

Trapping her in my arms, I forced her the last bit forward . . . and "Bohemian Rhapsody" went off.

Her lips slanted against mine, moist and ready. "Queen, Josh? Really?"

I pulled back with a muffled curse. "I have to take this. It's the kid."

Swinging away, I put the cell to my ear.

Ma started right in. "He had a bad dream, Joshy. Woke up sweatin' and cryin'. I just couldn't talk him down. He needs his daddy."

My throat closed in until it was hard to breathe. I shut my eyes against the sting of tears. "Put 'im on."

Sinking to the edge of Leelee's bed, I motioned for her to sit beside me. I curled my hand over hers, grateful for her presence while I tried to keep it together for the kid. I'd never had anyone beside me before, not like this.

I heard the sleepy-slow pat-pat-pat of his bare feet on the old oak floors. I imagined JJ's funny cowlick standing straight up as he sucked his index finger, wearing his favorite-for-the-month Hobbit pj's . . . and the shiny vinyl blue Superman cape.

"Hi, Daddy."

I swiped a hand beneath my eyes with his little tremulous voice in my ears. "Baby boy, it's late."

His hiccupping breaths hit the line, the kind that broke me in two. Leelee nestled against my shoulder. I tightened my hold on her as I listened.

"I had a wightware, Daddy. You didn't come back from L'Ana . . ."

"I'm always coming home to you, kid. Always." I swallowed down a salty wash of tears I didn't let fall. "Nicky and I are gonna pick you and Viper up Sunday night from Jamma."

"Jamma said Monday," he whined.

"Well, I can't wait that long. You wearin' the cape?"

"Yeah, but I still can't fwy to Momma."

I tried to find the words to reassure him one more time she'd left me, not him. "I don't want you to fwy to her, kid, okay? You stay with me. I'll always take care of you."

Reaching for a box of tissues, Leelee silently blew her nose, snuffling against me. Her lips were gentle, the touch almost nonexistent, across the ink on my chest.

"But I fwew off the divin' board at Jamma's pool today. No cape! I can fwy!"

Oh God. I need to get home faster. "That's cool, JJ, but just remember, kids can't actually fly, okay? And would you please stop wrestlin' with Viper while you're at it?"

"She wuvs me," he whispered the same old refrain.

"I love you too, that's why I prefer all your fingers attached to your body."

"I don' know what that means, Daddy. Sing to me." His demand was one step away from a final meltdown for the night.

Leelee right next to me gave me second thoughts about fulfilling his usual bedtime request. I wasn't a

135

crooner, not like my dad. The kid just thought I had good lungs because he didn't have anything but high-pitched Disney chicks to compare me to.

Aw, fuck it. You couldn't tell a little kid to just hit the sack when he missed his dad and had nightmares about his mother leaving. When all he needed to get a decent night's rest was a little musical ditty.

I knew the fastest way to send him to sleep. "*Little Mermaid?*"

"'Kiss the Girl', Daddy."

I grinned, the kid had no idea. "Kiss da girl, huh?" I used my best Rastafarian crab accent.

Leelee curled into me, a smile on her mouth against my neck.

Oh man, I can get used to this.

I sang the tune all about Eric making a move on Ariel complete with the bullfrog chorus. He giggled a few times before the other end of the line grew silent, and I softened my voice.

Ma came on. "He's out like a light."

"Thanks, Ma. Talk to y'all tomorrow." Turning off my phone, I shut my eyes, trying to get control of my emotions.

Leelee's fingers brushed across my shoulder. "A wightware?"

I shifted, my mouth moving across her cheek to her ear. "Nightmare. Because his mom left and he's scared I won't . . ." I shook my head, tugging her onto my lap.

Leelee whispered soothingly to me, her hands smoothing up and down my back. Her touch was amplified against my bare torso, heating my skin, changing the mood between us as surely as any words could. She pulled back enough to drag one hand over my chest, down to the muscles of my abs.

When her fingers skated across clenching muscles, drifting through coarse hair, I let out a hoarse curse. She teasingly dropped her hands lower then drifted them higher again.

With both hands pressed against my chest, she flirted, "Just kiss the girl, huh?"

"Yes," I growled, yanking her against me.

Her lips were perfect, so fucking soft. I attacked her. Spine-tingling, ball-bursting pleasure exploded inside of me when she met the ferocity of my kiss with a moan. Her tongue grazed my mouth and that was it. I pulled at her top lip then the bottom, tasting them one at a time and twisting my hand around her ponytail. My tongue thrusting in and out of her mouth like I intended to tongue-fuck her pussy, my other hand ran inside the back of her sweatshirt, grasping her to me.

Breathy whimpers spilled out of Leelee. Our heads angled for the kind of fit that made fireworks go off in my body. I broke away with a groan but didn't go far. I pulled her ponytail until her neck arched.

"Oh, God, Josh."

That's right.

Her neck to her sexy bared shoulder was mine for the taking. I wielded the flat of my tongue along the sensitive skin of her throat, and she shivered in my arms. As soon as she moaned, I stayed right where I was, at the dip of her collarbone. Kissing, nibbling, sucking her sweet flesh until she started a hypnotic grind on my cock and my name escaped her mouth with every gasp.

My hands slid around to her tummy. My mouth moved slowly to her shoulder, leaving love bites along the way. Under the sweatshirt, I caressed from hip to hip, and upward until the backs of my fingers grazed the undersides of her breasts. I wanted to palm those heavy tits, and I wanted to gorge myself on the sight of my tanned hands against her ivory skin.

"Take it off," I demanded.

Emerald colored eyes opened halfway. I ducked down to her mouth again, feverish for her lips. I scraped my teeth over her tongue and withdrew, commanding once

137

again, "Take the top off, Leelee."

She hit me with a smile that zeroed in on my cock crushed inside the leathers. With the hem of the sweatshirt clasped in both hands, she scooped it up. Over her belly, taut from her workouts but soft like a woman's should be, up to the bottom of her breasts, revealing full feminine curves I was gonna have a field day on. When she finally tossed the sweatshirt aside, my breath stopped.

"Leelee." Her name rasped from me, hunger in each note.

One second I was reclining against the headboard, the next I was face-to-face with the most gorgeous pair of tits I'd ever seen. They filled my palms, and just like I thought, my rough tanned skin against her pale softness was a major turn on.

I looked up at her. "These for me?" I squeezed until they bulged between my fingers and she gasped, nodding her head.

My palms scraped down her breasts, the workingman's calluses turning her skin pink and filling her nipples with deep color. I circled both handfuls lightly, teasing Leelee. Her head dropped down to watch me, and when she licked her lips, I leaped up to wet them for her with my tongue. Her cry filled my mouth when I pinched both buds between my thumbs and forefingers. I pulled her breasts taut then let them drop, a deep laugh rumbling from me when they bounced on her chest.

"Fuckin' gorgeous, babe."

When I lay back, I moved Leelee with me, using the notch of her small waist to guide her over me. Bed pillows beneath my head and twin pillows of flesh dangling over my mouth. *Fucking Heaven.* I popped one pink cherry between my lips and suckled hard. Leelee opened her legs wider over my thighs and pressed into my hard-on with tight licks of her hips.

She rode me like a goddamn pro, moaning every time our hips rocked against each other. Pushing both breasts together, I lapped the circumference until they were slippery between my hands then feasted off both nipples at the same time. My lips smacked, my tongue swirled. My teeth nibbled, and every chance I got, I pulled up to kiss the hell out of her again. I grabbed her ass, shoved her onto my thrusting hips, working her up and down my cock. My face buried deep in her cleavage, I thumbed her nipples while she went wild above me.

Her orgasm was loud, long, and the sexiest fucking thing I'd ever experienced.

I was so hard my dick was a goddamn rod inside the leather pants.

I didn't wait for Leelee to come down or calm down. One finger hooked in the low waist of her sweats, I tugged. "Let's see that pretty pussy, babe."

Her dazed eyes slowly opened. Her lips curved. Her breasts were swollen, wet, shiny. Leelee took over from me, slipping her fingers into the sweatpants. She lowered them from her hips, popped them over her ass and slid them down her thighs and off her feet.

Rising up, she kneeled between my legs. Her thighs were closed but I saw enough to know I wanted more. I wanted in. I wanted now. A fluff of downy red curls lay in a thin strip above a peek of pussy lips that curved inward, hiding all her hot secrets. I reached for her inner thighs to spread them wide, but she gripped my wrists.

"Uh uh. Not so fast, Stone."

All that creamy skin called to me, and damn if her pussy didn't glisten. I could've broken her hold and had her beneath me screaming for more if I wanted, but I relaxed back. "What do you want?"

"Stand up and show me what you got, stud."

Rising to my elbows, I plucked her lips between mine. I made one pass, then another, going back for more as I ran my hand between her thighs, seeking the promised land of her pussy.

Leelee withdrew. She growled. "Get 'em off."

139

"Hair down first, babe." I laid my hand on my cock and stroked it through the pants. "You wanna see this again, I want to see your hair down." Fuck, I wanted to feel it, all over my skin.

Her arms raised but I was there first. "Allow me."

I unrolled the elastic and her hair tumbled over my arms, along her back. It was soft as silk, just like her skin, and smelled like her perfume. I grabbed her to me. I crammed my hands into her hair, licking the shell of her ear.

Her moist breaths gusted against my cheek. "Josh!" Fingernails digging into my biceps, she struggled back. Pointing at my pants, she said, "Off. Now."

I lifted my hips to do the honors and hesitated. "Are you sure?"

"You know I'm not a virgin."

"You make me feel like one." Heat filled all my extremities, extended my cock, made me flush. I had never felt like this—unsure, hopeful . . . completely goddamn desperate. I wanted her, beneath me, beside me, in my bed at home. I wanted Leelee for years to come. "I'm not wearing anything underneath," I warned.

The throaty laugh of a temptress trickled over me. Her fingers traipsed across the rigid length of my shaft busting at the seams. "That's been pretty evident all night, sug."

She sat there on her knees before me like an angel. The haze of her red hair fell around her shoulders and over her gravity defying tits that were too plush to be anything but *au naturel*. Her legs pressed together as more filthy words fell from her mouth. "If you don't take 'em off, I'm gonna make you come in your pants and that won't be half as much fun as coming down my throat, will it?"

No, it wouldn't.

The excruciating metallic grab of the zipper set my nuts on edge. Once undone, the placket held tight to my thickness. I scraped the leathers down my thighs and calves, kicking them off my feet. A drop of sweat rolled

140

down my temple just as a drop of pre-come released from the head of my cock.

Thick, long, fully hard, my cock stood against my belly, absolutely ready for Leelee.

"Whoa, big boy."

As if my dick needed any more encouragement. My balls plumped up harder, heavy weights lifting on command.

"So beautiful, Josh." She crawled toward me, fingers skimming me.

My groin jumped. My hips pumped. Her touch fell away.

"You certainly don't have a problem getting it up for girls, huh?"

If only she knew how little she had to do—starting with breathing, for instance—for me to get hard. "Correction, babe, I don't have a problem gettin' it up for you." In fact, all the other women were nothing but blips in my background compared to this, compared to her.

"I want to do this right."

Leelee wrapping her lips around my cock in any permutation sounded just about right to me. "Huh?"

She backed off the bed, those tits swaying, their bright pink nipples swollen from my fingers and my mouth. "I want to suck your cock right. Stand up so I can get on my knees."

Fuck me. Now I knew where she got her ideas. The sexy mouth on her just made every last ounce of blood pulse through my cock until it was so hard it hurt. I jumped to the floor. She stood before me. All that candy floss hair slipped over my chest while Leelee teasingly tongued my stomach, my groin, my thighs, going lower and lower, never once touching my dick.

Her hands curled around my thighs, cupped my ass. She licked my pelvic grooves, one side then the other, brushing her cheek against my bottle rocket cock. Pulling my length down—but not stroking, not sucking—Leelee lapped my abs.

Fists clenching, teeth grinding, I knocked my head back.

"Put it in my mouth, Stone." A naughty glimmer shone in her darkening irises. Her dirty mouth drove me crazy and I wasn't even in it yet.

Shuddering from head to toe, I fisted my dick with my hand covering hers and lifted her chin. I tapped my rod against her parted lips. "Want this, babe?"

She tossed her hair back. "I want your cock in the back of my throat."

"Open up."

She craned her neck, slid out her tongue. I placed my tip—so full it pulsed—into her mouth.

"Lick it," I said.

Leelee rolled her tongue over the head and I yelled. My hands balled beside me, every impulse screaming at me to plunge down her throat. I held off, watching her. She lapped every jutting vein, sucking my meat between her lips.

"Yeah, lick it hard," I grunted.

Slippery from her lips, I shouted when she moved down to my balls. She pulled one inside then the other and lapped like a kitty at a bowl full of milk.

A tantalizing grin formed on her mouth when she jerked my cock between two tight fists. "You can put your hands in my hair, you know."

Woman of my dreams? Fuck. Woman of my wet dreams. I didn't want to pull her, didn't want to rush her, but I definitely wanted some of that hair. I took two handfuls, spread my thighs wider, and fucked down into her mouth.

Her head moved between my hands, her lush lips tight over me. Her tits swung with every long lunge of my cock. She bobbed up and down with mind-destroying suction. Her nails on my stomach clawed down, leaving red trails and jerking muscle in their wake. Every joint in my body tightened when she nosed my pubes. I groaned when she sucked up and off my cock, and licked her lips.

"I'm gonna come in your mouth." I fucked her face hard and fast for several long thrusts.

Leelee pulled back long enough to flash a wicked grin. "Do it."

Then I was lodged in her throat, clasping her hair, her head, curling over her as come shot out of my cock and every muscle in my body seized. Drops of semen slipped from the corners of her mouth. I pushed it back in, groaning when she sucked my fingertips alongside the head of my cock.

"Sexiest damn thing I've ever seen, Leelee."

Licking her lips, she smiled. "I've wanted to do that since I saw you masturbating."

And I'm a goner.

I threw her onto the bed. Instantly, insanely hard again, I parted the lips of her pussy with two fingers, working my thumb up and around her clit. Her hips rose, following my actions as I leaned to blow across the fiery line of her hair. She was glossy, slick with want. Circling my thumb slowly, I chuckled when she gasped, dripping onto my knuckles as I held her spread and open. Easing one finger inside of her, I watched as I pulled it out, shiny with her juices. Tucking in a second finger, I pressed harder, listening to the wet slurp of her flesh gripping me.

Then my mouth was on her. I pulled her lips into my mouth, tonguing the sweet frills. Her fingers twisted into my hair the way her hips undulated up to my mouth. I murmured against her about how hot she was, how smooth and wet. More heat flooded my tongue, the tongue I used to lick her up and down, inside and out. Always teasing the tight swell of her clit. Our noises grew louder. Leelee mewled and moaned. I sucked and ate her out. Pumping her with three fingers, I snatched her clit between my lips, driving her into climax.

Leelee screamed in release, her head thrown back, her

143

eyes screwed shut. Drawing out of her, I replaced my mouth and hand with my cock. The head was purplish, veins throbbing up and down my shaft. The dark intense color looked unbelievable against the swollen pink spread of her cunt. I slid my length up and down her, catching the ridge of the crown against her clit. Her eyes opened, almost black they were so dark with lust.

I could barely breathe when I fisted my cock, lowering it slowly down to her saturated opening. "Condoms?" My voice was unrecognizable, low and animalistic.

I was in fucking heat. I had a couple in my wallet, but of course I didn't have my wallet on me, just the damn leathers, iPhone, and the lanyard, all long discarded.

She waved around the room, her slick pussy maddening me as it sucked at my cockhead, giving it hot wet kisses.

I clenched my jaw, slowly thrusting just my tip in and out of her. On another crazy short plunge, I held myself there, just at her entrance, barely inside of her. Her flesh stretched for me, from me. Lips puffy and full. Sliding my hand down my shaft, I gently plucked at those lips where they pulled out and around the rigid cliff of my cockhead.

"Where?" My hips jerked, my thighs quaked. The muscles in my stomach and chest stood out as I restrained myself. I needed to fuck Leelee. Now.

"Oooh, oh fuck, Josh!" Her moan almost set me off. "In my red suitcase. I have a stash."

"A stash?"

A dangerous smile played across her lips. She lay with her arms stretched overhead, back arched, breasts high. "*Mmm.* Oh, that's nothin'. All part and parcel of the job."

I slid from the bed, padding to the suitcase she indicated. Digging through her debris, I found a Ziploc full of rubbers. I returned, ripping one open and throwing the rest on the nightstand.

Her gaze dragged to my hands while I rolled the condom down my shaft. "You should see the collection of sex toys I've got at home."

And that was my breaking point. I pounced on her and in one long lunge, seated myself balls deep inside. She cried out and I grunted in shock at her tight fit. So fucking hard I could've devoured her in an instant, I could've gone off in a second, I stilled inside of her.

"Jesus, babe."

"Uhhh . . ." she whined.

Grabbing her ass in both hands, I drove even deeper, growling with the impact. The condom did nothing to hide her heat, her wet sheath, her tight cunt gripping me. I pulled completely out. I jerked her hand down and clamped it around me with a yell. I watched her palm the heavy weight as pure wild need crashed through me.

"That what you want?"

Leelee frantically nodded her head. "Yes, yes."

"You got it." I removed her hand and slammed into her, shoving her back to the mattress.

Sucking her nipples, licking her throat, groaning into her hair, I rammed her with my entire length, impaling her over and over again.

"I'm gonna, I'm gonna!" Her back bent off the bed. Her pelvis thrashed against mine as I ground down onto her.

With a rough kiss, I swallowed her scream. "Yeah. Come, Leelee."

I grabbed her ankles and drew her legs around my hips. Holding her there, I continued to fuck her like a madman. Her pale pink pussy engulfed me, squeezed me. Her shouts surrounded me. I finally succumbed to the orgasm tearing through my body. It pulled up my balls, rocketed through my shaft and exploded out of the tip of my cock. I clenched my teeth so hard I could've busted a molar.

I withdrew slowly. Leelee all but purred beneath me. The full condom pulled off, tied up and tossed away, I enfolded her in my arms. *Yes.* Her breasts teased against my chest, her fingers toyed with my treasure trail, her leg slid between mine.

And I got to play with all that glorious hair.

Later, Leelee rode me while I sucked her nipples, kneading her tits. She knew exactly how fast to go and when to hold off and swivel her hips with me fully inside her. On the edge of orgasm for what felt like torturous hours, she only gave in when I begged her to fuck me fast and hard. So hungry for her as she clenched around me, I practically ate her puffy pink nipples off her body like sugarcoated candy. A swift orgasm seared through me, violent enough to turn my vision white.

It didn't take long for me to want another go at her when she spooned in front of me. I slid one hand over her smooth hip onto her stomach, dipping my fingers into her slit. The condom went on fast when she lifted her thigh for me to take her from behind. It was slow and steady, this fucking. Unlike anything I'd ever experienced before. I leaned back enough to watch my cock enter and drag out of her, inflamed by the sight. But there was something else I wanted to watch more.

"Turn around, babe. I wanna see you."

She complied with a sinuous roll. Then I fucked her solidly for as long as I could, the same steady pace making her sigh and smile, then gasp and writhe. We came together when I speeded my thrusts, her face buried in my neck, teeth nipping.

While she slept, I stayed awake and held her. All the fucking and fleeing of my past, all the fucking and fighting with Claire had never felt like this. How the hell could I be falling in love with a woman I'd just met when I'd avoided it for so many years?

And why did that idea make me grin like a fool, instead of send me into a full-blown panic attack? I squeezed Leelee harder, and she shifted in her sleep. Moments later, she stiffened in my arms.

"You have to go," she said in a resigned voice.

146

Rubbing my hands up and down her arms, I tried to ease the tension running through her. "I know."

I had to get to my own room. We couldn't let any of the other attendees see me sneaking around behind Nicky's back.

Leelee disengaged from me. Cold empty space settled between us. Her hard emotionless eyes were the first hint that I'd really, truly messed everything up.

"No, Stone. I mean I need you to get out. Now."

Reality stole the last remaining warmth from the room. Leelee sealed off her expression, sat back against the pillows, and pulled the sheet to her shoulders.

My jaw hardened. She'd called me Stone, not Josh, not soft and sweet as she had during our lovemaking.

"Leelee, don't do this." I reached out to caress her leg. "I know what you're thinking. This wasn't a mistake. We're not a mistake."

"I'm so stupid." She pulled her leg away. "But hearing you with JJ, listenin' to you talk about your life? You're such a good father. I got caught up in the moment . . ."

"It wasn't a moment. It's something I want to last."

"Are you even really like this, Josh? Or are you Stone? Are you just a massive slut for men *and* women?" She smacked her forehead. "I can't believe I did this. Again!"

I was furious—angry with her and the situation. "Goddammit, Leelee. This isn't a one-night stand for me, and yeah, I've had enough of those to recognize when it happens. I want this to be something more."

"Well, it can't be," she spat. Stumbling from the bed, she dragged the sheet around herself. "I can't do that because I don't know what the hell you are, or *who* the hell you are. And it doesn't even matter because you are gay!" She flung my leathers at me when I jumped off the bed.

"Get out." She fired at me again.

I'd forgotten about her temper. And with mine about to catch fire, getting out was probably the best thing to do at this point. I hauled on the stupid goddamn pants with

147

plans to burn them later.

"All right. I'll go. But don't think this is the end of it, Leelee. Because I'm not some prissy little shit you can order around. When I want something, I go after it." And by God, I wanted her more than anything.

She slammed the door in my face once I stepped into the hall. Of course she did. I started Walk of Shame number two, or maybe three.

I'd fucked up. Royally.

And now I had to prepare to get my ass chewed by Nicky. Not in an *mm mmm* kind of way.

Chapter Ten

Friday: Magic Mike Nightmare

NICKY WAS WAITING UP. Of course he was. The man who used to go home with a different bird every night—sometimes two—had forgotten how to let loose. He shut his book, placing it aside. And he called me a throwback? The successful romance writer of the ebook era still insisted on reading from real paper.

I peeled off the leathers one final time and stuffed them into the trashcan.

Nicky asked in an even voice, all false calm before the whup ass, "Where ya been? Or do I already know?"

I strode into the bathroom to clean up so I didn't go to bed smelling like after-sex. Shoving a washcloth under the faucet, I turned on the hot then lathered all the necessaries. "Why? You jealous, lover?"

He leaned against the doorjamb. "Shit, man—Leelee? What're you doing with her?"

"Since she kicked me out of bed, out of her room, and probably completely out of her life, it looks like a whole hell of a lot of nothin'." I slammed the faucet off and

149

toweled dry. "You need to get laid yourself, ya know? Take the stick outta your ass."

"You do enough catting around for the both of us." Nicky turned away, stomping toward the bed.

"Just 'cause you gave up your man-whore ways because the heat from your fang-girls got much too handle, doesn't mean I have to be a monk too."

His eyes flashed as he pointed at me. "Yeah, you do, Josh, because you agreed to stick it out with me as my partner."

With a towel around my hips, I toed up to the opposite side of the bed. "When was the last time you got screwed? I can tell you didn't bang watermelon lips last night because you looked like you had a cramp in your ass rather than coming in fresh from getting the top of your cock blown off."

He heaved onto the bed. "You're right. I didn't do watermelon lips because I have some self-restraint."

"Yeah. That sucks for you." A pillow hit my back when I turned to my bag.

Nicky had always been the bad boy in high school. The girl-getter. He reeled 'em in, we traded 'em off. During our late twenties, we'd grown more responsible in different ways. He had his career, and I was in over my head with the garage and the kid, although I still found time for my famous weekly one-night-stands. He hadn't been with any woman I knew about in at least six months. That had to tangle his nuts. I was almost tempted to throw him a pity fuck.

He was easy enough to look at even if I didn't swing that way. His muscled chest filled out his shirts, washboard abs lead to strong legs. The longish wavy brown hair had been wrapped around the fingers of many a babe, most of them overcome by his pretty purplish eyes. They also liked the tat around his bicep, black ink weaving against the big muscle. All in all, if I were playing for the other team, I'd find him bone-worthy.

"You're still a pretty boy, Nicky." I smirked at him.

He flipped me off from both hands.

After yanking on a pair of clean shorts, I bounced onto bed beside him. "You need a fuck."

Closing his eyes, he nodded. "I need a fuck."

"Sexual repression isn't a good idea, especially when you write all about sex."

One eyelid lifted. "And romance."

"If that's what you wanna call it when your characters are knocking boots all the time, bro."

Rolling to his side, he twitched his nose like he always did when he was dog-tired. "Looks like you knocked enough boots for the both of us."

Leelee's final words stung me anew. I shrugged.

"Ended bad, huh?"

"The usual. Screaming, throwing things, *unrivaled vehemence*."

He crushed a pillow over his head, burrowing beneath the covers. "But you didn't want to leave this time."

"No. No, I didn't. I'd have stayed in her bed."

The pillow on top of his head puffed up. "You have the worst timing ever, you know?"

I nodded, my head ducked.

"Just don't get me blackballed here, Josh. Are you gonna be able to keep your pecker in your pants?"

"Unless I wanna ram it up your ass, guess I'll have to." I jerked a handful of sheets over my waist.

"I guess you will." He tugged back.

I turned off the light and slid further down in the bed.

Nicky patted my shoulder. "I'm sorry, dude. I don't want to fuck up our relationship over this."

"Our friendship."

He yawned in my face. Good think the fucker had excellent oral hygiene. "What?"

I put the pillow back over his head, the way he liked to sleep, half suffocated. "Night night, and never mind."

The alarm bleated a few hours later. I laughed when Nicky yanked the cord from the socket and threw the machine against the wall, muttering, "Write-off."

The next time I woke, faint lines of sunshine ran under the curtains, and my stomach growled loudly.

"I hate you and your stomach, Josh." Nicky's muffled voice was filled with venom.

I turned on the lamp and perused the room service menu, chuckling when Nicky cursed me a new asshole. The fucking, the shut-eye, the boyfriend moment made me hungry. I needed food.

When he sat up, his cheek was creased from the pillowcase he'd mashed over his face. "When was last time you ate something?"

Besides Leelee's sweet pussy? "Donuts at the Writer's Widows thing?"

Nicky grabbed the phone and dialed. "Jesus, you're gonna waste away, and I'll never hear the end of it from Gigi when I bring you back, looking like a bag of bones."

At two-hundred-ten-plus pounds of pure muscle, I wasn't likely to turn into a skeleton overnight. I listened to Nicky order room service, letting him foot the bill because of write-offs, whatever.

An hour later, after wolfing down two breakfast entrees, I sat back, patting my belly. "What's the deal for today?"

"An outing, it's a slow day." He checked his watch. "We've gotta meet the Hens in the lobby in forty for the shuttle."

I perked up like Viper when her leash was jingled for a walk-run-race around the hood. "The Hens—will Leelee be there?"

His eyes met mine. "She's part of the group, so, yeah. But you're gonna be a gentleman, right?"

"Absolutely." Not.

I blitzed through a shower, buzzed down my stubble, stumbled to my suitcase with a towel dipping off my hips.

Nicky quirked a grin at me. "Your phone's been going off."

"Ma?" I dried the last of the water from my hair and chest.

He made jazz-hands at me before tossing the cell over. "Nope."

"Lemme guess, the knuckle bust crew?" My jeans and a T-shirt pulled on, I had second thoughts about taking a look at the latest from my mechanics who seemed to think they were Comedy Central material.

"Bingo." Nicky rolled his shoulders into a vintage button down and waited for his morning entertainment.

I braced myself. What came up was the Stone's Auto Service homepage with me plastered all over it. I wasn't just famous for my ass anymore. Smartass tech-nerd Javier had cut and spliced the video of Leelee and me dancing the tango. But that wasn't all. He'd added a Stone's garage spin at the end with a one-of-a-kind graphic that read: *Stone's: At Your Service. Hell on Wheels & Hell in High Heels.*

I put a call directly in to the office, and Ray answered, "You saw it?"

"Get me Javier." I chomped through the words like they were beef jerky.

Bossman ain't laughin', Javier, I overheard Ray.

Javier got on the horn and started blathering in Spanish, but I barked right over him, "Take it down!"

I hung up.

Then I hung my head. Nicky glared at me and I stared at Leelee's book. I didn't need his silent disapproval to know I'd been a first class dickhead all because I was a cranky bastard over Leelee. I just thanked Christ I hadn't lost my temper with JJ instead of Javier. Javier was easy to soothe, while the kid required a million hugs, a trillion kisses, and promises of puppy dogs—the cuddly kind—and pony rides.

I redialed and asked Ray to get Javier for me, please and thanks.

When I heard the phone exchange hands and Javier's skittish, "Sorry, boss," I sighed, "Jesus fucking Christ, boy."

That was my form of apology, one the guys were acquainted with.

"*Mierda,* I thought you were gonna fire me. We already got new followers on Twitter and likes on Facebook. *Las muchachas* like it. You're a big hit with your woman."

"Leave it up, son. You done good." Putting on my leather jacket, I joined Nicky at the door. "Just no more mule-packin'-asshole pics, please."

"You got it, *jefe*."

* * * *

I prowled the lobby as we waited for the Hens to gather. They finally showed, admiring each other's hair or outfits or yadda yadda, yip-yip. Leelee stuck to the fringes of the group while we trudged outside to the muggy May air to board the bus. I stood to the side, letting everyone pass as a perfect gentleman should. Janice kissed my cheek and pinched my glutes. Her glasses were rosy, her outlook less so.

"Red sky at night, sailor's delight. Red sky in the morning, sailors take warning." She left me with the ominous proverb, bangles jangling in her wake.

Missy wore three strands of pearls tight around her neck, like a collar, I presumed. I'd since done my BDSM research. "I would dearly love to have you bent over and at my mercy in a dungeon one day, Stone."

"I never did get into D&D."

"My, aren't you full of spunk today?" She grinned.

"Wouldn't you like to know?"

"Well played." She winked and was gone.

Jacqueline was one class act in a bright dress and new nail art in tri-tone chevrons, a time-consuming process she described to anyone who'd listen. "Ready to have some fun, hon?"

I reckoned fun was off the table unless I could get Leelee to talk to me. Seemed that was off the table too as she cold-shouldered in front of me and hustled onto the shuttle as fast as her fuck-hot red heels could carry her. Taking Nicky's hand, I settled us in the middle of the crew. The bus took off for destination unknown.

The chatter from the Hens was so loud I couldn't help but listen. A squabble broke out; they were worse than Ma's smut-reading circle of blue-haireds for getting into a debate about who-said-who-did what in the last twenty-four hours.

"Did you hear the sounds coming from that woman's room last night? It rivaled a good old fuck-room bullwhipping." Peachtree practically choked with glee.

"Word is she was researching for her new *Dom of the Dawn* book," Jacqueline said.

More gossip ensued. I listened with half an ear, wishing Leelee were sitting right next to me and not half a bus away.

When their voices lowered, I tuned back in. Janice tried not to turn her head to glance at Leelee. It was like watching a dog trying to itch that unreachable scratch. Likewise, my ears pricked up as Viper's did when meat or man was headed her way. I was On Command whenever Leelee was concerned.

"You hear about what happened to Leelee?" Jacqueline spoke in hushed tones.

Oh, I knew the answer to that one. I flinched. Nicky winced beside me. I'd screwed her silly—several times—then she'd come to her senses and kicked me out.

"No. What?" Both Missy and Janice asked while Nicky gripped my hand so tight a couple of my knuckles popped.

At a low whisper, Jacqueline said, "She was in the lobby this morning, surrounded by fans when *He* weaseled up."

No one needed to ask who *He* was. Andrew La Fucking Forge. The idea of him even looking at Leelee, let alone approaching her one more time, set my teeth on edge.

The cocoa-skinned beauty continued. "Whatever he said to her made her race back to her room. She didn't even finish the final autograph."

"Oooh, it's *soo* cloak and dagger. Like a LitLuv cozy mystery!" Janice exclaimed.

There was nothing cozy or cute or cuddly about Leelee being harassed by that fuckwit. Cozy was gonna be my left hook when it hit his kidneys.

"Why's he so intent on getting to Leelee?"

"LaForge thinks people are sheeple," Janice answered me.

Missy closed the gap between her seat and mine. "Exactly. Adding her to his stable of writers when she's been so vocally pro-Indie would be a coup. He's sure others would follow her lead."

"Too many folks are taking their businesses into their own hands, drying up the new talent available to agents. He needs fresh blood," Jacqueline said.

Several seats away, Leelee was pale and the strain in her posture knocked another notch loose in my heart. Right now all I wanted to do was ask her whose ass I needed to kick to make her feel better.

"But you'll protect her." Janice squeezed my arm.

Damn right I will.

* * * *

It seemed I needed to protect Leelee from the seedy Atlanta cesspool as we pulled up outside of a cordoned-off club. The exterior flashed with bright lights and neon signs even though it was barely midafternoon. *Oooh, aaah, pretty sleazy.* The sparkly gold name on the marquee gave me pause: *The Golden Banana.*

I took Leelee's elbow and held it tight until all the Hens had packed into the vestibule, paid their entrance, and moved along.

"Let me go," she hissed.

I did no such thing. I escorted her into the depths of a darkened room where hints of crimson and gold glowed from groupings of furniture in lounge areas. Front and center was a stage, and I reckoned I knew what Golden Banana really stood for.

Nicky tailed me. Leelee glared at me. This was a train wreck in the making, especially when we made our way to the others at a reserved table right in front of the stage.

I held out Leelee's chair and tucked it in. She looked like maybe she wanted to bite my hand off. I moved into the empty seat between her and Nicky, vaguely listening to the excited whispers as more and more ladies packed in. These people I recognized—writers, reviewers, readers—all from the Con. Slow day or an excuse to spend their dollar bills, I wondered.

Oh and look. Whaddya know? The LolliPOP Grrrls. The licker lewdly slurped the sucker out of her mouth and waved it at me. Hoodie-broody girl nodded at me with a leer.

Janice jabbed Missy. "Looks like we've got competition for Stone's attention."

Leelee huffed and raised her hand to order a drink from a passing waiter. He wore no more than a shiny vinyl loincloth to cover his crankshaft. I seconded the drink order—not the dink order—and the rest chimed in, too.

As soon as the venue grew crowded, the dim lights lowered even more and three spots hit center stage. Strutting from the darkness beyond, a man with slicked back black hair and painted on leathers—I dared-fuckin'-

say they were tighter than the pair I'd trashed last night—threw his arms wide.

Women erupted from their seats, leaped onto tables, started throwing panties, money, wads of paper with phone numbers. Janice pounded the tabletop. A small smile flirted across Leelee's lips. Jacqueline blew a man-hungry whistle through her teeth.

Nicky smirked at me.

"Welcome to 'Lanta, y'all! When we heard there was a group of beautiful"—he thrust his hips once—"talented,"—twice—"freaky group of sexy romance writers in town?" The MC gave Jules Gem a run for her money, rolling his pelvis obscenely, and the ladies threatened to stampede the stage. His voice dropped. "Well, we just had to put on a special show for y'all!" He raised his arms again, shouting, "Welcome to the all-male revue, *Magic Mike Night* . . . erm . . . make that *Noon*!"

From every corner of the room, men appeared. Lots of them. Almost naked men. No worse than what I'd gotten up to last night, but then Leelee had been focused solely on me. Now she wasn't. Her mouth dropped open, her cheeks flushed in that pretty shade of pink—the way they did when she was on the brink of orgasm. Threading through the audience of bloodthirsty demons, aka dick-loving babes, the strippers eventually made it onstage in one piece, without their negligible outfits torn off their bodies.

A few kisses were probably stolen and asses squeezed, I knew, because I'd been on the receiving end of that before.

I sat, glowering.

Nicky snickered at my expense. "Remember? I told you I'd take you to a strip joint."

My smile was sickeningly sweet. "Lover, if I wanted to see more dongs boing around, I'd still be backstage at Balls and Dicks or whatever the hell Jules called that free-for-all."

Inside I was not a happy camper, but outwardly I tried to project something other than jilted-lover rage every time I looked over at Leelee. *Great.* Now I had to watch her drool over the Chippendales. Sausage-fest take two only this time I wasn't performing and a bunch of limber-jointed, bendy bastards held Leelee's attention. *Joy.* They were all waxed to within an inch of their lives. At least I had chest hair like a real man should, thank you very fucking much.

I threw in a few wolf whistles, acting the part.

Leelee strode forward to shove a wad of cash against the wad of the oiled-up asshole doing the wham-bam on his knees at the end of the stage.

I sat and stewed.

Magic Mike day/night or not, there was no magic. I was *not* feeling the magic. The gigolos grinded, the groupies groped whenever they got close enough. And I had to act gay and salivating when in truth I was so hot under the collar, I wanted to throw Leelee over my shoulder, stalk to the nearest exit and have it out with her. Or have her under me. Either one would do me good.

That's when the construction worker started dry humping his sledgehammer. Literally. There was so much bouncing going on, someone's eye was gonna get poked out even though he was still somewhat bridled inside a pair of bright pink briefs cut-out around his ass cheeks. Jesus. *I* was blinded.

A sailor took the stage next, doing his best Gene Kelly MGM musical moves until he ripped off the pristine white uniform via the wonders of Velcro. He stood there with his sailor's cap cupped over his cock. The ladies went ape shit. A short, stocky policeman followed. I didn't really wanna know where he was going to ram his nightstick. This was a white-collar woman's wet dream about blue-collar workers, and I wanted to stand up and shout I was the real deal. Men at Work? *I'll give them men at work. Just take a trip to Mt. Pleasant and over to Stone's.*

159

The cop stripped down to his jockstrap and Janice swooned in her seat.

When Missy stood up, the whole table shook and I guarded my beer. She bellowed, "Yeah, beat that nightstick, boy! BEAT IT!"

I lowered my head to my arms on top of the sticky tabletop. Of course, the clever MC-turned-DJ immediately pumped out "Beat It" by Michael Jackson. Fuckin' A.

I only opened my eyes, peering through fingertips, when Leelee said, "Would you look at the Jesus crease on that one?"

It was a fireman, of course it was. Coyly flipping his helmet off, red suspenders dangling from his hips, he danced his shiny ass off under the lights. Leelee's fingertips moved to her lips as she watched the stripper, never blinking.

Nicky laughed like a hyena until I wanted to hit him. "Didn't know you had it in ya, L."

Jacqueline's gaze ran up and down the fireman's hose. "I'd tap that."

"I'd hit that." Missy cheered.

Probably literally.

Janice wiped the steam from her glasses. "I wouldn't kick that out of bed." The round robin had reached me, and she asked, "Stone?"

The tableful waited expectantly, except Leelee. She stared past me as she'd done ever since she kicked me curbside in the wee hours of the morning.

"I . . ." I trailed off. Then smiled at Nicky and stroked his arm. "I'm a one-man man."

"Le sigh." Almost everyone simpered.

Leelee gave a derisive snort.

Nicky started talking to Robo-Cop, playing it up. "We're looking for a third for the night."

Titters and twitters went off like light bulbs sparking.

I almost decked him . . . God, I was gonna murder him, bury his body next to the grease monkeys out behind the garage. Nicky had half a lifeline left before I Godfathered him, and he'd be taking his long sleep goodnight beside a head gasket, not a horse head.

The po-po went to rub up against another stripper pole, and I tanked back my beer.

The DJ appeared through a cloud of smoke. "I hear we have a few famous writers in the house. Is there a Leelee Songchild out there?"

Whoops, hollers, *oh hell no.*

The fireman with the so-called Jesus crease jumped down. He hunkered between Leelee's legs and flicked her calve with his tongue. The next thing I knew, his ass snuggled her face and his nuts tapped her chin. She gathered his suspenders like they were horse reins and hauled him in.

Missy hollered.

My knuckles turned white.

If Leelee got one more oily crotch that wasn't mine in her face, I was gonna blow.

I wondered who set that shit up for all of a second until I saw the evil grin Nicky aimed at me. "Payback's a bitch."

On second thought, murder was too good for him.

The black-clad host mic'd over the melee as the fireman slid his ass off Leelee's lap. "Give it up for our birthday girl!"

I ignored the clapping and the catcalling. If any other fucker got close enough to touch his crotch to Leelee's lips, I was gonna blow a gasket. And, *oh no*, she was not getting birthday jizz on her face. And it wasn't even her fucking birthday, for fuck's sake. I'd Googled that shit.

"Enjoying the show, darlin'?" Nicky asked.

"I hate you." I was fed up with playing follow the bouncing balls.

"You're kinda blowing our cover."

"As long as I ain't blowing you."

A waitress in a short skirt and half shirt served fluted

glasses full of frothy red liquid. Another fruity cocktail.

"Drink up!" Nicky clanked his glass to mine as Captain Dick took his place on Leelee's lap.

Drink up or bust the place up . . .

By the time she got free I was seeing red. She excused herself to the ladies. I waited a reasonable amount of time—all of twenty seconds—before I headed to the john.

I had two days left to bring her around. Time-wasting was not on my agenda.

She exited the restroom and I blocked her way. "You want a show, babe? I got it right here."

Hauling back, Leelee smacked me across the face. "Fuck you, Stone."

The slap was so hard it stung, but I shook it off. I grabbed her other wrist before she could come at me a second time. "Please do, Leelee."

"You infuriate me!"

"That makes two of us." I hustled her into a dark corridor.

When I had her caged beneath my arms and between my thighs, my anger melted away. Leelee the tigress turned all soft kitten.

Her eyes glistened and her lips trembled. "I already screwed my life up by myself. I don't need to do this dance again."

"I'm sorry." I bent my forehead to hers. "I am such a fuckup." My voice gentled.

She yielded when I clasped her face between my hands, intending only to comfort her. I laid a soft kiss on her cheek. I let her hair run through my fingers a final time.

Stepping back, I raised my hands. "I'll let you run from me this once, Leelee. But trust me, next time I see you, next time I'm with you, I won't let you get away."

She hesitated for a moment before she turned on her heel. Leelee walked away without a backward glance.

Chapter Eleven
Friday: Second Dance, Last Chance

THE SHUTTLE RIDE BACK to the Ramada was another exercise in *this fucking sucks*. Leelee's brittle smile combined with my broody mood, tension arcing between us. Thankfully the rest of the Hens peck-peck-pecked about the Magic Mike not-Night, oblivious to the undercurrent of awkwardness. Disembarking, I let Nicky take my hand and tug me inside. Everyone was in my way, the crowd more congested than ever. The lobby overflowed with balloons and posters and camera flashes. It seemed a Big Name Author had made her appearance.

I didn't care about that shit. I just wanted to keep track of Leelee as she slid away from the group. I planned to hunt her down later. Craning my neck, I glimpsed her on the escalator that rose to the second floor. I considered storming after her, but she needed time to blow off some steam without me in her direct line of fire.

Nicky made his excuses to go hobnob, and I grabbed a sandwich from the over-priced in-hotel deli, heading upstairs. One hoagie down and digesting, bottle of water

163

glugged, gym shorts and workout ignored, I flipped open *Ride*.

> *Jase fucked women for money. He dressed in a monkey suit for wealthy society broads, women who had too much bank and not enough bang in their bedrooms. He undressed for them and made sure their orgasms weren't the fake kind screamed out to massage the egos of their high-powered 'daddies'. He pocketed the cash and got out as quickly as he could.*
>
> *Going home alone, he relegated each lady to a memory of money made that had nothing at-fucking-all to do with lovemaking. They were distilled into dollar signs and decimal points as Jase reminded himself he was lucky he could use his body as a business transaction. He'd hit the shower—painfully hot water, strong soap, three complete washings—hit his studies, and study his bank account.*

"Oh shit." Jase was a bigger fuckup than me.

> *All his tats, his motorcycle, his rep—it was to keep people off his back. He let people think what they wanted because their opinions didn't matter. But Ave's did. She was the only person he wanted riding his back. She could never find out how he kept them flush.*
>
> *So maybe he was a rent boy who let women use him for easy money, but at least he paid the bills on time. That usually included Ave's share too so she could concentrate on her studies. He managed to keep his grades at dean's list level, which wasn't too shabby. And it meant his dad continued to foot the bill for tuition and fees even if he didn't bother with those pesky necessities*

like food, shelter, clothing . . . condoms.

When Jase slunk into the kitchen stinking of high-class perfume, Ave closed her books and stood to make her escape.

She was clean, she was innocent. That's why Avery was so special to him. She didn't make him feel dirty no matter how filthy he felt. Ave made Jase want more, from her. And frankly, her skittishness after a long evening of riding some woman he hoped he'd never see again made him a little on the tetchy side.

He grabbed her elbow.

"I have an exam tomorrow, Jase." But her protest died on a whimper when he curled his arms around her.

"So fuckin' beautiful, baby."

She covered her face with her hands. "I'm horrible."

Every moment with Ave showed him a new side. This one had him growling, "Who told you that?" Tears slithered down her cheeks and he scooped them away. "Stop, honey, stop. Please."

Hesitant fingers slid through his hair when his lips replaced his fingers on her face, his tongue collecting the salty teardrops. "Jase?"

Immense hunger ripped through him with that one little question. He shed his leather jacket and wondered how much Ave was willing to give. Because for her, for the first time, he'd give everything.

This kid was killing me, his thoughts so precisely mirroring mine. Jesus, maybe I could pick up some pointers from him about how to win Leelee over, especially since she was the one who'd created him.

"Are you using me?" Ave asked, pulling her

165

skirt down around her thighs when he tried to tug it up.

"You've gotta be fuckin' kidding me." The kiss he brushed along her neck made her sigh. There was no duplicity in his actions, just sheer want. For her taste, her feel, her freshness he'd never experienced.

Soft starving eyes slid to his. "Don't do this, Jase. Not if you're going to hurt me." Her shoulders rolling forward, she tried to hermit her way back into her shell of protection.

Everything. Ave meant it all. Her shy ways, her bookish looks, her need . . . she needed him like no one ever had.

"I wanna make love to you. Wake up with you." His lips tripping across her mouth again, he aimed inside.

Tentative licks met him. Then wild wet heat. Every motion, every intense and deep emotion, she met. The lapping, the teeth scraping, the lashing in and out as their mouths meshed had Jase on the edge of dragging his jeans off and grabbing his cock.

He let her go to get rid of his shirt, chuckling in a tight, low drawl when her fingers traced the grooves of muscle and the trail of hair from his stomach to the top of his pants. His cock rapped hard against the zipper. He was full, erect, eight wide inches of dick begging to be fucked or sucked.

Pulling her hands off him, watching her eyes widen, Jase smirked. "Want it, darlin'?"

He was pushing her, he knew it.

The stain on her cheeks and the flush up her neck was a telltale sign she liked it. He breathed against the small curl of her ear, tasting her earlobe, as sweet as her lips. "I know you do.

You wanna see me naked again, you wanna fuck me. You want my mouth on your cunt and your hands driving into my hair to hold . . . me . . . tight."

Her whimper drove a spike of need through him. He slipped his tongue into her mouth, hauling her into his arms. He'd never been kissed like this. Little pants of breath, small sips of lips in between deep, heady, all-seeking lunges. His hands dragged up her nape, into her hair, clasping, winding, tightening.

Breaking away from her addictive lips, Jase clasped Ave's face. One hand fell to her waist, bunching up the blouse, touching bare skin he'd never seen. "Are you gonna insult me again by asking about my intentions with you?"

"No!" Her mouth was so swollen he wanted to fuck it with his cock, slowly.

"Are you gonna tell me what happened to you, baby, to make you think you're anything less than goddamn perfection?"

She gasped and turned to flee, but he grabbed her around the waist before she could get away.

A whip of her hair flicked across his face, and fury filled her expression before being buried inside. "Not now, Jase." She slid her hands into the out-of-shape cuffs of her sleeves. A nervous twitch. One Jase wanted to break her of once he found out what had caused it.

Touching her cheek, he sought her eyes. "Sleep with me tonight, Ave."

She shook her head.

He wrapped his arms around her and rocked side-to-side. "Sleep with me. Every night. Goddamn it, I want you however I can get you." He kissed her neck, her lips, her lowered eyelids,

167

murmuring all the time. "I'm not what you think."

He was worse, though. Dirty, inside and out. Used, paid for, a fuck for money. But not for Ave, never with her. She didn't know. She had no idea. And he planned to keep it that way.

One silent nod of her head beneath his chin and Jase groaned. All the months of wanting, the years of searching, of finding Avery, and she was going to sleep with him. He wanted to strip off and do a victory dance before bending her over the table.

He was pretty sure those wicked ideas gleamed in his eyes, but he tried to extinguish them.

"Now," he tilted her chin up for a quick kiss, "put on your ugliest nightgown and get to my room. I'm holdin' you all night long."

And that was it, all he wanted.

A sniffled weak laugh came from her before she turned away.

Jesus Christ. I gave a watery laugh, too. Who knew Jase had it in him? The story Leelee wrote was explosive, emotional. It was full on, hands-down-your-pants hot, and I'd gone and gotten myself all worked up over her again.

"Fuck." I closed the book. All I wanted was Leelee as she'd been last night, open and fresh-faced instead of armored in attitude as she'd been today.

Checking the time, I saw it was coming up to eight already. I did a round of redneck washing in the bathroom then commenced my hunt for Leelee. She'd had enough time to cool down, and I'd had enough to heat up.

* * * *

I checked the second floor bar first, figuring that's

where she headed after the shuttle dropped us off. No such luck. I scoped out all her hideouts and hangouts. I pounded up and down the halls and that elevator at least half a dozen times, fedora angled over my eyes not doing a damn thing to hide my growing scowl.

An hour had passed by the time I returned to the bar, intending to swallow down the bitter taste of regret with a couple brews. There she was. She sat alone at the bar, nursing a glass of white wine. Her shoulders were practically up to her ears as she hunched forward. Classic get-out-and-stay-out posture. Too bad I didn't read body language so well. I plunked down beside her, not bothering to ask if I was welcome because I already knew the answer to that. Ordering a beer, I chanced a look at Leelee's profile. On second thought, I added a shot of bourbon, too.

She might've been sitting all hunched up to keep people out, but that was because otherwise she looked completely defenseless. Vulnerable, unprotected, undone Leelee sent a piercing blow to my heart.

She flinched from the hand I set over hers. But that was okay, I deserved it. Besides I knew how to handle her, just like my Camaro when I'd restored it back to its pristine bragging-rights glory—lovingly, tenderly, and with patience. I'd worked methodically on that machine, coaxing the engine until new life burst from the old. I did the same with Leelee. Murmuring quietly, I stroked her fingers and then her palm when her hand fell open. I knew how to take care of her: by telling her as I did then that everything was going to be all right because I was gonna make goddamn sure of it.

She let me caress along her arm so I could pull her closer, sheltering her with my body. Only then did the tension ease from her shoulders.

"LaForge won't take no for answer."

I knew how to make sure he'd take no, with my fist making it so. "What'd he say to you this morning, babe?"

She wiggled closer in my embrace but wouldn't look

169

at me, didn't answer me. Instead she tipped her wineglass up for a long drink.

"You've gotta tell me. If you don't, I'm gonna throttle it out of LaForge." I held my rage at bay, barely, because I was all about the comfort, but I couldn't stop from gritting my teeth.

"The usual. He's just findin' new ways to deliver the message that if I don't sign with his agency, he'll bring me down."

Lifting her chin, I stared hard into her eyes. "Something else you're not tellin' me here?"

Her gaze skated aside and she shook her head. Suspicion crawled all over my skin. But I'd let it slide until tomorrow, because I was a selfish SOB, and if Leelee was talking to me again, I didn't want to rock the boat by throwing around a bunch of macho vibes.

I settled for slow strokes up and down Leelee's side. After several long minutes, she purred contentedly against me. We had a couple more drinks, shared a basket of Buffalo wings, fighting over the last celery stick and blue cheese dressing. I almost gagged when she dumped half a bottle of ketchup on our order of fries. I smiled when she belatedly interrogated the bartender about what brand of ketchup it was, because she hated Hunts and preferred Heinz.

I complained about carburetors and handsy female customers, to which she nodded in understanding, even talking shop with me. She cursed about writer's block and handsy male agents . . . and I knew exactly what she was talking about. She told me about Sunday dinners with her folks—usually ending up in the garage with her dad as they fiddled with his latest project—just like me and the Stone's gang all converging at Ma's once a month. Leelee lived alone in the condo she and Patrick the Fuckstick had purchased. She'd replaced his candy-ass with one feisty kitten named Mews. Writing and her girlfriends were her life, just like JJ and the guys were mine.

It was easy, being with her, but beneath our innocent, getting-to-know-you conversation, the sexual current raced headlong. The compulsion to kiss her was so strong, I stared at her lips. I remembered licking the bow-shape. I couldn't forget how she'd opened that pretty mouth and sucked on both my balls.

The din of the crowded bar gradually drifted away. It was getting late; tomorrow was the book fair. Writers and readers wanted a fresh start for a day of pimping, promoting, autographs, freebies.

It was time for last call when I heard the music piped in from the speakers, Leelee and I the only ones left in the place. Soft strains of jazz drifted over us, and I recognized the Chet Baker tune.

We faced one another on our stools, Leelee's knees pressed between my thighs, while she talked about her plans for the sequel to *Ride*. Her hands waved in the air as she explained the next chapter in Jase and Avery's lives.

When I heard the next song, "Alone Together", I interrupted her, softly kissing the lips that called to me.

Dark forest green eyes widened on mine when I pulled away.

"This song reminds me of my folks." Drifting my fingers lightly through her hair, I teased out the curls.

"What were they like together?"

"I grew up on music like this. Ma and Dad were all about dancing, the old crooners, you know?"

"You get your singing voice from him." Leelee's fingertips trailed a line of fire down my arm until she held my hand, bringing it to her mouth for a kiss on each of my knuckles.

Her simple sweet touch blew me away.

"Nah, he was much better than me. It's just one of the things I hold onto about them. I remember one night at the garage after it was closed . . . I was eight or so. We'd had take-out in the reception so Dad could finish up an order while Ma completed some invoices. I'd fallen asleep on

171

three chairs pulled together, clean coveralls for my blanket, the smell of oil in my nose. The garage has always been a second home."

Leelee's smile grew. "Me too, at my parents. I used to wander into the garage during naptime. Mom wasn't a fan, but she finally broke down and made up a pallet with my favorite blankets in there."

"Goddamn. Can you get any more perfect?" The heat of the fire stoked inside my chest.

"Shush, now. You'll make me blush."

I grinned when more heat crept up her cheeks in spite of her words. "I woke up alone in the dark. Remember, babe, I wasn't always the rough, tough, buff dude you see now."

Slapping my shoulder, she rolled her eyes. "Please."

I captured her hand and nuzzled the soft skin of her wrist, drugging myself on her warmth as the song spun me into memories. The trumpet's slow sensual music wafted around us, weaving us inside a spell. "I crept behind the desk, and that's when I heard him singing. That's how Dad put me to sleep, same as I do with the kid."

The higher notes of the song dragged us closer until we were almost kissing.

"I tiptoed to the door of the first bay, and there they were. Dad was singing this song to Ma. He swirled her around between two cars on lifts, over the grease-stained floor with no candles and no orchestra. No one but the two of them."

I'd never imagined having what they shared.

"What a beautiful memory." Her rosebud lips burst into a teasing smile. "But I figured you for more of Chili Peppers fan."

"Chet Baker, old school all the way." I leaned in those last few inches, licking the crest of her mouth, snicking her with a gentle bite of teeth.

"That explains the fedora then."

I tugged the brim lower before angling in for another

short pull on her lips.

She moved closer to whisper, "And it explains the *Dancing with the Stars* moves. You really are a romantic."

I never would've thought so before her. "Only for you, babe."

This is it. The feeling of being all alone, together. It raced up my spine and pounded through my body, slamming right into my heart. What my folks had, I'd only experienced with Leelee. The night of the tango, in a roomful of people, we'd been intent only on each other. She was heaven in my arms and I wanted nothing more, no one else.

"You miss your dad." Her fingertips rasped against the stubble on my jaw.

I flipped my hat onto the bar. "All the damn time. But I don't want to miss you. Not tomorrow, not the next day."

She shifted off the stool, offering her hand. "Dance with me."

"I think that's my line." I brought her hand to my chest.

Warm and soft, her hip filled my palm, her skirt rustling between us as I stood. Leaning down, I nipped her shoulder, drinking her in.

"I'm re-writing it." Her body aligned perfectly with mine.

"For All We Know" began. There was nothing but the song and the sway of our bodies around the emptied room. Bartenders watched, quieting their movements as they cleaned up around us.

Wrapped around each other, we danced. Her hand skimmed up my back, mine slipped to her neck. Our lips hovered but no kisses were taken.

Leelee's cheek lay against mine—her soft to my rough. "Sing to me?"

No candles, no one else, my voice rumbled with the rich tones of old times. There was no fancy footwork, only feeling. And she felt so fucking good in my arms.

173

The music ended slowly. My hands snuck up her back, holding her against me, unwilling to let go.

The seduction broke when Leelee left my arms. She spoke softly, her voice filled with regret. "This doesn't change anything. I can't do this, Stone. Not after Patrick, and I don't wanna get between you and Nicky. I won't be burned again."

I'd made her feel good for all of a few hours. I wanted to do that for a lifetime. I felt as empty as the room we stood in. Tossing a few bills on the bar, I took up my hat.

"Can I walk you to your room?"

"No. No, this time you can't." Her head held high, no looking back, she strode through the doors.

Even though I said I wouldn't, I watched the girl of my dreams walk away from me one more time.

The bartender rapped his knuckles down. "Closing time, bud."

Isn't that always the way?

Chapter Twelve
Friday: Thrown a Bone

DETERMINED NOT TO BE a stalker-gawker—*that guy*—I gave Leelee a ten-minute lead before I began my trudge upstairs. The elevator dinged and as the doors opened Leelee barreled straight out into me. I caught her as she fell into my arms.

"What is it?"

"He was there, waiting by my door." Her eyes were wild.

"The fuck did he do?" Rage pumped through me, pure and primal. "You need to report him. Right now. I'll go with you." My teeth were clenched so tight I could barely scrape out the words.

"I can't." Her voice was a mere whisper.

"Why the hell not?"

"Because I can't afford to piss him off! He's in with the old boy network. He has connections, he's at all the conventions. He could really screw up my future . . . and Nicky's too."

"He mentioned Nicky?"

"Yes. He's scamming some kind of smear campaign. He knows exactly who Nicky is, and that you're supposed to be his partner, but he said he's not falling for it."

Fuck. The truth was so simple but it could end up being a big wrecking ball to Nicky's career. I couldn't blow his cover in public—he'd cultivated his gay persona for years. Then there was my slim hope with Leelee coming down like a roof on top of my head. If her *no second chances* rule applied to that no-good liar Patrick, I was certain I'd be next on her shit list as soon as she found out the truth.

"Fine." My jaw jumped. "You're staying in my room tonight." *And I'm gonna pummel LaForge's face tomorrow.* Bright and early. And maybe all damn day long.

"How's that gonna work, with you and Nicky?"

"I don't know, babe. You take the bed, I'll sleep on the floor, Nicky can have the couch."

When we reached the door, I slid the key card home and ushered her inside. Nicky looked over from tap-tap-tapping on his laptop then closed it down and stood up. Leelee shuffled backward into me and I grasped her around the waist.

"What's up?" he asked.

"She's staying with us tonight."

Turning into me, Leelee said, "This isn't a good idea."

"LaForge is darkening her door, and I don't think Leelee should be alone tonight." I kept my arm right where it was around her waist.

"Probably not." Packing up his computer, phone, and cords, he crossed to us. Leveling his gaze on Leelee, he said, "I think we got off on the wrong foot, but Josh'll rectify that soon. Have a good night, y'all."

He brushed past me to the door. I was right behind him. "What the hell are you doing?"

"Leaving you to it." He gripped the back of my neck

and squeezed. "Don't say I never did nothing for you, man."

I slapped him on the shoulder in thanks and watched him leave. *Damn.* I owed him, big time.

"He left?" Leelee spun toward me when I came back into the room.

"Yeah."

"Why? Why would he do that?"

I placed the fedora on the desk, pulling a hand down the back of my neck. "Because he knows the truth."

"So I'm the only one in the dark here?"

I was at her side in an instant, cradling her close. "Not for long. You've gotta trust me on this."

"Well, I guess it won't hurt to stay the night." She gave me her best glare then sent it around the room with a harrumph. "This place sure is tidy for two guys."

"I suppose so, compared to the detonation zone of your room."

I managed to step back before her fist made contact with my stomach. "That was uncalled for, Stone."

"Hey, I call it like I see it, lady." I winked.

She stood beside the bed, eyeing the fluffed pillows. "I don't have anything to sleep in."

Because that was a problem. Naked was definitely preferable, but I figured I was lucky if I could *get* lucky later. Besides, it wasn't about that right now. I'd just watched the woman who held my heart in her hands walk away, now I had one last chance with her.

"Sit," I said.

She blinked at me before doing as I bade. "What about Nicky?"

I stripped off my shirt and crouched at her feet. "I already told you, it's not what you think. And if you're still talking to me by the time this convention ends, I'll tell you everything. But for now, it's you and me, and not another word about him."

Heat flashed into her eyes, making them shine. "You don't tell me what to do." She jumped to her feet. "I'll go stay with Missy."

Hell no to that. She'd be tied down, trussed up, and possibly gagged, too. "Don't. I'm sorry." My hand crushed to my heart, I begged, "Stay, please. I'm sorry. You just make me so . . ."

"So what?"

I peered up at her, both palms coasting from her calves to the backs of her knees, bare beneath the skirt. Bending low, I kissed the turn of her ankle. "You make me crazy to have you."

"You're confusing me," she whispered.

"That's the last thing I want to do. I'm just"—I blew out defeated chuckle—"between a rock and a hard place."

Her soft hands touched my hair until I looked at her again. She was scared and she'd been scarred and it showed in her guarded eyes. "You've got me on uneven footing here."

"I don't want that either."

"What do you want?"

Skimming my palms along her legs, I said, "You."

"You can have me, tonight." Her tone dripped with seduction as she pressed back onto the bed, watching my every move.

"Just tonight?" I lifted her foot and kissed the instep, guiding my tongue to her delicate anklebone.

Her back bowed. I licked her leg to her knee, slowly caressing the trembling skin in my hand.

"I think that's best," Leelee gasped.

I'd show her what was best, with my cock in her pussy and her pleading for more, every damn day, all the fucking time. Stilling the beast that reared inside of me, I skimmed the high heels off her feet. I ran my tongue along each arch, listening to Leelee moan. She grabbed the bedspread and tried to spread her legs to me, but I held them closed.

"Not yet, babe."

Her eyes flew to mine, full of desire. Just the way I liked her. On. Fucking. Fire.

I jerked her forward, half off the bed, above my face. "Want me to eat you?"

She nodded.

Reaching higher, I grabbed the inside of her bodice. I ripped the dress from top to bottom, quickly doing away with her lacy bra and tiny panties. Leelee arched when my open palm slid up her mound, between her breasts, to her mouth where my fingers teased her lips open. Rising above her, I angled my lips to hers. The kiss I gave her was a seductive roll of tongues, the slow motion of mouths. Nothing like my caveman move to get her naked. She coiled around me as our lips lingered until I tracked back, getting to my feet with her wide open before me.

"You, sir, are a cur." She eyed the torn dress with a half a smile on her lips.

Damn right about that.

My gaze raked from her hips, to tits, to teasing smile. I snatched up one of my T-shirts, dangling it in front of her before I dropped it onto her belly. "You can sleep in that, or you can sleep with this."

My jeans rode low on my hips and I unbuttoned them. The wallet chain clanged. My cock punched through the opening the second I started to shuck the denim down my thighs. After sliding them off my feet, I towered over her.

Taking my cock in one hand, I squeezed my base and groaned. Inches of shaft pumped up, engorged, so ready to fuck into Leelee. "What's it gonna be, babe?"

I was going to screw every single runaway instinct out of her until she lived, breathed, and thought about me.

No shit. I was turning into a barbarian over Leelee.

Licking her lips, she threaded her hands through the long curls of her hair. The red lengths spread over her shoulders and across her breasts, teasing me with glimpses of ruby-red nipples. "Screw the T-shirt. I want you inside me, Josh."

A harsh laugh escaped my throat. I slapped my meat against my hand. "This?"

Her feet arched against the bed as she pressed her knees up and open. "Yes."

Kneeling over her, I thumped my cockhead against her clit. "More?"

She grabbed my shaft too, pumping me with slow strokes. "Not yet."

Her warm hand left me hungering for more when she let me go. Fingertips slid across my lips and I bit them, nuzzled them. She caressed my chest and stomach, tickling along all the muscles while I struggled to breathe.

Reclining against the pillows, she pointed a finger at me. "Stay."

"What?"

"Well, sug, you're such a big boy. I've gotta get myself ready for you."

Holy Christ. I watched Leelee, all that pale red hair shimmering around her creamy curves. Hot, naughty, and tempting, she dipped her fingers between her legs, spreading her lips to show me the glistening jewel inside. She circled outside and up, making all those frills and folds wet. I heard how drenched she was; strands of clear silk slipped between her fingertips.

With my gaze riveted to her, I left the bed, dug through my wallet for a condom, and turned the lights low. I snapped the rubber down my shaft and listened to the wet sounds, her soft low gasps as she fingered herself for me.

"Fuck. You are incredible, Leelee." My voice rumbled from deep within, my muscles flexed to pounce.

Heavy eyes drifted to mine while she circled her mouthwatering clit. "You think so? Just wait until you're inside me, Josh."

That was it. I lunged for her. Her plump cunt was in my mouth before she had a chance to gasp. She came hard as I filled my lips with her taste. I ran my pointed tongue up and down her glossy slit, drinking it all up. My stubble on her pussy, over her clit, between her legs, I ramped her right up again.

Yeah, Leelee was ready all right.

On my knees, I hauled her onto my thighs, spearing inside of her. Her back arched off the bed. I stayed deep, breath sawing out of me, and she fucked me with wanton rolls of her hips.

I pressed her back, into the mattress, kissing her. Soft and slow because she pulsed around me, nearly blinding me. "Babe," I groaned.

"So good, Josh . . ."

While I ground inside of her in slow deliberate circles, she clawed down my back. Sinking her nails into my ass, she silently begged for more. I rubbed my pubes against her swollen clit until she shivered. But I didn't want shivers or silent begging. I wanted Leelee screaming.

I sped up. The impact of my pelvis hitting her, my cock drilling into her, was overshadowed by her wails.

"I can go as hard as you want. You just have to ask me for it."

I slipped out of her pussy, groaning when my cock withdrew completely. My dick was covered with her, the wetness evident when I stroked myself above her, so close to her opening it was a torturous test not to drive inside.

Leelee writhed against me, whimpering. "No one's ever made me feel like this. No one's ever needed me so much before. Please, Josh, please. Fuck me."

"If any man touches you again, I'm gonna kill him." With her knees held against her tits by my arms, I plunged inside.

"Stone!" She bloomed into instant orgasm.

Her nipples in my mouth, my pelvis pile driving into hers, I heard nothing but her cries and the roaring of blood through my ears. She clamped onto me so hard, I fought to fuck her. Every long-lasting, deep internal throb inside Leelee rippled through my entire body.

Nostrils flaring, teeth grinding, I pulled free of her

vise. My shoulders shuddered and my breath stuttered. Ripping off the condom, I straddled her hips. Using two fists and two pumps later, I spilled all over her belly and breasts.

"Tryin' to prove a point?" Her husky voice worked its way inside of me, and I released one last jet.

My voice was nothing more than a hoarse whisper. "Not trying. Think I made it."

I rolled onto the bed and took her in my arms. Warm come slipped between our bodies, but neither of us cared. In fact, it felt real damn good. Pulling a blanket over us, I tangled my toes with hers and curled her hair around my fingers, bathing her neck with small kisses.

"What about you?" she asked.

I couldn't believe she was still breathing, let alone conscious and talking after the fuck of the century.

"*Hmm*?" Her long locks filtered through my fingertips. Her distracting display of full curves and creamy flesh took my libido on another loop-de-loop.

"What do I get to do if anyone touches you again?" Her elbows bit into my chest when she pressed above me.

"You can call me out and kick my ass."

"Even if it's Nicky?" Her timid question was an arrow to the heart.

I touched her with tenderness and waited until her lips sought mine. Our skin was fiery hot and we were too close, too electric to do anything but touch and taste. With her soft and open and me hard and ready, words took a backseat to base need. Another condom was rolled on before I pulled her leg over my hips to join our bodies.

Her ass filled my hands as she sank onto my cock from above. Her gasp—"Oh, God, Josh!"—was music to my ears, but it wasn't enough.

Her arms curled around me, pulling me closer. "How are you doing this to me?"

"It's all you." Lying below Leelee, I spread my thighs wider and opened her up more. I braced my feet on the bed and held her hips still with my hands. Pumping my hips, I hit every sensitive place inside of her. My lips ran down to her nipples, drawing them into my mouth.

The slow luxurious drag of my cock in and out had us gasping against each other's mouths. Her breath sweet, her cunt a tight heat pulling me in, Leelee cried out every time I withdrew. I pushed, and she arched for me. This slow motion lovemaking melded us together. Blazing need poured between us.

I didn't want to come. I wanted to stay inside her forever.

Fifteen minutes later, maybe more, we were slippery to the touch, still going at it with the never-ending pace.

"Jesus." Leelee's nails sheared against my straining shoulders.

I gathered her in my arms until we stretched against each other from toes to joining to lips. I sucked the pulse on her neck so hard a love bite immediately rose. Her cunt rippled around me. She bucked against me but I held her back so she'd come slowly, over and over again.

"Just like this." I curled my hips and thrust into her.

Leelee flew apart in my arms. Her pussy feathered over me and I shouted, "Yes!"

The long and smooth became heavy, heated, gasping, needy. Rolling her to her back, I pulled her up onto my shaft and planted her feet on the bed. She was gonna take my cock and milk it good. Her hands slithered down my belly, between my thighs, to my balls.

"That's right, Josh. Fuck me hard." Her mouth turned to my ear and she bit down. Hard.

My toes curled. The wet smack of our flesh almost made me come. I withdrew from Leelee, so slowly she moaned. My cock was covered in us. Veins rippled beneath my hand as I fisted my shaft. Leelee looked so good, so open.

Raising my ass up to pound into her, I poised at her entrance. I fell on her with a growl, driving the hard spike of my shaft inside. She climaxed the instant I cupped her ass and pulled her up tight. Grabbing her hair, hauling her head back, I used the handhold of her waist to piston inside of her. Every thrust shuddered through us.

My chin scraped up her neck to her ear and I groaned, "This belongs to me."

"Yes!" She fastened me in wet, velvet heat, hurrying my orgasm.

I shattered apart. The condom filled with come I wanted to overflow her depths and run back down our thighs.

One more night. Fuck that. An entire life was what I wanted with Leelee. Covering us up, I ran my hands all over her. Our kisses were the sweet, satisfied kind. Afterward, she nuzzled my chest, slowly slipping into sleep.

I turned off the bedside light and held her. I kissed her temple and she snored lightly. A laugh rumbled in my belly. Her cute nose burrowed closer to my chest. Her legs twined between mine. I couldn't stop feeling her skin, touching her, finally settling my palms on her ass.

An hour or so later, I was still awake, taking Leelee in with all my senses. I glimpsed my phone sitting beside the bed. The screen was blank. No missed messages, no missed calls. God, I missed the kid. He was the joy of my life. I wondered what he'd make of Leelee; he'd probably consider her his own personal Disney princess come to life. I snagged the cell and clicked to a photo I'd taken the week before heading here. Big goofy smile, dimple in his chin, huge hazel eyes, JJ was the spitting image of me before I'd given up on love. The phone glowed while I caressed the screen across his face.

"I miss you, baby boy," I whispered before I set the phone down. I squeezed Leelee tighter, trying to decipher what she thought of me, if she'd love my son as much as I did, getting way the hell ahead of myself. "But I'm gay," I muttered.

Quiet, sad, defeated, she answered, "I know."

I'd probably squished her awake. I clenched her even closer, hating the tears that tripped from her eyelashes.

"I can't be with you like this." Her silent sobs almost broke me down. "We have to stop doing this."

I whispered, "Why do I already miss you?"

"Don't. Don't miss me, Josh."

"Then don't leave me, Leelee." Leelee for lust, Leelee for love, Leelee for so long-gone. Soft and warm and pretty. Wholesome and innocent minx.

She snuggled deeper and I didn't want to lose this thing I'd never had. I wrapped her tighter in my arms. *Fuck me. I've become a cuddler.* "You feel good."

"*Mmm.*" She murmured, her thigh sliding between mine. "You feel hard, Stone."

"It's Josh."

"I know. I just like you hard."

Killing me.

"Gonna stay 'til morning?" I asked.

"No choice."

With my fingertips beneath her chin, I made her look at me. "That's not the answer I'm lookin' for."

Wariness and want clashed within her eyes. "For now. For you."

Smoothing her hair away from her face until it coiled along my chest, I lingered over her lips, kissing her softly. After she slipped back into sleep, I released a ragged breath. I imprinted the feel of her on my body before finally drifting off.

In the morning, I woke up, alone. I scanned the room, but she was gone along with a pair of my shorts, the T-shirt I'd offered her last night, her heels and bag. The dress I'd destroyed lay in a heap on the floor, just like my heart.

Ravage the fair maiden much, asshole?

I crossed both arms over my face. Emptiness surrounded me. The last time I'd felt this heavy weight was when my dad died. I didn't even consider looking for

185

a note from Leelee. She wouldn't leave one. It wasn't her style, and besides, she'd pretty much said it all last night when she told me we had to stop doing this.

I pulled her pillow on top of my face, smothering myself in her scent. I lay like that until I threw the pillow aside and stood up.

"Screw this." I wasn't some fancy-pants pushover.

This time I knew just where to find Leelee— someplace she couldn't hide, someplace she couldn't run from me.

The book fair.

Chapter Thirteen
Saturday: Book Fair Fiasco

I DIDN'T KNOW WHAT I was going to do when I got to Leelee, but I had the fastest shower on record. I was even speedier than the kid when he thought I wasn't paying attention at bath time and tried to get away with a splash and dash. I tried telling him Daddy has eyes in the back of his head, but that just wigged him out.

Dressed, deodorized, and aftershaved for the non-shave, I hustled into jeans and whatever shirt came to hand. The green Henley. It highlighted my hazel eyes and rugged good looks, at least that's what Ma had said when she'd given it to me. Fuck it, it passed the sniff test, it'd do. Striding to the grand hall, I thought about making a big Lifetime *Movie of the Week* scene. Chicks liked that weepy, get-your-Kleenex-out shit. Or maybe a John Cusack *Say Anything* grand gesture . . . minus the boom box and serenading, although Leelee did have a thing for my singing.

Maybe I'd haul her into my arms, drag her back to my room, and tie her to the bed until she listened to common

187

sense, then fuck her silly again.

That sounded like a plan.

The line was backed up beyond the room leading into the book fair, and it had already been going for an hour and a half. These romance readers were hardcore junkies. Growing increasingly impatient, I finally made it into the room *before* the room I needed to reach. Inside, dozens of random companies hawked their wares from body art to glass bongs, to cover model agencies. When I came up beside Big Blond from the Guys with Balls competition displaying *his* wares, we bumped fists. He introduced me to the Bad Boys for Books rep, talking me up like I was the next big thing since Fabio. I shook hands and gritted my teeth in a smile.

I accepted a business card with a, "Sure, yeah. I'll call you if I'm ever interested"—*not likely*. I made my way forward slower than the kid getting ready for Sunday School when I took him to church once a month.

Nametag checked, I finally entered the promised land of pervy books . . . and a squealing mass of arms, legs, and—what the fuck—feathers bounded up to me.

Jules Gem. She didn't have a megaphone, but she was still attached to her mic. She gestured for her camera guy to get a close up. "Stone! We've been waiting for you to show. You're *such* a dark horse celeb at LitLuv."

"Uh . . ." I frowned down at her, trying to come to grips with her outfit du jour. It consisted of some white feathery sweater thing that made my nose itch. "Hi, Miss Gem?"

"Oh, look at you!" She slapped my arm, not so playfully. "You remembered not to call me ma'am, aren't *you* a darling. Can you say that to the camera for me?"

"Huh?"

"Darling. Go on now, put some of that sexy southern feeling into it." She simpered into the lens with a huge conspiratorial wink.

Remembering the trouble I'd gotten into during the

flash mob, I asked, "This thing live?"

"Of course, Stone. Nothing scripted here. As we always say at the beginning of our broadcasts: You *LitLuv* it, we *live* it!"

I grinned at the sheer audacity of the woman. *Nothing scripted my ass.* "Sure, darlin', whatever you say."

Flapping her hands around in some sort of funky swoon-dance, she cut back to me. "Are there any authors you want to meet today, Stone? Who's your *favorite*?" She shivered in a display of delight.

"Nicky Love's my man. But I've also been taken with Leelee Songchild." In more ways than one, and hopefully in more ways to come.

"Isn't she just *gorgeous*." Jules's eyes widened dramatically.

Hell yes, she was.

"And can our Leelee ever write!" She turned to the camera, aiming a massive smile at it. "New Adult author has Stone under her spell. New Adult, everyone! It's the *new* black."

Giving a practiced view of her profile, Jules slanted her eyes at me. "And we'll have a *huge* feature on Stone coming in the August issue of *LitLuv* magazine. Because he's big, he's brawny, he *is* all that. I'll be in touch with Stone after the convention, folks, because I live right down the road from him on Isle of Palms." She pointed at me for the viewers. "All of him, for all of you. Isn't it purrrfect?"

What the hell? She was about ten minutes down the road from my garage. Life was never gonna be the same. "You're just a stone's throw away from me, huh?"

She smiled at the camera then motioned for the dude to stop rolling. "That's right. Great tagline, Stone, I think we'll use it. And the feature I'm doing on you? Full photo spread, mm 'kay?"

"I'm not sure how comfortable I am with that, Miss Gem."

She swung toward me, pure feminine menace. "You

189

don't have to be comfortable, just hot. And you can do that with both hands tied behind your back." Her eyes clouded. "Oh! Now there's an idea . . ."

Oh hell no, there is not!

Before I could stage a protest, Jules sauntered off, back in full Queen of the Con mode. I could just imagine her at the shop, digging up all my old dirt and getting cozy with Ray over a goddamn latte or some such Starbucks shit.

I'd worry about that later, after I made my peace with Leelee.

I scanned the cavernous overcrowded, overheated room, looking for any kind of landmark. Spotting big banners swinging above tables arranged in long lines, I read the genres boldly splashed across them in flames of red until I located New Adult. There was only about half an acre of concrete floor, sweating book hungry mobs, and possibly another Jules ambush between me and the most populated area taking up the far right corner.

I smiled when I saw Leelee had her own special promotional banner above a table heaving with fans. *That's my girl.*

I started in her direction. Unfortunately, I saw Nicky off to the side in the Paranormal lane, flagging me down. His suspenders dripped from his waist, the collar of his shirt was undone three buttons, and some broad had her hands all over his chest.

Obviously caught in the middle of a heated moment he wasn't all too happy about, he gave the man-to-man distress signal of wide-eyed horror.

"Goddammit." After last night I owed him a save.

Making my way over with lots of shouldering, elbowing and "'Scuse me, ma'am, pardon me, miss,'" I planted my hip on the table. I enjoyed several moments of Nicky's unease while his fangirl fawned all over him.

I cleared my throat. Arching an eyebrow, I went for the highhanded, he's-mine look.

Chicky looked up, blinked big brown eyes, and pressed her lips together.

I leaned over her to Nicky, "Is there a problem here, lover?"

Chicky backed up. She scowled between the two of us with *impressive* fury. I moved between her and Nicky, and she craned around me, sputtering, "But—but, you said it wasn't true!"

Ha. "Yeah." I caressed up my man's arm and into his hair, jerking him to me over the table. He murmured death threats under his breath. It was funny. My thumb rode up and down the pulse of his neck, making sure Chicky saw he was mine and I owned him. "There seems to be a lot of that goin' around."

Guess I knew where he'd spent the night . . . because we were both so good about the hush-hush, down-low shit. *Shee-it.*

Chicky's glare turned lethal, but hers was no comparison to Jules Gem's weapon of mass intimidation. I did feel bad when she marched around me to lay a resounding smack on Nicky's cheek. Fucker deserved it though, as much as I had when Leelee slapped me at The Golden Banana.

She stomped away and I turned Nicky loose.

"So, you're hitting that?" She wasn't his type—too easy—but I'd be willing to bet he'd docked, cocked, and loaded the Good Ship Hot-to-Trot.

"It was either that or bunk with Missy." He carefully rearranged his books, his swag, his PDA running a mini-slideshow of his book covers.

"Thanks for your sacrifice last night."

"Thanks for the bro-move just now."

We exchanged back slaps. "Think nothin' of it. At least you got laid, man."

He was already smiling and inviting a group of women to approach him. "You too, huh?"

"I don't fuck and tell." Rubbing my mouth, I looked

191

out over the crush of people, regaining my compass point on Leelee. My heart knocked around like a loose piston in my chest.

"Since when?"

"Since Leelee. That's when." I patted my palm to my tat, and he knew exactly what that meant. It was right over my heart and held the other two things I loved—cars and the kid.

"Shee-it."

"Yeah." I met his eyes, nodding, just as surprised as him.

Nicky pulled me to him with a long, hard hug. "Jesus, Josh."

"Yeah." I grinned as I backed away.

I threaded my way through a cluster of teen girls and their mamas converged around a YA author, all glittery nails, sparkly faces, and too much floral perfume. I ended up face-to-face with a well-endowed woman who grabbed both my arms.

"Stone! I saw you in Guys with Balls. I've gotta get your autograph."

"Mom! You are not getting your boobs signed again this year." Her teenaged daughter sounded mortified.

I'd have been a little shocked myself if the same thing hadn't already happened with another busty broad, right after said show.

"Oh yes, I am. It's tradition. Besides, this is The Stone." She shoved a Sharpie in my hand. Yanking a side of her shirt lower, she bared a good acre of tit. "Use as much space as you need. Make it out to Marianne with an *i*, okay?"

We were drawing a crowd so I kept it short and simple: *To a beautiful lady, Marianne. All the best, Stone.*

I accepted her hug then hurried off before any other body parts became available for autographs. I'd made it all of ten feet when I heard the tail end of Jules's high-pitched screech. I thought about her promise, aka threat, to track

192

me down in Mt. Pleasant. At the rate my day was going, maybe I oughtta head her off at the pass. Pulling out my phone, I called the garage.

"Stone's, just a stone's throw away," Ray answered.

I tore the phone away from my ear and glared at it. Then I snarled into it, "Excuse me?" Oh hell no. And how the fuck had they heard that bullshit already?

"Just saw you on the convention broadcast online. We thought it sounded catchy."

"Yeah? I *catch* you using it one more time and I'll make sure all of y'all never collect another phone number from the female clientele again." I gripped the phone harder. "It's Stone's, at your service."

"Isn't it just." A feminine voice simpered beside me.

Christ. Missy Peachtree, not at your service.

I muffled the phone. "Shouldn't you be signing—I don't know—whips or something?" *Hell, I was signin' tits, why not?*

She smacked my ass with a wide-open palm. "Great idea. But paddles have much more room to personalize." As usual she gave as good as she got before melting into the crowd from which she'd materialized.

The phone pressed back to my ear, I listened to Ray ramble on. "We hooked up the laptop to the big TV in the reception area so everyone can watch the goings-on over in 'Lanta."

I didn't know you could do that. I wished they didn't know either. Now all my escapades would be the talk of Mt. Pleasant.

"And just before you called I got off the phone with that Jules Gem. She wanted to check your schedule for next month. I figured we could use the publicity, so I offered her a free oil change."

Too bad she thought I was a foreign car dealer. Thank God most of this shit wouldn't hit the fan until after the Con. "Good idea about the oil change. Maybe we can keep her sweet."

"If anyone can, it's you." I heard Ray ringing up a sale and shouting a loud *hello* as the bell over the door chimed.

Damn, I missed that place. "Is the garage still standing?"

"Yup."

"Everyone still working his ass off for me?"

"'Course, boss. So long as you don't come back and try to fuck our asses." He snorted loud and clear.

"Keep it up, funny guy, and I got a tire iron with your name on it." When I looked back over to Leelee's corner of the room, I still couldn't get a visual on her. "I'll see you Monday. Make sure someone brings a box of condoms and a big bottle of lube. Limber up, motherfucker."

I hung up on him wheezing with laughter. *Yeah. Let's see what they make of that.*

"Yo, Stone!" Fawn flagged me down from the opposite direction of Leelee's table.

Dressed in a chambray shirt, cowboy boots, and a tangle of turquoise jewelry, she reached me with a smile on her tanned face. "Come meet my girlfriend. I told her all about you and Nicky."

I liked Fawn, I really did, but people needed to get out of my way. "Can I take a rain check? Maybe meet her at the banquet tonight? I'm trying to get a book signed for my ma before this thing finishes." I lied through my teeth.

She prodded me on my way.

Ducking and diving around the masses between Leelee and me, I slammed my hands over my ears when I heard a shriek attached to my name.

Petite Felicity was flushed to her hairline. Her catwoman glasses slid down her nose as she bounced up and down in excitement. "You've got to see this! I just had my picture taken with Leelee Songchild and I posted it on Twitter." Hugging my arm, she scrolled through her photos. "She's such a sweetie. I'm totally following her *on everything.*"

194

I was tempted to stay long enough to drink in the picture because, by God, this might be the closest I got to Leelee all day judging by my luck so far. But I had a fucking grand gesture to make.

"That's cool, Felicity, but I'm trying to say hi to her myself before the fair closes."

She slid her glasses back up and gave me a toothy grin. "Good luck with that. Her readers are like *über* crazy. You've got half an hour left."

Hunching my shoulders, I maneuvered in the right direction, silently cursing every single motherfucker in the hall. Swinging my head to the left, I saw Fred leaning against a table in the Contemporary lane. He sent me two thumbs up, and I saluted him with a one finger wave. He must've been sweating his balls off in that tweed jacket.

I put my head down and motivated until I ran straight into a wall of muscle even bigger than me. Steadied by a pair of dark hands on my arms, I rolled my eyes.

The last of the Widows, Devon, leaned over me. "Looks like you've got yourself some more admirers."

I followed his stare and thought about diving behind the slightly larger man. I was being targeted by the LolliPOP Grrrls. Devon loped away with a laugh, leaving me to face the blatant eye-fucking of the book review bloggers. Or, bloggesses, as I'd been informed.

"Hey, Stone," Blow Pop sucker simpered.

I wondered how I was gonna get away from them as they cornered me like I was schoolboy prey to their two-fold sexual attack. "Hi, ladies."

Hoodie grrrl plinked a tongue ring against her teeth. "Do you have plans for tonight?"

"We saw your dance with Leelee Songchild. You may be a butch gay, but it looks like you're bi, and we'd like a taste of that." The blonde tease twirled her tongue around the tip of the glistening red lollipop.

In the old days, pre-Leelee—precisely four days ago—I might've taken them up on their offer. However, no one got my motor revving like Leelee, and I surely wasn't into easy pussy anymore.

"Sorry, ladies. I'm not available."

I left them whispering behind me when an announcement rang out of the loudspeakers stating the book fair would close in fifteen minutes. Jesus Christ. I'd been here a full hour and a half, cockblocked north, south, east, and west by all the usual suspects. I'd yet to get to Leelee, let alone make my huge fucking gesture that would have her turning into a pile of mush in my arms.

I skidded to a stop with Leelee's table finally in sight. The pack gathered around her had slimmed down, but the person I saw shining from all the attention didn't resemble Leelee. In fact, I didn't recognize her at all until the big apple green of her eyes lifted to the person whose book she was signing.

Dear God. Another wig. I loved her as she was, but when she pulled out the wigs it made me think about role-playing. Naughty Nurse. Sexy Secretary in my office at Stone's. She took me from zero to sixty in an instant.

This wig was another black affair cascading down her back and across her shoulders. Her blouse was sapphire blue, laced together and low cut, giving a prime view of cleavage to anyone who stood over her. Like all of her fans, for instance. I needed to get over there pronto. I wanted to rip her blouse open and tear the wig off. I wanted to stare into her eyes as she climaxed while riding my fingers.

Grand gesture as fucking her on her author table during the book fair? Probably not a smart move.

Achingly hard, my lips almost chapped from all our kisses last night, I started toward her. I was a yard away when something tall, dark and sinister slithered up to her behind the table.

Andrew LaForge. I couldn't believe he had the *cojones* to corner her at the book fair. No one messed with my woman, not after she'd walked through fire all morning doing the meet and greet with a beautiful smile on her face. I stalked forward. When I saw Leelee swivel around and stand up, her expression undaunted, I stopped.

Holy shit, my girl was gonna give him what-for.

Close enough to read her lips, what came out of her mouth made my blood race. *"Get the fuck away from me, you creep."*

Sliding nearer so I could hear, I made myself stay put a little distance away. Leelee needed to do this. Leelee could do this.

She stomped forward and LaForge backed up, hands raised. "I've had enough of your dirty remarks, and this latest attempt at bribery? You're worse than slime. You have a reputation for being a prowler of new talent. Don't think for one second all the women you've oh-so-innocently fondled during group pictures while giving promises of sweet deals between the sheets and on paper haven't spread the word. Just because I'm new doesn't make me naive." One stabbing finger went to his chest and pointed there. "You might have your cloak of decency, your offers of contracts, your people who play off our complaints and try to make us look like 'oh-those-silly-women-writers are at it again', but we're strong. We're successful. We are not gonna put up with dickheads like you anymore."

Surprise melted into shock on LaFuck's face. He bowed from the waist, taking his leave to jeers and claps scattered around from those who'd witnessed his beatdown at Leelee's hands.

Once he disappeared, her shoulders fell. The smile she gave her remaining fans was shaky. I wanted to kiss her softly. Hold her close. Tell her, *atta girl.*

The final bell ringing, the book fair over, I started my approach.

Leelee looked up. Her gaze hooked mine and didn't let go. Everything I felt was reflected back at me: hope, want, need. Then her pain and distrust. She dropped her gaze,

197

shaking her head. Because of all she'd been through, me to blame for at least part of it, I remained where I was, several feet away.

She packed her books and materials, exchanged goodbyes with her tablemates. I wanted to be right beside her, doing the heavy work, easing her hurt. I wanted to be able to tell her I'd take care of everything. Run her a bath, massage her back, and hold her while she slept off the exhaustion of being on show.

I didn't say a word when she swept past me, but I damn sure tagged her heels. The midnight black wig bobbed up and down, her rolling suitcase pulled behind her. At one point the crush of people swallowed her up. I was tempted to pull a Rocky Balboa *Adrian* move, but she was spit out again, just a few yards away.

Shadowing her all the way the elevators, I knew she was aware of me. The protective starch melted from her shoulders. Before she stepped into the elevator, her eyes dragged back to mine and they were teary.

I planted a hand on the door, keeping it open. I reached inside to her, cupping her face. "You did so good, babe."

A single tear dripped over my fingers.

"Not now, Josh. Please. You are everything I want and nothing I can have." She stepped back with a gasp.

I withdrew my hand. The door closed. With my forehead thunking against the wall, I swallowed hard. What the hell had I been thinking anyway? What could I have done during the book fair, besides screw up an important event for her? My grand gesture was an asinine idea and I was an ass, straight up.

And it wasn't that I wanted her to need me to look out for her. But goddammit, I wanted her to need me, full stop.

Chapter Fourteen
Saturday: Sex Shop and Write-Offs

LIFTING MY HEAD FROM my head-butt move against the wall, I glanced at my watch. It was only one o'clock in the afternoon, too early to drown my sorrows in bourbon or dunk my head in a barrel of beer. In my room, I stripped off, hauled on my shorts, and yanked on a pair of sneakers. I grabbed a towel, a bottle of water, and pounded to the basement-level workout room.

Work it out, that's what I needed to do. Work Leelee out of my system . . . what a joke. One delusional part of me hoped I'd find her stretching out on the blue mats in the gym. No such luck and just as well.

Pouring with sweat through the punishing CrossFit reps, I cursed myself to infinity . . . and beyond. Dumbass. Asshole. Fuckhead. Jerk off. That was me. I finished with two sets of fifty crunches, squats, and pull-ups each. Only when my mind shut down and my lungs inflated for O2 intake did I stop. I downed my water, crushed the plastic, and tossed it into the recycling bin. I wiped off in front of the mirror. The muscles on my chest flexed, giving life to

199

the chrome pipes, the stylized heart, and my little anchor in life: JJ.

A harsh laugh cut out of my throat. I'd already pictured a beautiful scroll of *Leelee* wrapping around the tattoo, maybe even going flowery and shit with small, colorful songbirds and vines until the tat spread into a sleeve over my biceps.

Dumb shit, asshat, fuckwit—maybe I'd have those inked instead.

Upstairs, I shoved everything off, including the boohoos, and slipped under the hot shower spray. My muscles loosened. My cock did not. We were at a standoff. Every-fucking-time I gave in to the urge to whack it, somebody interrupted, so I wasn't even going to tempt fate. I gingerly toweled dry, avoiding my dick. It could misfire with a mere touch, and I already had enough messes to deal with. My last clean pair of jeans pulled on, I left the fly undone for breathing room. I ordered room service on Nicky's tab, slipped a Benjamin into his shaving kit for damages done, and studiously avoided all social networking outlets.

As soon as my cock subsided, I buttoned up. Breathing a gargantuan sigh of relief, I dialed Ma.

"Joshy!"

"Hey, Ma. The kid around?" Christ, I wanted to hear his little pipsqueak voice.

She returned with a whisper, "He's snug as a bug beside Viper. It's naptime."

I looked at the clock, two-thirty on the dot. All routine, one I was used to. I swallowed past the large lump in my throat. "Okay, that's good." He didn't even need me to sing him to sleep anymore.

"He's adjusting." The sliders whooshed as Ma stepped out onto the deck.

"Well, damn, Ma." Not that I wanted the kid tied in knots about me being gone, but it would've been nice to know someone missed me.

"Oh shoot, don't be all glum like that. What's crawled up your behind and made a nest there?" A clink of ice against glass came from over the phone—Ma was enjoying her afternoon refresher of bourbon and water.

"It's this girl."

"Speakin' of girls, I just couldn't wait. Now, you got me that signed book from Leelee Songchild, right?"

Yeah, she'd autographed it all right, and I'd scrawled my name in come all over her body several times since then.

Nicky walked in mid-conversation. He dumped his stuff on the floor, mouthing, "Gigi?"

I nodded.

Shoving off his boots, toeing off his socks, he padded over on bare feet. "Viper and JJ okay?"

I gave the A-okay sign. The kid was probably snuggled side-by-side with the badass bitch in her dog bed.

Ma said, "I downloaded it to my Nookie thingy, and mah Lord, that girl can write! Her book's hotter than my kitchen on a ninety-degree day."

"It's called a Nook. And you can follow Leelee on Facebook, Twitter . . . everywhere." I planned to do exactly that once I got home if she still wasn't speaking to me.

As I rummaged through my bag, searching for the paperback I'd gotten for Ma, I thought about the clothing explosion from Leelee's suitcases. I imagined her napping the morning off, cuddled between all those dresses and wigs and books. The idea of her sleeping amid her mountain of stuff made me smile. The Princess and The Pea. Goddamn, she'd wreck my house, turn it inside out just as she'd flipped my heart upside-down.

"I already Googled her, so don't treat me like I don't know anything about The Machine, sonny."

"Sorry, ma'am. And yes, I got your book right here." I unearthed her copy of *Ride* from my duffel.

Ma added more ice to her glass with a chink-chink.

"Why, she's just as pretty as a picture, could've been a starlet back in the day."

Turning the book over in my hands, I studied Leelee's headshot. "Yeah, she's gorgeous."

"Oh my. Are you blue over this Leelee?" I heard her hissing away from the receiver, "Shoo now. I said scat! I don't have nothin' for you vermin."

"Did that family of coons come back?" I held the phone out, speaker on, and Nicky heard her telling off the latest round of scavengers that came from the woods surrounding her house. We both kept our laughter quiet.

"This time it's that damn garden snake, Mr. Bojangles. Now I don't care if he comes around and eats the moles and mice, but I will not have him in my rafters." Mr. Bojangles had once been found hanging from the support beams in the garage area beneath the house. She'd named him Mr. Bojangles because she liked to tell folks she had a real live boa constrictor on the property. "I just threw my glass at him from the balcony, almost hit him too. And you didn't answer my question."

"Nah, I'm not blue." I was worse than blue. I was goddamn inconsolable.

"That's right, because Stone men don't piss and moan about what could be. They make it happen." She smooched into the phone and sent extras for Nicky, because, "I heard him chuckling in the background. Y'all can't fool me."

She was right. Stone men didn't sit around and mope. We took action and asked questions later.

* * * *

Unfortunately, the big Alpha Male Saves the Day moment had to wait once again. Figured. Half an hour later, I stood outside the hotel with the Hens, waiting while they boarded the bus.

"Field trip!" Janice clapped. Today she was back in her Steampunk gear, and I still hadn't managed to figure out what the genre entailed except maybe *Gunsmoke* meets *Doctor Who*.

Jacqueline winked. "Road trip."

Head trip, more like.

Pushing right up to me, Missy the Mistress licked her lips. "Research."

"Yeah, yeah. You keep trying to scare me, lady, and I'll be forced to show you who wields the bigger stick."

"I sure hope so." Her gaze flicked to my groin.

I adjusted, just because, and she threw her head back with a raucous laugh. "Touché."

Damn right.

I waited another few minutes, watching the carousel doors of the Ramada for a glimpse of high heels and red hair.

Nicky reappeared at the top of the bus steps. "She just texted Janice, she's not gonna make it, baby."

Climbing on board, I ducked down the aisle. I settled in next to Nicky and let him pull me into the lee of his shoulder. Swear to fuck, if we ended up back at The Golden Banana strip joint, I was going to lose my mind. This sitting around, stuck-on-repeat socializing wasn't my style. I missed getting my hands dirty. I missed the kid. I missed the garage. I fucking missed Leelee and she was only staying a couple floors above me—that just wasn't right.

Gossip about what went down during the book fair between Leelee and LaForge started up. I dropped my head down and shut my eyes. I'd had a ringside seat, but I wasn't going to join in and fuel the fire. Trying not to pay attention to their secondhand stories, I remembered Leelee's fierce expression when she'd told LaForge where he could pack his fudge. She'd been so damn glorious.

But afterward . . . the night spent with me, her shout-out with LaForge, her morning being in the limelight had taken their toll. It occurred to me her wigs weren't sexy disguises at all. They were her shield, a way to protect herself in public, to project the persona she had to. A barrier between everyone who wanted a piece of her and the real person she was inside.

I made a disgusted noise. I was beyond *numero uno* asshole ranking now. Shrugging off Nicky's arm, I turned around to Janice. She was hacking away on her phone, muttering about skanky agents and *hashtag predators*.

"Why isn't Leelee here?"

"Packing." Everyone chimed in without lifting their heads from their technological lifelines.

"She's leaving tonight?" My voice raised several octaves higher.

All eyes lifted to me.

I schooled my face into an unconcerned mask.

Jacqueline piped up. "Have you *seen* her room?"

Yes. "No."

"That girl blew . . . it . . . up! If she didn't start packing today, she'd have to hire a moving crew to get it done in the morning."

"Amen to that." Janice high-fived Jackée.

The shuttle stopped in front of a nondescript strip mall. Everyone hopped off. The store looked innocent enough on the outside, but one step through the door and I was thrown into a deep, dark cavern of forbidden delights.

A sex shop.

Of course.

Nicky wrapped an arm around my waist. "Are you gonna be okay?"

Like I was a virgin or something. I knew my way around cock rings, thank you very much. "Yeah, lover. I reckon I'll find something here we can make use of in the bedroom. Or in my office. Probably with you bent over my desk."

Janice dashed out a quick *#overheard #LitLuv* tweet.

The gaggle got over their swooning moment and scattered in different directions. Left to my own devices, I detailed the interior of The Gee Spot from corner to corner and back to front.

Double-pronged and plain dongs in every color from flesh to fluorescent.

Vinyl chaps: I made a note for Fawn.

Handcuffs, collars, the aforementioned cock rings.

Dog leashes, and pony tails . . .

There was a wall of butt plugs and ball gags—because I'd have to be gagged to get a plug up my ass.

A case of vibrators ranged from rabbits to butterflies, we-vibes, and sleek, silver bullets, as well as the notorious *it's really a back massager* heavy-duty variety that took 9-volt batteries.

Lube sold by econo-two-for-one bottles, by the gotta-hide-it mini bottle, or the single-use sachet: edible, flavorful, for him, for her, for *us* . . .

Porn flicks arranged by: mainstream, XXX, Extra XXX, ménage, boy-boy, girl-girl, and spoofs.

In short, nothing suitable to take home to the kid as a souvenir.

Nicky roamed up to me, his hand falling to my ass to goose me.

Mindful we were in public and surrounded by the social savvy Hens who could tweet, Facebook, or Instagram in an instant, I pushed him into a corner. "One more day, dude."

"Then you go after the girl?" The handsome motherfucker slanted a smile at me. Jesus, for a second I could even see what Stone might see in him. Too bad I knew everything about him, from how he liked his coffee, his favorite frigging USC sweats to write in, and which side he dressed to *and* slept on.

"It might be too late."

"Don't be so fatalistic." His chin jerked up. "You know what Gigi would say about that."

"Bullshit." We grinned at each other.

Mistress Peachtree sidled up beside us. "Lover's tiff?"

"As if." Beckoning out to the hazy, red-lit depths, I

dared, "Why don't you show me your piece of this playground."

I didn't know a Domme from a Doberman Pinscher. Both were brutal in my mind. But when Missy stepped ahead of me, she slipped into a different persona just as surely as Leelee donned her wigs to protect herself.

Kinks, fetishes, costumes lined the walls as Missy led me to the BDSM section.

Taking down a crop, she slid it across her palm. I smiled and grabbed a bigger one.

"It's not always about size, Stone." She plied her instrument in an arc that whistled beside me.

I performed a Zorro move in front of her. "Oh yeah? Tell that to my last conquest."

The slap-slap-slap of the crop on her palm rode the fine line of my nerves. I danced back as she sauntered forward. "It's about the exchange of trust. The power lies in the one who gives it up. The person who submits has all the control in a D/s relationship." Plying the slim weapon, she slashed the air between us.

On her next pass, I grabbed the crop and cracked it in two. "I don't submit to anyone."

"You've never let yourself lose control."

My teeth snapped together. I bent forward until we were nose to nose. "Yes, I have." I'd given up my control with Leelee, no one else. I looked at the broken pieces of the crop in my hand. "I'll pay for this."

"Yes. You will." Her look was intense. "Don't miss your chance, Stone."

Shit. She knew about me and Nicky, me and my feelings for Leelee. She had to, to keep making comments like that. I stalked away from the whips, chains, and nipple-clamps. Just in case, I picked up a box of Magnums—ignoring the hot pink size-and-style chart above the shelves, because really? I squinted at a sleeve of pillow-packet lube and decided to purchase that too, to keep up appearances.

At the register, I found Felicity haggling with the cashier as if this was a frigging flea market.

"Write-offs. These are write-offs, right?" She waved a handful of—*whoa*—crotchless panties in front of my face.

I batted them away. "Anything having to do with the conference—write-off. Booze, food, your registration as the assistant of an attendee. Call this research for your husband's stories and you're golden."

"Oh-em-gee! Thank you, Stone." Felicity whipped out her plastic and collected her bag. "I can't wait for tonight."

* * * *

Later in the hotel room, Nicky was in the bathroom. Steam poured from beneath the door, and it was a strong possibility he'd fallen asleep standing up in the shower. I left him to it. Condoms, lube, and crap I might never use waited in a bag by my duffel to be packed up and lugged back to Mt. Pleasant in the morning.

I kicked my feet up on the desk, opening Leelee's dog-eared book. If I couldn't get back in Leelee's bed, I was going to get inside her head.

> *After their first night when Jase showed super-human restraint, he went to bed in briefs, Ave in panties and one of his T-shirts that hung huge on her. He kept everything top shelf—and, man, she had a rack on her—above cloth, except when his tickles on her belly pulled his wandering fingers closer to the generous bottom curves of her tits.*
>
> *They lived together, loved together, and for the first time, Jase took a girl, his girl, on dates.*

That must've been where I got it all wrong with Leelee. Snatching a dance, a kiss, a fuck whenever no one was looking was no way to treat a lady. I'd probably made her feel cheap and tawdry instead of cherished and treasured.

The night Jase hoped to make love to Avery, he took her to a nice restaurant. It was nothing flashy or expensive, but the food was great, the place cozy. He was murmuring into her ear, describing what he wanted to do to her later when her eyes dropped the hooded look of pleasure. Her troubled blue gaze flashed across the restaurant.

Jase inched away and turned his head to look at the tableful he recognized from campus. They all thought they were hot shit. They whispered and giggled, pointing at the couple. Jase thought they were talking about him until he heard Ave's choppy sigh.

"What's that all about?" He jerked his head in the direction of the other table.

Ave pulled her sweater back on. With her armor back in place, she cowered. Hands tucked inside the hems, fingers curling over, she cast her eyes down. "Nothing."

The fact that she could withdraw from him so completely pissed him off. "Bullshit it's nothin'."

"I'm not a virgin, okay?" She hissed, head still down.

Shit. He wouldn't have expected any twenty-one-year-old to be a virgin, but given how chaste Ave had been when he'd first started rooming with her, he'd let himself hope so.

Swallowing his instinctual reaction, he said, "Oh-kay?" He tried to find her hand within the folds of her sweater but she flinched away. "And what's that got to do with them?"

Her hands appeared on the table from the

loose cuffs but only to compulsively fold and unfold the cloth napkin. "He told them, he told everyone, *it was consensual.*"

Jase sat erect in his seat, fists forming, his heart thundering. "Who exactly is he?"

Her voice was almost too quiet to be heard. "Their ringleader, Duncan Locke."

Jase knew Duncan. He hadn't liked him before, and now he was gonna kill him. "Are you saying Duncan raped you?"

Oh hell. My little piece of escapism just turned serious. I was only glad the same thing hadn't happened to Leelee, that she'd stood up to LaForge and given him the verbal smackdown before anything bad happened.

"I don't expect you to believe me. My RA didn't. That's why I had to get out of the dorms." *She still wouldn't look at him. In fact, she scooted her chair back, ready to walk out.*

Jase grabbed her hands, the napkin falling unheeded to the floor. He pushed up her sweater cuffs and pressed her palms to his face after giving a gentle kiss to each center. "You think I don't believe you, Ave?"

"Why would you?"

"Because I love you." *His voice was hard, unyielding.*

Her eyes shot up. Her lips fell open before she pursed them tight, shaking her head.

"Don't believe me?" *Jase's nostrils flared. When he received more silence from her, he shoved back his chair and stood.* "Right."

"Jase, I'm sorry! Don't, don't leave me."

He swung toward her, dropping a deep, full kiss on her lips. "Never leaving you. I'll be right back."

Rolling up his sleeves, he stalked to the table full of twats. He watched their shock as they took in his angry expression. His violence was barely held in check. Knuckles rapping down on the table so hard their water glasses spilled and several of the girls gasped, Jase got into each and every one of their faces.

"Are you talking about my girlfriend over there?"

The dumb fucks stared at him.

"That's what I thought." His voice vibrated with rage. "Listen up, you preppy, prissy little shits. I don't care who your daddies are, I don't care if you're varsity-this or sorority-that, I'll fuck you up. I'll ruin your social lives. I'll destroy your academics. I will run you out of this school. You know who I am, right?"

One of the letter-jacket wearing pricks answered, "Yeah, you're Jase Everly."

"Fucking bingo. So you know what I can do, right?"

Bingo nodded and the others followed suit.

"And that is Avery Greene. She's worth more than any of you can imagine. I love the shit out of her. You mess with her, you deal with me." Straightening up, he crossed his arms over his chest. "You can tell dickhead Duncan, I'm gunnin' for him."

Jase pivoted around and returned to Ave. Her face was burning, her eyes trained on the floor. Watching the group of shitheads rush to pay up and get out, he felt a little bit of satisfaction. But he was still enraged, so angry his ears buzzed. He couldn't handle the idea that some guy had hurt Ave, had raped her! There was going to be hell to pay, but he had to look after her first.

He pulled her from her seat into his lap, holding her against him. Her breathing was erratic. "I didn't want any attention. Never wanted anyone's attention after what he did to me."

That was why she dressed the way she did. Why she kept up the quiet mouse routine, except with Jase.

"Well, you got my attention now, Ave." Tunneling his hand under her hair, he tipped her head up. Her eyes met his, so bright blue they reminded him of tropical waters, revealing a little less hurt, a little more hope. "You've got all my attention. I love you."

When I'd first started reading *Ride* the story had fueled my fascination with Leelee, a sexy-shy woman I wanted to fuck. Not anymore. I was searching for pieces of her within the pages, looking for a way to reach her heart. Because if tomorrow came and I let her go without knowing the truth, her words would be all I had left of her.

Chapter Fifteen
Saturday: Big Bang Banquet

THE BALLROOM WAS SET to perfection for the final night of the RAWRing Twenties LitLuv convention. Decorated in black with hints of gleaming gold and rich pops of burgundy, I embraced the *flair* of the moment. Cigarette girls held wooden trays strapped to their necks, handing out programs instead of coffin nails. The room felt as off-limits as a true blue speakeasy.

I noted the Widows with a nod, swerved away from the LolliPOP Grrrls, and almost crawled under a table to hide from Jules Gem. I'd dressed with care for Stone's Last Stand in the fedora and a well-fitting suit, garnering wolf whistles from my bros, the Coverdale crew.

Nicky swaggered beside me as we wound through the high-tops at the back of the room to a six-top reserved near the stage.

Jacqueline stood up, shouting, "It's Nicky Fucking Love and Stone!"

Nicky grinned behind the two fingers curled into the corners of his mouth, pealing out a whistle worthy of a construction crew . . . or all the horny ladies at the Magic Mike Noon/Night male revue. "It's that Big Name Author, Jacqueline!"

Shaking my head, I helped Janice down from the top of the table where she'd whoop-whoop-whooped at us. They sure did love their spectacle.

She grabbed my biceps and then my ass. Her feathered headband slid over the sky blue Lennon glasses. "Holy shit. Your ass is *so* tight!"

She passed me over to Jacqueline. Her jet beads glinted against the soft coffee of her skin. "This g'on be a good night."

I dipped away from Missy's forthcoming embrace with a feint to the left. "Fight the good fight, Stone."

Yeah, all right.

I held out Nicky's chair, waited until everyone else was seated, then pulled up between him and the sole remaining seat. Leelee was MIA. Again. Or maybe not. For all I knew she could be wearing yet another wig, hiding behind her protective veil. The longer her chair stayed empty, the more I felt like I was going to crawl out of my skin.

There was a big bulb-flashing brouhaha when the publishing BFD of the moment swanned up to the table next to ours, complete with entourage. Janice's head coiled back. Missy smacked her crop across her palm. Jacqueline, the classiest of the group, spat into her palm and rubbed her hands together.

Romance writer turf wars.

Bubbly was served, lukewarm appetizers too. I ate like an automaton—food, mouth, chew, swallow, get it down. A few drinks later, a warm buzz spread to my stomach. I held Nicky's hand, even kissed his knuckles.

His eyes caught mine. "Watch it."

"Or what, you're gonna drag my suit off and screw me right here?"

"Oh my." Janice flipped her program into a fan.

Jacqueline's gaze was glued to us. "Yes, please."

"Get that in writing, Nicky." Missy went one step further.

Nicky's cheeks burned bright. I laughed from my belly, letting all the worry and stress go. If I had to play gay or go home, I was going brass balls homo tonight, especially since Leelee wasn't lurking around to catch me out.

Fuck it all.

Several courses later, Nicky was announced the winner in the Paranormal category-established author. When he strode off the stage, straight into my arms, I felt the heat of the moment. Stone's Last *Gay* Stand. With one hand curled behind his neck, I kissed him full on the mouth, sucking in his pouty bottom lip. Our tongues touched for an instant before I reeled mine back and sealed that shit shut tight.

We broke apart, shock written on both our faces. The room erupted as if the University of South Carolina Gamecocks had scored a last-second touchdown to beat the Clemson Tigers, and I stared into his violet eyes.

"That was weird." Nicky juggled his bronzed plaque in one hand.

"Yeah." I resisted the urge to scrub my mouth with a napkin.

He sat down. I grinned beside him. With my lips to his ear, I murmured, "Just so you know, rimming is still off the table."

"Frotting too?"

Douche. I'd have to look that one up.

What seemed like hours later of fidgeting with my wineglass, fiddling with Nicky's hair while daydreaming about silky red-gold curls, I startled when Nicky nudged me. "This is Leelee's award."

"Come again?"

"She's a shoo-in for this one," he whispered.

Bat ears Missy heard him. "Our baby girl's got this in

the bag."

I slapped both palms onto the table and half-stood, performing another sweep of the room. No Leelee that I could see. I hated that she was missing this, her big moment, possibly because of me.

"And the 2013 Award for Breakout New Adult Author, self-published or traditional, goes to . . ."

Fuckin' A, get on with it.

The presenter opened the envelope. She glanced around then coughed. "Um, yes. The five-thousand-dollar award for this prestigious new genre goes to Georgie Saunders!"

I growled at Nicky, "I thought you said it was a sure thing."

The room was alive and buzzing, apparently I wasn't the only shocked by the outcome. Maybe it was a good thing Leelee wasn't here after all. I could only think of one reason Leelee could have been passed over and that reason started with L and finished with Forge.

Jules took the stage amid shouts for a recount—Hens, Widows, and the like sounding the same as they had the night I'd lost the Guys with Whatever contest, but this was more serious. This was Leelee's career.

Jules called out, "Let's not be rude, friends. I believe Ms. Saunders deserves a standing O for her win tonight! Yes?"

She clapped ferociously, and everyone followed suit. Jules might be a bulldog in a cocktail dress but she had a fair point. Saunders collected her award and the big check, looking a little flummoxed.

"Now, let's keep this party going! In the tradition of LitLuv, slideshow time. A faaaantastic presentation of our fave moments from the past four days of writers, readers, romance, and RAWR!" Jesus. If nothing else, Jules could go into UFC announcing after she finished her gig here.

Lights dimmed. The show proceeded through the craziness of arrivals and registration to some shots of the more popular panels. Then there was a flash of Leelee and me in the bar, dancing before closing time. *What the fuck?* Jules hurriedly clicked to the next frame. More innocent photos—the book fair, the loco writers and fans at The Golden Banana. Then the goddamn tango-kiss.

My face hardened. I felt a million eyes pinned on me. Nicky slid down in his seat.

Jules clicked the PowerPoint. Again and again. And all the photos on the frigging massive screen were of me and Leelee in almost every compromising position possible. Kissing, touching, dancing, kissing, goddamn *gazing* at each other. Me coming out of her room looking well fucked. Her slipping from mine wearing my shorts and shirt. Every private motherfucking moment had been photographed. Making me out to be a big bad liar in terms of my gay cover story.

Pretty much the only thing not being big-screen-revealed was me actually making love to her while we burned up the sheets.

"Gotta be fuckin' kidding me!" I pounced to my feet.

"Holy shiznit!" Janice stared at me.

Jacqueline smirked. "I knew."

"You did not!" Janice threw down her glasses and full on glared at me. "You're gay, right, Stone?"

Missy stifled a snort and patted my clenched fists.

On stage, Jules was shutting down the slideshow as quickly as possible. "Well, that was interesting, no? We do pride ourselves on providing the *very* best in entertainment, people!" She waited for applause, teeth gritted. "However, there seems to have been some tampering with the presentation, and never fear, I will get to the bottom of this. No one messes with my PowerPoint and comes out alive."

An almighty scream splintered my ears and shivered down my spine. "You son of a bitch!"

My head whipped to the left. Leelee was with LaForge, coming down hard with her heel on his instep as she choked him with his own tie. "You said you wouldn't go after Nicky and Stone."

Oh, no. My woman was not protecting me against that dickhead.

Total pandemonium ensued. Through the blood pounding in my ears and the rage blinding my vision, I saw Jules leap from the stage, beckoning her cameraman after her. The Widows scrambled in her wake. The LolliPOP Grrrls grinned at the spectacle, one tonguing her gum, the other swirling her fucking sucker in and out of her mouth.

The Hens tweeted. I heard:

#LitLuv13 #popcorn

#AgentTakedown

I was gonna break their damn smart phones, after I broke LaFuck's neck.

"The rules changed, Leelee, after you publicly humiliated me." LaForge's voice was tight due to his strangulation by tie.

Leelee glared at me when I stormed up to them.

"What the fuck's goin' on here?" Every muscle in my body tensed and my jaw pulsed dangerously.

Leelee yanked hard at the silk in her hands. "Why do you think I blew up at him at the book fair? He showed me the photos, told me he was prepared to take them public if I didn't agree to sign with him. Ruin me, Nicky, and you."

Every single moment of LaForge's dirty tactics brought me to boiling point. Punching one hand against his chest to keep him back, I got down in Leelee's face. "And you didn't think to tell me? You didn't think I'd want to protect you?"

"I was trying to keep you, Nicky, and your son off the radar, you jackass!"

Yeah, enough with the talking. I pulled Leelee behind me to keep her safe.

Small hands beat at my back and Leelee shouted. "You have no honor, Stone. How do you expect to defend mine?"

"Like this." My fist slammed into LaForge's jaw.

A low moan clattered between his teeth. Not for long. I shut his trap with a fast uppercut to his chin. Satisfaction came in the echoing snap-crunch connection of my knuckles against his face. It came in his boneless body, crumpling down to the floor.

I swiveled around to Leelee.

With her hair down and wild around her face, her green irises absolutely spitting, she hissed, "I saw you kiss Nicky."

I nodded. There was no way around that.

"Remember what you said I get to do if anyone touches you again?"

You can call me out and kick my ass, babe.

"Yeah. Do it," I answered.

She primed her fist and kept her thumb tucked inside. Her dad had taught her well. One fast snaky jab to my midsection and another to my shoulder made me grunt with surprise at her force.

Suddenly everything was dead quiet apart from Jules commentating in hushed tones and the tap-tap-tapping of fingers on phones.

Leelee stepped onto one foot and I knew what was coming next. A kick to the gonads would have me writhing on the floor, hocking up my testes. I placed my palm on her thigh to block that particular blow, but she twisted away from me.

A thin voice piped up. "Leelee? Is Leelee Childes—I mean Leelee Songchild here?"

Who the hell else now?

"Patrick?" Leelee looked around.

No way has Patrick Pin Prick Waddell turned up on our final night.

A tall dude, all pink-faced and scrubbed clean with no rough edges what-so-fucking-ever, parted the crowd. He fell to his knees in front of her.

I pushed off the wall, but Leelee's hand on my chest stopped me from stomping his face in with my boots. Suddenly, absolute emotional terror sliced through me.

"You came all the way from Shreveport?" Her fingers grazed his face.

"I was so wrong. I'm not gay." Patrick glimpsed up.

Oh, now you've gotta be shittin' me. I was the one who wasn't gay, goddammit.

"Tell me this is not happening." I grabbed Leelee's hand before she made another pass over his face. "Tell *him* this is not happening."

Camera flashes blinded me. Whispers niggled at me. Leelee glared at my hand.

"I want you back, Leelee." He anchored his arms around her legs.

Screw this. I wanted her back too. I kept my hands off him by clenching my fists at my sides. My knuckles already bruised and bleeding, I hoped my expression was as scary as I felt as I stared down at him. "Okay, you? Shut the fuck up. Your voice is not heard in this conversation."

Leelee extricated herself from Patrick. "You ditched me for the guy in the china shop when we were picking out wedding patterns. You *left* me with a mortgage on the home we lived in. I've heard the gossip—you got laid off, you're in deep trouble. You think you can just weasel your way back now that I've finally found success with the writing you called a self-absorbed pastime? You destroyed my confidence! But you know what, Patrick? I'm a phoenix. " Her voice was honey all over, poison underneath. "I hope you choke on my flames. Get the hell outta my sight."

She turned her wrath on me before he even wriggled away. "You said you and Nicky were over."

I grabbed her hand and planted it on my chest, over my pounding heart. "Goddammit, woman. You've got a stubborn streak a mile long." Her gaze dove between my lips and my hand that held hers in an unbroken grip. I

219

wanted to kiss her so badly. I stepped closer. "I like it. No, I love it. I love—"

"Stone?" Nicky's smooth voice rolled over me.

Shit-fuck.

Everyone gawking, squawking, Christly tweeting every single second of my public stoning, and I didn't give a flying fuck as the words flew from my mouth. "I'm not a foreign car dealer. I'm a mechanic. And I'm not gay!"

"Oh my God. Not you too." Leelee peeled away from me.

"I'm not gay and I never was. I'm not Patrick. I'm nothing like him. You know that." Darting in front of her, I wouldn't let her escape.

"I let you in."

"I know you did, and I honor that. I have no excuse, Leelee. I did it because, because . . ."

"Because I asked him to," Nicky said.

Her head whipped between the two of us. "Bullshit."

"It's not bullshit. Never with you, darlin'. I've never felt like this about anyone else before."

"You're a liar, Stone. Just like him." She screeched like bald wheels on blacktop, pointing toward Patrick's exit.

"I'm in love with you, Leelee. Every sweet and sassy thing about you." Tipping down toward her ear, I whispered, "No woman has ever gotten inside my heart like you have."

When she backed away, her bottom lip quivered, and I silently begged her not to cry. *Leave me in a fire of flames as well.*

Leelee jabbed at me. "Let's get this straight. I'm not a damsel in distress, and you're not a knight in shining armor."

I begged to differ about that. LaForge was still a skin-sack on the floor.

"We aren't living in a romance novel. I don't care if you're bi-straight-gay. Because I don't care about you," she spat. "You, Stone, are a liar *and* a scoundrel. You probably don't even have a son."

From one of the onlookers, I heard a quiet, "This is an epic black moment."

I clasped my hands behind my neck. "Fuck." She couldn't have hurt me more about the kid. "He was never a lie. Neither were you." My voice rasped.

"I didn't mean that," Leelee whispered. She was pale and shivering.

"Yeah, you did. It's okay." My smile was wintry. "JJ's mine. He's real. No one messes with my kid." A blanket of regret spread across her face. "About everything else, maybe you're right." I angled my fedora over my eyes.

This was done.

I watched her walk out, her head held high. At least that was something to be thankful for. She hadn't been defeated, at least not in public.

"Show's over, folks." I slumped against the wall.

Nicky appeared beside me. I couldn't meet his eyes, couldn't meet anyone's. "I'm sorry, bro," I said.

"Yeah, me too." He ran a hand through his hair then over his face. "Are you coming up to bed? Long drive tomorrow."

I glanced around the emptying room, never at him. "Nah. I'm goin' nowhere."

I never had. I'd been content with my life. My garage. The kid. My Friday night tits-and-ass. I hadn't ever wanted anything else until Leelee hit me like a fucking hurricane. I laughed darkly, shrugging away from Nicky.

So raw my emotions were bleeding out, I staked out the lobby. I sat unmoving, oblivious to the commotion around me. The giant undertaking of the convention being cleaned up and cleared out. I wasn't leaving until I saw Leelee one last time.

A couple hours later, the lobby finally silent, I caught a streak of red all the way across the room. Leelee was sneaking out the far doors. Clever. I jogged across the lobby, stumbling through the merry-go-round doors. I stopped behind her as she struggled with the cobbled-together luggage cart. A car idled next to her.

"Leave me alone." She kept her face angled away from me.

I grabbed the cart in one hand and steadied the sliding suitcase formation with the other. "You're not getting away that easily."

"You think this is easy? My heart is breaking, Josh." Turning to me, she hugged herself tight, looking so small and so hurt.

I staggered back on my heels, breathless from pain. "Then don't do this."

The downward crescent of her mouth tugged at my heart like a goddamn hook had ripped through it. "I can't do anything else. This is—you, me . . . Nicky, my writing—it's a mess! And your son . . ."

My vision got watery. I swallowed, the lump in my throat immoveable. "So you're just gonna run away?"

"Don't you dare judge me." She popped open the trunk and yanked her belongings into it, any which way they landed.

"At least let me help you with your stuff." Anything to buy a few more minutes with her.

Leelee nodded, moving out of the way.

I jigsawed it all into the tight space of her compact sedan, making sure nothing would jostle during the ride. Too soon, everything was organized. I closed the trunk. The finality of the sound banged inside my head.

Gathering her hands, I pulled them toward my chest. "Tell me you're not drivin' through the night." The idea of her driving in the dark on her own just about threw me into a tailspin of worry.

"Just a few hours. I need to get away. I'm so overwhelmed." She lifted up until her face pressed against my neck.

Oh Christ, she felt good, so right. I wrapped my arms

around her, caressing up and down her back. What if I never felt her again?

I choked out, "Are you calling someone to check in on the way home?"

Call me, please call me.

"My folks. I'll be safe."

I cupped her face. My fingertips grazed her cheeks to her bow-shaped mouth. I kissed her forehead, her temples. Brushing my lips over hers, I waited a heartbeat. She returned that simple kiss, winding her arms around me. Her moan was all the surrender I needed.

Dragging my hand through her hair, I held her the way I wanted to, needed to. In full possession, slanting her face and sliding my lips more deeply against hers. The touch of our tongues was the perfect invitation to groan in pleasure. To hold on before the pain of goodbye. It was a kiss I hoped she wouldn't forget, couldn't walk away from.

Breath rushed from me when Leelee stepped back. I held my hand out to her for more. So much more.

She'd melted during the kiss—but not enough. The hurt in her eyes was worse than straight-up hate. And with it was anguish, desire. One hand pressed to her mouth, she stumbled to the car door. I was there in an instant. I hung over it, hungry for every last sight of her.

Reaching to stroke my face, Leelee leaned up for what I expected to be another kiss, but she turned away at the last second. "I'm sorry. I'm so sorry!"

The car door slammed as soon as I stepped away.

There on the walkway I crouched down, bracing my hands on my knees. Pain punched me in the gut. But I wouldn't look away, wouldn't blink. Not until she was out of sight.

Leelee left in a May haze of heat, exhaust fumes, red taillights. She left me with a hard stone taking center place in my heart.

My woman got away.

Chapter Sixteen
Not Romancing the Stone

AFTER UMPTEEN HOURS ON the road, driving on autopilot, Nicky and I arrived in Mt. Pleasant. Sitting in my ma's drive, I prepared to rip the door handle off the rented Volvo to get to the kid when Nicky placed a hand on my knee. My stabbing glare made him remove it.

"Next time, we're flying," he said.

"Next time?" I turned in my seat. "Dude, I pretty much just wrecked your reputation and screwed my love life. Or did you miss that tweet?"

"I've been checking all day long, in fact." A wicked grin slid across his mouth. "That stunt gave me more hits than a whore spreadin' her legs for a two-for-one-fuck."

Crude, but effective. Aaaaand, that goddamn fucker. At least he'd forgiven me. I didn't even have to send flowers. Asshole always came up smelling like roses.

I shouldered through the doors of the house ahead of Nicky. Ma sat on the sofa with her cross stitch, which she used to camouflage her current book-smut-of-the-month from the Sunday clutch of church ladies who called at all hours of the day.

She took one look at my face and slapped both book and fake old lady's craft project aside. "Uh oh, trouble in paradise?"

"It was 'Lanta. I wouldn't exactly call that paradise." I dropped my head. "Fell in love, fucked it all up."

Nicky squeezed my shoulder before we were wrapped in a tight maternal embrace, encompassing both of us.

Slipping back, Ma narrowed her eyes. "Now listen here, sonny boy. Unless this woman spat on your name, slashed your tires, or tried to run you over, you ain't fucked it up. And kindly don't use that word in my house. Leave that garbage at the garage, I don't need you dirtying up my domicile."

Nicky snickered behind me. I elbowed him, fighting a smile myself. Yeah, she had her dirty books to dirty up her *domicile* already.

Ma clapped both hands over her mouth. "Leelee! Leelee Songchild! Oh, son, you caught yourself a live one, didn't you?"

A flush heated up my neck to my cheeks, cheeks she pinched to pull me forward for a loud smack of lips on my mouth.

I wrestled back and swiped at my lips. "Ma!"

"Oh, you've gotta get that woman now. Mah Lord in Heaven. I swear, if you did her wrong, I'll be givin' you a dressin' down the likes of which y'all never seen. *Mm hmm.*"

At the sound of the patter-patter-skid of bare feet on bare floorboards, I turned around, opened my arms, and caught a wriggling bundle of boy. My eyes welled up. I sniffed hard, the knot in my throat swelling until I couldn't speak.

"Daddy!" JJ's scream about shattered my eardrum. It was the best sound I'd ever heard.

I tucked myself around him, breathing in sticky sweetness, baby shampoo, wet dog, and dirt. I kissed every

225

inch of skin I could find. Bouncing him in my arms, I pretended to groan due to his weight because it was either that or break down and cry. "Jesus. You've grown. What's Jamma been feedin' ya?" Tickling his little potbelly, I nuzzled his neck.

"Daddy, you scwatchy." JJ was giggles, wiggles, all things good.

Setting him down, I crouched at his level.

Pudgy toddler fingers touched beneath my eyes. "Daddy, your eyes is weaking."

"Yeah, I guess they are leaking."

As soon as that mystery was solved, he barreled into Nicky. "Uncle Wicky! I missed you. I missed Daddy more. Viper and Jamma kept me company. Can I come stay with you soon?"

Ma met my questioning eyes. "Orange Fanta and a Creamsicle an hour ago."

Sugar rush plus galactic levels of excitement . . . tonight was gonna be awesome. But it didn't matter. I couldn't wait to get the kid home, snug in his bed and sung to sleep so I could ease half the ache in my heart.

No sooner had Nicky answered the sucrose-fueled fire of questions than the kid jumped back into my arms. "What'd ya bring me?"

I'd brought myself a whole lotta heartache from a woman who'd driven away in the night, but I shook that off. I pulled JJ's gift from my back pocket. The pint-sized Georgia Bulldogs baseball cap was snatched from my hands. He didn't give a shit what it was. He whooped and hollered, racing around until Viper joined in the mad dash of boy and beast.

"Just might not wanna wear it in public round here, unless you wanna get your ass kicked," I warned.

The kid didn't hear me, but Ma sure did. She cuffed me on the back of my head. "Language."

"C'mere, c'mere." He towed Nicky and me to the sofa side table. Grabbing Ma's phone, he scrolled down like he knew what he was doing—more so than me—and tapped the screen. "Lookie. Jamma took pictures of me and Viper."

In the photo he used the massive, sleek-haired Rottie as a headrest. One had a tongue lolling out between big boy-eating teeth; the other had his hand tucked under the muzzle. Both were asleep.

"Sweet, dude-man." Nicky ruffled his hair.

Yeah, that's fuckin' precious. I loved seeing the kid snuggled up to eighty pounds of vicious-looking bitch.

An hour later, with the kid passed out and Viper hogtied in a car-harness, Nicky dropped us off at home. I carried JJ upstairs to his bed while Nicky brought in our bags. After slipping off JJ's sneakers and shorts, I left him in skivs and T-shirt, covering him up with a kiss.

Nicky waited on the porch. My house sat on a little knoll above the Cooper River. From this vantage point of the Old Village we could see the Charleston Bay as it narrowed into a deep waterway delivering cargo ships to the port terminals farther up.

Under the moon, sleek silvery bodies of dolphins arced through sluggish waves. Briny water scented the air, and night blooming jasmine. Damp, heavy heat clung to my skin like the honeysuckle vines on my porch. The swing moved with the breeze, just big enough for two, the perfect place to sit with Leelee.

Pulling me to him with an elbow crooked around my neck, Nicky inhaled. "Home."

"Yeah." I squinted out over the famed Ravenel suspension bridge that was always lit up like every day was the Fourth of July.

"You worry too much."

"And you don't get laid enough."

We grinned.

Viper slobbered on the rental's windows.

"I'm headin' off. Thanks for the week, man. Thanks for . . . you know." Brief, but hard, profound, Nicky's hug

227

meant a lot. Friends. Best buds. That shit was important. "Leelee will come around."

"Of course." I gestured over my body. "I mean, look at all this."

He snorted all the way to the Volvo, flipping his hair out of his eyes for one last wink. As soon as he rumbled off, I slumped to the steps. Glossy black wood, sanded and painted by me and my dad.

I sat there for a while, breathing it all in. Harbor and river, flowers and heat. Slapping my hands against my thighs, I stood up. There could've been a million miles between Mt. Pleasant and Shreveport—it sure felt like it. I wanted to kiss the kid goodnight one more time before I loaded the laundry and had a shower. Before I sat out back with a beer, cursing the crickets and bullhorn bullfrogs.

I had work tomorrow.

The boys better be on their A-Game. And that did not mean Ass Game, for a change.

* * * *

In the morning, I dropped the kid off at Ma's with more scratchy, stubbly kisses and squeezes, addicted to his laughs. Grabbing a mug of coffee and a homemade ham biscuit, I drove back down 17 to the shop. Red awning, huge sign, pre-dawn, renewed pride jolted through me.

This was where I belonged.

I let myself in the side door and switched on the lights. The bays filtered into bright illumination. Clean surfaces, scrubbed-down floors, cars undercover—fucking perfect. The scent of motor oil after a week away almost made me high. I'd come dressed in clean coveralls, as clean as they'd get, and checked a clipboard. Pulling the sheet off a truck, I started right in.

Half an hour later, all four tires were changed. Sweat dripped down my neck, and I hunkered back to enjoy a job well done.

Dusting my hands on my thighs, I cruised through the other bays and into the front of house. Tidiest motherfuckers on earth. Loved those grease monkeys. The magazines had been switched out, restrooms Spic and Spanned. Roses chilled in the fridge. I sat on the counter waiting for clocking-in time. That was when I spied the banner slung above the neat rows of chairs in front of me:

Welcome Home, Stone!

Fuckin' crackers. There better be some cake later, too, since I'd already brought them Krispy Kremes.

Ray's key scraped in the lock. The bell jingled. The men filed in. Fourteen of them, all dressed in their dark blue jumpsuits with red and white nametags stitched on, grins in place.

I hopped down and stood at the forefront. Fuck if I was gonna cry, but this shit was emotional. Back slaps, hard hugs, a little razzing, I greeted everyone and got it all back in return.

Idjits.

Gerald stuffed his massive hands into the pockets of his uniform. "No way he's been into the office yet. He's being too lovey-dovey."

Ray whistled, off-tune, and that was my clue the bastards had been up to something other than welcome backs and back slaps. Warning bells went off.

I stalked to my office and they all trooped after me, tripping over each other in the narrow hallway. Banging open the door, I flinched when I saw what was inside.

A veritable warehouse full of sex toys had been arranged on every available surface from my desk to the two-seater sofa, the chairs, and the tall metal filing cabinets.

No, not sex toys . . . fake cocks—dildos, dongs, schlongs made of every substance and in every color. Oh, and my favorite, the double intruder. I had flashbacks to The Gee Spot shop in Atlanta.

And I was surrounded by a bunch of dickheads who

229

crowded me into the penis palace. They tuned me around so I could see their extra special treat: a giant glossy poster of their Stone's Roses snapshot.

I couldn't even keep a scowl on my face; they were such assholes, but they were mine—true grit, funny, and goddamn creative. What could I say? They were my favorite assholes. When I started chuckling, they all let loose.

"Ya know, we just wanted to do up your orifice." Ray could barely get it out between gusts of laughter.

"Where the hell did you get all these dicks?"

Gerald stood by the door. "I bought a load of them at Generation Sex up on Dorchester Road."

"Batteries Not Included, it just opened in West Ashley." Javier pulled a toothpick out of his pocket, cleaning his oil-encrusted nails with it.

"Moan-A-Me had just gotten in new stock. I think I'm their favorite customer now." Mick slapped his thigh with a grungy baseball cap.

"And what the fuck am I supposed to do with 'em?"

"I don't know. Try them out on your lady love, that Leelee, *comprende, amigo*?"

Gerald smacked Javier on the back of the head. "The fuck? Didn't you check your Facebook last night?"

"What? What I do now?" Javier frowned.

Leaning against the desk, knocking over a few plastic pricks, I muttered, "'S'over."

"What? It can't be!" The boy looked as horrified as I felt. "Tell her you're not gay already, *si*?"

"Did that." My scowl turned black.

Ray's bushy blond beard twitched. "Tell her you love her? That always works for me when the missus gets pissy."

"Tried that."

A collective groan swept through the room.

"Flowers? Hey, send her some of our roses, why don't ya?" Mick offered.

"I don't think that's gonna cut it. I'd say she's beyond the flowers and an apology stage." Before they could shower me with any more pearls of piston-jockey wisdom, I looked at my watch. I toughened up my bark. "Hey, any one of y'all notice what time it is?"

"Opening!" Ray hustled out to the front.

The others shuffled away with well-meaning smiles and pats on my shoulder—in other words, pity.

Shit.

Before long, I heard the air compressors singing, impact guns trilling, the bell over the door chiming as down-home folk shouted hellos to my familiar crew.

It wouldn't do to sit around sulking all day in my cave-o'-dicks, so I headed out to get my grime on *after* I rolled up the poster. I snuck outside to Javier's pick-up truck and picked the lock. Unrolled over his windshield like a sun shield, the assholes faced inward. Then I returned to the office and crammed the cocks into the top two empty drawers of a filing cabinet.

Satisfied that every last dildo was out of sight, I walked outside. The buzz of traffic on 17 and the hum of work inside the open garage bays were comforting. The same old cronies sat out front. Some of them were Dad's friends. Some from as far back as my granddaddy's era. They were here for nothing more than people watching, old man gossiping, and shooting the shit. I'd even provided a few tables for them, umbrellas and all. They showed every day, setting up their checker- and chessboards. I was pretty damn sure money exchanged hands, but they kept it friendly. They ate my donuts, drank my coffee, used the facilities and were so deeply ingrained in the place they were family.

Stone's was family.

I greeted them with respectful handshakes. They called me sonny-boy with wide smiles in return.

It almost brought tears to my eyes.

I passed the benches, not listening to the women

whispering as I walked by with a simple "how-do". I didn't even look at them. I wasn't looking for anything anymore. I'd found it all in Leelee and let her slip away.

Balling my fists, I headed to the Pit, bay one. That was where we tackled the hard cases. I joined in on the ambulance the boys had promised to get back in business in forty minutes or less. Happy to be busy, my mind turned over like a well-tuned engine for a change instead of being hung up on Leelee. We rolled that big bastard out in thirty-five minutes, complete with interior detailing and exterior wash down.

Fist bumps all around.

I got stuck into the thick of the garage for the rest of the day. I'd be up to my eyeballs in bills and paperwork come the weekend, but for now, I was up to my elbows in grease. I worked the boys double hard and busted their nuts. I couldn't wipe the grin off my face, and that hadn't happened since I'd been with Leelee our final night in my bed.

After the last customer left, the open sign turned over, I headed out back. There was a strip of grass behind the garage, a couple picnic tables, and an icebox I'd filled with beer, soda, and Popsicles during my lunch break. Ma showed up with hotdogs, hamburgers, a giant tub of slaw, and the kid. The boneheads presided out back as I fired up the grill.

The kid was hefted into the air and tossed around like a potato sack. I turned my back, and shook my head, listening to his squeals of laughter. By the time we sat down to chow down, he was already two Popsicles too far gone. I was going to cut sugar out of his diet. Tomorrow. Just like I was gonna cut Leelee out of mine. The detox would be "epic", as Felicia would say.

That's when it slammed into me. I'd miss them all. The Hens—including Missy—the Widows. Most of all, Leelee. I tried not to imagine her here. It didn't work. I knew she'd love it, especially the garage. Of course I'd have to blind motherfuckers so they didn't stare at her perfect tits, but that wouldn't be a hardship. I still had the tire iron handy.

Ma touched the side of my face. "You miss her."

I struggled to put it all into balance. I was grateful as hell for what I had. This was a good life, but one huge part was gone. "Yeah, I do."

I stared out over my friends and family, listening to their laughter and chatter. And I wanted more.

* * * *

Over the next couple of weeks Stone's was busier than ever, and I partnered with a new automotive parts company. Being so busy I was run ragged was good. It kept my mind off Leelee: where she was, what she was doing, and hoping to high hell she wasn't doing anyone else. On the weekends, I added the final touches to the house, like . . . Jesus. Was I nesting? What? Just in case Leelee walked through the front gate one day out of the clear freaking blue?

It didn't matter. Hope wouldn't die. The last thing I had to do—after new curtains, color-matchy cushions, candles, and new crockery—was fix the loose toilet handle in the master bathroom. The handle Dad and I were supposed to repair the day he'd died.

Saturday evening, I put down my tools. I wiped my palms and gave the flush a go. The bowl whooshed like a charm, no jiggling required. Some of the old ache uncoiled from my chest but it still hurt like a bitch.

After a shaky breath and a swipe under my nose, I opened two bottles of beer. Clinking them together, I flopped onto the floor. I set one of the beers across from me. "Here's to you, Pops. I'll always love you."

I leaned my head back and shut my eyes. I tried to remember what it felt like to hug him. My shoulders shook and I let it go. I didn't hear tiny feet approaching, didn't know the kid watched me until I took another swig and peered around.

He popped his sucking finger out of his mouth. "Daddy, why is you sittin' in the bathroom, drinkin' next to the potty?"

"Why *are* you," I corrected on reflex.

"Huh?" The kid scratched that goddamn adorable cowlick. His Superman cape had been traded out for Batman. "And why is you weaking again?"

I pulled him onto my lap. "I love you. And it's okay to cry sometimes. I was thinking about your granddaddy. I miss him."

"Like I missed you in 'Lana?" His mousy voice twisted my heart and put it all back together again.

"Yeah." I pressed my nose into the back of that downy soft neck. I blew a raspberry, laughing when he giggled. "Something like that, kid."

* * * *

The house felt empty even with the homey touches I'd added. Even with the kid and his nonstop chatter from dawn to dusk. I couldn't get Leelee out of my mind, and I couldn't get in touch with her. Since the only thing I had from her were memories and *Ride*, I wound down each night by soaking in her words that were already part of my soul.

Jase found Ave huddled over in her room, the one she hadn't slept in for two months. Two aching, beautiful, amazing months.

As usual, her bedroom was tits-up, end-over-end. His lips twitched as he held in a laugh. "Watcha doin'?"

The night had fucked him over from start to finish, but not as much as her jerking shoulders while she struggled to pull together a . . . a

Stone, At Your Service

canvas bag full of clothes?

His amusement from moments before curdled on his tongue. He tried again, this time sterner. "What the hell are you doing, Ave?"

Long brown hair clung to her damp cheeks when she snapped her head around. "Are you still doing it?"

His confusion turned to coldness. Fear ran through him like sharp shards of icicles injected into his veins. "Doing what exactly?"

"You left your phone, I answered it." The bag closed, she turned and stood. "Doing them. *PS. You're two hours late for your date with someone called M Delesseleine."*

Colder than fear, worse than shock, the instant loss of Avery immobilized him.

"Are you still whoring yourself out for money, sugah?"

Getting in her face because he'd rather deal with her fury than the grueling pain if she left him, he roared, "YES! Damn you, yes!"

Ave shrank back.

"You think I like it? Fucking those women? Getting bankrolled and bed-rolled by broads I couldn't give a shit about? Do you think I wouldn't rather be here, with you?" His fists clenched, released, clenched. "Who else is gonna pay the bills, huh? How else will I make this much, this fast, so I can still have time to study and finally get what I want!"

"How can you slut around every night with a new . . . what? What am I supposed to call them, Jase?" She sent a ringing slap to his cheek when he didn't answer. "How can you fuck them when you've never made love to me?"

"I can't be with you, Ave. I'm dirty inside."
His head bent, his whole body did too until he

235

> *kneeled on the floor in front of her. Eyes shaded*
> *with loss, longing—the world of emotion inside*
> *them—found hers. "I'm too dirty for you."*

I put down my beer, inspected my hands. Oil stains
were embedded beneath my short nails, turning the lines of
my knuckles dark. Maybe I wasn't good enough for
Leelee. I wasn't the smooth-talking Stone she'd met. I was
just a car mechanic, a single dad . . . a lonely man.

> *"Have you forgotten I'm broken too? I'm*
> *broken without you." Tears streamed down her*
> *cheeks. "What do you want?"*
> *"I want you, Ave. Only you, always you . . ."*
> *He crawled closer.*
> *She strained away from him. "Is that where*
> *you were tonight? Did you double book? Lose*
> *your calendar?"*
> *"No." His laugh held no mirth. Lifting his*
> *hands, he blew across bloodied, cracked*
> *knuckles. "I was kicking Duncan Locke's ass,*
> *like I swore I would." His heart found a new*
> *rhythm when she lifted his hand, kissing the*
> *swollen mess.*
> *"You're hurt."*
> *He hooked his discolored fingers under her*
> *chin. "Not as hurt as you. I'm sorry."*
> *"Did Duncan apologize?"*
> *"Yeah, after he screamed like a girl. I only*
> *broke a couple ribs." With his boots. Jase*
> *grinned, remembering the crunch of bones. "And*
> *his nose."*
> *"Why?"*
> *"Because he took what wasn't his. Because*
> *he tried to break you." Jase's throat closed tight*
> *and he wanted more of Ave's hands, her*
> *embrace. He needed it to erase the image of her*

being fucked against her will. "*Because you are a treasure. No one has that right. Fucking no one.*"

"*I'm whole with you, Jase.*"

A thick choking sound preceded him crushing her to him.

I got up from bed and opened a window. The curtains flipped against my bare legs. Emotions similar to Jase's spun through me until I crouched on the floor.

"*You are so . . .*" *Ave's words ran out for once.*

"*Stupid?*"

She pressed small kisses all over his face, lastly to his lips. "*So honorable.*"

His gut clenched. All those women. Night after night. Premeditated fucks. Dollar signs and decimals instead of names and phone numbers was what they added up to. "*I'm not. Those women, they're jobs. I don't have fun. I fuck and get off 'em, get out.*"

Ave winced but stayed wrapped around him.

"*I'll stop. It's just you, it's only ever been you, Ave. Just forgive me, forgive me, please.*"

"*Yes. Always yes, Jase.*" *On her feet, she extended her hand.* "*Let's clean you up, bruiser.*"

After she'd cleansed his hands, she unbuttoned his shirt. He shivered when she traced the muscled mass of his pecs, a lone finger trailing through the line of brown hair that bisected his abs.

Ave breathed a laugh when his stomach muscles contracted under her touch. Half-lidded and heavy, that blue gaze found his. "*Will you?*"

"*Stop? Yeah, I said I would.*" *He shuddered*

237

through a long groan as she pushed the shirt from his shoulders.

She stood back in her white shirt, which was his white shirt. Dropping her hands from him, she removed her pants and panties. His ears hummed, blood rushed to his groin, engorging him. Heavy, round breasts filled out his shirt in a way that made the masculine cut insanely fucking sexy.

Ave touched the buttons of his jeans, beneath which his cock stretched the faded fabric. "No, I meant, will you make love to me tonight, Jase?"

Avery popped the top button free, and this time her hands were sure.

* * * *

He picked her up, which was good because her knees gave out. In the bedroom—their bedroom—he sat on the edge of the bed. "Finish what you started."

A moan skipped from her throat. She knelt between his wide-open thighs and thumbed the last three buttons free.

Sounding harsh, Jase said, "Take my cock out, Ave."

Oh God, this was what she'd wanted. Opening the jeans, her hand burrowed inside. He didn't lift his hips or shift a muscle, he wouldn't help her, she realized. Anticipation tightened her nipples into hard points and curled inside her belly. He groaned when she made contact, circling her fingers around his base, fingertips not meeting around that thick shaft. Lying on his belly, his cock was irresistible. The backs of her fingers glided up and then down while Jase watched, lips parted, breaths ragged.

"Stop. Stop, Ave, or I swear to fuck, I'll come right now."

With sudden violence—the best kind—Jase snapped forward and ripped her shirt open down the middle. "Better." He bent her forward and sucked her nipples with long endless draws of his tongue and mouth.

Her hips circled in time with his teasing, biting sucks. Avery threw her head back, moaning uncontrollably. Jase released her. Riding his shaft within his fist, he wriggled free of his jeans. He flitted two fingertips across the clear liquid on the head of his cock and pushed them into her mouth.

The taste, his taste was indescribable. Salty. Sweet. Musk and man. Addictive.

He returned to stroking. "Show me your cunt."

The words alone tied her in tight knots only he could release. She brought one leg up, placing her foot on the covers beside his hip.

He sat up, his face nearly at the juncture of her thighs. His breath spilled across her, followed by deep licks of his tongue. "So wet. For me?"

When Avery nodded, he sank her onto his lap. Coarse brown hair rasped against her thighs. His hands on her waist, his tongue trailing along her neck, he dragged her back and forth over the silky hot rod of flesh.

"Please now, Jase."

"Yeah? Need me now?"

A whimper, that was all she could utter, but he knew. He pulled her with him all the way onto the bed. Her head rested against the pillows, her legs splayed. Their kisses were deep and drugging. And when he entered her, Avery could see, she could feel it was with tenderness so vast it drew from a well of deep emotion, not just

239

desire and need.

"Feels like my first time, Jase." Her lips strayed from his jaw to his mouth.

He stretched all the way over her, filling her deep. "Then it is. I'm your first. Your first lover."

His words catapulted heat and hope inside of her heart.

Her lips pressed to his, she breathed, kissed, gasped. "First love."

"Only love, Ave. My only love."

* * * *

Three weeks after the convention, the kid had been broken of his sugar habit, but I still held onto my Leelee addiction. I ditched a different one instead. The minute I'd arrived back in Mt. Pleasant, I'd turned over a new, non-man-slut leaf. I took myself off the Friday night fuck market. When I went to bars, I didn't pick up chicks. I sat with my drink and stared at the wall. And I remembered one night, one song by Chet Baker, and a gorgeous woman in my arms.

Getting an earful from Janice over the phone and Javier in person, I was double-teamed into setting up a Twitter account, hoping Leelee might make contact. The tweets poured in and the texts did too. I was followed by Devon, Jacqueline, Felicity, Missy, Fred, and the rest, as well as many friends I seemed to have picked up in Atlanta, and over the years around home. I hankered after every secondhand word on Leelee.

As for Nicky, our fake break-up hit the social network radar and his novels went supernova viral. He'd had to deal with the fallout from the Hens—two years of deception didn't sit well with them. Until he found out they'd been placing bets on his sexuality the entire time. After he learned about that little piece of grifting, he was golden. I didn't see him much, and I missed him, too. He'd dived back into the whirlwind of writing, playing catch up, deadlines . . . and he had his own stalker-fan to deal with: Nicky's Chicky from the Con.

Unlike the constant tweets from *@Felicity, @Dev, @Jaque_line*, I got nada from Leelee. I understood why. She'd been burned by a guy who'd come out as gay weeks before their wedding. I'd come out as not gay the same time as ten tons of shit fell on her head.

LaForge had been named and shamed, his agency going down in flames. Indicted for harassment and extortion, his career was dragged under and drowned as others followed Leelee's suit. All this I heard over the goddamn Twitterverse, which was my only lifeline to the woman I wanted an entire life with.

Someone else managed to track me down. It wasn't hard, just follow the fucking bouncy cursor. *@The_JGem* tweeted me, from ten miles away:

U'll b cover 4 August LitLiv Mag, yes? Gud. Coming with photag 06-30 2 Stone's

The bastard little birdy didn't allow me enough characters to express how much I vetoed that idea. My phone calls and messages to her went unanswered because Jules Gem knew she had me by the balls.

The dreaded day arrived. Punctual as ever, she swooped into the parking lot with a photographer in tow. She climbed out of her SUV, transformed from a bulldog in a cocktail dress to a beach girl in a sundress. She still had bite though.

"Stone!" She imparted two fancy air kisses. Snapping her fingers at the shaggy-haired photographer, she said, "Scout it out, pronto. I need natural lighting"—she paused, squinting at the interior of the Pit—"and check the meter in that area. We could get some *amazing* affects from the overhead glow. Yes?"

During that day, the definition of hell was Jules posing me, oiling me up and buttoning me down. She ordered me into a perfectly tailored suit she'd pulled out of a bag and my own fedora. She told me to bend over and show her some ass while I had my head stuck under my Camaro's hood. All this was because of *great juxtaposition* between the expensive suit, my dirty hands, and the all-man mechanic interior of the Pit.

"Outfit change!" She briskly clapped her hands.

I backed out from around the support rods, whipping off the tie that hung loose around the open collar of my dress shirt. Greasing up the nice suit on purpose was liberating, especially since it didn't belong to me. Claps, catcalls, hoots 'n' hollers greeted me. I flushed scarlet to the roots of my hair. My photo shoot had attracted a ridiculous crowd filling the entire parking lot. *Fuck my life, right?* The old cronies grinned with toothless gums. The odd assortment of customers whooped it up. Every now and then I thought I saw a glimpse of stunning orange-gold hair, but that was stupid. No way was Leelee here.

I definitely spotted a few past conquests though. That alone made me rush to the office for my outfit change. Returning in coveralls, I wore the top looped around my waist to reveal a white bro-tank underneath. Jules subjected me to a couple more hours of "pose with your arms flexed", "tank top off and close up on the tat".

For the final shots of the afternoon, I loosened up, remembering my easy-come, easy-go Stone persona. "Hey, Miss Gem. How's about I pull the top of my coveralls back on but leave 'em open and keep the tank top off?" The air screeched with whistles and screams. I tugged the zipper at my crotch. "And maybe lower this a little too?"

"Like at Guys with Balls?" Jules asked.

I slid the zipper low enough to tease, reaching my hand inside. A tangle of pubes pushed over the top of the dark blue uniform. I couldn't hear myself think through the roar of the onlookers. Fuckers better remember to bring their cars back here next time they needed an oil change after the free show I was giving.

"*Purrrfect.*" Jules grinned with all her teeth. "Now spread those big thighs, Stone. Yes. Lean back, open the top more, more, more, *yes*. Elbows on the hood, head tilted back, eyes closed. *Hawt-hawt-hawt.* Now hold it, hold it, think about . . . Leelee Songchild, right between your legs."

Oh fuck. That did it. I sprang a boner in the blink of an eye, and me, like that, all spread out and horny? *Click-click-click.* Yeah, I was gonna have Leelee exactly this way when I won her back.

That was the last shot. Good thing too because I needed to get back to my office to make a come-shot, pretty goddamn quick. Stumbling through the emptying garage bays, I barely made it to the privacy of closed doors before I pulled out my cock with a deep groan.

Getting right down to a quick pump action on my shaft, I leaned against the desk.

A loud knock-knock hit the door.

I ignored it. My jaw clenched, my thighs shook. My cock throbbed. I was not going to be interrupted like every single time I tried to jerk off at LitLuv.

"Yo, Stone!" Ray pounded on the door.

"Motherfucker. Is the place on fire?"

"No, but—"

"Are we getting robbed?" I shouted.

"No, but—"

"'No buts' is right!" I cracked the door and shoved my head out. "I need five minutes, man. Five. Because my dick is gonna explode."

Ray stood his ground. "The thing is there's a lady outside, lookin' for ya."

"You've gotta be kiddin' me. What? Another broad who wants my autograph on her tits? One of the chicks who just watched the photo shoot?"

"All I know is she's a hot piece in a pretty dress. You

243

might wanna get to her before one of the guys snaps her up." He whistled as he walked away.

I slammed the door then slammed my forehead against it. I hiked the coveralls over my hips and managed to zip up around my raging erection. Striding down the hall and behind the counter, I tied the sleeves around my hips. I'd forgotten my fucking tank top in the office.

Screw it.

Cutting through the bays, I exited the building. Sweat flashed across my skin as the sun pounded down on me.

I'd almost reached the benches hidden beyond the Coke machines when Ray leaned out behind me. "Forgot to say, killer heels, man."

Killer heels. The last time I'd seen a pair of them was on Leelee. I didn't reckon I wanted to see them on anyone else but her.

Jules pulled up beside me and rolled down her window. "Now we're even."

"What?"

She did the kissy-kissy-face-smooch thing and smiled. "Besides, I just *love* a perfect HEA. Don't you?"

"Huh?"

She pointed behind me before driving off.

I swiped a forearm across my brow and turned around. I didn't move another muscle. "Leelee?"

Chapter Seventeen
Hell in High Heels

JESUS CHRIST, LEELEE LOOKED good. Leelee looked amazing. Here. In Mt. Pleasant, at my garage where I'd hoped to have her but never expected her to show up.

Scrubbing a hand across my jaw, I groaned because I hadn't even made a halfway decent scrape of my stubble that morning, per Jules's instructions. I walked toward Leelee, head cocked, scoping her out.

She sauntered to me, expression unreadable, checking me out.

Her hips shifted in the tight, knee-length, call-me-secretary skirt. Her tits moved too, those nice full handfuls swaying with every step closer. Her hair loose and down her back, just the way I liked it, shimmered in the sunshine. Perspiration clung to my temples but the flush on my face came from the vision in front of me.

In four-inch, taupe, patent leather stilettos.

Hell on wheels? She was totally hell in high heels, wearing a dress that worked its way over her banging bod like my hands itched to do. The lightest yellow with lilac

245

flowers and little sleeves that bared her shoulders, her collarbone, and a great big mouthwatering amount of cleavage. My eyes bored into her. My cock made itself known. My arms flexed, ready to grab her.

The boys hung out of the open bays like a barrel of monkeys. Their yeehaws and whistles filled the air.

Slicing my eyes sideways, I said, "Unless you wanna get fired right here, right now, get back to work and keep your traps shut."

Leelee stopped two feet away from me. She was half-in, half-out of the shadows of the awning. "So, this is you." Sweet as ever, rich as honey, her voice hit me in the groin.

Once again, I was reminded of my small-town business, my scruffy appearance. Jules had dirtied me up with grease stains for *visual pizzazz* and I hadn't cleaned up yet, too intent on beating the come out of my cock.

I scratched the back of my neck, thinking she could've just tweeted me to give me the old heave-ho instead of wasting the plane fare. "Yeah."

"Foreign auto imports?" The breeze picked up, flipping red tendrils of hair over her shoulder.

"Like I said. I lied. I'm sorry, ya know?" I stared at the low neckline of her dress, drowning in the sight of her rocking body before I met her eyes, lingering over her lips on the way up.

"Did I ever tell you how much I like the smell of a garage?" The wind changed direction, delivering her voice to me. A low, silky-rough temptation that slid like moist lips along my skin.

Oh shit . . .

Leelee came closer. Her movements were pure seduction. "How much I like a man who knows he's a man? Who protects his woman and"—closest now, her breath warmed the hollow of my throat—"knows how to satisfy her but still has a big heart beneath all the raunchy, macho instincts?"

246

I couldn't breathe except to get more of her perfume. Fuck, my brain was scrambled. I couldn't blame it on the heat, it was all her. "What are you doing here?"

"Jules told me about the photo shoot. I had to make sure you kept your pants on."

The dress, her body, her curves slid against me. My inhale was sharp. My fists balled beside me because I still wasn't sure if she was real or just a mirage. Or if she was staying, or what the hell she was really saying other than maybe I did it for her.

"My pants only come off for you, babe."

Her bottom lip pulled between her teeth before it slipped out, plump, pink, and wet. "I might just like to see that."

A zap of testosterone sizzled up my cock. I could barely speak my voice was so gruff. "What're you sayin' here, Leelee?"

Her hair waved with another whistle of wind, strawberry blond heaven. I captured a strand, teasing it between my fingers. We could've been on an island, not on the forecourt of my shop where Peeping Toms spied on us. The sun simmered, saturated us together.

"I love you." Clear and green, true and trusting, her gaze never wavered.

My heart flipped, it filled. So tense I vibrated on the spot, I asked, "But what about no second chance love stories?"

Shut up, Stone.

One hand lifting to caress my face, she murmured, "This isn't a love story. It's life. Our life."

The second she rose up on tiptoes to kiss me, my control snapped. All the frustration, the month of distance fueled the fire to feel her. My arms caging her, my mouth crushing hers, I took it out with teeth and tongue and lips.

Short, harsh breaths flared my nostrils because I wouldn't let her mouth go. Not ever. *So goddamn good.* I was one stroke away from tearing it up right here, right

247

now.

A gasp flew from Leelee's lips when I dove lower to her neck.

Claps came from the peanut gallery, of course, and "Way to get your woman back, Stone!"

I flipped them off, still kissing Leelee.

Her hands skimmed down my back to land on my butt. "You're an asshole though, for what y'all did."

I snorted. Did I give a shit? No. She was here, and I couldn't stop grinning. And she had a point. "Been called worse, babe."

Savoring one last, long suck of her lips, I held her by the hips and pushed her back. "I'm not exactly cleaned up here. Don't wanna fuck up your dress." God, she smelled like paradise, looked like a wet dream, was too good for me.

Leelee smiled. Her fingers skipped down to the crotch of my coveralls, slowly stroking. I grunted and thrust forward, but she lifted her hand off.

"I love the way you smell." She kissed my throat. "I love your rough hands. I really love your ink." Her tongue slid over my chest and found my nipple, toying with the flat disc until my dick almost reared through dark blue cloth. "Rip off my dress, buy a new one, get it dry cleaned, I don't care. I need your hands on me, *Stone*."

I grabbed her ass, jerking her to me. Her backside felt delicious in the dress. She'd be even better with it hiked up to her waist, panties pulled off and legs spread wide, dangling over my desk. "I need to fuck you now."

A slow smile etched across her mouth. "Office?"

Fucking hell yes.

Clasping her hand, I led the way. The clack-clack of her heels—not that I had a frigging shoe fetish or anything—blasted fresh, uncontrollable need to my balls. Against the wall, in the hall, *fuck*, I'd have it all.

A zippy Merc convertible with the top down cruised into the lot and careened to a stop in front of us. *Shit*. Ma exited the car, zeroing in on my hand around Leelee's.

All I wanted to do was hustle Leelee into my office, lock—no, *bar*—the damn door, and screw her brains out. I kept a tight hold on her hand, wondering if we could make a break for it.

I decided to cut Ma off at the pass. "Where's the kid?"

"He's over at Nicky's mimi's. I just stopped by to switch out the magazines." She turned her back on me to beam at Leelee. "And I am so glad I did."

I groaned. *Make nice, introduce, yadda yadda.* I needed to fuck!

"Ma, this is Leelee Songchild." As if she didn't know, Mrs. Google Fingers. "Leelee, I'd like you to meet my mother, Georgette Stone."

"Oh lawzy!" Ma's sterling silver hairdo swung with her head nods and handshakes. She was flustered, flabbergasted, and a bunch more f words I didn't need to elaborate on. She finally gave up on the polite form of greeting to grab Leelee in a hug. "I have been waitin' to meet you, girl."

Leelee hugged her back, giggling—cute, adorable, totally fuckable. "It's a pleasure to meet you too, Mrs. Stone. Josh told me so much about his family."

"Mrs. Stone. Pshaw."

Leelee asked, "Georgette?"

Ma reached out to smack me without even looking. She had good aim. "I don't know why he said that. Ah can't abide by that name. Everyone calls me Gigi or Ma."

"Okay, Gigi then." Leelee drew closer to me and I rested a possessive hand on her waist.

"And you bein' famous and all! Fancy that. Thank you for the book. I think your writing is delightful. A little naughty, and ain't nothin' wrong with that." Ma's cheeks were pink, her eyes lively. "I never did get the full story 'bout what Josh did to make you go off mad at him in 'Lanta, I'm sure he deserved it, but I am so glad you're here. He's been sorrier than a bluebottle stuck in a jar of jam since he got back."

"Well, I heard he was gay and that he and Nicky were an item," Leelee blurted.

Aw shee-it. Now we'd never get out of here, to the office, where fucking would happen.

"Gay?" Ma's eyebrows shot up her forehead, and then she started laughing. "Joshy? Oh, no. He's one hundred percent red-blooded male, all about the women, judgin' from the stories I've heard."

I grouched under my breath. This was worse than pulling out naked baby photos of me.

She continued, "You know how small town gossip is."

I harrumphed. Mt. Pleasant wasn't a small town by any means, anymore. People just acted like it was.

Leelee was laughing it up with Ma, although at the mention of my reputation as a lady's man, the green of her eyes turned laser sharp.

"Not that there's anything wrong with bein' a homosexual." *Oh, Christ, please, Ma, stop.* "Take Javier over there. Queer as they come." She waved over at him and he returned a thumbs up.

That got my attention. "What?"

"Where ya been, boy? Everyone knows it."

They do?

Well, all righty then. Maybe Javier hadn't minded the Stone's Roses poster I'd stuck in his truck after all.

I tapped on my watch to get Ma's attention. "Shouldn't you be getting back to the kid?"

"Oh yes. 'Course." She embraced both Leelee and me before standing back. "You'll come to dinner tomorrow and I'll drop JJ off at six-thirty tonight. Will that be enough time for you two lovebirds?"

"That'd be great, Ma. Thanks."

I didn't watch her pull out onto 17.

Office. Sex. Leelee. Sex.

I waved, nodded, grinned at everyone who cheered or whistled or wanted to greet *the lady*, telling them *later*. I took her behind the counter but didn't introduce her to Ray. I told him to keep everyone out of the back hall for a half hour—no, an hour, maybe the rest of the day—and guided Leelee to my office. One hand on her lower back, my fingertips touched the swell of her ass.

The door closed, locked, chair propped under the handle for good measure, I stalked to her.

She stood by my desk, a hand on her hip. "A real lady killer around town, huh?" Heels, dress, tits and ass, eyes smoldering—green, hot. "And here all I had to worry about before was Nicky."

"I'm not saying I'm an angel or a eunuch or whatever, but there's been no one since you, babe. Not even Nicky." I coughed over the last part, hoping she got my joke. I moved up to her. "No more carousing." With my hands buried in her sunshine-warm red tendrils, I pulled her head back to kiss her neck. "All that's over. Just you." I kissed her mouth, dipping my tongue inside, touching and seeking, finally retreating. "I love you."

Wicked, a temptress—that's what she was when she pressed me back. "Clothes off, Stone."

That I could do. Untying the sleeves of the coveralls from my waist, I attacked the zipper. I didn't get far. Leelee placed her hands on my chest and . . . shit.

I groaned. She toyed with my nipples until breath slammed in and out of me. Her touch, her mouth, her words against my skin with every suck and bite between my abdomen and my pecs accelerated my heart rate. All the blood in my body rushed to my stiff cock.

"God, I love your chest." Her fingertips grazed through the smattering of hair from my belly up. "Such nice soft hair on top, hard muscle underneath." Her fingers fanned out as she sucked and kissed my tat.

She walked me backward until I hit the wall. Bracing my feet wide apart, I leaned back and let her go to town. Her hands curled, fingernails digging into my ribs. I grunted, my balls full, huge, needing to come. Leelee's

251

tongue lashed over every inch of my torso before she nibbled the line bisecting my abs, one hand brushing my dick nonchalantly.

Hard enough to tear through cloth, I gritted my teeth, beating my head against the wall. She went for the arrowed indent of muscle to the left of my pelvis with long, deep strokes of her tongue and scrapes of her teeth. Goose bumps erupted on my skin, radiating from every place she touched. My dick slapped against my hip inside my pants. Awkward angle for such a massive hard-on, but I didn't care.

Goddamn. Leelee wasn't anywhere near to sucking my cock, but racing heat scorched the small of my back. It hit the dam of muscle between my ass and nads, pooled in my balls and made my shaft bulge even more.

I gripped her head in both hands, greedy for more. Pulling her up, I crushed my mouth to her swollen lips. I drowned her protest with my tongue, taking hers inside and hungrily sucking it.

With my lips against her ear, I rasped, "Get your fine ass on my desk, right now."

I smacked her rump when she turned, hurrying her along. I couldn't last much longer. I was definitely coming inside her pussy, but first I needed to eat her out. Lifting her onto the desk, I planted her down harder than I meant to.

"Hips up, babe."

She held herself up, and I rucked that fuck-hot tight skirt all the way to her waist. *Yeah.* Panties bared, legs falling open, she stayed still, her eyes on me. All for me. My own sexy Leelee Songchild playground with a tiny scrap of pale yellow, see-through material between her legs.

Whisking her panties down, I didn't give a fuck where they landed because they'd probably end up in my pocket later. I spread her thighs with my hands high enough to skim the wet, warm delta between. I bent over and put my mouth right on her, not subtle, not a Lothario, nothing more than need.

Heaven, she tasted like heaven. Floral, smooth, her fiery curls tickling my nose. Wet, wet motherfucking amen heaven. I was distantly aware when one hand grabbed my hair and two pointy heels stabbed my shoulders. Good pain. The best pain. Tongue inside, circling around, gathering moisture, sucking it down. My lips opened wide, French kissing her cunt, always a suck or nibble or drag across her clit. Her moans filled my ears, her thighs trembled beneath my hands and I went so far down on her I wanted to take up permanent residence in her beautiful pussy. The second her passage squeezed around my tongue and the two fingers I pressed inside, I grinned against her. I gentled, murmuring about how good she tasted. How perfect she was.

My voice gone, my tongue coated with everything that was her, I kissed all over her shoulders and neck.

Leelee dropped one finger between her legs. My eyes followed. I was gonna come if she pushed that finger inside herself. Her voice—low, velvety, strained—brought me back to her mouth. "Fuck my tits."

"What?" Screw it, I was gonna come from that thought alone.

She unzipped the back of her dress.

Fantasy, Life, Leelee, Love.

On top of my desk. I'd never get any work done here again.

I pulled the top down, yanking the lacy, fragile cups of her bra low too. She laughed when something ripped. Her tits spilled into my hands. Velvety domes, tight and high nipples, the same shade as her saucy mouth. Then they were inside my mouth. Making her sleek and slippery, I licked everywhere. My cock was going to explode, and then I was gonna die.

Stepping back, I lowered my pants to the top of my thighs. My cock jutted up my stomach. She turned lengthwise on my desk, her hair falling to the floor. She pressed her breasts together to create a deep chasm.

Holy fuckin' hell.

Guess I didn't need to ask twice.

I hoisted myself onto the desk, my knees spread beside her. One hand beside her head, the other curled around the base of my dick, I lowered my groin. Sliding inside the slickened clasp of her tits, I swore when Leelee bucked beneath me. The tip of my cock butted her chin. She lifted her head, licked her lips, licked me. I slid away, leaving her gasping. Throbbing inside the silky mounds of her breasts, veins standing out in my arms and on my shaft, I slid back inside the satiny heat. She sucked the head, loudly slurping every drop of moisture from me. Faster, grinding against her, I grabbed her neck to hold her up. At every touch of her mouth, I grunted as sweat trickled down my back.

I rutted against her a few more times, holding her by her tits, pinching her nipples. My head fell forward and I dragged backward, off her, away from the desk.

Barely able to speak, I jerked her up against me. Hot wet kisses joined our mouths. Hands grasped, pulling closer, always closer.

I had to be inside her. I tugged in rough breaths, watching her mouth, her eyes—half-mast, forest-colored. "I got tested."

"I beg your pardon?"

Suddenly nervous, I scratched my knuckles along my stubble. "You know, for STDs and stuff."

A small frown formed between her brows. "You . . ."

"I know, it was a little premature, but I guess I was hopeful." *Ah shit. Shit fuck, in fact.* With my hands on my hips, half a step away from Leelee, I waited.

Tits wet and out in the open, skirt up to her waist, she sighed.

Good goin', Stone. First with the fucking in the office of an auto garage when I should be seducing her in a high-class hotel, and now with the *I'm clean, let me come inside you because you mean so much to me* strategy.

I turned away.

She grabbed my arm.

One hand went to my pants, pulling them further down, the other splayed over my heart. "That's the most un-romantic romantic thing anyone's ever done for me."

"That gets you off?" I yanked her dress higher, loving it when she yelped.

Naughty, dirty, ready to take me raw, Leelee coiled a thigh over my hip. "I don't know. I haven't tried out the goods yet."

Her back hit the wall this time. Her legs slung over my waist. Just a dip of my hips and I thrust inside her. A slick fist against my fast piston, I yelled with every lunge. Rough hard raunchy sex. Leelee's dress rucked further up, her panties still dangled from one ankle behind my back. I was naked to my knees, and we went at it.

My chest, my legs, my heart burned. It all ratcheted up until I shoved her down by her hips, buried my face in her tits. I bit, sucked, slammed, fucked and hovered on the edge until she screamed. Wetness, heat, clamping down, Leelee's orgasm all over my bare cock obliterated every single thought I'd ever had until I was centered solely on her. I came, and the come—hers and mine—was a hot slick sleeve squeezing my cock. The afterburn laid waste to my muscles, shredded them in the very best way.

Catching my breath, I cradled her against me. "I love you."

Her head fell to my shoulder and she gave a breathy laugh. "That's 'cause I just let you fuck me against the wall and come inside me."

I had the decency to be a little sheepish—thank you very fucking much—but, well . . . *yeah.* I ducked my head to kiss her cheek. "Not just that, babe. For always, forever."

Before I got the full appreciation for my vow—which

would include kisses, whispers, and love in return—I leaned a shoulder against the filing cabinet beside us . . . and the goddamn drawers full of fake cocks tipped open. Rubber dongs spilled to the floor, bouncing off the carpet.

They came up to my ankles.

Leelee shoved her face to my shoulder, helpless with laughter. And every giggle tightened her around me.

Still hard, still inside her, I cursed those dildos. "Don't ask. Fuckin' jokers."

She swiveled her hips. "Maybe you can use them on me."

I was ready for her again. The scent of our sex filled my nostrils. With my forearms beneath her thighs, I lifted her higher, then dropped her hard onto me. "Why'd I do that when I got a good workin' cock right here, babe?"

She started giving me the lap dance of my life. Her head dropped back but she kept her glazed eyes fully on me while she fucked me slowly. "So I can suck your cock while you watch my pussy take it."

Fuck me. Now that had some merit.

After round two, Leelee lolled in my chair. I went for a washcloth, some water, and lunch, hurrying back. First things first, aftercare. I dipped between her legs, smirking when she squealed, smiling when she relaxed to my touch—cleaning up after myself.

I opened a bottle of water for her and spread out my loot. Hot pizza, all the works. Steam curled between us. The floor was our picnic table, and I fed her bites, kissing her after each one.

Her fingers brushed over my face. "My knight in shinin' armor."

"Hey, chivalry ain't dead, babe." My cheeks hurt from smiling so hard.

Later, I thought about work but decided to blow it off. We had four hours before going home so Leelee could meet JJ, and I didn't even know if she was staying yet.

Bent over my desk in the perfect invitation, she

studied the calendar we'd messed all the hell up. One finger circling September thirteenth, she said, "I veto the LolliPOP Grrrls spread."

"That so?" I came up behind her.

Leelee pivoted around and pushed me back. I splatted into the chair behind me, happy as hell to be manhandled by her.

"Yeah." She propped the heel of one stiletto against the sensitive tendon between my groin and thigh before sliding it over my stiff cock. "That's so."

Holy shit. There was nothing sexier than a take-charge woman. I shoved the coveralls down. My cock pulsed and a drop of pre-come pushed from the slit, rolling onto her shoe. I closed my eyes before I came at the sight of the pearly liquid on the shiny heel . . .

"Done deal."

I barely agreed before she leaned low and sucked me into her mouth.

* * * *

Leelee and I were headed out after the afternoon of destruction in my office. It wasn't half as chaotic as her hotel room, but it wasn't anywhere near neat either. This time I didn't give a flying fuck.

We reached my Bronco where I'd transferred her suitcases from her rental because I liked the idea of keeping her stranded at my house. Cro-Magnon? Not me. Nicky revved into the lot, his Jeep splattered in mud to the wheel wells. He hauled a trailer, on top of which sat a mangled heap of bike parts barely resembling a motorcycle. Hopping out, he sauntered over. The look he sent Leelee was probably meant to measure the possibility of her kicking him in the nuts. Satisfied with what he saw, he shrugged and pulled her into a hug.

She returned his embrace, I bumped his fist behind her back, and it was all good—the way it was supposed to be.

When he released her, I slung an arm over her shoulder, feeling like a fucking king.

Then I turned my attention to the trailer. "The hell's that?"

"The beast." He proudly patted the side of the bike.

One fender was dented, one missing, and the chrome pipes were corroded with flecks of rust. That was just the visible damage.

"More like a wildebeest left rotting on the savannah, dude."

"Fuck and You," Nicky said, treating me to the double bird. "I'm restoring it. I figured you wouldn't mind me keeping it here where I can work on it, since—ya know—I help out whenever you need slave labor."

"Yeah, sure, whatever. Knock yourself out, man, but I seriously doubt you're gonna get that scrap metal movin' again."

Leelee reclined against me, her hand flat on my stomach burning a hole through my shirt. "Actually, it's a 1946 Indian Chief, a fine machine. It's not in pristine condition, for sure, but these old bastards got more life in them than any other motorcycle ever made."

Nicky's mouth gaped open. Hell yes, she knew her shit.

"I told ya she knew her way around cars, didn't I?" I grinned.

Motion at the door of the shop stole his attention. With his hand half-raised to wave at Ray, Nicky dropped it as a woman joined my second-in-charge outside. His mouth hung open for a second time before it snapped shut.

"Never mind the bike. Who the hell is that?" Nicky asked.

The woman's head bent close to Ray's as they studied a parts book, her sleek jet-black ponytail a huge contrast to Ray's pale bushy hair. Her face turned in our direction, betraying not a single emotion. Nothing could be read from her eyes, the mirrored shades she wore reflecting outward.

"*That* is Catarina Steele. She runs the accounts side of things with her brothers at Chrome and Steele Auto Parts. We just started working with 'em."

Catarina was as cool as they came. Anyone could tell she had a great figure, a nice ass, even under the strictly professional cut of her suit, but no one touched it, touched her, or talked about wanting to tap that. Not in her presence or anyone else's.

"Maybe I might oughtta go talk to her about some parts I need." His wide grin dug deep dimples into his cheeks.

I thought about warning Nicky but decided against it. I could use some entertainment. Bringing Leelee in front of me, I looped my arms around her waist and set my chin on her shoulder as he ambled off.

"What's that all about?" she asked.

"*That* is a woman who is exactly Nicky's type. Hair color, her figure, none of that matters. He likes a challenge, and he ain't had one of them in as long as I can remember." I kissed the pulse on the side of her neck. She shivered in my arms. "And that is Nicky about to get his ass handed to him."

Sure enough, no sooner had he said hello to Ray—managing to get the dude to return to the building—Nicky exchanged a few words with Catarina. Her shoulders turned tighter than her features. He lifted his hand, presumably to twirl his fingers around a loosened strand of her hair, and said something else, his arrogant smile firmly in place.

The second his fingers made contact with her hair, Catarina grabbed his wrist in one hand and sent a crack across his face with the other.

I snorted at his stunned look and muttered, "Ouch."

Leelee elbowed me.

We stood to the side as Catarina roared from the parking lot, barely jerking her chin at me through the windshield of her car.

A little less full of himself, although not much, Nicky strolled over.

"What'd you say to her?"

He stretched his jaw back and forth with a wince. "I called her Wildcat, you know, because of her name."

"Oooh, burned. Hurt much?" I stared at the handprint spreading across his cheek.

Leelee stifled her laughter while Nicky glared at me. "Just tell me she treats all the guys like this."

I towed Leelee over to the passenger side of the Bronco. "'Fraid not. I've never even seen her crack a smile, let alone get so riled up she lost her shit. She's all about business, that's why I like dealing with her."

"Shit." A grin slid across Nicky's lips. "Looks like I hit a nerve."

* * * *

"Oh, Josh, it's beautiful!" Leelee stood on the walkway in front of my house. White picket fence, two-story Victorian with black plantation shutters, wrap-around porch, decent-sized yards front and back . . . the whole shebang.

I took her elbow as we went up the stairs and through the front door. Letting her wander around at her leisure, I hurried back to collect her luggage. I dropped the bags inside, tracked her down in the kitchen, and sandwiched her between the worktop island and my body.

Her eyes glowed. "What?"

Tracing the outline of her lips with my thumb, I frowned. "What is this? I mean, we love each other, yeah, but Louisiana, South Carolina?" My fingers slid up to cup her face. "I don't want the kid conflicted and I'm not thrilled about you being out of sight, let alone four states away."

"What do you want?"

Dangerous question. Basically everything, with her. "I want you to stay."

"For how long though?"

I snorted. "Yeah, about that. I was thinking maybe . . . forever?"

Her head shook until she rested it in the crook of my neck, but her smile had been soft. "I'd love to stay, Josh. I don't want to mess you or JJ around." Her voice turned into a whisper. "I didn't book a return flight."

I pushed her back so I could look at her. "Really?"

"Yes, but I think—since there's that little thing of only knowin' each other a week, and all the kerfuffle . . ."

"Kerfuffle?" One of my eyebrows lifted as well as a corner of my mouth.

"You, Nicky, gay, not gay . . . seduction . . . dancing." She ended with a sigh.

"*Hmm.*" I tangled my hands in her hair and went for her neck with a kiss that slid to her ear. "I like dancin' with you, Leelee."

I waltzed her around the kitchen, enjoying the feel of her in my arms and the enormous possibilities of her staying with me.

"So, I'll stay for a couple weeks, and then we can figure out if it works." Her voice melted against my skin.

"Oh ye of little faith. It'll work." I dipped her, my lips finding the hollow of her shoulder, sucking lightly. "JJ will be home soon. Let's get you settled."

I grabbed her things and propelled her up the stairs into my room. Our room. Clean and tidy, fresh and bright, I couldn't wait to see what sort of mayhem she made out of it. I emptied drawers—not that she'd use them as she seemed to prefer her belongings strewn all over the furniture—but the idea of her underthings in my dresser gave me a frigging thrill. I shoved my stuff to one side of the large closet and turned around to find Leelee staring at me with her hands on her hips.

"Are you sure you want to put me in your bedroom,

sug? What about JJ and confusion?"

I swaggered to her and pulled her into my arms. "This—you and me together—isn't confusing. He's gotta know where you fit in our lives."

"But you've never had anyone here before?"

Hell no. I'd booted them out as soon as the sheets cooled. Jesus, I'd been a bastard. I'd never been like that with Leelee, never would be. "No, not while he was home."

"What if he hates me, Josh?"

"Babe, the kid's best friend is Nicky's bitch pooch, a scary demon thing called Viper. He ain't gonna hate sweet you."

Her eyes twinkled and her long eyelashes fluttered. "Are you sure?"

I swatted her ass. "Yeah. Listen, I'm grubby as fuck so I'm gonna jump in the shower. You do your thing." I glanced one last time at my spotless room. "And keep a watch out for my ma?"

"Sure thing." She pinched my butt in return.

Ma hadn't arrived by the time I'd done a cursory clean up. Neither had Leelee demolished the bedroom, yet. She unpacked, tossing whatever came to hand into various drawers with no rhyme or reason whatsoever while I lounged on the bed, grinning like a fool.

I saw the smile flirting around her lips and the glances she sent me.

Jesus, she was gorgeous.

I kissed the side of her neck and headed downstairs when I heard Ma's car. She sped off with a toot of her horn as soon as I collected JJ from the car seat and his stuff from the trunk, the soft top on her convertible sliding down at her push of a button.

Suddenly my palms sweated. Shit, I was nervous. The two most important people in my life were about to meet.

On the porch, I set down the kid's knapsack and blankie, plus a bag of possible contraband sugary items. I crouched at his level. "Did Jamma say anything new to you today?"

His face scrunched up. "Um, she said she got the burn in her heart after we ate us some chili dogs at Cosmic Dogs, and dat the traffic on seven'een so bad she might well crawl us home." He scratched his tummy. "I think that it, Daddy."

I hugged him to me. Goddamn killed me every time. Bad grammar and all. "Well, we've got someone visiting for a while." *Maybe forever, hopefully forever.* "Her name's Leelee. I love her, son."

Fidgeting from my arms, he sat cross-legged in front of me, cheek in his hand, guileless green-gray eyes blinking. "I wuv everyone you wuv, Daddy." He held up all five fingers of one hand. "Jamma, Wicky, Viper," *ha!*, "I wuv Gerald and Way, Harvey . . ."

I laughed every damn time he called Javier Harvey.

He held up his other hand for more fingers to count. "I even wuv Momma. She didn't wuv me back."

My chest heaved several times and my throat tightened. I mashed him against me because I didn't want him to see me *weaking* again. "Momma loved you, kid. Your momma loved you, she loves you, okay? Sometimes people, they just don't fit." With my hand engulfing his entire head, I rocked him with me. "How could anyone not love you?"

"Will Weewee wuv me?"

Holy shit. If I hadn't been crying, I'd have fallen over laughing. We needed to work on his enunciation. "I bet she already does, baby boy. Are you okay with this?"

"Does she sing Disney songs too?" Wide-eyed, he wondered.

Well, shit, I didn't know. It hadn't been on my to-do list when I'd thought about winning Leelee back into my life. "Maybe we oughtta go find out."

I walked him inside. He only came up to my knees and his fingers curled around mine, reminding me of the way

263

he'd latched onto my thumb the first time I'd held him. Newborn, and sweet smelling, and the most fragile piece of bliss I'd ever known.

Another slice of the promised land waited beyond the doors. Leelee was all smiles and a few tears she blinked away as we entered the house. I couldn't speak. I opened my arm, inviting her into my family. I looked at Leelee pressed against one side of me, JJ on the other. They both peered up at me, and I had to swallow past the hard knot in my throat.

"JJ, this is Leelee." I patted her waist and squeezed his hand. Leelee's fingers dug into my chest, all of our emotions centered there. "Leelee, this is my baby boy." Love and hope so massive in that moment, they were etched in my soul and on my heart. "He wants to know if you sing Disney songs."

She slipped free of me, kneeling down to shrink herself to my son's height. "I sure do. But I'm a girl so I like the princesses better. That Flynn Rider has a lot to answer for."

Breath exploded from my chest when JJ nodded so very seriously at her. In fact, my goddamn heart reached up to my throat and stayed there while I watched the two of them meet, eye-to-eye.

Leelee gathered his free hand between hers. "Now, I do like me some *Little Mermaid*. What about you?"

"Ursuwa the sea witch kinda scares me." The kid shivered all over his body, and his hand slipped from mine.

"Me too." Leelee's eyes popped wide. "No one likes a witch, do they?"

"Nuh uh. Can I show you my new fairy stowybook? It's in my woom. Daddy don't care, do you?" He didn't wait one way or the other. JJ pulled her hand and she scampered to her feet.

"'Course you can, didn't you know I love fairytales, darlin'?" She toed off her high heels and padded to the stairs.

The kid hung back for a second, their hands connected, the both of them linked to me, to my heart.

"Daddy, she wooks wike Ariel!" And he was a goner, toddling off beside her.

My throat was dry, my eyes wet as I watched my son and my woman walk up the stairs, sharing secrets, hand-in-hand.

Chapter Eighteen
Stone: At Her Service

A WEEK AND A half later, the kid and I took up residence in the kitchen, making a total mess of the place. We fried up fresh catfish and I tried my hand at making jalapeno hushpuppies because Leelee had ordered them when we went to Red's Ice House. Friday night at home, I was happy to stay put instead of scoring on the bar scene. I laughed when the kid held up gooey, fish-battered fingers, trying to smear them on my face from where he perched on the counter.

Leelee looked over at us, a smile on her lips with a pen pushed behind her ear. She was in the living room, writing, visible through the open archway, and still here. She liked to move around the house at different times of the day, following sunlight like a sunflower opening, blossoming. The porches, the kitchen, and if she was really on a roll, she lugged her laptop upstairs later at night to the cozy office we shared while I scratched through paperwork. The writer's block was gone. The professional fears caused by LaForge and the anxiety to write faster and faster vanished. And just like her, the second story in her trilogy bloomed.

Sometimes she read to me from her day's work. The hot passages dripping from her low-toned voice made me harder than a plank, and made for good sex long into the night, but so did basically anything she did. Leelee laughing, her wet from a shower or pink from a bath, her tousled head pillowed on my shoulder as she woke in the morning. Lazy as a feline, stretching on top of me.

The flirting, the occasional fighting because she would never be less than feisty as hell, this thing about making a life—a home—together, got me right in the gut. It pushed up to my heart and filled it until I thought it would explode with happiness.

Fuck me. I'm turnin' into a Hallmark card.

I went back to helping JJ form misshapen balls that pretended to be hushpuppies. I kept sneaking glances at Leelee though. She stretched out on the floor, legs spread wide, leaning over onto her elbows as she tapped across the keyboard of her laptop. In faded sweats, her hair in a ponytail, wearing one of my threadbare T-shirts, she walked a fine line between relaxed innocence and getting her bones jumped. Jesus. I certainly couldn't go after her, not with the kid around. Some things wouldn't do even though he was used to our hand-holding, hugging, and even our kisses, because I wasn't going to hide my love for her. Touching Leelee was as vital as breathing. And he'd taken to her like she was the next best thing since chicken nuggets chased with a hot fudge sundae.

Starting up the fryer with JJ coloring at the table and possibly all over it, I realized I was almost one hundred percent domesticated and loving every fucking minute of it.

I pressed the timer on the range and sat across from the kid. "Whatcha drawing, baby boy?"

He shoved the piece of paper at me and kept doodling, on his hand. "Guess!"

Crap, I hated this game. I mean, how the hell was I supposed to know what a tentacle-mass of red waves and a tent-shape with purple flowers was supposed to be?

I ran a fingertip over the scribbles. "Gimme a hint?"

"Dat a pitcher of someone I like."

Squinting, I saw it then, in a surreal way. I dropped my voice. "Leelee?"

"Good, Daddy! She's wearin' dat dress from the day I met her!" He squealed, all semblance of being secretive off the table. Climbing off his chair and into my lap, he turned down the volume to whisper, "Can we keep her?"

Oh my hell, like she was a pet. Leelee and I had discussed it. We'd made it barely a week before both our minds were made up. We worked, *this* worked, the three of us together. Spending more time apart meant unnecessary pain.

She was staying. "I can write anywhere, but there's only one Stone's, Josh. This is your home, and I want it to be mine too," she'd said.

And it was. High heels, mountains of dresses, cosmetics, files, folders, books and all, strewn around our bedroom, bathroom, and the office. Fuck if I even wanted to change a thing. Leelee was a hurricane-level storm that upended my life, made it chaotic and crazy, and more complete than I'd ever thought possible.

"Yeah, kid, we can keep her." We fell into hair-ruffling, tummy-tickling awesomeness.

Walking into the living room after tucking JJ in at the table with a full-body bib, I hunched before Leelee. She blinked up at me, pulling out of the writing daze that captured her for hours.

I slid my fingers down her neck. "Hey, babe. Dinner's on."

Curving her arms above her head as she stretched and did that feline thing I liked, she said, "You know, you two are so cute, Josh."

Cute. My grin grew dangerous. The atmosphere

charged as her eyes strayed to my mouth and stayed there. Her breath deepened, her cheeks heated.

She'd eat those words later, with my cock in her mouth.

And she did. Not long after the kid had passed out cold for the night, she found me in the living room. "Still got that hat, Stone?"

"Why? You got plans for me, babe?" My hard-on formed in anticipation as I sat on the couch.

Leelee lifted off her T-shirt, slipped out of the sweats, and let her hair down. Completely utterly fuckably naked, she stood several steps away, moving her hips in a suggestive dance. "I think I wanna go for a ride."

"Hat's in the hall closet," I croaked.

"Don't move."

I watched her ass swish-sway away, in complete agony as my cock lengthened down the inseam of my jeans.

On her return, she wore my fedora at a sexy angle. She leaned over me so I could take long hard draws on her nipples while she slowly pulled my erection out of my jeans.

My aching length pumped in her enclosed fist. "Fuuuck, Leelee."

She put the hat on my head, lowering to her knees between my spread thighs. Her mouth engulfed me in one swift, wet move. All the muscles in my body screamed with pressure.

Her mouth worked me to the breaking point, her fingers ripping at the buttons of my shirt and pulling it open. I shrugged it off, one hand guiding the back of her head up and down.

Rigid, slick, shiny swollen, my cock slapped my stomach when she released it.

I pulled her onto my lap and thrust into her hot sheath without warning. I swallowed her yell with my mouth and grunted, "Josh Stone. At your service, babe."

* * * *

The following week, coming up on mid-July, Leelee and I headed out of town. We'd pick up a U-Haul in Shreveport, tow my car, and drive her belongings back to South Carolina. She planned to put the condo up for sale in hopes of making enough profit to cover the mortgage Patrick Fuckstick had saddled her with. It hurt like hell to leave the kid—only my second time—but we needed this time together. We craved it.

He gave his blessing with a book he'd stapled together complete with hacked-off edges from safety scissors that didn't even fit my fingers. The pages opened to gaudy, blobby drawings of castles and, well, I couldn't make out much of the rest until the end. The final page showed a picture of three people holding hands. The red hair was a dead giveaway for Leelee. The bright blue cape on the smallest figure was his. And between them both was a giant—shit, had he made me a Cyclops?—linking them all together. A lopsided heart surrounding us.

I tucked the book under the visor of my muscle car. Gripping Leelee's hand, I drove away, trying not to look back or turn the car around.

The '69 Camaro, on the road, with my woman: life couldn't get much better. She proved to be more entertaining company than Nicky's waxed ass by far. We took our time, doing the tourist thing through Georgia, Alabama, and Mississippi, staying at inns instead of dime-a-dozen hotels. Every night was a new romantic pit stop.

Romantic may have been stretching it. Once we left Mt. Pleasant, we were all over each other every chance we got. The domesticated animal gave way to pure male greed. Leelee was right there with me, as hungry for the clothes-tearing, hair-grabbing, wet, loud, horny sex as me.

By the time we arrived at her apartment to pack it up in the four days we'd allotted, my Camaro resembled the cracked-up state of her hotel room in Atlanta. It'd all started with one innocent straw wrapper from a Sonic Cherry Limeade and had grown to out-of-control proportions. I swore, she had a hundred changes of clothes stowed beneath the seats alone.

It was one thing to mess up my house. I could always hire a maid. It was another to annihilate the Camaro. On that last day of driving, I'd had to change a flat—no biggie—but that was work shit I didn't want to drag into our vacation. I hadn't been able to reach the kid all day, and I was in a *fine snit* when I finally parked outside her place.

It was sweltering outside, late at night. We had a couple hours to start clearing before falling asleep exhausted and meeting her folks for brunch the next morning. I needed a shower for myself as well as an excavator for the car to be able to see the floor mats again.

I slammed my door, stomping over to open Leelee's before she found the handle, probably because it was hidden under her usual debris.

My shoulders stiff, I formally bowed. "At your service, it seems."

Her long legs flashed out of the car. "You got a problem all of a sudden, *Stone*?"

She did not wanna pick that fight with me.

I pressed her against the hood, hot as the surface of the sun after driving four hours straight. "Yeah, maybe I do. When are you gonna start pickin' up after yourself?"

"You weren't complaining about how sloppy I was last night when I sucked your balls until you shouted my name so loud the manager called our room."

Her reminder made my anger over stupid shit morph straight into lust. Zero to sixty, three seconds flat.

"Maybe what you need is a homemaker à la *Father Knows Best* instead of me. That would suit your old school, macho image." She sneered.

Parting her thighs, I stood inside them, rigid against

271

her. "You're asking for it, Leelee."

"Look, I don't know what crawled up your ass, Mr. Pissy Pants, but you're not the boss of—"

"You might wanna rethink saying *you're not the boss of me*, babe." I pushed in tight. "I ain't your boss, don't wanna be. But I am your man."

"You arrogant pig!"

"Wrong words, woman." I lunged inside her mouth with a kiss so full of force and passion, I groaned with the way she gave it up, clinging to me, pulling me down.

She held me with one hand around my neck. She tried to drive me back with a palm to my chest. I smirked before attaching my mouth to the shivery point on her collarbone.

"Oh God, Josh, you're not gonna—" She gasped when I slipped two fingers under her panties, finding the warm, silky opening and her clit.

"I'm gonna fuck you right here, on top of my car." One handed, I unzipped. I stroked my cock, watching the way she draped on the hood, one knee raised. Sure she wanted it, positive she was ready, I slammed inside. "We're about to wake the neighbors."

Frustration, fury, fatigue boiled down to this hardcore, raw fucking. I powered inside of her. I wanted to be in her skin. The next best thing was Leelee supporting herself on one hand, her head dropped back, her hips pumping up.

Her pussy rippled around me, blanking everything from my mind but the pure ecstasy that burst inside of me—mind, body, sight, muscles tautened until I roared.

She burned against me, around me, shaking from her legs to her tits. I held the back of her head, protecting her from the unforgivable metal of the car.

When she slumped, I did too. Her fingers combed through my hair. "You been thinkin' about doing that for a while?"

"Maybe." I could fall asleep right there, her satisfied purr better than any engine I'd ever worked on.

"It's probably a good thing I'm moving out." Leelee

dragged herself back together as lights came on from inside a couple apartments.

I lifted her against me, one arm beneath her knees and the other around her back. "I reckon."

A messy car to deal with in exchange for one incredible woman who turned my world upside down, inside out, and perfectly right? Worth it.

The next morning the prospect of meeting her folks shot my nerves to shit. I compounded the frazzled edge by downing two cups of black coffee. On the drive over, I couldn't sit still. I was turning into the kid.

"What if I say fuck in front of them?"

Leelee's hand on my leg calmed the jumpiness. "They're not gonna hate you, Josh. They're just good, salt-of-the-earth people, and they want me to be happy. Besides, I don't think they ever approved of Patrick, and you're night and day from him."

Amen to that.

Unfortunately, I was in trouble almost as soon as we entered the house. Small and energetic as a hummingbird, Leelee's mom Patsy bounced from hugging her daughter to holding both my hands, pumping them up and down.

Her dad, on the other hand, looked like a woolly mammoth, staring me down with arms crossed over a barrel-sized chest. At some point Brian Childes's hair must've been nearly the same color as Leelee's, but now the wild beard and thick curls were steely grey shot through with what was left of rust-colored red. His moustache didn't even twitch when he shook my hand.

"Mr. Childes, Mrs. Childes, pleasure to meet y'all."

"Oh, Leelee, you were right. What a lovely baritone he has." Patsy linked her arm through Brian's and petted his bicep. Only then did the stoniness of his face thaw, and only when he looked down at her. "She said you're a wonderful singer, Josh."

I was not breaking out the show tunes for them when Leelee's father looked like he wanted nothing more than to break my legs.

"Dad." Leelee left my side and gave the forbidding man a hug. His features softened a second time.

"You're looking a hell of a lot better than you did when you left here, sweetie." He touched the back of her head with his big paw.

"Well, you can thank Josh for that, and JJ of course."

"*Hmm.* Are you sayin' I should cut the boy some slack?" The fact he'd called me boy let me know he had no intentions of cutting me any slack at all.

"That's enough now, Mr. Childes. It's the Lord's Day, Leelee's home and happy, and we finally get to meet the mysterious Josh Stone." Patsy pinched his arm lightly. "Now be polite, like I finally taught you after thirty years."

"Woman." His voice was gruff with warning, his face sterner than ever, but a hint of playfulness showed in his eyes.

Maybe the old man isn't gonna take me out back and skin me alive after all, at least not before we eat.

We made it through brunch with me still in one piece. It wasn't too awkward once we got rolling. Patsy drew everyone into conversation the way Ma would have, and both she and Leelee paid careful consideration to me. Brian did too, but with a hostile look in his eyes.

I tried to help Leelee's mom in the kitchen after we ate—anything for a stay of execution—but she told me she didn't want menfolk messing up her domain. Fair enough. I slunk out when Leelee's dad entered the room, rubbing his hands together and reaching for Patsy. I overheard their conversation.

"You lay off that boy, now, Bri. He's done a good thing, bringing our Leelee back, and bringing her back to herself."

He harrumphed.

She twined her fingers behind his neck. "If you play nice you get pie later."

A huge grin finally broke through the old dude's bark

and bite. "I like pie," he drawled, grabbing a piece of Patsy's ass.

I had a feeling they weren't talking about the apple pie set out on the cake stand in the middle of the table.

I'd barely managed to sneak back to Leelee in the living room when her dad beckoned me. "C'mon then, Josh."

Time to duke it out already? My food hadn't even settled yet. I stood and followed him into the garage, or to the gallows, as it were.

His grin turned dark. "Just us men now, huh?"

I gulped and said a prayer. At least we were in familiar territory. I looked at the covered bulk of a car sitting center stage on the cement floor. "What're you working on?"

He swept the cover off with all the flair of a man about to show off his pride and joy. "Pontiac GTO."

"'67, right?" I admired the dark maroon hardtop he'd revealed.

He nodded once, pulled the lever under the dash, and popped the hood. "Come have a look."

"She's a beaut." Glancing at the woodgrain vinyl dashboard, taking in the chain-link grille on the Pontiac's nose, I joined him under the hood. We inspected the shiny V8 engine that would growl like a lion. "Something to be proud of."

"I'm just finishing the fine tuning now. After that, I'll be working on the interior. I'm gonna take her back to her former youth." He winked at me and I began to breathe easier.

Lowering the hood, he left the GTO uncovered and we continued to appreciate the lean mean lines of her. He looked out the open garage door to my Camaro. "Did you restore that one?"

"From scrap to what you see now."

Resting against the trunk, he scratched along the steel wool beard on his chin. "I've gotta admit, I've got a hankerin' for that model. Did you and Leelee have a nice trip out here?"

It probably wasn't a good time to tell him what I did with his one and only daughter on top of the car last night. I swallowed that thought right quick. "Yeah, we did and we needed it. I know this all seems real fast, sir, but it's the real thing. I'm the real deal." Jesus, I sounded like an eighteen-year-old idiot come to pick up his daughter for the prom.

"I hope you don't think just because we share a love of cars I'm gonna go *real* easy on you?"

"I wouldn't dream of it." I leaned against a workbench. "Just like I wouldn't dream of letting any harm come to Leelee through me or anyone else."

Spreading his thumb and forefinger over his moustache, he smoothed it down, all the while scrutinizing me. He suddenly asked, "Is it after noon yet?"

I glanced at my watch. "Twelve-twenty, sir."

He stealthily closed the door between the kitchen and the garage, stepped over to the icebox, and nodded at me. "Time for a beer."

He took one, handed me another, and sat on a stool, pushing its neighbor out for me. After a long guzzle, he wiped his mouth. "You go to church?"

I got the picture. I was in for a Q/A session with Pops. I could do this—I'd handled Jules, for chrissakes.

"Once a month." I sipped from my beer, figuring it wouldn't do to act like I wanted to down an entire six-pack.

"Do you run around?"

"I used to, I'm not gonna lie. But I was responsible, never did anything in front of my son, never intentionally hurt anyone." I twisted the beer bottle between my hands, its condensation mixing with the sweat on my palms. "I'd for damn sure never cheat on Leelee, sir."

"Ever cheat on your ex?" The grilling continued.

"No, sir. She left me because . . . well, we never had a good relationship and, after JJ was born, shit went to hell in a handbasket. She suffered from postpartum depression, and I don't think she was cut out for motherhood. And we definitely weren't made for each other."

He placed a hand on my shoulder and squeezed. "That had to have been tough."

"Yeah, and no. The hardest part is watching JJ try to figure out how his momma could leave him." I shrugged. "I think we've been a better family without Claire. I never thought we needed more until I met Leelee. She's one helluva woman, Mr. Childes."

"Intentions?" He cut to the heart of the matter.

"That depends on whether you've got a shotgun stashed around here somewhere."

He clinked his bottle against mine. "Good answer, and I do."

Setting my beer on the workbench, I looked him square in the eyes. "Sir, I expect you to make my life a living hell if I mistreat your daughter. I want you to know that isn't ever going to happen. I've fought for her. I've thought of no other woman but her. She's inside my heart."

"She deserves to be treasured, not treated the way that twiggy piece of shit Patrick did."

"If he's still in town, I wouldn't mind paying him a visit." My jaw hardened.

The hand resting on my shoulder tightened as anger flashed across Brian's face. "Only if you bring me with you."

Another beer later, I laid down my cards. "I want to ask Leelee to marry me, sir, with your blessing."

"All I want is her happiness. You know how that is."

"I can do that. I'd be honored to do that."

He squinted at me for a long time while I sat perfectly still. "I bet you can." He nodded, the matter settled.

Leelee found us like that, drinking beer, talking shop. She took one look at the empties and rolled her eyes. "It's not even five yet, Dad."

He pointed at the Frigidaire—one of the old ones, baby blue, chrome handle—and she grabbed one herself before calling through the door, "They're out here gettin' plastered, Mom."

The Queen Bee, the hummingbird, entered, taking a seat on Brian's lap. "Where's mine?"

Everyone gave cheers and thanks. Leelee stood beside me with her arm draped around me. We talked about our trip and the weather, the upcoming college football season . . . Basically nothing at all but with the all-important feelings of belonging and acceptance.

Then Leelee's dad blindsided me. "Do you wrap it?"

I choked on my beer.

"Dad!" Mortified, Leelee flushed to her hairline. Not a bad look on her.

I settled a hand on her hip, stopping her from baring her claws at Brian. "It's okay, babe." I answered her father, "We're both clean and monogamous, so no, I don't."

"I'm on the pill, Dad, Jesus." Leelee moved into the shelter of my arms.

Patsy pounced. "Got that out of your system, Bri? Leave the kids alone, they're happy."

"Yes'm." Just like that, she brought him to heel.

* * * *

A few weeks later, we were completely settled at home in Mt. Pleasant. We'd pushed it on the return trip, eager to get back to the kid and start our life together. *The Stone family is everyone's family.* And now I had my own.

As well as a motherfucking cat. I'd had to listen to Mews mewl all the way across four states. Now the calico furball was being tortured by the kid as he ran off his sugar buzz from the strawberry shortcake Leelee had made for dessert.

She and I sat on the back porch watching JJ playing in

the grass below. Evening dipped down, painting the sky in colors that reminded me of her dresses. She wore one of them tonight. A sundress with little straps, and she was barefoot, which I really liked since it meant she couldn't run away. Yeah, I was a barbarian where she was concerned. She hadn't complained yet.

"Why's it called Mews, Weewee?" The kid asked, the furry bundle squished in his arms.

I snorted. *Weewee* still cracked me up.

"It was a little joke; Mews, because that's the sound a cat makes, for Muse, m-u-s-e, like a writing muse." Leelee stroked her fingers through his hair.

"I don't get it." His brows knitted together.

"No worries, kid. Me either, Leelee's got the brains of the family." I heard her sharp intake of breath and looked over. I hadn't even realized what I'd said. It just came naturally—her being part of the family. I put my hand on the nape of her neck, playing my fingers up and down, smiling at her reaction.

JJ scampered away, holding the cat over his shoulder before placing it on the grass to cajole it toward him with promises of dog biscuits and ice cream. He acted like Mews was a trainable canine—maybe I should've bought a leash from The Gee Spot after all.

"Hey, kid! Remember what I told you about letting animals lick your face, right?"

He flapped his hands in my direction, the only indication he might've heard my warning. With him occupied with cat-agility lessons or whatever he was attempting with the hula-hoop, I turned to Leelee.

"Got somethin' to show you."

She cut her eyes to me. "I just bet you do. I think you showed it to me this morning."

Arousal, swift and immediate, pounded through me. "Not my cock, babe, not this time." I pulled on her hand until she left her chair and slid onto my lap. "I'll give you a hint, it rhymes with cat."

I laid my lips against her neck with firm, moist kisses up to the corner of her mouth. "Gonna guess?"

"You didn't, Josh." Her fingertips hovered over my shirt.

I winked at her, a grin forming. Taking the hem in both hands, I peeled the shirt over my head. My biceps, pecs, shoulders flexed for her, showing off the new design I'd had finalized earlier on my original tattoo, extending it even further.

Her eyes enormous, she gasped. "You did, you're gettin' . . ."

"You can touch it." *Oh yeah, she can.*

Cautiously, she slipped her fingertips across the tat, stroking first around *Joshua James December 13 2009* before following the circumference of the heart to the stenciled addition of her name. Beautiful calligraphy sat inside the top chrome pipe: *Leelee Songchild.* From there her fingers skimmed to my shoulder where a dense, sometimes delicate design of vines and chrome as well as a few songbirds intertwined as I'd imagined for Songchild.

When she stayed silent, I said, "It's not done yet. I want a sleeve down to my elbow at least, eventually. But I needed to get your name on me. Whaddya think? Wanna come to the studio with me tomorrow and watch them fill it in?"

"Yes." Lips—soft and slow—replaced her fingers. Gentle, worshipping, she moved to my mouth. Her tongue coiling inside, seeking and finding mine, she moaned when I grabbed her hips to twist her to me.

Breaking away, she whispered, "It'll be breathtaking, Josh. I love you so much. So much. I feel like I can never get enough of you." So close our lips still touched when she spoke, the heat in her eyes changed.

"Turns you on, huh?"

When she breathed against my lips—"Yeah"—and dipped in again, I decided it was JJ's bedtime.

We got him sorted out, read to, sung to, and snuggled

with together. I kissed him and stepped back to let Leelee do the same. We moved toward the door and I switched on his nightlight.

He watched us with eyes growing heavy. "Weewee?"

"Yeah, JJ?"

"I wuv you and your pwincess hair."

She squeezed my hand and I squeezed back. I figured she had a lump in her throat similar to mine when it took her a moment to reply. "I love you too, sweet boy. Goodnight."

"'Night, Weewee, 'night, Daddy."

She acted like she wanted to linger a while longer, but I tugged her away. "Don't even think about it. If you make eye contact with him, you'll never get out of here. I know how he operates. And you're all mine after dark."

Leelee giggled, allowing herself to be led back outside. I brought a glass of wine out for her, a beer for me, and beckoned her to sit in front of me on the lounger, between my spread legs, her back to my chest.

"I know why you wear the wigs, Leelee."

She turned, and I framed her face in one hand. "You figured it out. My shield, huh? Pretty lame, I guess."

"You never put up a front with me."

"I tried to . . . I should have . . ." Her voice faltered. "I'm so glad I didn't, Josh."

Wrapping my arms around her, I rocked her a bit. "I'll be your shield, babe, you know that." Her head rested back and I smoothed her hair, the gorgeous, unforgettable hair down her back. "Why though? Why hide all of this?"

"Being a redhead was horrible. Before you, I used to wear it up all the time. I was teased a lot when I was a teenager—freckled, gangly, ginger hair—the girls weren't nice."

I burst out laughing and she turned to take a swipe at me. "What?"

"Hate to break it you, babe. But those girls, teenage bitches makin' fun of your hair? It's because they were

281

shit-jealous of you." And I was jealous of all those teen boys who probably choked on their tongues every time they saw her.

Her face brightened when she saw things my way. "So you like my hair?" Leelee lifted the whole mass of curls and red in both hands before letting it tumble down.

"Fucking love your hair." I buried my nose in that fine, red-gold sheaf. "And don't think your ma didn't break out the high school yearbooks when I was there. Goddamn gorgeous then, even more so now."

She put her wineglass down and straddled my lap. "And I know what you really think about my wigs, Stone."

"Do you?"

"Secretary, starlet, or naughty nurse?" With her lips close to my ear, her husky words sent a shot of thick arousal straight to my groin.

What about a triple header? My cock about exploded in my jeans but despite my one-track mind, I declined. "Not tonight. I've got something else in mind."

Surprise widened her eyes as she leaned away from me.

"But I'll definitely take a rain check. Here, lift up a sec? I got somethin' else to show you."

"Didn't you just say not tonight?" She gave a teasing laugh, rising off my hips so I could dig a hand into my pocket.

Pulling out a box, I presented it to her. It was small, square, and gold leather, its meaning unmistakable. My heart thudded to a faster beat as I watched a world of emotions cross her face: shock, bashfulness that heated her cheeks to the prettiest pink, and hope when she lifted her eyes to mine and tears shined there.

Fingers trembling, she lifted the lid, revealing the ring. I plucked it from its white velvet bed, and the tears on the edges of her lashes glistened as they traced down her cheeks.

I tried to find my voice but it was rusty because hope

and want and love threatened to consume me. "I know it's early days, Leelee, but I'm old-fashioned when it comes to you. You don't have to say anything right away, or even wear it, but I need you to know how much I love you." I caressed her face, taking the tears away on my fingertips. "I would be the happiest man, the most honored if you'd be my wife."

My face turned hard with emotion I tried to contain. The ring shook between my fingers—nothing too fancy or flashy but a nice-sized diamond set within a circlet of emeralds.

With her hands on my cheeks, Leelee pulled me into her kiss. A kiss so intense and deep, it felt as though she poured her entire heart into my soul. "Yes. I want it, I want you. I love you," she whispered.

I squeezed my eyes shut and clenched her hard.

"Gonna put it on me, sug?" She rubbed her face, so soft and smooth, against my shadowy cheek, playing with the hair at the back of my neck.

My fingers still shaking, I slid the engagement ring home. I kissed her fingertips until her hand curled around my jaw. When our kisses changed from joy and happiness to intense and hot, I slid from the chair, taking her with me.

Upstairs in our bedroom, I turned down the lights and closed the door. I crooked a finger at her. "C'mere, babe."

Kissing her insistently—her mouth, her neck, the tops of her breasts—I touched every part of her body I slowly uncovered. I lingered on the sexy curve of her waist and suckled at her nipples until they became puffy and deep pink. Closing my lips around the swollen pearl of her clit, I licked and sucked, groaning at her taste.

Her hands in my hair urged me to my feet. Leelee shed my clothing with just as much care, murmuring when her lips brushed my tat, making my muscles tense and tighten. Her fingers whispered down to my ass and over my ribs while she settled on driving me insane with her mouth. She

283

licked my chest and scraped her teeth across my abs. With my cock in her mouth, she found my eyes and watched every flicker of emotion, sucking me off, making me slick until I was delirious and panting.

We moved to the bed. Leelee settled below me, her body open to take me. Our mouths met, lingering when I pushed inside. Only a gasp and a moan escaped our lips. I hooked my arms beneath her shoulders as her legs slid to my waist, and we were so close nothing could part us, nothing ever would.

I rocked into her, and it was quiet except for our breaths and the sound of skin against skin. Slowly grinding inside of Leelee and pulling out, I waited until she arched against me and did it again, and again. The blankets fell from the bed, followed by the pillows. Leelee's foot slid up and down the back of my leg, and I twisted her hair between my fingers. Slow and easy, long and deep, gliding in and grunting when I withdrew, we had all the time in the world.

Our lovemaking was aching flesh. It was long and intense. It was wet, and tight, and so very fucking right, I couldn't stop touching Leelee, fucking her, feeling her move against me.

She came suddenly, striving up to gasp into my mouth, a silent scream I swallowed. Heat fisted my cock, slick, tight suction drawing me after her. My muscles froze and my body unraveled. Her name tore from my lips when my final thrusts soared into her and I flooded her pussy with come.

"Oh God, Josh!" Another orgasm took her with me one more time.

Released from the vise grip that had locked me into climax, I lowered over her, letting her feel all my weight, all my body. Her hands slid up and down my back while I kissed her neck, her face, her lips.

Complete, that's what this feeling was. Finally complete and whole. I smiled, moving onto my side, sliding my legs between hers. I leaned across her to grab a blanket from the floor. With her head resting on my biceps, I went back to kissing her. Her eyes remained closed but her lips curved into a sleepy, satisfied smile.

And like that, she drifted asleep. My woman. As close to me as possible from heart to soul to body. *Damn.* Hallmark card again. I laughed quietly. I filtered her hair through my fingers, teasing out the snarls from my rough treatment. I didn't want to wake her, I wanted to keep breathing her in, feeling her.

Her hand rested on my chest over the new tattoo design. The ring on her finger sparkled, with emeralds to match her eyes.

And I was no longer alone.

**Keep reading for the
first chapter of
Love
In The Fast Lane
Carolina Bad Boys #2**
Coming in December 11, 2014

Now available for preorder exclusively on Amazon.

Chapter One
Potluck, Rotten Luck

I ARRIVED AT GIGI'S house on the last Sunday in August carting along my mimi, my Rottie, and a piping hot casserole dish of homemade mac 'n' cheese. Mimi had made it. Top Chef I was not. Neither was I Queer Eye/Straight Guy material after the failure of my fake relationship with Josh at the LitLuv convention in May. I blamed our bust-up on Josh's inability to keep his cock in his pants. He'd defected after no more than three days, switching to the other team to be with a woman he just couldn't get out of his system—Leelee Childes, known to the reading and writing masses as Leelee Songchild.

Shee-it. I hadn't been any better, bedding the first piece of fluff I could find right after him. Pandora had been no more than a receptacle for my erection that night in Atlanta, but she was one seriously determined, slightly freakish stalker. Even being half a country away didn't keep her from sending me all sorts of pictures of her . . . well . . . *Pandora's box.*

At least she hadn't begged me to reenact one of the squirm-in-your-seats sex scenes from my books. That was bonus material right there.

Cut loose from my *boyfriend*, I was back in the game, no gay cover story to keep the chick-fans at bay. Not that it mattered. They weren't catching me. I was about as far from relationship material as any man could get. Top romance writer I could do, but I had no frigging clue how to woo a woman anymore. Case in point, Cat Steele's open palm to the side of my face a month ago. Now that woman, she had some spark.

My cheek still burned. She sure packed power behind her punch, I'd give her that. And screw my cheek, every time I thought about Wildcat and how she'd gone off on me at Stone's garage, my cock fired to life. She was nothing like the revolving bed of babes I used to partake of whenever the mood hit me. That was a bad habit I'd outgrown in my late twenties.

These past few years, my octogenarian grandmother had been all the woman I could handle. Not that she needed handling, she'd have you know. With her health on the decline and me the only relation nearby to look after her, I did my best to provide for her. She'd done the same for me when no one else had cared enough, not even my parents. I kept her comfortable without letting her think she was incapable of doing for herself. One thing my mimi still had was an impish grin to go with her mean ear-pinching move if I stepped out of line or made her feel like a doddering old lady.

Gripping Mimi's elbow, I guided her over to Gigi Stone, who was holding court just like she used to at Stone's Auto Service back when her husband—Josh's dad—was still around. Gigi used to call James her silver fox, but she was still the foxy one. She and Mimi hugged, Mimi's long braid streaked with white and Gigi's cutting edge bob pure silver. They'd both weathered age and the losses of life well, even if it showed sometimes in the sadness of their eyes. It did in all of us who'd lost someone near to our hearts.

Gigi wheeled around to me after I set the casserole on the long table overflowing with potluck fare. She took my cheeks in her hands and pulled me down for a kiss on my forehead, the same way she had since Josh brought me home with him during my first days as the new kid at Wando High. I'd been abandoned by my folks and left to be raised by my mimi. Gigi's welcoming kiss that day had caused a thick lump in my throat. It still did, every damn time, but fourteen years later, I was better at covering up the emotions tugging at me.

Draping my arm around her shoulders, I planted a kiss on top of her head. "Hey, Gigi. Have the bozos eaten you out of house and home yet?"

I scanned the crowd of folks consisting mainly of Stone's garage crew—old and new—and their wives, partners, and kids.

She wrangled from beneath my arm and patted her hair where I'd mussed it up. "I figured you and Joshy would take care of that. You been keepin' each other out of trouble, now? 'Cause you know I don't like to hear about my boys behaving badly, 'specially not when it comes secondhand from my church ladies."

She accused me before the fact of any wrongdoing with a withering glare. She'd done the same when Josh and I had made devious, detention-bound plans during high school.

"Ain't up to nothing, ma'am. Just writing and riding, enjoying this fine southern weather, and your fine southern charm."

"Oh, you always were the sweet talker. Don't know how Joshy managed to hook that Leelee. If she ain't a prize, I don't know who is."

I glanced around until I saw the pair . . . Gigi's son and

his lady love.

"Reckon I don't wanna know what you're ridin', either." She sniped with a hint of a smile.

I barked a laugh so loud, it startled a tiny baby in the arms of a woman across the table. Ray's wife hushed and rocked the little pink infant before popping a bottle between her lips.

"And I reckon Josh won't be getting into any more messes now Leelee's here to stay. Besides, I was talking about riding my Jeep. The bog's been good this summer—"

"*Sssht*. You can just save that mud-runnin' nonsense for the boys. Tell me about your writing instead." Gigi's eyes gleamed, her cheeks tinged pink. She was hankering after a new release date.

I slipped the leather tie from my ponytail and ran my fingers through my hair. "I signed that three-book contract in June for the witches series. Beating my head over a title for it, but I'm just finishing the first edits—"

"That's enough now, Nicky. Leave me and Miss Myra to it. We gotta catch up, and you don't need to listen to no more woman's stuff, you get enough of that in your books." Gigi nudged my mimi like they were schoolgirls about to steal kisses with the boys behind the bleachers.

"But you just told me to—"

"Sonny, don't tell me what I just told you to do. Haven't you learned anything yet? No wonder you haven't managed to snag the right woman." Gigi's impatience was evident in the cutting way she called me sonny.

"You know you're the only woman for me, Gigi."

"Oh, hush that now. I'm likely to get the heart palpitations. Anyway, I still remember that time you and Josh decided your first box of rubbers would be better put to use as water balloons so don't you even try to flash that lady-killer grin at me."

I was sent packing with a final sparkly laugh from

Gigi and an in-cahoots grin from my mimi, Miss Myra. The pair of them were thicker than thieves when I sauntered away, whistling for Viper to keep up at my heels.

"They're probably comparing notes on sex scenes from the latest New Adult releases," I muttered as I ambled off.

They were part of the same old-dames book club that met once a week to read and discuss every single sex-riddled book under the sun, including mine. Gigi and Mimi had once convinced me to "give a talk" to the group. It was a frighteningly funny affair during which I felt like a retailer for Pure Romance. Except I wasn't selling sex, I was selling romance . . . with a side of smut.

Far enough away from the food to give Viper free run, I let her loose and sent her in the direction of little dude-man, JJ, the kid. Might as well give Josh a few gray hairs while I was at it. He was living large with the love of his life and too smug for his own fucking good. A little scare wouldn't hurt him none, and my dog would never hurt the kid. They'd practically grown up together, sharing dog beds, baby beds, and chewtoys during the teething stage.

That hadn't gone down well with Josh.

Ray, Javier, Gerald, Mick, and all the other guys were in attendance, as were the old coots who shored up the checkerboards and headed up the town crier gossip outside of the garage on 17 North. Their kids, grandkids, and all the hangers-on always showed at the Stone homestead for potluck every last Sunday of the month. Directly after one's church of choice.

I listened to the laughter, the murmurs and chatter. The sun beat down, spreading the smell of the giant white magnolia blooms with their lemony scent. Inhaling the heady fragrance, I started toward Josh who was half laughing, half telling JJ off about sharing Popsicles with Viper. Again. Ever the shit-stirrer, Gerald held out an unwrapped orange icy treat to JJ, replacing the one Viper had licked down to the wooden stick, flipping Josh off behind his back.

Yay me. I'd get to clean up bright orange dog puke tonight. No matter. The kid would have a tummy ache, Viper would have a tummy ache. Josh and I would commiserate by phone in the morning.

I watched Leelee nuzzle Josh's neck and him smile down at her. I smiled myself when he leaned over to kiss her.

Man, he finally got it all.

I couldn't have been happier if he truly was my brother.

I shifted my aviators with one finger to brush beneath them, ducking my head while I swallowed the emotion filling my eyes out of nowhere.

Pressing through the beer-drinking, loud-talking crowd, I drew up short when I saw the sexy, black-haired vision of my dreams. Wildcat aka Catarina goddamn Steele. She got the steel part down, all right. She'd gone off like a powder keg at me, but she was back to her cool, untouchable self today. I could see that from several yards away.

She wore a dress as befitted a lady who had recently sung her Sunday psalms. But everything about Cat screamed hellfire more than O Heavenly Father to me. The white sheath stopped above her knees, snug on her willowy frame. The lightweight cardigan hid her arms to the wrists, but neither the dress nor the sweater could cover up the goddess body beneath. Ripe curves, long legs. Fiery as fuck, cold as ice, and just waiting to be melted by passion.

The sight of her rippled an arrow-shot of heat to my groin. My jeans became snug at the crotch as I took in her slanting cheekbones and the haughty tilt of her chin, her eyes hidden once more behind mirrored shades. She was exotic, erotic, and aloof. With jet black hair pulled straight back in a neat knot, Cat sent out a siren song that sizzled all the way up my cock.

I wanted to see her hair down. I wanted to tear off her sunglasses. Goddammit, I wanted to know what color her eyes were.

Her fingers flirted into JJ's hair when he dashed passed, her low laughter following the boy who had a whole gang of kids gunning at his heels for a game of tag.

When Cat looked up, her gaze swung to me. I didn't shift, breath, swallow. I didn't move. Neither did she. *Take the shades off, darlin'*. Mick from the garage careened past her, chasing after the kids, and our look was broken.

I was free to move on. But did I? Hell no. I stood stock still, taking in my fill of her. Cat didn't have a problem ignoring me though, turning to crouch down and scratch Viper's ears when my dog nuzzled against her legs.

"Got it bad, huh?" Ray asked, handing me a beer.

I snorted. "Not."

The burly blond guy took several long gulps of his beer then swiped a hand across his moustache and mouth. "Yeah right. Listen, Nicky, you don't wanna tangle with *that*." He pointed the beer bottle at Cat, who I'd already been staring at for far too long.

"She's pleasant enough with you."

"'Cause I ain't tryin' to get into her pants."

Unfortunately the grease monkeys—or assholes as Josh affectionately called them—were more perceptive than a room full of shrinks, and I'd had my fair share of those, too.

"Hey, I was being friendly to her that day." I avoided his shrewd look by inspecting the label on my microbrew.

"Yeah, I don't think the woman does the friends thing. I heard she had some trouble in her past, so you're best leavin' her alone. Also, if you fuck up Josh's new partnership with Chrome and Steele, he's gonna get all pissy again like he was after the Leelee/Atlanta fiasco."

He had a point. Josh did excel at being a first rate dickhead when he was down in the dumps. And a woman with a troubled past was a headache I didn't need. I had too many skeletons in my own closet. I didn't have any room for anybody else's.

Ray cocked his head to the side when he heard his name called. "Aw hell, the old lady's hollerin' for me. Probably wants me to change another one of Emma Jane's diapers. The girl's so goddamn tiny, man, how can she dump such a huge load? And the smell? I'd rather put up with Gerald's BO." He complained like any new father would, but the twinkle in his eyes and the way he stepped-to on command gave him away as a proud papa.

I strolled around, drank more beer, and shot the breeze, maintaining a safe distance from Wildcat. My fingers started getting itchy when I hadn't checked my phone for texts or emails or Facebook updates after the first hour. I didn't always like the fact I had to run around like Viper chasing her tail on the social media loop to keep my author presence alive, but I still suffered from withdrawals from the Internet, the one addiction I allowed myself. Stone Sunday was a wifi-free zone, as anyone running the risk of Gigi's formidable wrath found out. One good thing: it meant my con stalker-chicky couldn't reach me via any outlet from Twitter to Facebook to G+ for at least one day.

Josh found me drumming my fingers on a table, watching Javier court danger as he hunkered over his phone, tapping away with speed.

"Watcha doin'?" Josh asked as he slung a hefty arm around my neck.

"Waiting for Javier's imminent execution by your mom." I peered at the black-eyed, black-haired boy. Then I knocked Josh's arm off my shoulder, standing up straighter as Javier furiously typed on the screen of his

iPhone, giggling quietly to himself. "Holy shit, he's like—
"

"Janice."

"Yeah, man, if she was a Hispanic homosexual."

Beer spewed out of Josh's mouth, landing on me. Oh well, no worse than Viper's slobber. We continued to laugh our asses off while Javier imparted two regal middle fingers in our direction without looking up. He better be careful, Gigi was liable to snap them off. A young dude with surfer blond hair approached Javier, leaning in to kiss his neck.

"So that's his guy?" I took an appreciative look.

"Yeah, Tate."

"How come we didn't know about this?"

Josh shrugged. "'Cause we're dumbasses?"

He was probably right about that.

"They make a cute couple." I nodded over to Javier and his All American jock. "They make a better couple than you and I did anyway."

"We sucked at that, huh? And not in the way we were supposed to." Winking at me, Josh asked, "Which one do you think is the bottom?"

I squinted at the pair. It was hard to tell. Tate had some muscle on Javier, but maybe that just meant he was the tight-end receiver. Javier was the youngest of the garage crew at twenty-three and his boyfriend couldn't be much older. "Maybe they're switches?"

"The only switches I know are the ones Ma used to brand our behinds with when we misbehaved. Missy Peachtree would know all about that." There was a fond smile on his face when he mentioned the Domme/grand dame from my writing group, the women we referred to as the Hens.

"Hey, Stone!" Javier was no longer giggling, he was outright guffawing.

"What up, ace?"

Just then, the rest of the Stone's crew surrounded us, each brandishing his cell phone to show us . . . *Oh, fuckin' hell.* Lookee there, a do-over of the infamous "Stone's Roses" photo the guys had cobbled together while Josh and I were away in Atlanta last May. This time it was tiled and titled "Ring Around the Rosy", their hairy assholes and all in close-up. Now I knew what Javier had been working away on; he'd emailed it to all the gathered gang.

And that shit was funny.

"Y'all, it's gonna be your puckers full of posies if that bullshit ends up anywhere near Twitter," Josh boomed.

We all laughed at his expense until Gigi yelled, "Chow's on! Now put them damn gadgets away and get your grub on."

One large table crowded onto, Gigi held everyone at bay with a nod to Josh. "Say grace, son."

His deep voice began to rumble, and I held his hand on one side of me and Mimi's on the other. Holding them both tight. "We thank the Lord for the bounty he provided, for the family and friends we're given, for the life and love granted us. For those missing, and those we will always miss, we take this time to remember."

"Oh, Josh," Leelee sighed from the other side of him, knowing as I did he was thinking about his dad.

I squeezed his hand and released it so he could embrace his woman, pretending I wasn't blinking too fast when I kissed Mimi's wrinkly cheek.

Stuffing her hankie away, Gigi started sending platters around. "Eat up, y'all."

There was a saying from Gigi, from way back. *The Stone family is everyone's family.* I looked around the table bursting with people. She had that right.

Everyone tucked in and talk turned to Leelee's book *Ride.* Copies of it were everywhere in the lowcountry. The whole town of Mt. Pleasant was enamored with her. All the boys had read it, their wives, girlfriends, lovers, too. I could just imagine all the jealous broads who had bought that book simply for a hint about how Leelee had snagged the long-elusive Josh Stone.

"How do you feel about sharin' the limelight, Nicky?" One of the jackasses asked.

"Yeah, you ain't the only romance writer in town now." Someone else chimed in.

I chewed a mouthful of slaw. Slowly. My writing and Leelee's were about as far apart as you could get, apart from the gasping-for-breath sex. She was New Adult, I was Paranormal. Never the twain did meet.

Giving a smug grin to the group, I tipped my head toward Leelee. "Y'all can ask me that question when Miss Songchild has another five years under her belt."

"Booyah!"

"Snap."

"Oh, it's on," Leelee said as she reached for me while Josh leaned out of the way. Grabbing the collar of my shirt, she growled, "Romance wars."

"You got it, L." I spat in my palm. She did likewise and we shook on it.

"Y'all about done hauling out your dicks yet? 'Cause I've got something else to say," Josh grumbled.

Leelee slid her hand across his chest. "First of all, I don't have a dick, sug, which you well know by now. I have brass balls. And second," she whispered something in his ear and his hand around a bottle of beer tightened until white knuckles appeared.

His voice came out low and gruff to her, "Yeah. I want that later, babe."

Leelee's laughter tinkling, she sat back, a pleased smile on her face. Her haze of pale red hair brushed Josh's shoulder as he stood up.

With his hands on the table, he looked over all of his, shaking his head and smiling. "I asked Leelee to marry me, and she said yes. Would you believe it?"

The table erupted with victory shouts. I kept my eyes on Josh and Leelee, capturing the way she curled her fingers around his, silently mouthing, "I love you so much."

Tears shined in her eyes, in his—*fuck*—in mine too. I couldn't even bear to look at Gigi, but I knew she'd hauled out the hankie again.

Lifting Leelee's fingers to his mouth, Josh stared at his fiancée. "She's wearing my ring and that makes me the proudest damn man in the whole world. I don't deserve a woman like her, but I'm gonna do my best to make her happy. And I'll kick any motherfucker's ass who hurts her again."

Leave it to him to go barbarian/romantic. The table shook when everyone rapped on it.

"Date, date, date," we chanted.

He brought Leelee to her feet and into his arms, to a kiss that would've simmered off the pages. Breaking away, he was choked up. "We decided to get married on Thanksgiving. It seemed—shit." He backhanded his eyes. "It seemed a good time to get hitched 'cause I'm so fucking thankful for her."

I stood up and clasped his shoulder. "Cheers, man."

"With beer!" Some wiseass cracked.

But those bastards couldn't fool me. Their wide grins and claps and shouts showed how awesome they thought this was. The boss finding his woman, falling in love, making her his wife.

JJ piped up, "Weewee's gonna be a pwincess!"

He was passed down the table for squeals and hugs and gentler than usual high-fives.

We raised our bottles and everyone shouted, "To love!"

I gave Josh a hug, and one to Leelee after. "Tamed by love."

"I wouldn't say tamed," Josh groused. "Watch it, bro,

you're next."

Later in the afternoon, Gigi cornered me. "Now we've got Joshy settled down, what're you waitin' for, son?"

My gaze skidded to Wildcat. *Hell no to that*. Put a stop to that impulse right there. Fuck, my cheek still stung from her smack last month. I did not need a ballbuster for my woman.

JJ interrupted the ill-fated love match, breathless and doped up on sugar. "Uncle Wicky! Uncle Wicky!"

He grabbed me by both grubby hands until I hunched down. His sweet breath spilled across my face, and he grinned at me. "Wuv you, Uncle Wicky. And Weewee's gonna be my momma!"

Jesus. I knew what JJ did to Josh's heart . . . he just about flipped mine upside-down too. I'd been part of his life from newborn to now, helping my buddy out when Claire, his ex, left them high and dry.

These people were my family. The only family I needed.

"Come see, we built us a fort!" he shrieked in my ear.

Tugged along after him, I flagged down Leelee. "Just how much sugar has the kid had, L?"

"Ice pops on tap, Coke on repeat." She tallied off his cocktail of high octane sweets while the dude-man vibrated beside me, hopped up on his sugar rush.

"Josh is gonna have a field day with that."

"You know as well as I do all it takes is a Disney song and a reminder we aren't leavin' him to settle him down, Nicky." She smoothed JJ's rumpled hair.

"Weewee sings the bestest!"

His fingers slipping from mine, I turned to Leelee. "Nights in the rocking chair?"

She watched Josh's son, soon to be hers, as he joined the ragtag bunch headed into the forest. "A few, but he's getting better. I'm never gonna be Claire to him even if he barely remembers her, I don't want to be. I just want him to know I love him, and I'll never let him go like she did."

"I'm really happy for you and Josh, you know that, right?"

"It shows, Nicky." She reached up to pat my face.

I shoved my hands into my pockets and looked at the ground. "Does it?"

"You are Josh's brother in every way but blood." She squeezed me close for a hug before letting me go.

Josh had got it right with her. He was one lucky sumbitch.

It sounded like the kids were playing a cross between Marco Polo and Zombie Attack in the surrounding woods, but I couldn't find JJ. Confident the older kids would keep their eyes out for the youngsters, warning them away from the creek and the pluff mud, I ended up at the plankboard bar where the cooler of beer, water, and juice boxes were stored along with an arrangement booze. Making myself useful beneath the flowering canopy of crepe myrtle, I played bartender to all and sundry.

I stood up from restocking the beer cooler, coming face-to-face with Cat. I slotted my aviators into the neck of my shirt and wiped my hands down the front of my faded-to-fuck jeans. I'd shaved in the morning but the evening stubble tickled beneath my fingertips when I scratched lightly on my jaw, never taking my eyes off Cat's face. Her mouth parted, her tongue wetting the pouty bottom lip. I could take care of that for her.

Bracing my palms on the rough wooden bar top, my biceps bulged and my forearms flexed with muscles. "Pick your poison, Wildcat." *Hell, pick me, darlin'.*

Suddenly, I didn't give a shit about Ray's warnings or her hot temper . . . in fact I was more intrigued than ever.

Especially when her voice rolled over me like raw silk, delivering another stinging barb. "If I had any poison, I'd have slipped it into your drink already."

Yeah, that definitely got a rise out of me. My cock

took the wake-up challenge and thumped against my jeans. Hot damn, I was gonna have this woman sweet-talking in my ear and eating out of my lap by the time I was through with her. If she was determined, I was goddamn stubborn.

"Hey, you don't need to prove to me you're tough as nails, I got it."

Moving around the bar between us, I slid in front of Cat. Close enough to feel the heat of her body, not near enough to touch although at this point I wouldn't say no to another slap across the face. Wildcat riled me up and made me feel alive like no other woman had.

She pursed her lips and the only hint I affected her at all was the fluttering pulse in the dip of her collarbone.

"So, what'll it be, Cat?" My voice a low, rough rumble, I made sure she knew I was offering more than a refreshment.

"Sweet tea with lemon please." Then her smile opened up, planting a perfect dimple beneath the apple of her right cheek. "Guess I could do with something to sweeten me up."

I laughed, strolling back to get her a cup of sweet tea from the large silver tank of sun-sweetened brew. Serving her a red Solo cup filled with ice, lemon wedges and Gigi's own recipe, I crossed my arms over my chest. "So, are you telling me your bark is worse than your bite?"

She took a sip, swallowed, and slowly grinned. "Oh, hon, my bite is so much worse than my bark. You don't even want to know."

Cat strolled off on long legs in a white dress, leaving me desperate to know, needing to know. I wanted to feel her bite, all over my body. Her words shook me, sent me straight into fuck fantasies I needed to expel onto paper, into my story, if I wasn't going to get my hands on her.

The getting-my-hands-on her possibility looked even less likely when I saw Cat later. She was speaking heatedly to a new dude. Her hands waved around, her black hair came loose, and hot color painted her cheeks. The guy talked over her, getting down in her face. *The guy* had wavy blond hair to his shoulders, golden scruff on his face, and full tattooed sleeves down his arms and onto the backs of his hands where several heavy silver rings weighed on his fingers.

It looked like Wildcat had her very own wildman with an MC crew.

A bolt of jealousy jolted right through me.

Oh no, I am not goin' there either.

Not with her, not just because she was a challenge. A very sexy, tight-lipped, straitlaced challenge who made my bygone days of bedding broads look like a walk in the park.

I knocked back the last warm dregs of my final beer of the day, prodding Josh with my elbow. "Think that fucker has enough tats? Wonder what he's trying to prove."

"Who? That guy with Cat?"

"Yeah. *That guy* with Wildcat." I gritted the words through clenched teeth.

Josh took both our empties and sailed them into the recycling bin. "Yo, that's one of her brothers, Brodie."

My pissed off mood immediately lightened. Which was stupid as hell. "Well, they don't look like they're related."

She was dark and gorgeous, he was light and . . . whatever. I was not paying attention to the relief spinning inside of me. Not.

"Word is Catarina has full sleeves on her arms, too. Must be a family thing," Josh added.

I hardly heard what he said. I was too busy picturing tats, all up and down Cat's arms, colorful sleeves over soft skin. Was it an intricate masterpiece or unconnected designs? I was turned right the hell on, wondering what story her ink would tell. Dammit.

After rubbernecking Cat and her brother's showdown,

I hunted down Viper—who I hoped hadn't been made into mincemeat by Josh yet—and Mimi, who was probably up in the house trading her latest ebooks with Gigi, splashed out on bourbon.

I didn't get far before the blond biker stood directly in my path.

And here we go.

"I saw you staring at my kid sister."

Who the fuck was this dude kidding? There was no way Wildcat was a kid what-so-fucking-ever. "One might even say I was ogling her," I smart-assed.

This Brodie Steele was as ripped as me. And maybe he had an extra couple inches over me, but that just meant I could move faster. Josh didn't call me scrappy for nothing.

"She ain't interested," he growled, popping his knuckles where three fat silver rings sat for extra menacing measure.

"Huh. You see, that's funny." I scratched the side of my jaw and then loosened my neck. "I got the feelin' Cat was capable of taking care of herself when she slapped me across the face."

His fists uncurled and he smirked. "She did that?"

"Yeah, the first time I dared to say hello." A mistake I was willing to make again, but big brother didn't need to know that. Her smart slap awoke so many impulses inside of me, I'd let her beat the crap out of me just to see the passionate fire win out over the cold ice queen bondage.

"Sounds like her."

No shit.

"Hey, you're Nicky Love, right?" Brodie extended his hand, pumping mine.

"Nick Loveland, yeah."

"I probably shouldn't tell you this—Cat would kick my ass to Timbuktu and back—but she's got all your books." He chuckled.

Storing that little secret away for future flirtation.

"Lay off, Brodie."

That throaty voice, the one right there, made the hair on the back of my neck stand up and electricity course to my cock.

Brodie put both hands up in front of him to ward off Cat. "Just exchanging pleasantries, sis."

She came up beside me, her hands on her hips, long sleeves covering her arms and possible tattoos I wanted to see. "I know all about you and your pleasantries and you can fuck off, *brother*."

Backing away, Brodie grinned between us. That grin made him look like a devilish little boy, except for the fact he'd been ready to pummel my face in a few minutes ago.

"Walk me to my car?" Cat asked.

Invitation, question, command . . . I didn't care. I took Cat's hand in mine, lacing my fingers through hers, smiling when she audibly breathed in at the touch of skin against skin.

Yeah, spark.

And Christ, as if I needed another reason to ignite that spark. Cat's car? It was nothing but a top of the line, special edition, drag-racing demon with a thick black widow blood red stripe down the center . . . A Dodge Challenger Rallye Redline. The kind of road-beast women took their panties off for. Or, in my case, the kind of muscle car I tried not to drool over as I held her door open.

Waiting until she was seated, her long legs pulled inside, I lingered.

"That's far enough. You've done your job." Wildcat closed the door.

Most chicks invited me inside so they could take a ride on my cock. Forget about eight pistons pumping under that badass hood, I had one piston in mind for her.

I caressed the roof as if I was caressing Cat's body. The half-shaded, black-tinted window rolled partway down.

"My job?" I was not used to getting the brush-off.

Cat gripped the steering wheel with both hands, her eyes aimed out the windshield. "Proving a point to Brodie." Her mirrored shades reflected up at me. "And now we're done."

We weren't done, not by a longshot. But I let her roll up the window. I watched her peel out in a cloud of dust and gravel, mashing the pedal to the floor to fishtail it away from me.

For whatever reason, I got under cool Cat's skin.

I was so very fucking far from done with her.

Also by Rie Warren

Sugar Daddy, Lowcountry Heat #1
New edition, January 2014
Contemporary erotic romance

She needs a job. He wants a mistress. Hearts and contracts are bound to get broken.

Shay Greer is pure GRITS—a Girl Raised In The South–but nowhere near a demure southern belle. She's looking for a way out of her broken down marriage when she lands an unexpected job offer she really should refuse. Position? *Mistress*. Fringe Benefits? *Of course*. Fraternization with sexy CEO Reardon Boone? *Required*.

Shay signs on, lured by the promise of intimacy missing from her failed marriage. She's barely survived a hellish year of heartbreak and needs a fresh start. Little does she know a clean break is the last thing she'll get with the mysterious millionaire.

Reardon sticks to his tried and true rules: no-strings-attached seduction, no messy emotions, absolutely nothing resembling a real relationship. This sassy, sultry woman fits the bill precisely…until she arouses more than his erotic appetite.

A shark in the boardroom and a lady killer in the bedroom, Reardon is as irresistible as he is unattainable. Shay falls hard, but his inability to love could tear them apart. She finds out that beneath Reardon's seductive mask lies a man as tortured as she is.

Deep Water, Lowcountry Heat #2

Coming in 2015
Contemporary erotic romance

Wounded Navy SEAL warrior, Captain Ransome Boone is a man with a mission: to stand on his own two feet in time for his brother's wedding. Moving into his own place, he's just taken the first step toward independence. He's expecting old Mrs. Curry as his caregiver, but gets the shock of his life when her daughter shows up instead.

Solange Curry was the gangly girl he teased in childhood. Now she's all grown up–a gorgeous Gullah goddess who captivates him. Living with the sexy, no-nonsense woman is infuriating, exciting, and fraught with erotic possibilities. But Solange won't bite.

Despite her undeniable attraction to the sexy former soldier, she won't risk her professional integrity for a quick romp. Not for a bad boy like Ransome with a reputation that extends far beyond their little corner of South Carolina.

For Ransome, dealing with his physical setbacks is one thing. Coming to grips with the idea he might not be a good enough man for Solange is a brand new obstacle. One he's hell bent on overcoming. He's fought for his life, now he must fight for her love and prove he's an honorable man.

Don't Tell Series
Grand Central Publishing/Forever Yours

In His Command, Don't Tell #1, m/m
RT BOOK REVIEWS TOP PICK!

On Her Watch, Don't Tell #2

In His Sights, Don't Tell series novella, m/m

Under His Guard, Don't Tell #3, m/m
Coming in 2015

Freebies available at www.riewarren.com:

Jingle Bell Rock

A short, hot festive m/m freebie

*A bashful bouncer, a Cajun rock boy, and a Christmas Eve
kiss that changes everything . . .*

Heart Beats, m/m

A Valentine's freebie following *Jingle Bell Rock*

*Candy hearts, birthday cake, and the most important
question of all.*

In His Heart, m/m

A Don't Tell series freebie, 'Blondie' POV.

Acknowledgments

I'm going to keep this real simple. Who? Me? Inconceivable, I know. Many thanks and much love go out to my very good friend, beta, and editor Gillian Littlehale. In this last round of editing she has a. put me in the time-out corner, b. told me to stop whining, and c. offered me Ativan. Not many people know you or your writing well enough to do that. Massive thanks to my critique partners. They are one cool and dedicated bunch: Jenna Barton, Christine Cox, April Gasaway, Kari Haines, Joelle Mendes, Lisa Pinney, Tracey Porcher, and Heather Savage. Enormous love to my street team—you all rock my world!

I'd like to thank my agent, Saritza Hernandez, for keeping up with my mania. And by extension, Cate Hart who helped slap *Stone* around so it became the published novel it is today. (Please know I live in mortal fear of forgetting anyone or anything all the time so if I managed to miss someone, feel free to spam me until I cry)

Extra heartfelt love and appreciation to my family, friends, readers, and fans—wow? I have fans!—who feed my addiction, otherwise known as writing.

About Rie

Rie is the badass, sassafras author of *Sugar Daddy* and the *Don't Tell* series–a breakthrough trilogy that crosses traditional publishing boundaries beginning with *In His Command*. Her latest endeavor, the *Carolina Bad Boys* series, is fun, hot, and southern-sexy.

A Yankee transplant who has traveled the world, Rie started out a writer—causing her college professor to blush over her erotic poetry without one ounce of shame. Not much has changed. She swapped pen for paintbrushes and followed her other love during her twenties. From art school to marriage to children and many a wild and wonderful journey in between, Rie has come home to her calling. Her work has been called *edgy*, *daring*, and *some of the sexiest smut around*.

You can connect with Rie via the social media hangouts listed on her website https://www.riewarren.com. She is represented by Saritza Hernandez, Corvisiero Literary Agency.

3208

Made in the USA
Lexington, KY
23 March 2015